OTHER PEOPLE'S SECRETS

OTHER PEOPLE'S SECRETS

A NOVEL

MEREDITH HAMBROCK

CROOKED LANE

NEW YORK

Copyright © 2022 by Meredith Hambrock

Published in the United States by Crooked Lane Books, an imprint of The Quick Brown Fox & Company LLC.

Crooked Lane Books and its logo are trademarks of The Quick Brown Fox & Company LLC.

Library of Congress Catalog-in-Publication data available upon request.

ISBN (hardcover): 978-1-63910-098-9
ISBN (ebook): 978-1-63910-099-6

Cover design by Nicole Lecht

Printed in the United States.

www.crookedlanebooks.com

Crooked Lane Books
34 West 27th St., 10th Floor
New York, NY 10001

First Edition: September 2022

10 9 8 7 6 5 4 3 2 1

For my mom.

PROLOGUE

THE CITY WAS heaving hot, sun baked and panting. Sanitation workers had walked off the job six weeks previous when the union couldn't reach a deal, and black bags of garbage were tossed over park fences, cooked in piles for eight, nine, ten, twelve hours a day, leaving the air smelling like a hot banana. Here, on September 1, just a few minutes after seven o'clock in the evening, the Dumpster Baby, pink skinned and screaming, was discovered behind a grocery store, nestled on a bag of Flamin' Hot Cheetos.

For a brief moment, just after she was pulled from the trash, the Dumpster Baby was considered a miracle, a tiny, screaming wonder, stared at by a pack of grocery store employees who stood in a circle around her, cooing, waiting for an ambulance and the police to show up to take this distraction elsewhere. Once she was taken into custody, leaving the cellophane Cheetos bag behind, she became something unremarkable. Another orphan Jane Doe, case number #45BN6ab9. Dropped into the system, bundled in blankets passed between hands as paper shuffled from one county to another until, finally, she was adopted by a grizzled woman in her early fifties named Hannah who lived on the edge of Bitborough Lake, four hours outside any sort of metropolitan center, eight hours from the dumpster that delivered Baby unto this world.

Hannah kept the name Jane Doe—because, Baby deduced later, Hannah was very susceptible to any sort of suggestion—insisting until even the day before she died she just thought it was a pretty name, an innocent one. *Jane Doe*. Like Bambi. Jane Doe. An unidentified female on the news, her sins lost to the world, a beloved blank slate.

Baby inhabited her true name without any kind of shame and demanded everyone call her Dumpster Baby, Baby for short; forced the story down their throats so she walked through the world honestly, at least. *Herself.* Because that was all she knew. There was no Mayflower in her history, no flag planted into the ground that could give her a measure of herself, tell her how to love or who to become.

This ancestral black hole, the absence of definition, took root and drove Baby to turn into what she was. Because even though Hannah loved her in her own quiet, sighing, drunken way, an absence can grow in the spaces of not knowing. Questions. Dumpster Baby tried not to wonder. She tried not to think too hard about it, and eventually, *not thinking too hard about it* became Baby's primary trait. She embraced ignorance and, well, ignorance became her. And she grew older and started working and drinking, and partying, and best of all forgetting, because that was what she was best at, everything she truly loved—beer, pot, men, heaving dance floors and old friends—isolating her from any hovering expectation, any definition, any hope about who she was or where she was going or what she was supposed to become.

So instead of striding out into the world to confront it, Baby hid inside a summer resort on the edge of Bitborough Lake, inside a town so boring it was simply called Lakeside, home to 672 people, inside a dive bar called the Bloody Parrot, with ceilings that were caving in, thick drops of water constantly condensing and falling on heads and shoulders, paint curling off the walls, a constant smell of deep-fried something thick in the air, with a floor so sticky it was impossible to clean.

And now, here's Baby, stuck, twenty-nine years old, eyes closed to the world, waiting for a breath, for a reason, for a slap to the cheek, god, anything, to force her eyes open, to wake the fuck up.

"WHAT DO YOU mean I have to pay for a coffin?" The itemized invoice shakes in her hand.

"It's protocol for cremation, Baby," Duffy says. He takes a pull on his e-cigarette, then offers it to her and she waves him off. His fat raspberry-scented clouds are making her nauseous.

"So I have to pay for a box that you already burned?"

"Listen, I'm sorry, I really am, but this is like a legal thing."

Baby sighs, closes her eyes, and tries not to panic about how the slowly depleting wad of cash in her pocket is getting a whole lot smaller while Duffy talks about wood and temperatures and how hard it actually is to burn a body, did she know? Not easy.

"She couldn't have just raw-dogged it in a sheet or something?"

Duffy has, at least, the courtesy to laugh. Baby takes the remains of Hannah's bank account out of her pocket and starts counting. "How much?"

"It's normally thirteen hundred—"

Her heart drops. She wants to throw up.

"Thirteen hundred dollars? For something I could've done by myself, in the woods?"

"We already agreed on the price," Duffy says, and he's right, Baby knows he's right. She was in a state when she signed the papers, turned over the body, can't really remember anything other than the dull ringing in her ears, the mushiness of time, since the moment she discovered Hannah's body when she came home Sunday night after DJ's birthday, stinking drunk. Baby found her adoptive mother on the kitchen floor, eyes wide open, hands frozen in the air, fingers twisted into mangled claws, as if she died trying to fight off invisible ghosts.

Duffy sighs, and Baby can tell he feels bad for her. They always do. "Listen, I can give you a friends-and-family. I can do it for seven hundred and fifty dollars. Because it's you. And we all loved Hannah."

Baby grins a little. "Friends-and-family deal at the crematorium. Jesus."

"Hey. It's a funeral home," Duffy says, then softens, remembering that he likes Baby. They always remember. She counts out the cash fast, used to it, reminds her of the end of the night at the bar, the bills are just less soggy. She slaps the money into his palm without ceremony, and Duffy says he'll go get her.

"What?"

But he's already ducked into the back and returns, moments later, with a thick white bag of Hannah's ashes that he places on the counter with a soft thump.

"Seriously?"

"Urns are extra. And they're not cheap—you can't believe what I have to deal with. The supplier—"

"Okay, okay," Baby says. "Thanks." She rushes outside, her stomach suddenly turning, flipping over on itself, and pukes in the garden out front, one fist squeezing the bag of ashes, the other clutching at the *O'Shea Funeral Home* sign. It's an hour away from Lakeside, this funeral home, and she knows she'll be waiting for more than a minute for her ride from DJ Overalls, who went to pick up the party sub for the wake and said she'd be right back.

Baby spits, then digs into her backpack for a beer, the warm cans at the bottom, grabs one and cracks it open, takes a swig and cleans the vomit out of her mouth.

It doesn't make sense to Baby, Hannah being here one minute and gone the next. It should make sense. Hannah was a drunk, full-on liquored up, glassy-eyed, ruddy cheeked, and pissed off Baby's entire life. It just seemed so random. Alive, shouting at Baby about god knows what one moment and less than twelve hours later dead on the floor of their little house. Sure, she'd been in her seventies, but she still charged around, as if the booze were powering her very soul, the stubbornness forcing her to stand upright.

Baby takes another long drink from her beer and sighs, so lost in it that she gasps when the car horn sounds.

"Baby!" DJ Overalls shouts at her out the window of her purple hatchback. The party sub is so long it's hanging across the back seat, wrapped in tin foil, sticking out both windows.

Baby waves and hurries over. DJ can be a stick-in-the-mud about drinking in the car, which is ridiculous, because it's not like they'll run into the police. The rule is usually that once they leave paved roads, they're allowed to crack one. Today Baby thinks she can get away with it on the highway, and her suspicions are confirmed as she slides into the front seat, beer in hand, and DJ says nothing. Baby drops the bag full of ashes onto the floor between her feet with a thud and takes a long drink. After all, she is in mourning.

* * *

When Baby was picking up Hannah's remains and DJ Overalls the party sub, Crystal Nugget apparently took it upon herself to deck the entirety of the Bloody Parrot in an explosion of black—black balloons, black streamers hanging from the ceiling, black paper chains, black plastic tablecloths. When Baby arrives with the bag of ashes in one hand, Crystal takes it in two fingers and carries it over to the table where she's set up a guest book and a framed photo of Hannah and puts it down in front.

"Should we put . . . her *in* something?" Crystal asks, and Baby shrugs, opens another beer and takes a long drink.

She sits in a chair, in the middle of the room, and waits.

The wake doesn't have a set start time, not that Baby knows of, but all of her friends show up, some of them behind the bar, some of them just standing around, drinking, opening bags of chips and restocking coolers because they don't know exactly what else to do. All of their regulars, their customers, mill in small circles. Lakeside is a small town and news travels fast. Even Baby's neighbor, Betty—who rented them the rickety little cabin on her property—shuffles in and stands alone in the corner, her ratty white dog under one arm, baring its teeth at anyone who comes too close.

Louise is the last to arrive and when she does, she and Baby make eye contact across the bar and their bodies move toward one another. They've never embraced, never in all twenty-nine years of Baby's existence, but they throw themselves at one another in a boob-smashing hug that makes Baby lose her breath. "I'm so sorry," Louise whispers into Baby's neck.

"It's not your fault," Baby says, surprised at the level of emotion Louise is expressing—Louise has always been an eye roller, a gruff back slapper, but now she looks small, like she's shrunk a few sizes, her white hair glowing in the dark like a neon sign flashing *I'm old, I'm old, I'm old.*

"Yes it is. It's my fault," Louise says.

"I should've done something," Baby says. "But I don't think she would've stopped drinking. There were a few times she tried. Didn't stick."

Louise says nothing, just holds Baby. Baby knows exactly what she's feeling. That maybe if they'd sat Hannah down, if they'd tried harder, maybe she wouldn't have had the stroke so early. Could've lived out a few more years. Happier. Lighter.

But it's a stupid thought, really, and it leaves Baby as soon as Louise lets her go, walks out of the room to hide in her office, do her crying out of sight of her employees.

"Eat this," DJ Overalls says, appearing next to Baby. "You need something in your stomach." A sizable chunk of the party sub, Hannah's favorite food, sits on the plate and Baby picks it up, the dull, now cold sandwich in her hand, and takes a bite. The meatballs squish against her teeth, making her want to throw up, but she manages to down the entire thing and does feel marginally better.

She sits in a chair next to Crystal, who alternately holds her hand and fetches Baby drinks for the rest of the night, switching between beer and water. For once, Baby just sits there and lets them all fuss over her, wipe the drool from the corners of her mouth, hug her, squeeze her shoulders. Eventually, though, Baby's had enough of this attention.

She wants the bar emptied out, she wants it to be just the three of them, maybe Marco too if he wants to stay, but it seems like the whole town is still hanging around, waiting for something.

"How do we get them to leave?" she asks Crystal and DJ, who's just returned from her stint behind the booth, changing the Steely Dan to Hannah's other favorite, Tony Bennett.

"I think they're waiting for your speech, you know—"

"The eulogy," DJ says.

"What?" Baby says.

"Just say some things you loved about Hannah—"

Baby interrupts her with a loud *psh*, and DJ slugs her in the arm. "Don't speak ill of the dead."

"Hannah spent most of her life speaking ill of me." Baby says. "It's about time I returned the favor."

"Listen," Crystal says. "It's just what people do. Besides, there must've been some things you loved about her."

Baby didn't think about this before she arrived. It would be hard to define their relationship with its odd power dynamic, to find a balance between Hannah her savior, the woman who pulled her out of the dumpster, and Hannah the broken drunk, with a tongue like a whip and eyes so sharp she noticed everything and held back nothing.

Baby takes a long sip from her drink, can't tell if it's ice water or a very watered-down vodka soda designed to keep her hydrated. Either way, she just wants to get this over with.

Crystal reaches down and squeezes her hand.

Baby stands up and watches DJ scuttle over to the booth, where she turns down the music. "Hey!" Baby shouts, and her voice comes out quieter that she expected. She takes a swig from her drink as the room turns to face her, then a deep breath. "Shut up!"

A chuckle, a murmur, then quiet. Even Louise seems to have heard the change in the volume, has emerged from her office, eyes puffy, to lean on the doorjamb and listen.

"Uh, thank you for coming," Baby says. "Obviously, if you didn't come, you'd be an asshole." The room chuckles again, warmly. "And it's a Friday. If this resort was open, most of you'd be in this bar anyway." Another chuckle.

Baby relaxes. "God yeah, Hannah. She loved this piece-of-shit resort almost as much as I do. Oakwood Hills is home. That's really dumb, I know, but it is. Hannah taught me a lot."

Baby stops and takes a sip from her drink and smacks her lips, feels like an actor, someone else, performing, shakes her glass a bit, then gestures to it. "And not just that."

Another chuckle.

"She taught me that you can choose your family, even if it means picking them up out of a dumpster or shacking up with them in a bar. God, what is it now, for fifteen years?"

"Sixteen!" Crystal shouts.

"Right," Baby says. "But seriously, without all of you, without her, I wouldn't have anything at all. And that's, well . . ."

Baby stops to look at the ceiling, feeling the tears coming.

"Baby's gonna cry!"

"Fuck you!" she shouts, feels the tears arriving, takes a deep breath, trying to hold them in.

Crystal steps up next to her, DJ on the other side, and they raise their red plastic cups in a silent toast. Everyone in the room follows suit, murmuring, "To Hannah."

It's then that Baby feels the tears stream down her cheeks, the shock that's caused her mind to fog over these past few days opening up, the clouds bursting full, letting it all go. Letting it all out.

2

WEEKS LATER THEY'RE opening the Bloody Parrot, the lot of them, Baby, Crystal, DJ Overalls, Marco, Louise, pulling equipment out of storage, stocking the bar full of liquor, sanitizing the fridges, when Baby's phone buzzes in her pocket. Everyone she knows is in here, which can only mean one thing. She fumbles with it at first, the butterflies that accompany the text message she always receives at the beginning of the season punching at her stomach. It's the text message that always defines her summer, for better or worse.

She stares at the cracked screen, her hands shaking just a little, at the text Peter Pomoroy sent to let her know he's back: Why don't they just hang out, just the two of them? He has some family stuff to do, but maybe he can swing by later?

The summer doesn't start for her until Peter comes back, but instead of any sort of buildup, Baby just feels anxious that this will be the last summer they see each other, the last time he slides back into her life sideways.

Baby waits a beat and tries to quash the voice that always flails up, that whispers to her, low and harsh and honest, about how Peter always appears and disappears at will, never accountable to her, to anything, that it's just a summer thing. *But still.* Another voice invades the subconscious drag that's happening, a peppier voice that tells her he does always show up. No matter. He always shows up.

Not true! the other voice wails. *Not when it matters.*

"Shut up," Baby mutters, and Crystal looks up at her from the floor, where she's attempting to scrub the linoleum clean, a truly fruitless gesture.

"What?" Crystal says. "Did you say something?"

"No," Baby says, then goes back to cleaning their ancient register with a toothbrush, with a focus that makes everyone in the room suddenly suspicious.

"Who texted you?" DJ asks.

"Spam," Baby says. "Viagra ad."

"Sure," DJ says. Baby knows they hate it when Peter makes his entry each year. No one says anything this time, though, and Baby can tell it's because they pity her, they've all pledged to stop giving Baby a hard time. And she takes the break gratefully.

A few hours later, once her phone buzzes again and Louise gives her an *Oh, go on* tick of the head, Baby emerges from the Parrot, sweaty, exhausted, a little drunk from the cocktails they sipped using years-old booze Louise had deemed ancient enough to throw out. When she reaches the steep, paved pathway that winds down to the dock, she looks out at the lake and inhales, tries to relax. She doesn't see Peter's boat, but that's normal. He usually parks around the side, under the cover of a fat pine tree so no one can see them, and she sets off in that direction, her chest tightening.

The boat is what gives Baby hope for her future with Peter Pomoroy. It's old, from the nineties, with torn orange leather seats and a big old outboard motor strapped to the back that pisses when he starts it up. The boat has scratches all over the body, the brand of it rubbed away—where it used to say *Evin-rude*, now it just says *rude*.

Baby loves that Peter Pomoroy, who could've sold this boat and bought another years ago, can't let go. It's almost as if he's holding on to things at the lake that matter to him, even though he's getting too old for them. She knows that for as long as he has the boat, he'll come back to her, every summer.

Her hope punches her in the stomach when she steps onto the dock, rounds the corner and sees him, stretched out on the floor of his boat, hands knit together behind his head, a hat slung backward over his head, an old green T-shirt with thumbed-out holes all over it hugging his body. Dumpster Baby is so many things at once—excited, terrified, horny, but above all, happy that he is the same. Everywhere else he is Peter Pomoroy, one of the twin heirs to the Pomoroy Pharmaceutical fortune, but here, in this boat, he's exactly the kind of guy Baby can see herself with, the kind of guy Baby isn't afraid of.

"Hi," she says, the awkwardness of seeing Peter for the first time since last summer making her sweat. When he looks at her, it feels as if someone has just rung a gong.

"Baby!" he says, excited. He stands and reaches out with his arms. She kicks off her flip-flops, puts one hand on either shoulder, and hops down into the boat, the edges of it slapping the water. He pulls her toward him and gives her a long kiss, his tongue sliding between her lips, and she welcomes it, the happiness of the moment completely obliterating the doubt she stared down all night, forgetting about the waiting, the smugness of everyone in the bar, the fear that this time they'd all be right, that this time he wouldn't show up for her.

Baby relaxes into it, into him, and starts yanking at his shorts, forcing a chuckle out of his throat, and his hands slide under her shirt and it's just like it always has been.

"Buy me dinner first, why don't you," he says, but lets her wrestle him to the scratchy gray carpet and impress upon him just how much she missed him.

When she rolls off him, he holds her tightly to his body with one arm, kisses the side of her head.

"Wow," he says, a mildly shocked expression on his face. "Hello, Baby."

"Missed you too," she says.

Silence arrives between them and it's still uncomfortable, nudging at her, the fear of what will happen when they run out of things to talk about. "You're up early this year."

"I graduated," he says. "And I'm supposed to be looking for a job, but I thought . . . I don't know. Might as well enjoy the last summer I have, you know? The bar can wait."

"What bar?"

"The bar exam," he says. "You know, lawyer stuff."

"Oh." Baby flushes, embarrassed that she didn't know that. "What do you mean by last summer?" She tries not to panic. *Last summer.*

He laughs. "Well, I mean, law isn't exactly a seasonal job."

"I know. But no weekends? No holidays?"

"Did you meet Wade last summer?" he asks.

"No," says Baby. Peter never brings his friends from the city to the Bloody Parrot, but usually after they visit, Baby will hear from him about the wild parties on his parents' island, a vagueness to the details, the attendees, making her wonder if there were girls there, other girls he's purposely not telling her about, girls who go to college, girls who will one day become wives and mothers, girls with pedicures, girls who vote.

"I didn't bring him to the Parrot?"

"No," says Baby, trying to keep anything accusatory out of her voice. DJ said it's because he's ashamed off all his trashy townee friends, but Baby doesn't think that could be it, not by a long shot. He's here, isn't he?

"He would've loved it," says Peter. "Anyway, he's a year ahead of me and he started clerking for this judge last September and I haven't seen him since."

"Oh." It felt like it was happening too soon. "Why do you want to be a lawyer anyway?" she asks, trying to keep it casual. "You'd make a much better ship's captain."

He laughs and tucks a strand of hair behind her ear, reaches behind her and finds her discarded Oakwood Hills baseball cap, puts it back on her head. "We've got to grow up sometime, Baby."

"Do we?" Baby asks, poking him in the belly button. He has an outie and sometimes when they're drunk, he stands up and pushes his stomach out, hard and round, and he looks like a pregnant teen, the hard watermelon of skin all stretched out. "Are you saying you want me to become a Dumpster Teen?"

"Or just a normal teen," he says. "Or a grown-up."

"But grown-ups work twelve months out of the year," Baby says. "Disgusting."

He chuckles and hugs her to him a little tighter, his stubble rubbing against her ear.

"You're right," he says. "Dumpster Baby can stay right where she is."

"Yes!" she whispers.

"Sometimes I think you have it all figured out," he says. "Work five months a year, spend the rest relaxing."

"Occasional part-time to keep the unemployment checks flowing, but yeah," Baby says. "That's the idea."

"You don't want more than this?" he asks.

Baby looks up at Peter Pomoroy and then out at the lake. The deep blue-gray water is the color of iron tonight, and the subtle breeze causes ripples that grow into tiny waves. This is the moment to tell him, to tell him what she wants. It won't happen once the summer settles into its own subtle rhythm. She takes a deep breath and pauses, then lets it out.

He laughs. "I get it," he says. "If I were you, I'd be doing the same thing."

Her cheeks flush. DJ Overalls doesn't know shit. Baby kisses him again, right on the mouth. Of course she's imagined a million different futures where Peter Pomoroy abandons whatever boring corporate Richie Rich life he has in the city to move up here full-time and they open some kind of business together. Like a frozen yogurt shop or a marina. She can still hang out with Crystal Nugget and DJ Overalls as much as she wants, and in the winter they can take trips to the Caribbean or Italy or Mexico for some sunshine.

"I know, you think it's stupid, since you're from here and I'm not, but I mean it."

"I know you do," she says, squeezing him tighter to her body. It's so much easier to have these conversations lying down, when they don't have to make eye contact and can just stare up at the sky or across each other's bodies, press lips into shoulder blades and forget the rest.

"Did I tell you my sister is up here this summer?" he asks.

"No," she says. She knows he has a twin sister she's never met because the girl spent her summers at some fancy all-girls camp and never came out to any bush parties or the Parrot or anything. Baby's always assumed she's a snob. "What's her name again?"

"Amelia," he says. "She just graduated from business school and wants to start a small business up here."

"Really?" Baby asks, surprised. "Why here?"

"I don't know, she has lots of charts and graphs. Something about real estate prices and market share. She's being a real nerd about it. You should meet her."

"Really?" Baby says again, even more surprised. The Pomoroy family has always been off-limits, the island especially. Peter always comes to her. Baby has never been over there, never dared set foot on the property in case they have cameras—even in winter, when all the palatial vacation homes are deserted, leaving the townees and the tall trees to commune with the dark.

"Of course," he says. "Speaking of family, when's Hannah making spaghetti? I've been daydreaming about it for months."

His question stops her cold, and she sits up and looks at the edge of the boat, the dock, which desperately needs to be sanded, to where her flip-flops sit, the casual way he brought up Hannah making her heart physically hurt. Of course he doesn't know Hannah's dead, didn't bother to open Baby's emails. He never does. Whenever September rolls around, he packs up his stuff and leaves, forgetting about this town until he needs it again.

"What?" Peter sits up and grabs her shoulder.

"Hannah's dead," Baby says simply.

"What?" he asks. "When?"

"A few weeks ago," Baby says. "I emailed you. Twice." She picks at her fingernail, listens to him swallow once, his stomach gurgling.

"I'm sorry, Baby. I didn't get it."

She pictures DJ holding a megaphone, standing on the edge of the dock screaming *bullshit!* right into her ear.

"Why not?" she asks.

"What do you mean?"

"No internet at that fancy law school?"

"I just didn't get the email," he says.

"Everyone else got it." This is as close to a fight as they've ever had. It's not like they're exclusive, not like they've had honest conversations about who they are to each other and what that means.

"I'm sorry, Baby." Peter reaches for her elbow, massages the skin there. "I didn't. Why didn't you call?"

A question she can't let herself consider for too long. Enough hurt for tonight. The breeze kicks up and the waves knock the boat against the dock, as if it's time to go. Baby stands.

"Can I give you a ride home?" he asks, and she knows he thinks she still lives five minutes away, just around the point in the little cabin she used to share with Hannah. Baby let the lease drop when she realized how expensive it was to live there alone. Betty, the divorced old woman who owns the property, always hated her. Probably because Baby took her only son's virginity, but she can't be sure.

"I don't live there anymore," Baby says, stretching her arms up over her head and yawning. Definitely time for bed. She steps back into her shorts and hops a little, pulling them up and over her hips, finds her shirt in the back corner of the boat, tucks her underwear in her pocket.

"Where do you live?" he asks.

"Up there," she says, gesturing to the boathouse.

"Louise lets you?"

Baby steps out of the boat, slipping her feet into flip-flops. "She hasn't figured it out yet." Baby shrugs. "Free Wi-Fi."

"Baby, I can lend you some money," he says. "If you need help getting a place."

"I don't need your money," Baby says. "Once things at the Parrot pick up, I'll be fine."

"You've got to live somewhere."

"I'm good," Baby says, spotting a six-pack of beer with four left in it on the back bench of his boat. It's nice, too—fancy

German beer in a green can. Baby grabs it with two fingers. "This is my home."

"Hannah didn't leave you anything?"

"Of course she did," Baby says, lying, thinking about the nearly depleted thin roll of bills she has tucked into her old hiking boots. "It's fine." Baby swallows, and the rest comes out harsher than she means it to. "It'll all be fine."

"That's really sad, Baby. I'm so sorry." He speaks in a voice she doesn't recognize, and she suddenly feels desperate to get away from him.

"I'm going to go," Baby says, turns away before she starts to cry.

"Good night!" he calls after her.

"Night!" She waves behind her and heads inside the boathouse, climbs up to the roof, and straddles the peak of it, the beers still hanging from their pack. She unsnaps one and takes a long sip, watches Peter's boat as it trolls back out into the middle of the bay. His island's ten minutes away at full speed, but the dork always trolls at night because when they were teenagers, a very piss-drunk Sig Marsh drove her aunt's boat up onto someone's dock and got thrown from it and died. She'd been heading home from a bush party. Baby can't remember the name of the cottagers who owned the dock she ended up on, but they found her body hanging from a tree by the life jacket she'd been wearing, her neck lolling off to the side.

After that, Peter always kept a sleeping bag in his boat, and if he was really drunk he would sleep wherever he was docked and go home at sunrise. Baby has spent more than one night in that boat, their bodies pushed together by the confines of the space more than romance. Usually she'd wake up first and pump the bulb connected to the engine to get the gas moving, and by the time she'd started the engine, Peter would have woken up and he'd take over. But more than one morning, while he slept on the floor, she drove herself home in his boat, docked at Betty's, and left him there, then crawled into her bed for a few extra hours before she had to turn around and head back to work.

Sometimes she'd go back down to the dock and he'd still be passed out, and she'd start his boat up again and drive herself back to Oakwood Hills. He'd sleep late into the afternoon and come up and hang with them in the Parrot and order twenty chicken strips with hot sauce. If they were doing housekeeping, he'd order his food to go and sit on their laundry cart on top of the piles of dirty sheets and towels and eat and talk while they stripped beds and Windexed the windows. Sometimes, if his hangover wasn't too bad, he'd help them out or bring them a joint and they'd all smoke it in a bathroom with the shower on hot and then go hide out in the woods until their pupils returned to a more normal size.

Baby finishes two beers and chucks the cans into the lake. It makes sense that he didn't open her email. Maybe it did end up in his spam. She doesn't know. If he was actually her boyfriend, she would've texted or called and he would've gotten back to her right away. And she knew it then, when she was writing the email, that he wouldn't come to the wake, and she knew it when she walked across the dock to restart this "relationship."

She's a smart girl, Baby, buried underneath all the horseshit and the boozing. She's not stupid. She can do the math. He's a hot, rich guy who has every opportunity in the world, and she's a Dumpster Baby, stuck in a nowhere town living paycheck to paycheck, and if they just hook up on his boat during the summer, that'll have to be okay with her.

3

"I'M NOT DANCING to this," Baby shouts, pounding her fist against the floor. "Do I look like a ballerina on her night off? Meat Loaf! Meat Loaf! Meat Loaf!" She sucks the dregs out of her can of beer, crumples the can in one hand and throws it over her shoulder.

"Hey!"

It's a city bitch. Baby can tell by the outrage in her voice. Anyone actually from Lakeside knows that when they step into the Bloody Parrot, they're in Baby's domain and any airborne projectiles are to be dodged or thrown back.

"What the hell?"

Baby's pretty sure she knows which one it is. A pack of them walked in earlier, but the tallest, a blonde in a pink tank top, seemed to have the most attitude. Baby ignores her and stomps across the dance floor, slamming her feet down to emphasize her point.

Crystal's at the DJ booth, shaking her head, and DJ Overalls is slumped against the wall, texting, one leg casually slung over the other, a flip-flop dangling off her toes. Tonight her overalls are a classic blue denim, rolled up to show off ankle bracelets made from embroidery floss she should've cut off three summers ago and hasn't.

"I'm not changing it," DJ says, ignoring Baby.

"Oh, come on," Baby says. "You've been playing the same song all night."

"I have not. It's an album," DJ Overalls says. "This is what the paying customers want." She gestures to a pastel-colored square lighting up the screen on her laptop.

"I'm a paying customer," Baby says.

"Yeah, but your tips are shit." DJ grins at her. "Come on, Baby, fuck off."

"You fuck off."

"Bitch." DJ smiles.

"How do you even dance to this?" Baby asks.

DJ gestures out to the floor with her chin, where the city girls are all swaying back and forth. The song seems to be designed for hair, and Baby watches, annoyed as they flip it back and forth. A breeze whips in through the patio door, and they all seem to be pretending they're in a shampoo commercial. Maybe this is just what's cool now. Baby can't quite fathom it, but if this pack of identically dressed faux blondes are all so fully committing to it without any trace of irony, it must be real.

"They look like they're having seizures," she whispers to Crystal Nugget, who snorts into her vodka tonic. "Come on." Baby grabs Crystal around her wrist. "I feel like jumping rope."

"Baby, no," Crystal says, but doesn't resist as Baby drags her back onto the dance floor. Baby pulls off her baseball hat and shakes out her hair, which is a hive of gnats and snarls and stinks of lake water, and starts skipping with an invisible rope. On a good night, she and DJ or Crystal or some drunk guy she's befriended for a few songs will get the entire dance floor to play pretend, sometimes throwing a giant invisible beach ball around, or grabbing hands and creating a limbo stick. Tonight it's double Dutch. But the city bitches don't seem impressed, clearly hate the idea of actually having fun at a bar, and keep shaking their hips around in circles.

"It's sort of like you're hula-hooping with no hoop," Baby says, abandoning the jump rope. She starts mimicking the hip waves and thrusts of the girl in the pink tank top.

"But also not bending anything," Crystal says, and they're both laughing and laughing and it's Tank Top who catches Baby's eye, the girl in the pink who's looking at them, a mocking eyebrow raised, and she turns and says something to her friend, and they both look at Crystal and laugh.

"What's funny?" Baby calls across the floor, gesturing to Crystal Nugget, who doesn't hear, is too busy laughing at herself. Sure, Crystal is a lot of woman, with piles of platinum-blond hair. Tonight she's wearing tight leather shorts and a leopard-print tank top her boobs are trying to escape. But she's a thoroughly kind person, and watching these city bitches giggle at her while she relaxes after getting her shift cut makes Baby want to smash some heads.

"Nothing," the girl says, then whispers again to her friend, who has the same haircut, the same straight white teeth, the same jean shorts riding up her ass, the same miniature cowboy boots.

And it's the laughter that gets to Baby, the smug, self-assured laughter, the tittering, the stares, that puts the rage on boil, a roaring filling her ears. She hates these bitches and their fucking city attitudes. Come up here for a weekend, try to claim everything. They're used to being invisible, a packed crowd surrounding them, stomping around in their high heels, buying seven-dollar coffees, video chatting on their nine-hundred-dollar phones paid for by careers they'll abandon in five years for whining children and farting husbands. Baby fucking hates it. *These weekenders.* Usually the cottagers, the real diehards, know what this place is. But these types of bitches just duck in for the weekend and want to define the world.

So Baby sort of can't help it when she chugs half her beer, then spins, throwing the remnants out at the two girls, watches with satisfaction as the foamy swill lands in the middle of the pink tank top and slides down.

"Jesus Christ!" the girl shouts. "Hey!"

Baby grins and flips her off. Crystal has stopped dancing, is standing with a fist on her hip, shaking her head.

"Baby, come on," she says. "Already?"

"It was an accident," Baby says.

"Excuse me," Pink Tank Top says, handing the vodka soda she was drinking to her friend, the straw on the edge of the cup threatening to spill over onto the floor. "This shirt is dry clean only."

"And . . ." Baby says.

Pink Tank Top glares at her, then rolls her eyes. "Pathetic."

"What was that?" Baby asks, now losing control.

"I said pathetic. You. I've been sneaking into this bar since I was seventeen. You've been here at least that long. Don't you want to, like, I don't know, get a life or something? I mean, come on. Coming back here's like visiting the world's most depressing time capsule. Let me guess, you work the summer, then surf unemployment for the rest of the year, waiting until you can make tips off of the rich kids who come up here on weekends? It's *pathetic*."

"I think you should leave," says Baby.

"Oh wow, really?" Pink Tank Top laughs, her eyes mockingly wide. "Says who?"

Baby steps closer, right up to the girl, can smell her perfume that reeks like a bag of Halloween candy. People are starting to look, but Baby doesn't give a shit, she really doesn't.

Pink Tank Top opens her mouth, but Baby cuts her off with a quick shove that tips her off her heels. She falls over into the pack of girls behind her, bringing two down with her, all of them disappearing into a very blond pile.

"Go home," Baby says, then turns to where DJ sits, shaking her head.

"I thought you weren't going to fight this summer," DJ says. "You just said, I shit you not, like three hours ago, 'I don't think I'm going to fight this summer.' And I said, 'You know, Baby, I think that's a really good idea. I think it'll be good for you and good for the bar.'"

"They need to—" Baby says, then cries out as she's dragged backward off her feet by a sharp yank to her hair. She stumbles and just catches herself on a table, straightening up. All the city bitches are facing her and Baby can't quite remember which one she's fighting, the army of them all so identical she feels a little woozy.

"Come at me, bitch!" Baby calls out.

"All right, that's enough." Johnny the security guy appears and in one motion throws Baby over his shoulder.

"Aw, c'mon, Johnny, I didn't even touch her," Baby says, as he carries her toward the front door.

"Sure, Baby," he says. "And I'm the sultan of Brunei."

"That's not real. You're making it up."

"It's real," Johnny says. "I saw it last night on *Jeopardy*."

Baby flips two middle fingers at the girls as she's carted away, feels all the eyes in the bar on her, hears some scattering applause—probably the Dickie brothers, who are the kind of losers who'd take video of a girl fight and probably have a catalog of Baby's greatest hits at home.

Outside, Johnny puts her down on the edge of the patio, and Baby's rage has morphed into blushing embarrassment. "You better kick them out too," Baby says. Johnny takes a slow, deep breath and rubs his shaved head, and Baby thinks about how she's never seen Johnny get mad about anything, ever, never seen any emotion that went farther or deeper than a sigh, a rub of his head.

"Just go chill on the balcony. I'll get rid of them," he says. "You're bad for business, Baby."

"We're fine. It's still early."

"They were tipping," he says.

"You can have my share."

"One day I'm going to take you up on that." Johnny shakes his head, a soft grin on his face, and Baby knows she's off the hook, as usual.

"Thank you!" Baby calls after him, her heart pounding in her ears. She takes out her phone and checks it again, hoping there will be a text from Peter asking her if she wants to hang out again. It's been weeks.

Instead, nothing.

DJ's going to be pissed at her; hell, they're all going to be pissed at her. Here she is, chasing this flock of girls away, city bank accounts and all. Baby heads down the balcony, around the corner, out of sight, and listens as the chorus of their shouting fills the air.

"No fighting, ladies, sorry."

"That ugly girl started it," the girl complains.

Ugly is a bit much. She prefers *lacking beauty* or maybe *undercooked*. Or poorly assembled. But ugly? Baby sighs, looks at her reflection in the greasy window, can just make out her big nose and wide-apart eyes, the ear that sticks out a little more than the other, the half-deflated boob and the overachiever next to it, and shrugs. It's not like there's anything she can do about it.

"And she's gone too," Johnny says. Baby can picture it now; she's seen him many times before, waving groups out with two hands, shepherding them to the bus in the parking lot as if trying to herd goats back into a pen. "Now if you give him twenty bucks, the driver will take you where you want to go. Good night."

"This place gets more and more depressing every year," the bitch says. The bus starts up with a rumble. "We won't be coming back."

"If you change your mind," Johnny says, always the politician, "we'll be happy to have you—another night." The doors of the minibus squeak closed, and the bus pulls out of the gravel parking lot. She waits for its lights to turn out onto the road before she slumps back around the corner, feeling like a proper asshole now, embarrassment turning to shame. The evolution of a normal night out for Baby. She definitely needs another beer.

Moments later, Johnny's back on his stool, a silver counter in his hand, even though he doesn't need it. Not tonight. Always a professional.

"Sorry, Johnny." She nuzzles her head against his arm, and he laughs.

"We've got a whole summer of this. Isn't it a little early to be losing your shit on the tourists? I've been kicking you out of this place for years. I'd say we're usually looking at late July, early August."

"Well, I am in mourning," says Baby, wondering if maybe she does feel worse about Hannah dying than she's let on, that there's something about it that just doesn't feel real or possible or even true.

Johnny wraps an arm around her shoulder. "You really did a great job with that party. She would've liked it."

"Thanks," says Baby. It wasn't totally unreasonable that Hannah died, but it was sudden and Baby's just not quite used to the freedom to move through the world without anyone leaning over her shoulder, telling her what to do. Whenever Baby forgot to shower or do her hair, Hannah would be there, usually six or seven drinks in, telling Baby she looked like a hemorrhoid.

"You going back in?" he asks.

"In a minute."

She hops up on the low wall next to Johnny. She's known him since they were in kindergarten, and he lets her stay quiet for a while. Her buzz is starting to fade. She flips her phone on and off and on and off, the blue light making her eyes hurt.

"What did she say?" Johnny asks. "The girl you were ripping on?"

"Just that we were pathetic because we've been working here for too long."

"I could've told you that," Johnny says, laughing.

"I know," Baby says. "All right? I know."

Baby knows she's not supposed to fight. She's always known. It's any number of things, though, on any given day, at any given time, that make her draw her hand back. She loves a slap. The sting, the sound, the spectacle. A hair pull. Oh, baby, Baby.

"Where are you living now, Baby?" Johnny asks.

"Oh, you know," she says. "Here and there."

"My cousin got a full-time job out on the rigs, if you want to look at his place," Johnny says. "You'd have to get a car, but it's quiet."

"Yeah, maybe," Baby says noncommittally. She thinks she might just tough it out for the summer and figure all of it out when she's flush in September and has to worry about it. She should've known Hannah would die broke, penniless, wasted drunk, leaving Baby in a similar state. Just the way things go, she reasons.

Baby stares off, up toward the road, and spots two headlights in the distance, cutting through the darkness. The car slows down and turns up the drive to the resort. "Uh-oh," she says. "You think they're coming back?"

"Nah, they were way too drunk," Johnny says. Baby agrees. City girls don't drink and drive, which leaves her curious about the familiar sound of the engine approaching. She can't quite put her finger on it.

As she watches the car get closer, she blinks, because she's seeing something that isn't possible. The car. The shape of the headlights and the roar of the engine. She knows the car. A sinking dread grabs hold of Baby. She punches Johnny in the arm.

"Fuck," she says, watching as the headlights get bigger and bigger, and it takes Johnny a second to realize what Baby knows for certain.

"No way." He looks over his shoulder to make sure no one's coming out of the bar and the two of them stand up, not sure where to look or where to go.

"We can keep him out, right?" Baby asks.

"I mean, yeah," Johnny says. "Listen, let me do the talking, and if anything happens, call Deputy Donna, all right? Her number's on the card." He gestures to the card pasted to the wall next to the little shelf where he puts his water bottle, his flashlight, a pack of Dentyne Ice, the remnants of a Band-aid.

Baby knows the card, has prank texted all manner of idiotic bullshit to the number on many separate occasions from random phones of bar friends she's made for one night only. *It'll be hilarious*, she always says. And it almost always is. But now they need the card, they need it, which is ridiculous in itself. How's a five-foot-four rent-a-cop going to protect them from this?

The car stops in the middle of the lot, gravel skittering in all directions. And sure as anything, Baby sees that the car belongs to Bad Mike, and that the figure climbing out of the front seat has a very distinct scorpion tattoo climbing up the side of his very thick neck.

CHAPTER

4

IT'S BEEN SEVEN years, but he looks the same. Shoulders so broad he has to step sideways through doorways, hair clipped short, the bottom edges of it freshly buzzed, the tiny black hairs looking almost blue against his pale scalp. Tattoos everywhere—pressing together on his arms, snaking up his neck, and poking out his shirt collar. He's wearing fresh sneakers, the soles glowing white through the darkness. His jeans are so tight that his muscles want to burst out of them. Two guys get out with him, probably the same idiots who followed him around before, wearing cargo shorts, basketball shoes, and hats ticked off in opposite directions. Baby thinks they also might be related, somewhat distantly, because they all have the same "eh doy" expression on their faces, Mike's masked only by a terrifying blankness.

Baby crosses her arms, leans against the wall, even, then straightens up again, settles for looking at her phone, pretending to check her text messages, her hands shaking.

Johnny walks out a few steps to meet them on the lawn, and Baby follows him out of the corner of her eye, biting down on her tongue. "Not tonight, boys," he says, a hand out and low. "It's pretty quiet in there, we're a few minutes from last call."

"We'll just come in for one," says Bad Mike, an easy smile, eyes flickering over Johnny's shoulder to Baby. He sounds charming, the grin making him look like a politician on steroids, but Baby knows Johnny isn't fooled.

"Not tonight, man, I'm sorry. I really am." Johnny's been doing this job since he hit two hundred pounds in the eleventh grade, and he's good at it. He knows when to be aggressive and when to keep his hands low, when to rip a girl's fake ID in half and when to hand it back to her and send her on her way. "The Legion has off sales. Truck was just by today." Johnny plays like they do just want a drink, even though Baby's sure that's not entirely what they're after.

Bad Mike wants to strut around, wants all the people who put him away to know he's back and he's here and their summers all just got a little bit different because of it. That he doesn't give a shit, that any shame they're hoping he's carried on his back since he was arrested has been sloughed off. And he hasn't changed, didn't find God behind bars, just found his way to the gym and a tattoo artist who probably didn't clean his needles.

"Baby, Baby, Baby."

"Bad Mike, Bad Mike, Bad Mike," Baby replies. "Doesn't have the same ring to it."

Bad Mike brushes past Johnny and strides up the steps toward her. Baby shoves her phone in her pocket, doesn't want him to see her failed attempt at a text message to the police and stands, chin up, arms crossed, to face him. As he stares her down, she really does feel the alcohol evaporating from her body, as if the beer is turning to piss with every second she waits in his eyeline.

"How's my girl?" he asks.

"Who?" she says.

"You know who I'm talking about."

Baby knows she's not helping it any by playing dumb, but she keeps at it, shrugs. "I don't," she says.

"Then I guess I'll have to remind you," Mike says, and he makes a move to walk toward the bar. Baby doesn't know why she does it, where she finds the guts, but she sticks out her foot as he's striding toward the entrance. And Bad Mike doesn't see it, stumbles and falls through the front doors of Oakwood

Hills, all two hundred seventy pounds of him, landing on the floor with a mighty crash.

"Uh-oh." The words tumble out of Baby's mouth and she makes a move to hop over him, toward the bar, not sure what she's doing, the urge to run away from him taking over, the lizard in her brain cracking the whip.

"Baby!" he screams, reminiscent of an angry dad in an eighties movie, the rage and humiliation trumping everything else.

The crash has drawn a crowd, DJ Overalls and Crystal among the gawkers at the front door, eyes wide, unsure that this is what they're really seeing.

"Baby! You are dead! You're fucking dead!"

Baby dives into the huddle of bodies and pushes past them as Mike's buddies help him to his feet. Likely not the entrance he was dreaming of, a humiliation at the hands of the town Dumpster Baby instead of the intimidation he was hoping to heap on them.

Inside the bar, Baby cowers behind the group of them. There's the patio; she could jump off the patio, maybe. The fall wouldn't kill her, but whatever damage she sustained would likely hurt less than what Bad Mike is capable of. She'll hunker down in the lake, maybe swim under the dock. They can't get her there.

She's about to turn toward the patio when headlights blast all of them, lighting up Mike and Johnny and his friends still near the front doors, all of them in silhouette. Baby didn't hear the car coming and almost faints with relief when she sees the red, white, and blues of Deputy Donna's cruiser lighting up the dark.

Luck. Dumb, stupid luck. It's not out of the ordinary for her to swing by the Parrot, the only fun bar in the area, just to make sure they aren't pushing capacity or overserving, seeing as they're almost always doing one or the other, and quite often both.

"Uh-oh," Baby shouts from the back of the crowd of people, her heart thudding in her ears. "Is someone violating their parole?" Bad Mike turns around, seems to be trying to decide what the smart move is, measuring his urge to choke her against the desire to stay out of prison.

"See you soon, Baby." He turns back toward his car, his two idiot cronies following him, brushing past Donna as she walks up the front steps.

"Have a great night," Baby calls.

DJ turns around and punches her in the arm. "Will you shut up?"

Deputy Donna, their last hope, truly, all five foot four of her, steps through the front doors, hands on her belt buckle. "Everything okay?"

"Did you see that?" Johnny asks.

Deputy Donna nods. "Do we need an ambulance? Everyone all right? Some drunk girls called the community line about a fight."

"Seriously?" DJ says, turning to her, but Baby's already across the room, taking a swig of whiskey right from the bottle to quell the screaming in her chest.

5

"IN A WAY, I'm the hero," Baby says. "If I hadn't pushed that girl, Donna wouldn't have showed up. You are all welcome."

The bar is now closed. Johnny's in the bathroom, went in there a few minutes ago looking a little green and hasn't returned. Baby sits at a table with Crystal and DJ, an open bag of just-expired chips they can't sell between them, no one but Baby eating.

Before she left, Donna spoke to Johnny, who told her about Baby and the fight and Mike. Apparently Donna hadn't known Mike had gotten out early; otherwise she would've spread the word. She left pretty quickly, claimed she wanted to follow him, check in to see where he was staying, then would make a phone call to the parole board to find out what kind of violations they should be on the lookout for. It's all they can do.

"At least I didn't have to talk to her," Baby says. "Donna really knows how to harsh my buzz."

"You shouldn't be so mean," Crystal says, her voice shaky. Baby can tell she's thinking of what might have happened if Donna hadn't shown up at that exact moment. DJ Overalls reaches over and squeezes Crystal's hand.

"Can't help it," Baby says. "She just brings it out in me." There's been bad blood between Baby and Donna their entire lives, the scales tipping back and forth between them for as long as Baby can remember. In high school, Baby had the upper hand, did whatever she could to make the goody-goody, the narc with the doting parents and the new clothes and the braces, know she wasn't special.

But as soon as Donna got the badge, she started repaying the favor. Almost everyone in Lakeside accepts a certain reality about Dumpster Baby. Donna, for whatever reason, decided not to. So if Bad Mike hadn't shown up, Donna probably would've hassled her about the girls she allegedly picked a fight with, tried to haul her off for drunk-and-disorderly.

Baby's phone feels like a giant brick in her pocket. She keeps wanting to check it, but every time she does, DJ Overalls catches her eye and shakes her head. It's the time of night when Peter might swing by or shoot her a text to tell her he's parked his boat at their spot. The subtext of DJ's disapproval is that they're not leaving Crystal tonight; they'll see her home together.

To distract them all from the dread of what's to come, Crystal leans over and lays her head on Baby's shoulder. "Did Peter text you?"

"Nope," says Baby. "He will, though."

"Of course he will, sweets," she says. "Don't worry about me. I'm sure Mike just wanted to scare me. And I'm not going to let him." Her voice wavers a little.

"Yeah, fuck him," Baby says. "I bet he's not even allowed out after ten. Donna will sort him out."

Silence falls, all of them lost in thought, and Baby reaches for another chip.

Very suddenly, Baby's phone buzzes in her pocket and she jumps, leans over so she can get her phone out of her jean shorts and yanks it out so quickly she almost drops it. The text reads *He's Not Coming.* Baby looks up and DJ's laughing at her.

"Fuck you!" Baby says, and the tension hovering over them breaks. At least this is normal, Baby holding out for Peter at the end of the night, drunk, waiting, while Crystal and DJ not-so-silently judge her. The specter of Bad Mike has evaporated. For now.

"Peter, prove them wrong . . . now," Baby says to her cell phone, staring at the screen, checking to make sure the dropping hasn't interfered with her reception. She sends herself a text. Her phone beeps immediately. She sighs and tosses it into the middle of the table.

Usually, once the doors to the Parrot are locked, the real party begins. It's Baby's favorite part of the night, the moment when they lock out everyone they haven't hand selected, when they play the music on low and sometimes dance together, all wasted, cheeks flushed on the dance floor, waiting for a guest to call down to the front desk and ask them to shut up, the group of them all in this one place, sweaty hot, richer than they were before, stress hanging over their lives evaporated, condensed into drops on the ceiling. It's the happiest Baby's ever been, three AM in the Parrot, playing pool or dancing, or smoking pot, or just sitting out on the deck in the quiet next to someone she's known her entire life, playing cards, staring up at night skies that exist nowhere else.

Tonight, there's a real air of defeat in the air, which Baby cannot stand.

"Can we start closing, please?" Marco asks, and everyone starts flipping chairs over on the tables and Baby is, well, she's drunk and still sucking on a beer. If the party doesn't continue, she's just going to be alone, here, waiting for Peter, like a ripe old loser.

"What gives, guys?" she asks. They all ignore her, turning their attention to usual tasks.

Baby gets up from the table and stumbles over to the bar, where Marco's wiping things down. She hops up onto it and lies on her back, rubbing her butt back and forth to make sure it's extra shiny, feels the spilled drinks and melted ice cubes soaking through her jean shorts. "You're not going home now, are you, Marco?" she asks, picking up the soda gun and spraying some Coke into her mouth.

"Judy is off tonight," he says. "In other words, as soon as I get home, I'm going to be welcomed to the Morkuary with open legs." He wiggles his eyebrows, clearly pleased with himself.

"Ew," says Baby. "I can't believe you're dating a cop. Fuckin' narc."

"No need for narcs in this town," Marco says, fishing a maraschino cherry out of his plastic tub and dangling it over her mouth. She opens up and he drops the red bulb, and it promptly lodges itself in her windpipe, forcing her to sit up, coughing and hacking, until it goes down.

"You're no fun now that you're old."

"Get off my bar." Marco pushes her off, then tosses a handful of receipts in front of her. "And make yourself useful."

"You didn't do the dinner receipts yet?" she asks.

"I was saving them for you."

"Did we really hit forty chits tonight?" She flips through them, checking the numbers, confused. "It felt so empty."

"People were in here until around nine," Marco says. "Your memory is getting crappy."

"Whatever," Baby says, flipping through the receipts and doing a quick tally. "One thousand, three hundred forty-six dollars, twenty-eight," she says. "And $161.52 in tips. That can't be right." She scans the numbers again, tallying in her head, her one good parlor trick, her only marketable skill, obsolete now that every idiot carries a calculator around with them. "No, wait, it is."

"It's almost like the service here sucks or something." Marco laughs at his own joke. "How much each?"

"Forty bucks and thirty-eight cents," she says. "Minus five each for the kitchen."

He pulls her tip money out of the register and hesitates. "You want me to—"

"Jar it." He puts her thirty-eight cents in the massive tub of change they keep behind the bar—savings for house parties, beach parties, bush parties, gravel pit parties. Crystal walks over, tosses her shoes at the bar. They hit it with a clunk and roll away.

"Where's mine?" she slurs.

"Flip some chairs first," Marco says. "You too, Baby."

"Hey, you got a text," Crystal says, snatching Baby's phone off the bar. DJ Overalls appears and grabs the phone away from Crystal.

"What the hell? Give that back," says Baby.

"This is for your own good." DJ sticks the phone down the back of her overalls. "He's a jerk," she says.

"Just on the inside," Baby says, laughing.

"Flip some chairs, Baby!" Marco shouts from behind the bar.

"C'mon, let me read it." Baby lunges at DJ again, tries to grab her around the waist.

"Flip five chairs," says DJ.

"I flipped ten," says Crystal.

"You did not," says Baby.

Baby flips an entire table of chairs, all eight of them, so DJ will lighten up. There are far too many chairs in the Parrot. Baby has this exact thought every single night. No one ever sits down for long anyway. The ceiling is too drippy.

"I'm going now!" Baby says, once she's done at least a third of her share of the closing. She tips DJ five bucks, and DJ pulls Baby's phone out from her overalls. "Nice and sweaty," she says, but Baby ignores the condensation, reads the text, fear stirring in her stomach. He's at the dock. *Coming down.* Her fingers are numb. *Be right there.*

She shakes her hair out and jams it back under her baseball cap, wishing she'd had the forethought to apply fresh deodorant.

DJ's finger loops through the belt on her jean shorts, holding her back. "Baby, I'm not going to listen to you whine all summer when he dicks you over."

"Noted." Baby knows the threat's empty, because DJ Overalls is just as bored as the rest when it comes to this tiny town and any kind of gossip is a distraction. Anything at all, even if it's your best friend being completely miserable because her on-again, off-again boyfriend won't text her back.

Baby looks over to Crystal at the door, leaning on the jamb and flirting with Johnny. Just like last summer and the summer before that, and the summer before that, and basically every single summer since they got jobs there. Crystal flirts with Johnny. DJ tries to talk Baby out of hooking up with Peter. DJ fails. The cycle continues.

"He made you take a morning-after pill," says DJ.

"It was for my own good."

"He blended it into your smoothie," she says.

"That was one time," Baby says. "He's just Peter. He knows I suck at swallowing."

"Oh god," DJ says, "ugh. I'm going to throw up. Use a condom," she says.

"I'm already wearing one," Baby says, wiggling her eyebrows. DJ laughs—can't help it, Baby knows. DJ lets go, rolls her eyes toward Crystal as if to say, *I can handle this*. Baby grins.

"Someone's getting laid tonight," Baby sings, and runs out of the bar, slapping Crystal's butt as she passes her. "And that someone is me."

6

THE NEXT MORNING, Baby stands at the bottom of the hill, just outside the boathouse, groaning. It's too hot out and the hill's too steep and Baby's already puked behind a birch tree and washed her mouth out with lake water, which tasted like the inside of a shoe. She and Peter were up until sunrise, drinking, listening to music, skinny-dipping. It's all a bit of a blur, but she feels like a gigantic pile of ass. There's a protein bar in her pocket that she was already dreading eating, but the emptiness in her stomach is making things worse, and she just isn't sure forcing herself to swallow a weird nut patty is going to make it better.

She's stuffing her hair under a baseball hat and shoving on sunglasses when Marco drives up in a golf cart. He likes to laugh at them in the mornings when they walk around pale faced, puking behind bushes and trees, chugging water, stinking of the night before.

"Baby's got a hangover, Baby's got a hangover," he sings, slowing down next to her so she can climb in. "And she's sleeping in on her housekeeping shift. Again."

"Ah, crap," says Baby. She has a bad track record when it comes to housekeeping.

It dates back to the first summer she got a job at Oakwood Hills when she was fourteen; Hannah had fixed it for her. Louise had caved because she, along with everyone else in town, loved Hannah and, like everyone else, treated Baby with a removed sense of pity. Baby always attributed it everyone knowing about her tragic backstory, the awkward, trashy way she'd emerged into the world, and they definitely all knew about Hannah. There probably wasn't a person living in Lakeside who hadn't at some point helped carry Hannah out to a car, stinking with wine or vodka or both, lain her across the back seat, driven her up to the cabin, and knocked on the door for help getting her into bed.

For Baby, the drinking had started early. At fourteen she was sucking back warm beers in town with boys too old to be hanging around high school girls. Baby was a weird one; she loved the taste of beer instantly. Imports, domestics, generic pilsners, fancy home brew. Hannah smelled her the mornings after, the yeast hovering around her like an aura, and knew it would be a problem.

Instead of leaving Baby to stay out all night, Hannah introduced her to what she liked to call "consequences," would wake her up with the sunrise and pile her into the boat and they'd drive up to work at Oakwood Hills. Hannah would get to work on the books, nursing black cups of coffee and plain slices of dry toast, and Baby was sent to housekeeping hell with a summer hire named Helga who smoked constantly and barked orders at her as if Baby were her personal assistant.

It took Baby three months to realize she didn't have to clean the bathroom with an old toothbrush and it really didn't matter if she dusted behind the toilet every day. If anything, her time with Helga taught Baby the least amount of work she could get away with.

"Are you getting in or not?" Marco asks, and Baby, fighting the nausea that seems to come with moving, does so gingerly, slides onto the golf cart's bench next to him. He slams on the gas and throws her body backward in the seat, her head, oh her head, the pain traveling up her neck to behind her eyeballs. "Come on!"

Marco laughs.

"You did this to me," she says. "You're a bartender. Haven't you ever heard of cutting someone off?"

"Ha!" Marco laughs. "Like that would work. Lucky for you, Louise has called an all-staff meeting."

"Oh no," she says.

Marco reaches back into one of the cardboard boxes and hands her a bottle of water.

"Thanks." Baby smiles at him as he takes off, the golf cart powering up the steep hill.

"Lean forward," he says, as they near the crest of the slope, the engine straining. They rock the golf cart, just barely making it over the top, and drive toward the main building.

Oakwood Hills isn't a giant resort. The capacity is under a hundred. The main building has fifteen rooms. Five cabins in various state of disrepair sit in the back fields right at the edge of the forest. Louise always says she's going to redo them, but the money never seems to stretch far enough. That's what she says, anyway. Baby's seen the wads of cash they deposit after big nights at the Parrot. Baby thinks Louise must be funneling huge chunks of it toward her retirement, doesn't seem to want to reinvest anything in the resort, is content to let it sag and leak and get chewed on by rodents.

The best thing about Oakwood Hills is its location. Close enough to Lakeside that you can walk in for pizza but far enough away that it feels like you're surrounded by forest. And the buildings sit up on a hill, on the edge of a cliff overlooking the lake. Louise told Baby once she had about eight business cards from major hotel chains sitting in her office, offers always just waiting for her, just sitting there. She could get out whenever she wanted, but she didn't want to, because this was her home too. She'd grown up here and she liked that there was something left, on the edges of the lake, that felt like it belonged to a human being, a place on the lake real people could afford to visit.

"You shouldn't drink so much, Baby," says Marco.

"So smug," Baby says.

"Yeah, well. Don't say I never warned you."

"A sober bartender. You're like that guy from *Who's the Boss?*"

"*Cheers*," he says. "Like the guy from *Cheers*."

Baby sighs and hits her knee with the half-empty water bottle.

"What's the word on Bad Mike? You worried?" Marco asks. She can hear the skepticism in his voice.

"No," Baby says. She's convincing neither of them. They ride on in silence. The golf cart's battery sucks and it's not moving as fast as it used to.

Baby takes a cursory look around at the property, up the driveway. She half expects to see Bad Mike roaring toward them. Instead, the morning is quiet, the road empty, a cheerful sun blinking at them overhead, smiling almost. The entire day is like a laugh. And yet. Seven years. Baby can't believe it's been seven years since they put him in jail. Her and DJ, and Crystal, almost dead.

Donna's father was sheriff at the time. Bad Mike was four years into his reign as the drug kingpin of Bitborough Lake and all of its surrounding counties, was responsible for deaths and disappearances and overdoses. And it was Crystal he'd been obsessed with, always. Crystal Nugget who'd fallen in with him after her mother took too much up her nose. And if it hadn't been for Baby and DJ, they all knew Crystal'd be dead now too, cold in the ground next to her own mother because she couldn't find a way out.

Instead, DJ and Baby waited for the right moment to call the sheriff, when they knew a trip up to Bad Mike's property would mean domestic battery charges, maybe even felony assault. It wasn't a trap, exactly, so much as good timing. The police didn't want to; they'd wanted to line up a drug case. Put him away for good. But times were desperate. The night Deputy Donna's father pulled Crystal out of a closet, well, if he'd been just a few minutes later, Baby's sure Crystal would've died. Bad Mike had a bunch of his product on hand, and it gave them good reason to tack a few more years onto his sentence. As if almost murdering his girlfriend wasn't enough.

But now here he is. Baby finds it hard to believe he was let out early for good behavior. Probably had someone on the outside figuring out who to shake down.

Marco pulls up in front of the resort where DJ and Crystal are waiting with the other employees. Baby falls out of the golf cart to her knees in front of them. "I'm dead," she croaks. "Please donate my organs. If they can salvage anything."

"Aw, poor Baby." Crystal smiles down at her.

"What you need is a grease coat," DJ says.

"Sure do," Crystal says.

Baby immediately knows they brought her breakfast. "Come on," she says. "Cough it up."

"That's not very polite," says DJ, pulling the greasy paper bag out of her backpack. She dangles it over Baby's head, waving it back and forth just out of reach. Baby grabs for it and misses.

"Come on," Baby says. "I'm going to puke."

"Maybe she doesn't need it," DJ says, taking a step back. Baby musters up just the smallest amount of strength and lunges and grabs it.

"I love you," she says, opening it and finding not one but two hash browns snugged up against a greasy egg-and-cheese. "You are both saints."

As Baby sits on the ground, shoving the sandwich into her mouth, Crystal and DJ sit next to her.

"Donna paid me a visit this morning," says Crystal.

"Wow, really?" Baby says, spraying little bits of egg onto the ground.

"Bad Mike shouldn't have been at the Parrot last night, and apparently she's going to go remind him of that this morning."

"That's good news," says Baby. "Are you worried?"

Crystal shrugs. "Of course I am. Aren't you?"

"Yeah," Baby says with a full mouth. "But there isn't really anything to do but wait, right?"

Just waiting, all of them, for Bad Mike to decide to hurt someone. Baby takes another bite, the yolk exploding out of the end of the sandwich and landing on her shirt. She swipes at it with a finger.

The front door to the resort creaks open, and Louise sees them all waiting out there and sighs. "Come on, let's go into the bar."

Baby stands up and swipes at the gravel and dirt clinging to her shorts. "When are the Walshes getting here?"

"They're not coming this year."

"What?" Baby asks. "Why not?"

"Just get in," Louise says, flipping through her clipboard. Baby studies Louise. Her eyelid twitches. The Walshes have held their annual family reunion at Oakwood since Baby started working there, and probably for at least a decade previous. They would book out all the cabins and usually half the main lodge, and Baby is pretty sure she's made out with at least five of the cousins, though it was really difficult to tell them apart. They always showed up wearing the same color khakis and the same reunion T-shirts. It was almost like they were doing it on purpose to confuse her. And the names. All rhyming. Larry, Gary, Mary, Terry, Barry. Ridiculous.

"So we're not sold out this weekend?" Baby asks, concerned.

"We're delaying," Louise says. "Not opening quite yet. I have to bring in an inspector."

"For what?"

"Foundation," Louise says. "You've seen that sagging ceiling in the Parrot. Might need to replace it."

"Oh," says Baby. "That's all?"

"Just get inside," says Louise, waving her clipboard after them, as if it would make them go faster.

"What's this all about?" Baby asks Crystal and DJ as they troop into the bar.

"I'm sure it's nothing," Crystal says. "She probably just wants to tell us not to be dickheads this summer."

"Like that'll work," Baby says.

"You never know," DJ says. "This could be the year."

7

B ABY, CRYSTAL, AND DJ are among the last to shuffle into the Parrot, and all the seats are taken. They hop up next to Marco and Johnny on the bar, and Baby fights the urge to pull the hood on her sweatshirt up over her head. The hangover still lingers, poking at the back of her head, throbbing in her forehead, and she turns around and pours herself a Coke with one hand.

"Who's that?" Marco nudges Baby and gestures to the front of the room, where Louise stands next to a blond woman in expensive clothing.

There's something familiar about her, but Baby can't quite figure out exactly what it is. Her hair is evenly dyed, eyebrows thick and maintained. She almost looks like a fashion model, beautiful enough that she could probably take a dump wherever she wanted and no one would care.

The woman's even wearing white pants, very crisp and pristine looking, straight off the line in a laundry commercial. Baby can't understand the audacity of someone wearing white pants. It's as if they're just bragging about how perfect their lives are, how they don't bother eating ketchup or any condiment, really, just survive off vodka sodas and undressed salads, the kind of food that bounces off you without leaving a stain.

The woman catches Baby sizing her up and Baby pretends to be studying the ceiling, even goes so far as to nudge Crystal and point at the gum cluster she spent last summer on. Baby didn't throw the original piece of chewed gum up there, but she sure as heck did her best to connect the clusters to make the gray constellation into a perfect giant penis.

"Your best work," Crystal says, patting Baby on the knee.

"Thank you," says Baby.

"All right, all right, settle down," Louise shouts. "I've got some news."

Baby stares ahead, feels her eyeballs glass over. These all-staffs are always a waste of time and are almost always either about customer complaints or the failing septic system. Stop flushing tampons and be nicer to the guests. If the ceiling drips on their chicken wings, replace all the chicken wings, not just the one that got dripped on. Really riveting stuff.

"You think she's one of those secret shoppers?" Crystal asks.

"A what?" Baby asks.

"A secret shopper. Businesses hire them to check up on their employees," Crystal says.

Baby squints at the girl at the front, suddenly worried she's part of the gang of bitches she fought last night. It's entirely possible. But not likely Louise would spend good money trying to figure out which of her employees is the biggest loser. Those truths are more than likely self-evident.

Baby's gaze shifts upward to the giant ship-in-a-bottle hanging on the ceiling over Louise. She's drunkenly gotten lost in it about a million times, almost fallen over trying to count the hundreds of little ship lines that hold the sails in place. Once, when she ate too many mushrooms, the tiny pirates standing on the deck performed a lively little dance routine for her. Louise's dead husband built it. Baby can't imagine how many hours it took him. She remembers him hanging it up in the Bloody Parrot after he finished it, just a few weeks before he died, and how delicately he carried it in. Now it's covered in dust.

"This is Amelia Pomoroy," says Louise, and it clicks, then, why she looks familiar. *Peter's sister.* "Last week she made me an offer on the resort, and after a chat this morning, I've decided to accept."

The room is silent.

"Shit," DJ whispers.

"What!" Baby shouts.

"Let's just get through this, Baby, and then we'll do questions," says Louise.

Louise keeps talking, and Baby doesn't hear any of it. Fifteen years. More than half her life she's been here. Fifteen years.

Louise thanks everyone for their years of service and talks about moving to the Florida Keys to open some kind of swordfishing business with her brother and his son. Says she's felt like she's given her all to this place but it's just not working for her anymore and she needs a change and she thinks Amelia, who spent all her summers growing up on the lake (lies!), can keep the spirit of the resort alive.

Baby feels about a million things in flashes all at once. She wants to know if Peter knew about this. Why Louise didn't tell her. What it means for the resort. If she and the others are even going to stay employed through the summer. She looks down and sees that her hands, which no longer feel attached to her body, are gripping the edge of the bar so tightly her busted-up fingernails are imprinting in the waxy fug. The questions start to spiral in her head, the terrible possibilities building up in a giant pile inside her skull.

"What the fuck," Marco mutters under his breath.

Amelia takes a few steps forward once Louise has finished and gives them a big smile.

"She looks like a real bitch," Baby whispers to DJ, who shushes her.

"I want to hear."

"She seems nice," says Crystal.

"Because she's wearing white pants?" Baby whispers back.

"No," says Crystal, her eyes forward. "Maybe. Yeah."

Amelia clears her throat and waits for them to quiet down. "I know you all have a lot of questions about what the plans for the resort are. I understand how important it is to you."

"Just our fucking livelihood," Baby mutters.

"Shh," says DJ.

"We're going to be doing a quick renovation," Amelia says. "Just sprucing up a few areas. If you'd like to take a look at the vision boards I've created for the future of Oakwood Hills Resort and Spa, check me out on Pinterest. I'm easy to find."

"Spa?" Baby says, maybe a little too loud. "Where's the spa going?"

"Down by the water at the edge of the property," Peter's sister says, smiling. "They going to start pouring concrete for the foundation on Monday."

"We're going to have a spa?" Baby asks again, struggling to keep herself from totally losing it, the word *spa* spitting out of her mouth as if Amelia had told them there would be a slaughterhouse parked right next to it.

"Exactly," Amelia says. "Otherwise, we're going to be freshening up the paint, bringing in some more soothing colors, and I'll be passing around a sheet at the end of the day with sizing for the new uniforms that will complement that aesthetic. If you'd like to sign up for construction or painting crews, we've got our team leads over here," she says, gesturing to a table where a burly guy Baby doesn't recognize sits next to Jerry, one of the landscapers. "Jerry, who you all know, will be leading the painting crew, and Charles is going to be leading construction. If you don't want to be involved, just simply head home and wait for me to call in a few weeks."

Amelia seems to expect them all to leap into motion then, but the news has everyone sitting in a stunned, dumb silence.

Baby raises her hand again, throws it up in the air so hard, the whiplash hurts her shoulder. Amelia nods at her.

"We're not keeping the bar open?"

Amelia shakes her head. "We'll be closing temporarily for renovations."

"But it makes money," Baby says. "Not to mention all the tips we'll be missing out on."

"It's still early in the season," Amelia says. "We'll be making some changes, and we'll have everything back open in two weeks. A month tops. And I'll have new contracts for everyone in the next few weeks as well. Everyone's jobs are safe. I can't reiterate that enough, so don't go looking for anything new, all right? Thank you. Just know that I'm really excited to be working with you all."

She clasps her hands together and takes a small bow. Baby decides it's because she probably thinks they're all going to start applauding, but no one does. The ice machine sputters, coughing up a few more cubes.

It's a low blow, a real low one. Maybe the lowest of all time.

Eventually everyone starts moving, making their way toward the tables where Jerry and Charlie have sheets out, sign-ups.

"Should I get us on painting?" DJ asks, hopping off the bar. A few of the maintenance guys are already up there, shuffling toward the tables, scribbling down their names. Baby fucking hates painting. "At least it's with Jerry. We know Jerry."

"Do it," says Crystal. Baby chews on the inside of her cheek and manages to get off a nod before DJ crosses the room and stands in line behind one of the kitchen guys.

Baby wants to reach behind her and start smashing the bottles in the bar, one by one, get rid of the last remaining glasses so it's all fucking plastic, dump liquor out onto the floor in lines and drop a match. But she can't and she knows it, and so she hops off the bar and storms across the room. Eyes are on her, she can feel them, so she slams the door, the door they're not supposed to slam, as she walks out, hears the grinding of the rusted-out hinges, the metal giving way behind her. A scream, a gasp as all of the employees scatter. Baby doesn't look but hears the door wrenched from its hinges, the pane of glass inside the metal smashing to the ground.

8

BABY SITS DOWN on the edge of the dock and sticks her
feet in the water, wincing at the cold. Now she sees all of
this was probably on purpose, the lack of bookings, the weird
busy work they've been doing around the property the last few
weeks. Louise knew and just didn't tell them. Just left out this
small, important detail. Couldn't even look Baby in the eye as
she cut the cord, the coward. Hannah was gone; sure, she was
Louise's best friend. But Baby can't imagine what could have
possessed Louise to abandon them. She could've at least given
them a chance to figure their lives out, one last summer to save
up some money and decide what they're going to do next.

Amelia Pomoroy, the scrubbed-clean professional Barbie
doll, has bought the whole resort, dusty employees and all, and
here Baby sits, not having shaved her legs or armpits for god
knows how long, and there's a dirt stain on her ankle, a black
strip of dirt just there that somehow is still clinging to her skin
and *fuck*. It doesn't even really make sense. Why the entire
resort? Why not some kind of dumb clothing store in town?
A juice bar or a yoga studio or something Amelia understands,
something inside her own world, something to cater to the rich
customers she knows so well?

Baby lies back on the dock, leaving her ankles in the water.
It's still cold, the kind that takes your breath away if you jump

in, grasping at your chest, clutching at it, and she waits as her feet slowly lose all feeling.

Here lies Baby, a broke-ass nothing with empty pockets to show for the last few decades of her miserable rotten life. And she can't believe Louise. She really can't. The selfish bitch. The idiot woman. How could she desert them like this? With that overplucked Barbie doll?

And she sits up, pulls her feet out of the water and almost gets up, almost storms up to the building to find Louise and tell her what she really thinks of her, but then she thinks of Louise's husband, gone suddenly too. The story of her husband is too horrible for Baby to write Louise off forever. The woman deserves a nice retirement in the Florida Keys catching swordfish and enjoying the sunshine and forgetting about all of deaths, so immediate and gripping and terrifying.

Baby barely remembers Louise's husband, Terrence. He was a writer who wrote travel guides and tried to publish novels but couldn't. He had a thick British accent that Baby would later learn was northern and low-class and gargled out of his throat with what sounded like a huge amount of effort. Baby would spot him walking around the property at strange hours of the day. He was always well dressed but looked like he'd been wearing his clothes for days, sweating through the buttoned-down shirts, dark splotches soaking his underarms, a harried expression as if he were always late for something.

Hannah had always thought Terrence had a gambling problem. Once, Baby saw him trip up the front steps of the resort in the early-morning hours, and chips from the casino went everywhere, rolled out from his sleeves and pockets like he was a cartoon. And then he killed himself so abruptly it seemed as if he'd never existed at all. So quickly, gone. Just like Hannah.

Baby lies on the dock until the sun sets. No one comes to find her, which she feels is probably intentional. People seem to be very intent on giving her room to grieve lately. Space. They all think space is important, which seems ridiculous to her. Baby wants late nights, beer bottle in hand, music blaring; she wants drunken dance floors, bodies pressed all around her.

She wants weed and vodka and tequila and 2000s boy bands and nineties rap and eighties pop screaming at her from their broken sound system. The last thing she wants is space.

Climbing up into the boathouse and trying to fall asleep sober among the moldy life jackets isn't really all that appetizing, so she heaves her body up off the wooden slats and leans into her walk back up the hill, back up to the Parrot just to see if anyone else is around and maybe to have a shot or a beer or both. Maybe even drop the shot into the beer. The possibilities are endless.

As she rounds a corner, she isn't looking, is lost in her head, and nearly bumps right into Amelia Pomoroy. She's standing sideways on the hill, taking small steps while she talks on her cell phone. "We're getting rid of this fucking hill," she says, spotting Baby and nodding at her. "Steps or something. Just come pick me up," she says into the phone. "Meet me at the dock. Please. Come on, I said, please. Thanks."

She hangs up the phone and smiles at Baby with her white, even teeth. "Hello," Amelia says, in a voice that asks a question.

"Hey," says Baby, pretending not to get it. Amelia can buy this place, sure, but they don't have to roll out the red carpet.

Amelia gives Baby a very slow once-over, diagnosing her on sight. Unshaven legs, bare feet, no pedicure, scabby cuticles, unwashed jean shorts with more than one mysterious sploosh, shirt just barely tucked in at the front, hair stuffed up under a baseball cap.

"You're Baby, right?" she asks, craning her neck down to the dock, where Baby knows Peter's boat has not yet arrived. She knows the sound of the engine. She knows it.

"Uh," Baby says, a bit worried by this sudden loss of anonymity. She thought she had more time.

"My brother's told me all about you."

"Uh-oh," Baby says involuntarily, and Amelia laughs, actually loses the bitchy furrow of her eyebrows.

"It's mostly complimentary."

"Oh . . . good." Baby's annoyed at how intimidated—momentarily—she is by this girl and her dumb eyebrows. Baby takes a deep breath and looks her in the eye. This is her house, after all. "So, what sorts of changes are you planning?" Baby asks. "Some kind of big-city juice bar? Kale and all that?"

"Just some sprucing up," Amelia says. "You know . . ."

"The spa," Baby says. "Is it going to be one of those sorts of spas? Because I'll really have to think about participating in something like that. My wrists aren't as strong as they were in high school."

Amelia doesn't take the bait. "What sort of spa?"

"You know," Baby says. "The kind where everyone leaves a little happier than when they arrive? I'm just saying, I'd have to think about it. I mean, I'd definitely need to start moisturizing more."

Amelia stares at Baby, not laughing. Clearly not used to being mocked by the help. Baby suppresses a grin.

"Did you sign up for a crew?" Amelia asks.

"Yup," says Baby.

"Which one?" Amelia asks. Baby realizes this is the beginning of it, the trials. The tests. The breaking in. She doesn't trust Amelia with the truth, decides to fib in case she's going to flex her managerial muscles, show Baby who's boss by swapping her to a different team.

"Construction. I just hate painting," Baby says. "The fumes are so gross."

"Right," Amelia says. "Well, I'm sure you'll be called in by your group leader soon."

"Great," says Baby, looking down at the dock, confirming what she already knows. That *Rude* still hasn't arrived and Amelia isn't going to move until it does

"Peter told me all about this summer camp for grown-ups. In my mind, it's a bit pathetic. Louise never really let this place grow into its potential. This resort needs to change if it's going to be as profitable as possible," Amelia says.

Baby tries to hold in a blip of laughter but can't.

"What?" Amelia asks.

"Nothing," Baby says, brushing past her. "It was nice to meet you."

"Is there a problem with trying to run a profitable business?"

"Of course not," Baby says, turning on her bare heel and heading back up to the resort.

"Then why are you laughing?"

"It's just how you said it. 'As profitable as possible.' I don't know." Baby knows she's digging a hole. She just can't stop herself. "That's just not the way this place has ever run. People don't like vacationing at a place that's trying to be as profitable as possible. They want to stay somewhere where they can relax, have fun, you know, enjoy themselves without worrying the people they're hanging out with are trying to squeeze as much out of them as they can."

"People like to feel comfortable and looked after," Amelia says. "Not like they might get hepatitis from drinking out of the faucet."

Baby bursts out laughing again at that one, but it's a forced laugh, her cheeks burning, flushed. This ignorant bitch. This idiot woman. She doesn't know anything. They haven't had a hepatitis outbreak since the eighties.

"All right," Baby says, leaving out the *bitch* from the end of her sentence. Thinks about how much she wants to slap her.

Amelia tilts her head, as if she's reading Baby's mind.

The roar of *Rude* powering around the corner shakes Baby out of it, and she turns away from Amelia and walks off before she does something she regrets.

"See you soon!" Amelia calls. Baby knows she will and hates it. Oh, she hates it.

At the top of the hill, she spots Amelia's shining SUV, parked obnoxiously in the middle of the driveway, and she waits until she hears *Rude* heading off into the distance to kneel down next to the tires and unscrew the caps, to press down on the valves one by one, smiling as the tires deflate.

9

S HE COMES BACK to a whole mountain of French fries, a big square of them covering an entire bar table, and Crystal standing over it, crying, holding a glass ketchup bottle and shaking it so vigorously it almost looks X-rated. And platters and platters of chicken fingers, too many chicken fingers, the guys—Marco and Johnny—slumped in front of the mound, chewing. DJ's lying on the floor, shoveling mozzarella sticks into her mouth from a paper basket that sits on her stomach.

"Like, where have you been?" Crystal asks as a blob of ketchup exits the bottle and lands on top of the french fry mountain. She put down the bottle and dunks a few fries, shoves them in her mouth.

"What are you doing?" Baby asks. The smell of grease hangs heavy in the air, almost a thick smoke of it.

"Amelia told the kitchen guys to throw everything out. They're redesigning the menu. Obviously, they didn't want to waste the food. That being said, I don't think we're going to get through all of these chicken fingers."

"No," Baby says, looking at the mounds of food. "Are you joking?"

"She said something about fresh ingredients, I don't know. Probably quinoa."

"Rich bitches always like quinoa," Marco says. "I read it in a magazine." He's drinking a beer. It's a rare sight, Marco with beer in hand. *Not good for the soul.*

The occasion calls for it.

"Why don't we just put all of our food in a box in the freezer and write *quinoa* on it. She won't know."

"Can you freeze quinoa?"

"Who cares?"

"That's actually a pretty good idea," says Johnny. "I'll go tell them to stop frying stuff."

"Free lunch all summer," says Baby. "I'm making margs." She heads to the bar. "Speak now, or you're drinking one."

"I'm driving," says DJ.

"Tonight? In our time of need?" Crystal shouts from the floor.

DJ shrugs.

"Yeah, okay."

Baby starts lining up glasses, her body on autopilot.

"She was brainstorming new names for the place," says DJ, her mouth full of cheese. "Maybe just Parrot. Or Parrot's. Or something totally different like 'Evergreen, to go with the tree theme.' A tree theme! Can you believe it's come to this? Themes? Themes!"

"We can't let her," Baby says, pouring shots of tequila over ice, shaking the grainy lime-green liquid they use as a mixer.

"It's done," says DJ. "Apparently they've been negotiating for weeks."

"How much did she pay?"

"Jerry says he heard from Mathilde that it was one-point-two," says DJ.

"That's nothing," says Baby.

"God, can you imagine just having one-point-two million dollars in your bank account?" Crystal asks. "I wouldn't be caught dead around here."

"Really?" asks Johnny, coming back from the kitchen with two plates piled with chicken wings. "Where would you go?"

"I don't know," says Crystal. "Mexico?"

"We can't let her do this," Baby says. "It's bullshit."

"This is a business," Marco says. "What can we do?" Johnny lets out a bitter laugh and picks up a few fries from the mountain and shoves them into his mouth.

"We can shut up and make some money," he says through the mashed potatoes in his mouth, spittle going everywhere. "And then get out."

Baby just knows that it'll haunt her if she doesn't try. If she sits back and coasts, lets Amelia dismantle this place, chase out the termites and bedbugs and the rotten floorboards and the skunky pillows. As if she hasn't lost enough. This is it for her, this place. This is all she's ever wanted. She's not going to let some city bitch take it.

"Baby," says DJ. "I know what you're thinking. We can't just chase her out of here and expect that we'll get to keep our jobs or that the building will stay open. So let's just chill out. It might not be that bad."

Baby ignores her and takes a long sip of her drink.

When they were nineteen, twenty, twenty-one, they used to sit on that front deck after closing, when the night was quiet and cricketing and everyone else had gone home, and they'd talk about possible imagined shared futures, or individual lives and the paths they'd take away from Oakwood Hills. DJ was going to the city, one way or another. Music school or maybe someone would hear her original mixes, the stuff she played sandwiched between whatever electropop hit had topped charts that summer, and they'd love it and get her some kind of job at a record label or a club or working as an apprentice. She had a cousin there, with an apartment she could sleep on the floor of, for a time anyway. The story had a clear beginning, middle, and end.

Crystal was going to marry a rich banker in his forties, hopefully someone who would love her hard and brief and then let her go with alimony, or at least a payout that would give her some freedom for once. Some fresh air, a deep breath.

Baby's future never existed anywhere else. She'd been to the city a few times and didn't care for it. It was too loud and smelly and full of people. It made her feel like she had to be something else—the people always brushing past her with their bags on the subway, hot air coming out of weird vents, cars doing stupid shit in intersections, bitches on cell phones elbowing her, everyone looking so goddamn clean all the time, so put together, like they had proper drawers in their homes, drawers full of clothes that they pressed and dry-cleaned or whatever. Why live there when you could live out here?

Years passed and they stopped talking about it. Whenever they came out of the winter, pinched, savings dwindling before their eyes, Baby knew the shared desperation kept them tight, close, together. They needed this place. They needed it badly. They talked about moving on, but no one ever did anything different. They all just stayed here. And from where Baby was sitting, that was for the best.

And now? Baby can feel it. She can feel the ground shifting beneath them. What she can't quite comprehend is the fact that no one wants to act with her, to do anything to preserve what they have. It doesn't make any sense.

10

B ABY WALKS DJ and Crystal out to DJ's little shit car, the
purple hatchback covered in stickers. Crystal carries three
large Ziploc bags filled with fries and another two with chicken
fingers. "We'll have to stop on the way home for more ketchup,"
she says to DJ.

"Nothing is open," says DJ, turning to Baby, arms crossed.
"Are you going to wait for him again?"

"No," she says. "He's already down there."

Baby worries, suddenly, that DJ's going to call her bluff,
march ten steps to the hill, and look down at the boathouse at
the empty dock, but instead she gets into the car and turns it
on, the bass from whatever music she was blasting on her way
in making the entire thing vibrate.

Baby watches them drive off, trying to squelch the feeling
rising up in her, the loneliness.

If there's one thing she knows about herself, it's that she's
annoying. She's been annoying girls like Amelia her entire life.
This could work. This could be her Olympics.

As DJ's lights disappear around the bend in the drive, Baby
is filled with a sensation that she's being watched. A light in
the main building is still on and she hears a crash, then a bang.
Swearing. There are still two vehicles in the drive: Amelia's and
Louise's. Amelia's with the flat tires. Louise's with the taped-on

side mirrors. Baby peeks into Louise's window and sees knotted trash bags, bloated suitcases, banker's boxes overflowing with receipts, the scrabbled-together contents of Louise's life jammed into the back seat. Baby's stomach sinks. Louise is leaving. Now.

She steps inside and almost trips over the filing cabinet, the old, rusty, broken one from Louise's office. It's on its side, abandoned in the middle of the lobby floor. The door to the Bloody Parrot still hangs on its hinges, and she spots Louise standing there, staring up at the giant ship in a bottle hanging from the ceiling.

"I saw your Jeep," Baby says.

"You," Louise says, unfeeling. Baby is momentarily struck by her own anger, by Louise doing this, all of this, so soon after Hannah died, like she was waiting for it. Louise, with her chubby fingers like sausage links, her wedding ring still on surrounded by red swollen flesh, trapped there until she cuts it off. Baby stands there and just looks. Does Louise owe Baby for all her years of loyal service or does Baby owe Louise for letting her be who she is, here?

"Hey," says Baby.

"Can you grab the other end?" Louise asks, turning around and walking toward her, gesturing to the filing cabinet. Baby obliges, surprised at how heavy it is. Louise picks up the other side.

"What's in here?"

"Oh, tax stuff, all that shit," Louise says. "Don't want to lose track of it."

"You're leaving now?" Baby asks as they shuffle out the front door.

"Yeah," Louise says. They step in silence, make it halfway to the Jeep before Louise speaks again. "You should too."

Baby drops the cabinet into the gravel, the force of it making Louise jump. The cabinet falls sideways and rolls over, the dented top drawer spitting out like a tongue. Louise immediately drops to her knees and tries to slam it shut.

"What the hell is wrong with you?" Baby says. "You're sneaking off in the middle of the night?"

"Listen," Louise says. "Baby. This town is dead. Go build a life somewhere."

"What are you talking about? This is my home."

Louise manages to slam the drawer shut and heaves herself up off the ground. Baby spots something black tucked into the small of Louise's back.

"It's not a home, it's a building. Just—"

"Is that a gun?" Baby reaches out and grabs it, unthinking. It's heavy in her hand, shiny new, may as well have a price tag on it.

"Shit," Louise says, grabbing it back and tucking it away. "Baby, just stop it. Okay? Listen to me. Get out of here. All right? Go."

"You know I'm never going to do that," Baby says. "You think I'm going to let some bitch from the city steal my home?"

Louise sighs and stands up in a squat, dragging the filing cabinet through the gravel. Rage fills Baby from her toes up, the same blinding rage she feels when the city bitches give her the once-over on the dance floor, trying to tell her who she should be. She wants to grab Louise by the shoulders, shake her, get a real explanation out of her. Why now? Why?

"Can't you just be straight with me?" Baby asks.

Louise ignores her, opens the trunk of her Jeep. She grabs a few trash bags full of clothes and tosses them into the back seat, then leans the filing cabinet up against the bumper and heaves.

"How am I supposed to leave?" Baby asks. "I've got no money, no job—"

"You need money?" Louise asks. "Here."

She reaches into her pocket and pulls out an old, crusty, folded piece of paper. Baby takes it. It's old, almost parchment-like. She unfolds it. It's a map of the lake about the size of her head, bays and tiny areas scratched off, large Xs through them. Only a small portion of the lake is left.

"The safe," Louise says. "I've always had reason to believe it has casino chips in it. If you find it, it's yours."

"Is it out there?" Baby asks.

"Should be," Louise says. "You know the story."

Baby does.

There used to be a safe at Oakwood Hills, a big old safe made of green metal. It even had a thick knob you turned to unlock it. This was before the bank opened in Baysville and you had to drive for an hour and a half, way up to Grover, to drop off deposits. So they kept a lot of cash on the premises most of the time, defended by the weight and heft of the safe.

One night Louise's husband wheeled the safe down to his boat, somehow loaded the giant thing into it, rowed out into the middle of the bay, and then chained his ankle to it, pushed it into the lake, and drowned himself. Eventually his body drifted back to shore without the foot, which only lit the rumors on fire.

But no one knew exactly where in the lake the safe had landed. Louise never even mentioned it. Eventually the gossip died down. But Baby can do the math and Baby has seen the books. It all went down back when the resort was in its heyday, booked solid, sold out, weddings and events, the Bloody Parrot always packed full of cottagers on the patio drinking until all hours of the morning. Back when the employees were paid in thick wads of cash held together by rubber bands. Back when no one had debit cards.

Hannah was a little obsessed with the safe, thought it held probably about a hundred thousand, easy. It drove her crazy, Baby knows, to think of the money out there in the middle of the lake, just lying there, left alone to time, to water. She'd only bring it up when she switched from white wine to vodka.

"Why casino chips?" Baby asks.

"Terrence liked to gamble. We were having problems that summer. He was having problems. It's a long shot, but it's the only thing I can give you."

With one last heave, Louise shoves the filing cabinet into the trunk and slams the door, then turns and pulls Baby into a hug, wraps her body up in her arms and holds her. It's not like the wake when Louise grabbed Baby and sobbed into her neck and apologized and her quiet grief made Baby feel like a real human being for once. One with a history and a future. There was an apology in it. *I'm sorry. I'm sorry I let you live with that abusive drunk for all of those years, I'm sorry you were never really loved all that well. I'm sorry. I'm sorry.* But now, this hug, there's a fierceness to it. Almost an anger. Baby can feel Louise's heart pounding between them. Her stomach hurts.

"Why are you doing this?" Baby asks, to her sweater, the words muffled. Louise sighs.

"I've had enough," she says. "I'm scared. It's time to move on. You should too. Hannah not being here, it changes things for me. Promise me you'll leave."

Baby shakes her head. She doesn't understand. "I can't do that."

Louise sighs. "Then just . . . stay away from Amelia, all right? I don't trust her and neither should you."

Baby steps back. Looks at the map, at the expression on Louise's face, as if there is much more to say and Louise is deciding now, in an instant, whether or not she should speak. Instead, she climbs into the front seat, turns the engine on. Eyes forward.

"Stay out of trouble." Louise puts the Jeep in gear, doesn't even look in the rearview mirror at the building where she lived and worked for thirty-five years, and drives off down the road, out to the highway, turns right and disappears into the night.

EVERYTHING IS TO be painted white. Or beige. Eggshell. Cream. Amelia's having them clear all the furniture out of the cabins and paint the floors, the walls, the ceilings, the bathrooms. Jerry has crews all over the place. In the main building. Outside on the Parrot deck (though, so far, she hadn't touched the inside). They're even painting the outside of the boathouse. The paint colors are idiotic, names like Llama White and Mystical and Au Naturel and Crusty Bread, delivered to them by Amelia herself, who dropped them off in a rented pickup truck wearing paint-splattered jeans Baby was positive she'd bought like that.

"They all look white to me," Baby says, as she climbs up a ladder and rolls a fresh strip of a shade called Winterwash on the ceiling. "But if I owned a paint company, I guess I'd be bored too."

"I'd make the names more memorable. Like Princess Teeth. Or Happy Ending," says DJ. "You know, just so the people know what they're buying."

"Smart," says Baby, laughing.

"Can you get high off paint fumes?" Crystal calls from inside the closet. "Because I think I'm almost there."

"Go stick your head out the window," says DJ.

"Nah, I kinda like it," she says.

"What are we listening to?" Baby asks. DJ has her cell phone hooked up to a speaker in the corner, and some kind of ambient orchestral music floats through the air.

"It's my new stuff," she says. "I borrowed some instruments from the library down in Huntsville."

"I like it," says Baby.

"Me too," Crystal calls from the closet. "But I'm high on paint fumes."

"Then you're my target audience," says DJ, sitting down on the toilet. "This is going to be a bitch to keep clean," she says. "White."

"Maybe we can get her to put us full-time at the Parrot or something," says Baby.

"I don't mind housekeeping," says Crystal. "It's mostly just hanging out."

"Because someone does all the work," says DJ.

"I know," Baby says. "It's really hard for me, being the most responsible."

They all snorted at that one.

"Mike came by my place last night," Crystal says suddenly, and the two of them stop talking. "Nothing happened," she says, cutting in before DJ and Baby can move toward her. "Nothing happened."

"What do you mean, came by your place?" DJ asks.

"He parked outside," says Crystal.

"How do you know it was him?" Baby adds. "It could've been his idiot cousin."

"It was him," Crystal says. "I know it was him."

"Did you call Donna?" Baby asks, knowing that it's sort of an idiotic thing to do, calling Donna. It makes the entire exercise seem ridiculous if the last and only thing standing between them and Bad Mike is Deputy Donna, a baby police lady who has a shotgun, sure, but also couldn't win an arm-wrestling match if her own life were on the line.

"Of course I did," Crystal says. "She came by, he left. It's fine. I just thought I'd tell you what happened."

"You should move in with me," says DJ.

"It's really fine," says Crystal. "And I think he'd burn the house down if I left."

The *he*, of course, is her grandfather, almost entirely deaf, barely able to get around. Not exactly the biggest and greatest defense against a giant criminal out for vengeance.

"Did you think on my proposal?" Baby asks, changing the subject before things get weird.

Baby had called Johnny, Marco, Crystal, and DJ into the Parrot that morning and shared what Louise told her, leaving out the part where Louise encouraged her to run for it. Baby talked up how easily she thought they could get Amelia to leave the resort behind, abandon the project, and then they could find some way to buy it. Finding the casino chips, if there were casino chips, could be the way forward. But she needed everyone in—and everyone was on board except DJ. Baby ran the numbers for them—there could be upwards of a hundred grand in that safe—but DJ hesitated.

"Let's just try to get through the summer," DJ says, avoiding Baby's eyes. "She's just a stupid rich girl. She'll realize it's hard work and then'll probably make someone like Jerry the manager and everything will go back to normal."

"She doesn't seem like that at all," says Baby. "She's going to gut this place—"

"Baby," says DJ. Baby can tell she's trying to shove it aside, avoid it so they don't have to face it, subtly allow the new normal to take over until they're all worse off than they are. She used this tactic to great success the summer Baby wanted to do a naked wakeboarding show.

It's not like Baby can't see her point. Amelia doesn't seem so bad when she's dropping off paint cans and everyone's doing what they're told. Sure. Everyone tries to play ball in the beginning. But Baby knows that their wages are slowly going to be sucked away, she just knows it. If profit is what Amelia's after, there's no human thing that will keep her from it. Baby's no fool. Pretty soon they'll all be fake smiling while they refill the fucking breakfast buffet, and they'll have to call their guests *sir* and *ma'am* instead of saying, "Hey, you, with the station wagon! Your kid's got a nosebleed."

"Would you still work for her if she closed the Bloody Parrot? Wouldn't let you DJ?" Baby asks.

"There are other bars I could DJ at," she says, though Baby senses a slight tremor in her voice.

"Nothing close," says Baby. "Next bar is hours away. What if she replaces the Parrot with some new age vegetable trough for salad freaks? Do vegan assholes even tip? She hasn't really said what she's going to do with it. You think we can all get by on minimum wage?"

"I just don't think the plan is very solid," says DJ.

"I'll figure it out," Baby says. "We just have to play it right. Have a little faith in your Baby. Has she ever messed things up for you?"

"All the time," says DJ. "Literally all the time."

12

AT LUNCHTIME, AMELIA actually blows an air horn and they drag themselves to one of several daily meetings. The entire staff is there, a real air of defeat in the room, all of them staring forward at this woman who seems to come from another planet.

"Great work, everyone, excellent progress so far. We're getting there. Can I get a volunteer, uh, you?" She points at Baby. "And you," she says, pointing at DJ. "Sorry, I'm still short on names." It's an obvious power move, but Baby smiles as Amelia walks up, a real wide fake one.

"DJ," Baby says, pointing as they stand up. "And Baby."

"Of course," she says. "Of course. I should get everyone to wear name tags. We'll have to pick something else for you, though; I don't think we can exactly have 'Baby' showing our guests to their suites, now can we?"

She delivers the line like a joke to the rest of the room. The entire staff just blinks at her, like she's speaking an alien language.

"Ready for the big reveal?" Amelia asks, her hands pointing toward the boxes. "Ta-da!"

Baby is starting to suspect Amelia's never had a real job before.

"What is it?" DJ asks.

"Open the box, silly," Amelia says. "Why do you think I called you up here?"

Baby rips open a box and pulls out a pair of bright-white pants, a real glowing white, like a nurse's uniform. The pants are a cross between a chino and sweatpants, with thick, cuffed ankles and a drawstring waist, the top a white T-shirt with a small gray logo stitched on the left.

"Uniforms!" Amelia says, her voice so loaded with excitement Baby thinks she's going to explode. Again, the entire room blinks up at her. "I read this study in business school about worker satisfaction going up after three months in uniforms," she says. "And I have to say, I really get it."

"What?" Baby asks, trying to keep her voice from straining, really unable to form any sort of thoughtful response to this excitement.

"You know, we had uniforms at my high school, and at my summer camp."

"At camp?" DJ asks. "You had uniforms at camp?"

"I know," she says. "It's crazy. But it actually works. You don't have to waste time wondering what you're going to wear, planning it. You just do your laundry and have your clothes ready right there."

"Right," says Baby. "Laundry."

"I've tried them on. They're so comfortable," she says. "One hundred percent sustainably sourced cotton." As if they all cared about the environment. They only started recycling a few years ago, and only because Louise said if they returned everything, they could keep the change. After a big weekend at the Parrot, it was usually worth about a hundred for the party jar.

"And a brand-new logo," Amelia says, completing the sale. The room is silent.

"Did we ever have a logo?" asks Marco.

"We have a sign," Crystal says. "Does that count?"

Marco raises his hand and doesn't wait for Amelia to acknowledge him before he starts talking. "Are we supposed to wear it when we're landscaping?"

"Yes," she says. "Well, you can wear coveralls."

"We'll have to order some," he says.

"All right," she says. "I'll make a note of it." She pulls out her phone and starts typing.

"What about when we're serving?" Baby asks. "Are we going to have aprons?"

"It's not really the aesthetic I'm going for," Amelia says. "Plenty of restaurants have a waitstaff that don't wear aprons."

"Where do we put our order pads?" Baby asks.

"Parrot is going to be a new concept," she says. "We'll be reinterviewing all staff before that happens."

"Reinterviewing?" Baby asks. "What? I thought we weren't being fired."

"No one is going to be fired," says Amelia. "But we will be placing workers in permanent departments. Studies have shown—"

"Wait," Baby says. "Hold up. You're not going to let us rotate through the Parrot?"

It was the only way to make money, rotating through the Parrot, so they could take a turn making tips. Everyone did it if they wanted to. And people who stayed at the resort actually liked it. They got to know the staff that way, everyone by name.

"I'm still working on the restructuring plan," Amelia says. "I'll let you know."

"When is that going to be?" Baby asks.

"It's not high priority right now," she says. "We'll talk more about this after everyone tries on their new uniforms. Step right up. We've got lots of sizes."

Everyone stays in their seats, the shock spreading through the room. A new concept, new uniforms, new jobs. Baby looks over at DJ Overalls and knows she can't do it—she won't. DJ Overalls wears the overalls, everyone knows why, everyone understands. DJ avoids Baby's eyes. It's like abuse, almost; it feels like abuse, Amelia, dancing around DJ, unknowing of the history, the past, the people, real people, individuals standing in front of her, Amelia with her sustainable cotton, her white sustainable cotton and the gray logo, crowing about studies.

"It's just a uniform," Amelia says, her voice strong and dismissive of all that they're going through right now. "Here." She starts pulling them out and putting them into people's hands, and they take them and stand up. The room is moving, the eyes aren't on them anymore, and Baby sidles up to DJ, whispers in her ear, as everyone walks forward to get a set of what might be the least practical decision in the history of resort management.

"Want me to grab you some larges?" she asks. "Maybe they'll fit over your clothes."

"I can't," DJ says. Baby knows she can't, and the tone of her voice, the hopelessness of it, only makes Baby angrier.

"We can get rid of her," Baby whispers to DJ, as everyone around them mutters in small groups, picking up the shirts and measuring them against their bodies. "But I can't do it without you."

Crystal returns and passes them each a set. "I just thought I'd get us sizes before they run out," she says, holding three piles, misreading the expression on DJ's face. "I can put them back."

"It's fine," DJ says, sitting up and looking at the uniforms, the two pieces of fabric on the table, picking up the pants and standing up, squeezing the waistband between her thumb and forefinger. "I can't wear this," she says, in a dull voice. Baby knows it's not about the uniform. Of all of them, DJ—if she could—would roll her eyes and strap it on.

"What are you waiting for?" Amelia trills. "Go try them on!" She throws her arms around Crystal and Baby, squeezes them against her, like she's their goddamn track and field coach. Even her fingernails are painted white. "I really need you on board with this!" she whispers, then scampers off to the next group.

"Let's go try them on!" Baby says, louder than usual, and leads Crystal and DJ out of the room. The subtext was there;

Baby can smell it. *Put on the outfit or I'll find a way to make this terrible for you.*

They head down the hallway to the emergency stairwell. Crystal puts on the outfit. Baby stands, watching DJ, who just sits, slumped on her knees.

Baby feels like a military commander standing in front of a map, trying to figure out how to keep out the enemy that has somehow already made it inside the gate. It's not that Baby doesn't believe in progress; she likes Netflix and the internet and smartphones. She just doesn't believe that the new car's always better. That everything has to be shined up and dusted off.

A home can just be a place that stays. Maybe you buy a new fridge. But what makes a home a home is how it smells, how it feels, the imprint of your ass on the couch cushions, the chipped mug that sometimes cuts your lip but you can't bear to throw away.

There's magic in it for people, too, she knows it. She's seen it. This feeling that you can go out into the chaos of the world, let it beat you up, and when the time comes to book a vacation from your boss sexually harassing you and the doctor telling you to cut back on the red meat and your kid getting suspended from school for watching porn in math class, Oakwood Hills is waiting for you.

A magic to be found in coming back to a place that's almost always exactly the same, with all of these employees still here, having frozen themselves and their lives in place for you. Baby sees it. Everyone knows her name, her story. They give her tips just to tell it. The guests see her, they see *her*. Pouring their morning coffee, drunk on the dance floor at closing, up at nine or ten to push the housekeeping carts around, teaching their kids to dive at the end of the dock at sunset, holding them over the water by their ankles while they scream with laughter. And they always come back. Mostly. The last few years have been tough.

If Amelia can't see the beauty in that, Baby knows she has to be taken care of.

"We're going to look like inmates at the psych ward," Baby says, stepping into the pants, pulling them up over her jean shorts.

DJ sits up, straightens her overalls. "Let's do it." Anger radiates from her body, seems to be escaping in waves, her voice shaking. "Let's run this bitch out of town."

13

DJ DUMPS FOUR cans of chili into a pot and puts on a very epic instrumental soundtrack, complete with organs and a choir that makes it feel like they're sitting underneath the world's angriest church. Baby stretches out on the old orange couch in DJs basement apartment, looking at an old CD, a Christian speed metal band. "Why do you own this?" Baby asks.

"It's hilarious," DJ says.

Baby tosses it to the side. They drove up here after work. Baby was hoping Peter would text her to hang out, but she hasn't heard from him lately. She's been wondering if he's avoiding her. The wimp. *My sister is opening up a small business*? Please. He could've warned her and he didn't.

"So here's what I think," DJ says. "Because I know you've just been waiting with bated breath."

"Oh, go on," Baby says.

"I think this whole 'find the safe and buy Oakwood ourselves' idea is too risky."

"How so?" Baby asks. DJ answers that comment with a harsh, sidelong look.

"First off, how are you even going to look for it? It's not like you're a triathlete. It's dangerous. And you don't know what's in it."

"I talked to Louise—"

"Still," DJ says.

"She has a point," Crystal adds. "I don't want you to get hurt."

"I won't," Baby says.

DJ keeps going, ignoring her. "I think what we do is annoy Amelia. We annoy her and help her see that it's better to have a local in charge, someone who knows the employees, has been here awhile. Someone like Jerry."

"Sure," says Baby. "Okay." But Baby knows it won't work. Amelia has a stubborn streak. There's no way she'll give them what they want, how they want it.

"The soup's boiling over," Crystal says, jumping up and running over to the stove.

"I still think the safe is a good idea," Baby says.

"How are you going to get out on the lake every day?" DJ asks.

"I'll just get Peter to help me," Baby says. "Easy."

DJ rolls her eyes.

"Treasure hunt? Come on, it's right up his alley."

"Is it?" DJ asks. "I would never have guessed. What does he need treasure for?"

"Everyone wants soup, right?" Crystal calls from the kitchen, poking at the dishes DJ has let pile up in the sink.

"Yes, please," Baby says.

"I'm just worried. None of us can make it through winter without working," DJ says. "There's also the question of how we would run a resort if we could buy it."

"I've been looking at the books for years. And we've all been working there for like a decade. We know better than that dewy bitch," says Baby.

"She does have really nice skin, doesn't she?" DJ says, picking at a cornflake dried to her coffee table.

"Okay, we're all eating out of yogurt containers," Crystal shouts from the kitchen. "Don't worry, I washed them." Crystal walks out with two yogurt containers full of soup and puts them down on the coffee table.

"We have to somehow sabotage her without making her hate us so she'll consider selling it to us. It's got to be cheap."

"Do you really think there's conceivably enough money in a safe for us to buy it?"

"Maybe for a down payment . . . then we get a mortgage," Baby says, trailing off.

"Who the hell is going to give you a mortgage?"

"I think my yogurt container is melting," Crystal interrupts, sitting down and taking a slurp of soup.

"Eat faster," says DJ.

Crystal shrugs and takes a sip. "We need to be aggressive," she says. "I heard she's planning a big 'reopening' weekend in a few weeks or something."

"So we have a little under a month to make Amelia hate her new job and get her to sell."

"Not sell. Pick a manager," DJ says. "By being challenging. That's it. And you don't go looking for that safe with Peter. You'll get hit by a boat—"

"Chopped up by the propeller," Crystal chimes in. "See, it does have a hole in it!" She holds up her yogurt container and points to a brown drip as it falls off and lands on a white napkin on the table. "Those uniforms are psychotic," she says. DJ takes a long slurp of her soup. "I'm getting a plate," Crystal says, heading back into the kitchen. "Seriously, do you have any clean dishes?" she shouts from the kitchen.

"No!" DJ calls back.

"You need to take better care of your stuff," says Crystal.

"Why?" says DJ. "It's all trash."

"It's depressing," says Crystal. "It's really gross, too. Look at this." She holds up a frying pan she shoved sideways into the sink next to the pile of dishes. "It's got mold on it."

"It's a science experiment," says DJ. "'How grossed out can I make Crystal before she cleans my apartment for me?'"

Crystal rolls her eyes and turns on the sink, sticking her finger under the hot water, testing it, then picks up the dish soap bottle and dumps in far too much. "This is love," she says, prying half of the dish stack away from the other and putting them on the counter.

Crystal sighs and starts scrubbing. "Could we plant some drugs on her?" she says. "Then she'll have to hire a new manager, because she'll be in jail."

"Amelia?" DJ asks.

"We're not bringing meth heads into this," says Baby. "We're not talking to Bad Mike."

"We wouldn't have to talk to him," says Crystal. "We could get someone else . . . Marco, maybe."

"Rich white girls don't go away on drug charges," says DJ. "They just don't."

Crystal shrugs matter-of-factly.

Baby knows Crystal's seen more than they have, the criminal side of it all. "You're not afraid of Mike?" Baby asks.

"I'm terrified," Crystal says. "But I'm more afraid of what will happen to us when we're out of jobs, you know? You remember last time."

Last time . . . Baby knows Crystal is talking about her mother. There used to be a mill just twenty minutes away by car. The town used to be a whole lot bigger too. But when the mill closed, that was its undoing, the beginning of the end. Hundreds of people lost their jobs. Bad Mike pounced on everyone he could, brought in new customers, hooked people, ushered a new kind of murderous crime to Lakeside, to its dying population, the quick and speedy decline of a once bright and sunny vacation town. A population of thousands became hundreds within a few years.

"And here I was thinking we could end this entire thing by putting gum in her hair," says Baby.

"We're not talking to Bad Mike, end of story. It's off the table," DJ says. "We're not engaging."

"He took my grandfather grocery shopping today," Crystal says. "And paid. People are going to start OD-ing again. He still has money. It's going to be just like last time."

"No," says Baby. "Donna's all over him."

Crystal lets out a bitter laugh. "Yeah, Donna versus Mike. We all know how that one'll end."

"Why did he take your grandfather grocery shopping?"

"Because he wants me to know he's still around," says Crystal. "Right? He wants me to know he hasn't forgotten. He blames me. He blames you guys too, you know? He wants us to know he's out there."

DJ sighs and leans back into the armchair, takes out her phone and spins it around in her hands. Silence falls over them. Baby thinks of those terrible months when Crystal took a few steps off the road and fell in with Bad Mike. Her mom OD'd, and you'd think that would've made her want to steer clear, but she's always had a lot on broil, Crystal, just close to burning, just crispy. She tried it a few times. They pulled her out of it before it went full-on, but Bad Mike went ballistic and things unraveled from there. Baby's surprised they haven't heard more from Mike about it. There's a reason he drove to the Parrot his first night out, and it's not because he wanted a drink.

Baby doesn't want to linger on it. "It's not like we can do anything about it," she says. "Let's focus on the thing we can change. And we're not bringing him into this. We don't want Amelia dead, right? We just want her out of Lakeside."

"Right," says DJ.

"And if Bad Mike comes around, we'll take care of it," Baby says. Crystal sighs and picks up a fork, starts scrubbing it fast, dunking it into the grimy dishwater, her fingers slowly turning red.

"Right," she says, after a long pause.

"And Baby won't go looking for that safe," DJ Overalls says.

"Right," says Baby.

14

"DID SOMEONE SAY treasure?" Peter Pomoroy asks, strangely awake for the early hour, the engine already cut. He's standing with one leg propped up on the dock, fists on his hips, posing like a pirate surveying the horizon.

"Ahoy," she says.

"I didn't know you were able to wake up this early."

"It's not by choice. I rise with the sun these days," she says, grabbing the cardboard box and shoving it under her arm, picking up the shopping bags that contain everything they'll need for this mission and stepping down into the boat. She bought them secretly, made sure DJ and Crystal didn't find out. She knows the real reason they don't want her looking for the safe is that they don't want her spending time with Peter, relying on Peter, bonding with Peter, setting herself up for the same huge disappointment that befalls her every September. But she can't help it. She can't. She has to try.

"Yeesh, you really mean business, eh?" he says, and leans behind her to pump the bulb on the gas line.

The boathouse, well, what it has in charm and low-cost living, it lacks in ventilation. The mornings are freakishly hot; Baby usually wakes up covered in sweat, the sleeping bag she desperately zips up in the middle of the night morphed into a damp cave. She's taken to climbing out the window and across the roof and jumping into the lake, the cold making her swear and scream but ultimately feel pretty incredible, eyes flying open, heart pounding. At first, she thought the shock might kill her, but she's starting to love the dread that descends when she wakes up, the fear that grips her as she climbs the roof, starting the day with some light masochism.

Last night she sent Peter a couple of texts: *Treasure hunt?* and *6 am? Don't tell anyone.*

And he just said *Yup,* so she wasn't sure if he'd actually show up, what with his record of sometimes not showing up. But here he is.

"So what's the treasure?" he asks, speaking too loudly, over the dull groan of the motor.

"Let's get farther out, away from the dock," Baby says, suddenly aware of the lake, the speed of sound across water, the attention they could draw simply by being awake at this ridiculous time of day. "I don't want anyone to hear."

Peter laughs and shrugs, putting the boat into reverse. "What's going on, Baby? And what's that?" He gestures to the box and the bags she loaded in the boat. Everything still in its package, including the special batteries she had to hitch an hour out to Dorset to buy.

"I'll tell you once we're out," she says, casting an eye around the bay. A fishing boat at the far end. Nothing suspicious about it. The lake is calm. No wind. Great diving weather. "Just head to the middle of the bay."

Peter listens, lets the boat drift out, steering with one finger while he watches her unpackage the metal detector and the batteries. The detector looks exactly like the ones in Archie Comics, with a flat end, like a Frisbee attached to a stick, but this one has a sling that slips over her arm, kind of like an exoskeleton, and a pair of fat headphones that are supposed to be waterproof and aren't going to electrocute her—according to the reviews she's read online.

Apparently the detector works to a depth of thirty feet, which Baby doesn't think she'll need. The lake isn't that deep. Most of it, she figures, is shallow enough that she can probably swim down with flippers. She studied the map Louise gave her last night; only certain parts of the lake were unmarked. Not a ton of ground to cover, all told.

"Are we on a secret mission?" Peter asks, a mocking smile on his lips.

"Listen," Baby says. "You're going to have to start taking this seriously, or I'm not going to tell you about the secret mission." She feels paranoid, exposed, out in the middle of the lake. Anyone could be watching them. Anyone at all.

At the dead center of the bay, Peter turns off the engine. She'd call his expression bemused, but there's far too much joy in it. He turns sideways in his seat and watches as she pries open the little home for the batteries. "Baby, tell me. I'm dying over here."

"You can't tell anyone," Baby says.

"Okay," he says, smiling at her. "Are we ditching a body piece by piece?"

"You promise? This isn't a joke," she says.

"I promise," he says.

"There's a safe sunk in the lake, and it might have a bunch of money in it," she says. "And if I find it, it's mine."

Peter blinks at her. "A what?" he asks.

"A safe," she says. "Money. A lot of it. No one else to claim it. It's mine, if I find it."

"What?" he asks.

"It's my inheritance," she says.

"Hannah sunk it in the lake?" he asks.

Baby tells him no, gives him an abbreviated version of the story. The money and the gambling and Louise and her husband, and she fills it with optimism and possibility and excitement and he just sits there, staring up at her with a totally blank look on his face, an unreadable one that turns sad.

"How do you know the money's in there?" he asks.

"Louise told me before she ran off. She gave me a map and everything." Baby pulls it out and hands it over. Peter unfolds it and studies.

"So she was looking for it."

"Exactly," Baby says.

"Is money waterproof?" Peter asks.

"It's not bills," Baby says. "It's casino chips. Maybe. Hopefully. I don't know. But that's what makes it fun."

"And that's a metal detector?" he asks. "Are you sure you can use this underwater?"

"I did my research," Baby says, surprised by all the questions. She didn't think he'd have so many questions. "You still have that anchor in here?"

"Yup," Peter says, opening up the cabinet under the bow and fishing around. She hears the rattle of a few empty beer cans, the clink of beer bottles. It smells like wet Styrofoam. He unearths an ancient rusty anchor with a frayed yellow line attached to it, a clip on the end.

"Does it work?' she asks.

Peter picks it up, weighing it. "I barely use it," he says, clipping the end of the rope to the cleat on the side of his boat and tossing it overboard. Baby drops her jean shorts and grabs the mask and the snorkel. She stares at the water.

"Are you okay, Baby?" he asks.

"Sure," she says. "Honestly, not very excited about getting in there, but otherwise . . ." She trails off, thinking of just how cold it was this morning when she dunked her body in, the grasping, stinging kind of cold.

"Can I just give you some . . . can I just help you?"

"You are helping me," Baby says.

"I'm sorry I didn't tell you about Amelia. It kind of came out of nowhere, to be honest. I didn't even know she knew Oakwood Hills existed . . ."

"It's fine," Baby says, tossing the mask and the flippers into the lake. She jumps in because she knows that the longer she and Peter talk, the easier it'll be for the truth to arrive, and she'd rather not. Definitely not before noon.

Baby screams a little to herself as the cold water attacks and she grabs at the mask and snorkel, panting a little as she puts them on, trying to warm up. She dives, experimentally, down toward the bottom of the lake, the pressure of the depth pushing at her ears, making her feel like the water is squeezing her head between its hands, and just when it's seconds from exploding she pushes back up to the surface, treading water as fast and as furiously as she can to keep her body from numbing, taking big, deep, gasping breaths.

Peter watches from the boat, doesn't say anything when she turns her head. "Can you pass me that thing?" she says, pointing to the metal detector. He picks it up.

"Is it on?" he asks.

"I think so," she says. She isn't sure. He passes it down, and she slides it up her arm. It's heavy but not unwieldy. A burst of static immediately comes out of the headphones, and she puts them on and listens. It's definitely something. She dives straight for the bottom of the lake and starts feeling around and realizes it's the damn anchor, pushes herself to the surface, taking another gasping breath.

Peter sits, watching her patiently. She takes off in a different direction, the detector stretched out in front of her, and glides, hearing another burst of static, her heart rumbling with a weird hope, even though she knows it's so idiotic, in the back of her mind, just so plain stupid to think they're actually going to find it a few minutes after they start looking.

She dives again, the temperature of the water dropping when she reaches the bottom and feels around, her head screaming. Everything around her has a green hue, the sun filtering down in streaks and waves as she pats the ground with her fingers. It's certainly not a giant steel box.

Her fingers capture a long, thin scrap of metal. She picks it up. A wrench. An old one. Lungs empty, she pushes back up to the surface and takes a giant breath, her body starting to shiver in earnest. "Anything?" Peter asks.

"Rusty tool for a rusty tool," she says, tossing the wrench up into the boat.

He grins. "Aren't you freezing?"

"Yeah, I think I'm going to need to see if I can find a wet suit. I can go for a little while longer, though," she says.

She pushes away from the boat again, this time in a different direction, staring at the lake's floor, searching, and spots a sunken tree on the bottom, its skeletal hands reaching up toward her as if there's a pirate ghost inside, attempting escape. The static explodes in her ears, loud enough it's making her body tense up. She sweeps the scanner left and right, and everything seemed to be lighting up. Baby's heart swoops in her chest. Maybe this is the safe.

She takes a deep breath and dives, kicking her legs, freezing, numb, the chills starting to prick at her, stiffening her muscles. By the time she reaches the bottom and starts patting the muck, her legs are screaming. The static keeps pulsing in her ears, and she desperately scrapes at the sand. Her fingers close around a handle and she pulls, then pushes up to the surface without looking, worried she might pass out.

She examines what's in her hand—a bright-red toolbox covered in muck. She passes it up to Peter.

"Should we start a museum?" he asks, grabbing it. "Things from the deep."

"Pull me up," she says, tossing the mask into the boat, her breath coming in gasps between shivers. His boat doesn't have a ladder on it. He grabs her under the pits and lugs her over the edge. She slides onto the bench and lays flat out, feels her body shaking uncontrollably.

"You okay?" he asks again, and then, "Shit, you're bleeding."

Baby looks down at her leg. A deep, bloody gash, so dark it's almost purple, the blood running down her leg. She can't feel a thing.

"My skin is numb," she says, in halting breaths.

"I don't have any Band-aids," he says.

"It's okay," says Baby.

"I think there's an old shirt under here," he says. Baby presses her thumb against the torn skin.

Sirens. Sirens on the lake? Baby think she's probably hallucinating, then looks up. "Oh for fuck's sake," she says.

Racing toward them in a small police boat is Judy Mork in full uniform, standing at the bow, holding a rotating red light in one hand and a bullhorn playing a siren sound in the other.

Donna sits at the back, driving. Baby chokes on a laugh, which is drowned out by her shivering.

"Morning!" Deputy Donna shouts as they near, the horn still blaring. "Judy, cut the horn."

"The button is stuck," Judy says, slapping the megaphone against her hand. The blaring cuts off with a strangled yelp.

"Nice to see you again!" Peter calls back, flipping on a smile. Baby scrambles for a towel.

"Mr. Pomoroy," Donna says. "Welcome back."

"Thanks," he says.

"Hey, Donna," says Baby.

"Jane," she says.

"May I ask what you're doing out there? Engine trouble?"

"None of your business, Donna. It's not illegal to park in the middle of the lake," says Baby.

"Actually," Mork interrupts, "there is a bylaw against trolling now that the algal blooms on this coastline have increased by point-oh-five percent. Were you aware?"

"No," says Baby. "Not caught up on my algae news. But the engine isn't on, so scram."

"Baby, if you don't shut up, I'll take you in for drunk-and-disorderly."

"It's six AM," Baby says.

"Wouldn't be the first time," Donna snaps back, and Peter chuckles. Donna adjusts her belt, clearly pleased with the attention. "Why are you bleeding?"

"Here," Judy Mork says, passing some Band-Aids from their first-aid kit to Peter.

"Thanks," he says.

Donna narrows her eyes, and Baby can tell she wants to ask more questions but can't figure out a way to force them to answer.

"Well, make sure you don't troll," Judy says after a drawn-out silence.

"You got it, ladies," says Peter, flashing them a smile. His teeth are so white, Baby feels like they could be seen from outer space. The sun catches them and blinds her. "Have a great day now."

The cops head off, toward the only other fishing boat in the bay, and Baby relaxes, annoyed that they're out on the lake, bothering her, when they could be checking up on Bad Mike, trying to find a way to muscle him back into the clink before he can do any real damage.

"You think you need stitches?"

Baby's still shivering. She unpeels the Band-aid and sticks it onto the gash. "Nah," she says, looking down at the water.

"Are you sure this is a good idea?" Peter asks, still rubbing her shoulders. Baby's embarrassed at the shivering, the endless shivering, as he pulls her to his chest, and she closes her eyes, presses her cheek into the cotton of his tank top.

"You don't like treasure hunting?" she mutters into his shirt.

"I'm just worried about you," he says.

"Why?" she asks. She wants him to say something. Anything. Is it just guilt? That's the real question she wishes she could ask. *Is it guilt that has you out here? Ten years of it built up in your chest like pneumonia, the gunk that sticks in your body, the gunk you can't get rid of?*

"Is this really what you want to do?"

"The treasure hunt?" Baby asks. "Absolutely. But you can't tell anyone, okay?"

"Why not?" Peter asks.

The lie comes quick and easy. "I want it to be a surprise."

"Okay," he says. "But why don't we go back for today? You're freezing." He leans around her and pumps the bulb attaching the gas line to the motor. Baby takes a deep breath and pokes the wound.

15

Hours, days, weeks, whole lifetimes of painting, neck craned up at the ceiling, turning brown walls white, turning wood paneling cream, change and evolution, fumes and green tape and a sore back and the boring thrum of work. Baby hides out at the end of every day in the loft of the boathouse, waiting for everyone to go home. Tonight is no different, except she needs to find the wet suits, wants to claim them before Amelia orders the messy storage area underneath the deck cleaned out.

Amelia's got an intense relationship with the dumpster, can be seen at any hour of the day hauling old paintings, wooden ducks and bears, all of the kitschy decorations out to the bin and tossing them in. Other staff have taken to hopping up at the end of the day, poking through the trash to see what they can salvage. Even Marco took home an old wooden mallard.

But Baby's sure there are wet suits underneath the deck because she can't forget that sweet summer the staff bought a Jet Ski. All the summers blur together in one big sunburned, stoned, drunken mass, but Baby thinks it was eight or nine years back. A long time ago. Louise's nephew, Jordy, had moved to Lakeside, bringing with him a bit of a weed habit, and was smoking all day, every day, and boy he was fun. The Jet Ski was his idea, and it took only a few weeks of tips to pay for it.

Of course, it only lasted for a month, and then someone, driving drunk in the middle of the night, ran it up on the rocks over near Baysville and sunk it. No one would admit to it, of course, but everyone thought it was Baby, who knew it wasn't her because she'd been off with Peter in his boat. It had to be Jordy.

But then Jordy got his third cousin once removed pregnant, and she wanted to move to the suburbs so she could be close to her family, and then he became a paramedic and now every time Baby sees an ambulance she's very concerned that she'll see Jordy driving it.

Anyway, that Jet Ski came with two wet suits, and Baby thinks they must be in the crawl space beneath the Parrot deck.

Underneath the main lodge, off to the side where the Parrot deck juts out, a storage room everyone's afraid to go into sits, full of old life jackets that, if you cut them open, are probably pocked with black mold. A broken canoe, sawed right in half, lies in the back there, gathering dust, next to an old Elvis bust, the remnants of probably a hundred floating toys, diving rings, dried-out bottles of sunscreen, rusty tackle boxes, and warped fishing rods. The door that keeps out the elements is a short piece of cropped plywood with a combination lock, long rusted and broken, that leaves a good six inches of space between the bottom of the wood and the ground. Anything can get in, and does.

When the resort feels empty and Baby's waited long enough, she shimmies out of the boathouse, climbs down the birch tree, and looks both ways before heading over to the storage room. The padlock has disappeared, been replaced with an old pencil shoved into the latch, and she yanks it out, gravity pulling the door open, the hinge screaming as it swings downhill.

"Anyone in here?" Baby calls, stomping her feet in an attempt to scare off any rats that might be nesting in the old life jackets and trash. Baby hates rats. It's the tail. Really disgusting. She shines the light back and forth and waits for the rustling to stop. Definitely rats.

The neon-pink sleeve of one of the wet suits lies in the corner, draped over an old board for a Windsurfer that Baby forgot was down there. She hurries through the creepy closet and grabs it, tripping over an old coil of rope, and the second wet suit comes out with it, their sleeves Velcroed together.

"Hello?" a voice calls. Amelia. Baby's annoyed she ditched the heels, swapped them out for some very silent rubber-soled white sneakers that let her move around quietly. "Who's there?" she calls again, then rounds the corner. "Oh, it's you," she says, her hand over her heart, pressed flat, like she's physically trying to make it stop pounding. "I thought it was an ax murderer."

"There are a lot of those around here," Baby says, trying to duck past her.

"What are you still doing here?"

"Just looking for these," Baby says, replying too quickly. "I knew they were tucked away somewhere. I bought them a few years ago." Baby holds up the wet suits, blabbering, overexplaining as if she's someone who's definitely, totally guilty.

"Retro," Amelia says. "Very nineties."

"Yeah, they say *Splash Queen* and *Splash King*," Baby says, showing her, the lettering scrawled in graffiti letters across the chest. The stripes along the sides are pink and blue respectively, and geometric shapes dance down the edges.

"I love the pattern," says Amelia. "I was thinking of redoing the Parrot with something like that." She gestures toward the print. "Sort of a nostalgia thing."

"Oh," Baby says, annoyed that she actually likes the sound of it. "Cool. So you're here late. Are you living here now?"

Amelia laughs. Baby stares at her, suddenly realizing just how much she looks like Peter. Slap a mustache and a dick on her and they'd be identical. "Not really. I did sleep in one of the cabins last night, though," she says. "Peter usually gives me a ride in, but he said he was meeting up with you for an early-morning swim or something?"

"Yeah," Baby says. "I need an exercise buddy or I just won't do it." The lie falls out of her mouth so easily, it's just like Baby's telling her a real, true story. And it isn't exactly a lie; Peter has spent every morning this week watching her paddle around in the lake.

"What are you doing now?" Amelia asks.

"I was going to head out," Baby says, looking off down the drive, realizing the lie is a bit thin, since there's no car waiting for her, just the walk into town. It's not so unreasonable to believe she'd take the trip on foot; it's just not the likeliest of lies.

"Have a drink with me," Amelia says instead. "My treat." The expression on Baby's face must seem skeptical, because Amelia's enthusiasm slips away almost as soon as she makes the offer. "I mean, if you've got plans—"

"No, I can," Baby says. "Sure." Knowing her enemy isn't a terrible idea.

"I didn't realize Peter had so many friends up here," Amelia says as they trudge up to the Parrot.

"He does?" Baby asks. She laughs. "I mean, we barely tolerate him."

"He should've gotten a job here."

"I'm sure that never occurred to him," Baby says.

Amelia nods. "Probably not."

Silence falls, and Baby relishes the awkwardness of it, knowing that Amelia doesn't know what to say to her. Baby can feel her making the measurements in her head—what she should and shouldn't say, how to say it.

"Sorry, I'm just not used to how quiet it is out here," Amelia says.

"You never worried about psycho murderers at that fancy summer camp?" Baby asks.

"It was on an island," Amelia says.

"Murderers can swim too," says Baby. "Don't discriminate."

"Good point," Amelia says, chuckling, "I never even considered that."

Baby slides onto a chipped wooden barstool. Amelia walks behind the bar. Baby doesn't try to stop her or advise her of anything as she turns and clasps her hands together, stares up at the vast array of liquor towering over her.

"Well, what'll you have?"

"Caesar," Baby says.

"Spicy?" Amelia asks, ducking under the bar, rummaging around, trying to assemble all the ingredients. Baby leans on her elbow, smug. She could do it with her eyes closed.

"Oh, yeah."

"Gin or vodka?"

"Tequila," says Baby.

Amelia raises her eyebrows in surprise as she spins the glasses with rimmer and drops two handfuls of ice cubes in each.

"You're pretty good at that," says Baby, making sure to keep her tone flat, the surprise absent.

"I bartended for a few summers in Greece," says Amelia. "I get bored if I don't have a job, and I have all these friends from boarding school who'd go out to this island for the season and just lie around, and it started to drive me crazy, so I talked this guy into giving me a job at one of the clubs a few nights a week. I made homemade Clamato juice and convinced him I invented it."

Amelia pours a shot and dumps it in Baby's glass, then puts the bottle down.

"You forgot—"

"I don't drink," Amelia says, plopping a tiny mountain of olives in each glass, each of them floating like eyeballs. "Virgin for me."

"Right," says Baby.

"Voilà," she says, handing the boozy one to Baby and touching their glasses together before Baby even has a chance to pick hers up. When she does take a sip, she's annoyed to report that it's delicious, maybe the best Caesar she's ever had, just the right combination of salty and spicy.

"Peter told me you just graduated from some fancy business school," Baby says. Amelia nods, takes a sip of her drink, and leans back against the counter, resting her head lightly against the shelf holding up the midrange bottles, all of them gathering dust.

"That's true," Amelia says.

"So what the hell are you doing up here?"

Amelia laughs. "All my friends have big jobs or weddings or whatever. They all live elsewhere. I wanted to build something of my own. And Peter always talked about how fun his summers are up here."

So you have to ruin it? Baby doesn't say it, just smiles and takes a long sip while she considers the logic. Baby can't imagine hearing about a fun party and then showing up three hours before said party begins and demanding they make changes to everything about it.

"He is good at having fun," Baby says.

"I know," says Amelia. "I can't really imagine him at a law firm. It's weird, I always thought he'd want to do something like this," she says, gesturing to herself. "Start his own business or something."

"Me too," says Baby, very simply, deciding that the less she gives Amelia in this conversation, the better.

"My father is a difficult man," Amelia says. "Brilliant. But difficult."

"I bet," Baby says.

Amelia takes a long sip of her Caesar. "What do you know about my family?" Amelia asks.

Baby shrugs, feigns true ignorance, doesn't want Amelia to know how many nights she's spent staring at the blue light of her phone in the darkness, reading profiles on business websites, net worth estimates, Wikipedia pages. All of it. "What do you know about mine?" she asks.

Amelia raises her eyebrows as if to say *touché*. "I do have a question for you."

"Sure," Baby says, happy there's a reason for all of this, that Amelia isn't trying to make her a friend, that there's a quid pro quo.

"Were you really, like, a . . ."

"Dumpster Baby?" she asks. "Yes." Baby understands the curiosity; she's lived the curiosity. But most everyone around here is bored of the story, has heard it thousands of times since she's crowed for anyone who wants to hear it. Except this bitch.

"And you were raised by—"

"A nice lady who adopted me," says Baby, taking another long sip from her Caesar before continuing. "She never had any kids or a husband or anything, and she read about me in the paper and adopted me."

"Wow," Amelia says.

"I can also do a backflip on a wakeboard," Baby says. "Those are the two big rumors about me. Just thought I'd get that out of the way."

Amelia chuckles. "I'm sorry."

Baby shrugs. "I'm not. I like my life."

"That's lucky," she says. "Not everyone can say that."

Baby thinks about the nights she came home to find Hannah passed out, head down on the table in a puddle of puke, empty bottle knocked over on the table or shattering on the floor. Sometimes her pulse would feel so weak, Baby'd sit next to her bed all night, listening to her breath. Those lonely nights caused questions to worm their way into Baby's mind. Did Hannah adopt the Dumpster Baby because she wanted someone who'd feel grateful? Someone Hannah thought so little of she could collapse into the most pathetic version of herself without any kind of shame? It's a bitter thought. Baby always tried her best to push it aside, but it's always found a way to come back to her.

"You know, Peter really loves this place. I was surprised he put up half the money for it." Baby's heart stops when she hears the words. *The hell?*

"He just really wants to see it thrive," Amelia says. "He wants it to get better." She fishes an olive out of her glass and chews.

"What do you mean?"

"He's my partner," Amelia says. Baby feels her face flush.

"You said thrive—"

"You've seen the books, you have to know this place hasn't been living up to its potential. Louise was exhausted. I think you all almost killed her."

Baby's brain follows the logic for her. The staff haven't been looking after it, they haven't tried to succeed, they drove Louise away.

"Sometimes management just needs to be refreshed. The bones are here—"

Baby feels the anger rising, the same anger that comes to her in the bar when the bitches descend and tell her she isn't worth shit. She takes a long sip of her Caesar, almost finishes it.

"You guys are doing your best. It's just fresh eyes, new ideas. Modernization. I know what people in the city want. I know how to make this place become what it has to be."

Baby isn't sure how to have this conversation; her pulse throbs. *Has to be?* As if this were a necessary step of existence. As if Amelia were rescuing them, pulling the resort out of a dumpster, giving them a life. And they're just supposed to be grateful?

"Why don't you drink?" Baby asks instead, choking on the words, steering the conversation away from a dangerous place where she'll clearly lose it, especially if her thoughts dwell too deeply on Peter—Peter investing, Peter helping this woman ruin everything.

"I don't like the feeling," Amelia says.

"Why not?" Baby asks.

"I don't like losing control," Amelia says, very carefully, her eyes locked on Baby's. The moment feels like a threat, but it ends before Baby is sure if the intensity was there or if she imagined it. "You'll lock up?"

"Sure thing," Baby says, shaking her glass, the ice now half melted.

Amelia walks out from behind the bar and pauses, her lips right next to Baby's ear, breath hot against her skin.

"Find somewhere else to live," she whispers with an iciness that Baby has never heard from her. It cuts into her stomach.

* * *

After she leaves, Baby breaks a wine bottle against the wall, throws it from the middle of the room, red flecks of wine and glass exploding in an artistic grotesque array. She watches all of it in slow motion, the liquid dripping down the wall like blood.

Peter, the dirty fucking traitor.

CHAPTER

16

"OH, WHAT NOW?" Baby asks. It's early, probably around nine, and her hair is still wet from another fruitless morning of diving, this time without Peter. She texted him after Amelia told her he'd invested, told him she wanted to lie low for a few days, and then went out without him. She's been swimming out from the dock, examining the floor of the lake in wide arcs, has found about a billion beer cans that she's piled on the dock to return, but no safe, no lifesaving cache of poker chips. Just the quiet deep, the remnants of her own trash.

At least the wet suit works, despite a few mouse holes chewed out in small circles on the ankle and the butt. She isn't shaking with cold. Her hair is drenched still, and the good toweling she gave it hasn't done much. It's the worst thing about having hair, the wet clunk of it dripping down the back of her T-shirt. She just hates it and is lying on her back on the dock, trying to soak some warmth out of the warmed wooden boards before having to trudge upstairs for another day in the salt mines, when DJ appears, standing over her, blocking out the morning sun.

"It's retraining day," says DJ. "We're starting in ten."

Retraining day. They've heard Amelia muttering about it. Customer service retraining. Baby wants to scream.

"No warning," Baby says. "We could've at least had some time to—"

"So we could all collectively call in sick?" DJ asks. "Come on, Crystal's bringing breakfast." She reaches down and hauls Baby up off the dock, muttering and groaning and cursing, pushes her up the hill, hands on her lower back as Baby flops back and forth, pretending she isn't going to go.

"Why is your hair wet?" DJ asks, suspicious.

"Just went for an early-morning swim," Baby fibs, so off-the-cuff DJ actually seems to believe her.

Oakwood opens in a week, the insides, the guts of it, polished and primed. The small bits and pieces of sabotage Baby and the gang have tried to enact haven't been very successful. Painting the walls the wrong color (Amelia didn't mind it, actually), stealing the batteries on the new golf carts (she bought backups), pouring sugar in the cement mixer when she tried to lay the foundation for the new spa (that actually caused problems—the entire thing was being delayed). That, combined with natural bad luck (a few missed lumber deliveries, half the construction crew taking different jobs up in Dorset), hasn't done much to quell Amelia's entrepreneurial spirit. She's already taken deposits from three couples for weddings in the fall. Keeps walking around the grounds with a bright smile on her face, clipboard pushed into her hip, barking about morale in a sunshiny voice. Nothing they've done has mattered.

They slouch into the bar, nodding hellos to everyone slumped on the tables. Baby sits down next to Marco, notices the deep circles under his eyes, the scent of whiskey leaching out of his skin. "Yeesh," Baby says. "Broke your shower?"

"Takes one to know one," Marco bites back lamely, taking a long sip from the to-go cup in front of him, then pressing his palms into his eyes and rubbing. Crystal hurries in, holding a brown tray with three coffees in it. She sits down next to DJ, Johnny just a few steps behind her.

"You get here with Johnny?" Baby asks.

"Yeah," Crystal says. "Why are you so wet?"

Baby shrugs.

"Here," Crystal says, passing her a French vanilla, and Baby knows full well that this generosity is driven by Crystal's fixation on making sure she's beloved by everyone, that she'll be the first to bend over for Amelia, probably already has, quietly, behind the scenes when no one is looking, starting with a compliment, probably something about Amelia's hair, and working her way in from there.

This feeling of settling has relaxed around them, this inevitability, and everyone seems to be coping with it differently. Baby's the only holdout. Despite Amelia's threats she's still squatting in the boathouse, still trying to resist. She takes a hot sip of the French vanilla and burns her tongue. She's got to find that fucking safe before the other employees start talking about how much they like the uniforms.

Amelia walks across the dance floor, staring down at all of them, smiling big and fat and wide, a box of doughnuts in her arms. It's a truly incredible mystery to Baby—how Peter could be related to this? It's crazy. Amelia puts the box down on a table, and no one moves as she opens it. "Good morning, everyone!" she says. "Dig in." She sits down on the edge of the stage, examining a clipboard she's tucked under her arm. No one moves. Baby is at least heartened by that.

"Tired? I know you've all been working really hard, and I just want you to know, I really appreciate it." Amelia picks up the box of doughnuts and offers it first to Jerry, who looks around the room, smiling at everyone, as if he's asking permission, then leans forward and grabs one. "Do you mind passing them around for me?" Amelia asks, and Jerry nods, grabbing the box and handing it off to Marco next to him.

"The rumors are true," Amelia says, gesturing with her clipboard. "It's retraining day. I really want us to be a customer-focused resort—obsessed with making it the best weekend ever for the people who come up here. It's hard to relax when you're worried about the staff, your bed, your dinner, so I want to make sure that with our grand reopening just a few days away, we're all on the same page."

Baby slides down in her seat, her butt creeping toward the edge, and she gets low enough that she's almost lying parallel to the table.

"I'd like to do a diagnostic exercise, just to see where you're at. Do we have a volunteer?"

Amelia looks around the room, everyone blinking up at her, silently chewing. The doughnut box passes under Baby's nose and she grabs at it, eyeing what's left—crullers and jelly and a single Boston cream, which she snatches up just before DJ can get her hands on it.

"C'mon," DJ whispers. "You know I hate jam."

"Sorry," Baby says, and takes a big bite, the cream from the doughnut escaping out the opposite hole, landing on her thigh with a plop. Baby swipes at it with a finger, licks it off.

"Who's the best at customer service?" Amelia asks. "Anyone?"

The room seems to look up and blink at her, all at once, as if she's speaking a dead language. The phrase "customer service" has never been uttered inside these walls.

"I want to nominate someone," Marco calls out, too loud, and Baby's worried it's too drunk, his voice, that Amelia will notice. "Baby should do it. Everyone loves her."

Baby gets up without protest, because if Marco is called forward, he'll probably get fired for smelling like he slept inside an aging whiskey barrel. She crams the rest of the doughnut down her throat as she does, chasing it with hot coffee. She almost starts coughing, walks toward the stage, slipping through chairs, her tongue burning.

"Now let's work out a scenario, just to see how it would go. Can we get a volunteer to be the angry customer?"

Marco's hand shoots up, and he stands before Amelia agrees, drags his feet toward the stage slowly, adjusting his belt. Baby doesn't like the expression on his face, this sort of smug, condescending amble he's affecting.

"Why don't we use a table?" Baby says, pointing to one at the edge of the dance floor, a good few feet away from Amelia, hopefully far enough away that she won't smell him.

"Sure," says Amelia, and Marco sits. "Okay, so Marco, you're a customer, and Baby is your server. She brought you a regular Coke, but you ordered a Diet."

"I'm good with it," says Marco. "Aspartame is the silent killer. I'd rather drink a regular." A few titters from the crowd and Marco grins, shifts in his chair, arms crossed, smiling.

"But for the purposes of this exercise, do you mind just pretending you're angry, please?" Amelia says, her voice even. Baby can see her patience is already straining.

"But she's saving my life," Marco says, smiling. "I've got a family history . . . all sorts of cancers. Skin cancer. Ass cancer. Cancer of the face."

Baby spits out a laugh at that one, shaking her head.

"Right," says Amelia. "Let's try something else. Why don't you suggest a customer scenario. You're the bartender—you must deal with angry people all the time."

"Not sober ones," he says. "Most of our guests are usually happy to be on vacation. They like it here."

"Right, well, I'm trying to draw a few higher-end clients who might be a bit more particular. So please, let's just run a scenario."

"What if we switched spots?" Baby asks. "I can be the angry one."

"Go for it," Marco says, standing up.

"Okay," Baby says, staring at the coffee cup in her hand, pretending to be an asshole. "What the fuck is this!" she shouts, throwing her cup at Marco. "I asked for Diet Coke, you moron. Are you trying to kill me? I might have diabetes! Get me the manager! I'll sue! I'm going to repossess this place and everyone in it. My shoes cost more than your car! I vote for the meanest candidate in every election!"

Everyone busts out laughing, including Marco. "I don't have a car," he says.

"Drink it!" Baby says, putting him in a headlock, grabbing her coffee cup from the floor and forcing it toward his mouth. "Drink it, you asshole!"

Marco, flailing against her body, affects a high voice. "Help me! Help! I'm being assaulted."

"I'll save you!" Johnny says, running up to the front and grabbing Baby around the waist and pulling her off Marco. He spins her overhead with a clumsy kind of grace, then puts her down on her feet.

"Okay, okay," Amelia says, waving her hands. "Break it up." Amelia's smiling, sure, but only because she has to. Baby can tell. Can't do a grand opening in a few days without staff. Can't find staff around here unless she builds housing, trucks them in from the city, and for what pay? Definitely wouldn't be as cheap as hiring the locals. Shining them up, buffing the skin, reshaping their personalities like clay. "Let's try another one."

Hands rocket into the air. Baby feels as if she's inspired everyone, opened a cage. Baby sits down in the crowd and watches, her feet up on a chair, as Crystal and DJ head up onstage and Amelia gives them roles. Crystal is the customer, and DJ's the housekeeper.

Crystal and DJ explode into a long, drawn-out fight about some stolen jewelry, which culminates with DJ collapsing to the floor. Baby thinks this feels a little bit like the twelfth grade when their normal homeroom teacher, Mr. Carr, had broken his arm and leg in an accident and was in traction at the hospital for six weeks and they'd trucked in a green little baby straight out of teacher's college to cover for him. And it started off innocently enough. Her name was Miss Hartstone, and someone called her Fartstone. Things devolved from there. But Baby remembers the giddy feeling of power, the swelling of it inside her chest, as the woman slowly stopped trying to run homeroom, stopped reading announcements, as this collection of teenage bullies was slowly vindicated.

At the time, Baby had a real *Whatever, she's just a bitch* attitude, not really considering that Fartstone didn't necessarily deserve it. But now Amelia is standing up there, the real embodiment of someone who deserves it, with Baby the arbiter of all of it.

"I'm dying!" DJ shouts, rolling around.

"I don't know CPR," Crystal says.

"Yes, you do!" DJ says, clutching at her chest. "Save me!"

"Sorry," Crystal says. "You called me a twig bitch."

"Too late," DJ says, a guttering cough escaping her throat, like the spirit of her dead husband may truly be in this room, as if it's entirely possible the jewels will be found. Baby applauds as DJ surrenders.

Amelia pulls Marco back up onstage with Johnny, and they turn a prompt about overserving in the Parrot into two intensely grounded homoerotic soliloquies about their true feelings for one another. Tina and Gerard perform a short play about pissing in the gardens to keep them blooming and beautiful. As the entire staff gets on board, a wild fantasy takes hold of Baby, that Amelia will just walk out, get in her car, and never come back. Abandon the lodge to them. She's rich. Baby imagines she must just abandon things all the time. Give them away once she has no use for them anymore.

Amelia sits down, eventually, on a stool at the side of the stage, scrolling through her phone, sighing, but Baby doesn't detect any of the sadness, any sense of personal failure, any weakness at all. The room sees it, and Tina and Gerard sit down at the circular tables they're sharing with Jerry. Baby feels a distinct shift, the self-congratulation evaporating. Tina and Gerard are a couple with four kids, and the silence from Amelia, the fact that she won't play the manager, isn't even bothering to attempt to control them—the truth of this arrives and behind it the worry.

The room stares at Amelia; Amelia stares at her phone, deflating everyone with her silence. Eventually she sighs again, puts two hands on her knees, and stands up. "So do I have to fire one of you, or are we going to do this?"

Baby looks over at Marco, sees him raring to go, wanting to stand up, this being the moment he was waiting for to tell her off, to flex in front of everyone, tell the bitch she can't push them around. Instead, Baby stands, the one who got them all into it, ready to go.

"I'm in," Baby says, grabbing Crystal by the shoulder, who gets up, clearly unsure about what they're supposed to be doing, whose side they're on. Baby gets it, though. Amelia has a line.

Amelia looks at her clipboard, traces the edge of her list with pencil. "Here's your scenario: we've double-booked a room, and the customer is angry that the room we promised them isn't available."

Crystal walks up. "I'm here to check in," she says.

"What's your name?" Baby asks, examining an invisible computer screen.

"Why didn't you welcome her?" Amelia cuts in. "Start again."

Crystal steps back, shooting Baby a tiny eye roll before she steps up once more. "Welcome to Oakwood Hills," Baby trills in a voice so loud and phony she checks on Amelia to see if she's going to stop them again, but Amelia just watches, her chest rising and falling, a firm set to her lips.

"I'm here to check in," Crystal says. "My name is Crystal."

"That's a nice name," Baby says. "Let me look you up on the computer." She pretends to scroll for a few minutes. "We've got you in cabin four," Baby says, grabbing an invisible key from behind her. "You're just going to take this key and head out—"

"She booked a lakeview room," Amelia shouts. "Crystal, tell her you booked a lakeview room."

"I booked a lakeview room, not a shitty cabin," Crystal says, affecting a ditzy voice.

"There was a small problem with overbooking," Baby says. "Our cabins are in tip-top shape, with larger beds and more privacy."

"I bet they're right by the woods, which is where the bears live. And the ax murderers. I don't want to get my head chopped off." The crowd chuckles, and Baby rummages through her head. This scenario has never actually happened in the billions of years this place has been open, not even when they used to use a manual booking system.

"Unfortunately, our lakeview rooms are all booked," Baby says. "But I can offer you the forest suite, and we'll give you one night free for your continued, uh, loyalty."

"Thank you!" Crystal says. "What excellent customer service. I will continue to come back to this place for years to come." The crowd applauds, a caution in the air, eyeing Amelia, and Baby can tell she's enjoying the deference, is learning that everyone here is just that afraid of losing their jobs, that they'll play ball when they know their livelihood is on the line.

"Right, so let's do a constructive critique here. I like how you problem-solved the issues so quickly using the resources you have at hand, but I think your attitude could use some work."

"My attitude?" says Baby.

"Yes, I think that it's good customer service practice—and I'd like everyone to hear this—good practice to apologize. At first, say you're sorry. Most people who've worked in this industry for as long as you have should know that."

Baby feels her neck flush, feels all eyes on her, waiting for her to react. This is the moment where she'd reach back and slap a city bitch who dared talk to her like that. The entire room seems to be expecting her to, and she thinks, maybe they even want her to. That if Baby breaks open, they won't have to pretend, they can all just act like irresponsible idiots and walk out, forget about their livelihoods and their futures, throw them aside for principles they can't afford to live by.

But someone has to look out for everyone. Baby doesn't know how it ended up being her, but it is, all the same.

"Crystal, let's try this again," Amelia says. "This time, I'll show you how I'd like you to react in this sort of scenario."

"Okay," Crystal says, shooting Baby a silent apology. Baby shrugs.

"Should I go?"

"Just a second." Amelia centers herself, throwing shoulders back, neck impossibly straight, shining teeth glinting in the morning sunlight. She stretches her lips into a white, phony grin. "And action."

"Go now?" Crystal asks, confused.

"Yes," says Amelia, her voice final and flat.

"Okay," Crystal says, walking up to Amelia, fake angry. "There's someone in my room!"

"I'm so sorry about that. I'm sure I'll be able to assist you with this issue and we'll get it resolved. Which room are you in?" she asks.

"Cabin five!" Crystal says. "Someone else's stuff is all over the place."

"Let me take a look here," says Amelia. "Ah, it seems like we've doubled-booked you. I'm so sorry about that. It's never happened before. How about I transfer you to a lakeside room?"

"It's not as good as a cabin!" Crystal says. "I want privacy."

"It's got a wonderful view. The breeze off the lake is beautiful. And I can also offer you ten percent off your dinner tonight for your inconvenience."

"Is that it?" Crystal asks.

"How about I throw in complimentary turn-down service?" Amelia asks, still smiling. The more Baby stares at her lips, the determination set in the grin and Amelia's inability to let it go, the more Baby's worried that she's underestimating her.

"I guess I'll take it," Crystal says. "Thank you."

Amelia turns to face the group of them.

"But that's not fair. Baby offered that," DJ pipes up.

"Also, Baby offered her a comp night, which we want to avoid at all costs," Amelia says. "That's a completely idiotic way to run a business. Just offer a free turn-down."

"Turn-down service is already free," Johnny cuts in.

"It's true, but the customer doesn't know that," says Amelia. "Sometimes when you're serving customers, you have to tweak the truth a bit. But I think the big takeaway here is, don't offer a comp room without asking for permission from me or your supervisor."

"Who's our supervisor?" Baby spits out, worried now that someone else is coming into the equation. These sorts of structures, vertical ones, they always leave people like Baby at the bottom.

"We'll talk about this at another time," Amelia says. "For now, we're focusing on opening." She looks at her watch. "I think that's lunch. We'll come back here in thirty."

The crowd disperses for lunch, everyone shuffling out of the room, the somber weight of Amelia's pivot crushing them. Of course she wouldn't care about her deal with Louise not to fire them. Of course if they start acting like jackasses, they'll be out. Baby knows it's idiotic to act like this. To underestimate Amelia.

Outside, everyone stands in small groups, pulling out lunch bags. "This isn't enough," Baby says, once she and Crystal and DJ have made it out of earshot. "This dumb kid's stuff. She's too confident. We've got to do something bigger. It's got to matter."

"You okay, Baby?" Johnny asks in his quiet way, walking up from behind them, head ducked. "You did well."

The kindness in his voice embarrasses her. Of course she's fine. But the attempted humiliation, the way Amelia tried to root under her skin, she won't soon be able to forget it.

"I thought she seemed really annoyed," Crystal says.

"And then she almost fired someone," DJ says. "I don't think this is a good idea, Baby. Let's just ride it out. She'll get bored eventually. Start missing her sweet life in the city, her friends and her spin classes and her green tea facials, and she'll go back to her life and leave us be."

Baby shakes her head. She's seen more of Amelia. There's more to this than she's letting on. She's way more invested. "This is different," Baby says. "It feels different."

"Based on what?" DJ asks.

"We had drinks," Baby says. "She's trying to prove some-thing. If we don't stop her now, we're going to lose this place. I know. I can feel it."

DJ lets out a frustrated sigh that's almost a scream.

Crystal wraps an arm around her, around Baby. "What do you want to do, then?"

"I don't know," says Baby, still, staring out at the horizon, thinking. "But it's got to be big."

17

BABY'S LEANING AGAINST the tree with DJ and Crystal when Peter's head appears at the top of the hill, followed by his body, then his feet. Staff training continued throughout the afternoon. Amelia was relentless, running the same scenarios over and over until everyone was using her canned, corporate language, sanitizing them one by one. By the end of it, the employees were slumped over in chairs, legs stretched forward, listening with their elbows propped on tables as Amelia droned on and on and on. Slowly breaking them down like prisoners.

So when Peter shows up, Baby doesn't move. She knows she should stand up, go talk to him, make it easy on him, in the same way she's been making it easy on him for the entirely of their relationship, but instead she looks at the gravel parking lot, at his bare feet, which probably don't have the thick calluses hers do, thinking, *He's probably just here to pick up Amelia anyway, you dumbass; he's probably not even looking for you.*

Baby stares up at the leaves on the tree, an ugly tree that rises in an oval shape, sort of like a head of romaine lettuce. Wind kicks up and rattles the branches, which rustle loudly overhead. His ankles appear on either side of her neck, just brushing the edges of her earlobes.

"Hey, ladies," he says, which is a weird thing to say, no doubt. Baby laughs at the awkwardness of it, as if he's her friend's dad, popping his head into the sleepover to make sure they don't need more popcorn and aren't sexting any pervs on chat rooms.

"Hey, Peter," Crystal says, standing up, giving him a hug. "Why haven't you come to visit us yet?"

DJ ignores him.

"It turns out I'm working for Amelia too this summer," he says, chuckling, trying to make something of the absurdity of himself with a summer job. How ridiculous, how silly to think a guy like him could and would work. He's too rich, after all.

"She's really something," Crystal says.

"That's one word for it," says Peter, sticking out his big toe and brushing the edge of Baby's cheek with it.

"How's your summer going, DJ?" he asks. She keeps on ignoring him. Baby imagines she's lying down in the grass, just like Baby is, but staring at her phone, browsing through tracks, maybe with two earbuds snugged in, her gaze steadily forward. Peter switches angles almost immediately, not one to be shamed or embarrassed or to read anything into it.

"Is she asleep?" he asks Crystal, nudging Baby with his toe. She stays perfectly still.

"That wouldn't surprise me," says Crystal. "Li'l Baby's had a long day." Peter chuckles. All Baby wants is for him to walk off and leave her alone here, just stop trying, stop pulling her in.

But of course he doesn't walk off, he's never been capable of reading her mind, and instead he extends a hand down to her and she takes it, her body responding before she has a chance to beat back the instinct of it. DJ's watching her, she can feel the judgment, the *Here she goes again* of it all. The up and down and back and forth of it. *Weak girl, Baby, weak girl*, she thinks, as she follows him back across the gravel toward the hill.

Marco's walking across the lawn to his beat-up old truck and stops when he sees Baby being pulled away by Peter, narrows his eyes at her, shakes his head slowly, back and forth. He may as well be mouthing the word *traitor*. Traitor! Traitorous bitch! Baby turns away, ashamed.

She wants to be angry at Peter, to stomp her feet and yell and demand he explain himself. Insist on knowing why he didn't warn her. How he could be an investor. Why Amelia exists at all, why he didn't just eat her in the womb when he had the chance. But she doesn't. She just follows him down to the boat, lets him squeeze her hand and ask why the search for the safe stopped. Baby mutters an excuse, grabbing the wet suits from their hooks in the boathouse, and they head out again.

*   *   *

Peter finds a handful of rusty shotgun casings that he drops on the floor of the boat, then unzips his wet suit. "We need gloves," he says, sucking on the webbing between his pointy finger and his thumb. "Good thing I just got a tetanus shot." He flashes his hand at Baby, a thin line of blood dripping down his palm.

"Poor baby," says Baby, unzipping her own wet suit and rolling it down to the waist, the cool air prickling her skin, making her shiver as goose bumps rise up and down her arms. The sun is almost down and they still haven't found anything.

"We've covered quite a bit of ground." Peter looks back at the bay toward the resort, the lake stretching out in front of them.

"We just need to look over there," Baby says, gesturing to a bay just to the right of the resort, a quiet little inlet that doesn't see much boat traffic. No cottages either, parked on the shores, just a long strip of water bordered by trees. Baby's heard prop planes land there before, at night, seen them flying overhead. Rumor always was that it was Peter's dad, flying himself up for the weekend. Baby never spotted his person, never saw the plane taxiing to Pomoroy Island, just heard the buzz of it, the splash of the water, saw its yellow dot circling high up in the clouds.

"Getting too dark anyway," he says. "Want to go to town?"

"Town?" Baby asks. Town isn't much. A pizza joint, a strip mall, a blurt of a rocky beach to sit on with your socks off. Baby doesn't have anywhere better to be, but this doesn't line up with their activities, isn't on the list of things they do together, which is mostly drinking, fucking, partying, smoking weed, dancing, and beer pong. They've gone to town to hit the liquor store, buy boxes of beer for bush parties or cases of white wine for Peter's mother that cost more than Baby's paycheck, but town, for town's sake?

"Yeah, town," says Peter. "I'm hungry."

"Okay," Baby says, sliding out of the wet suit and tossing it on the rear bench of the boat, drying her body off, and pulling her jean shorts back on, her sweatshirt, unspooling her ponytail and twisting out the water.

"I'm sorry," he says.

"What are you sorry for?" she asks as they go through the motions of getting the boat started.

"Amelia," he says. "She doesn't have much experience . . ."

"Managing?" Baby says. "I can tell."

"I was going to say with people who aren't like her," he says.

"People like me?" Baby asks.

Peter doesn't answer and Baby doesn't push.

"I don't mean anything by it, but you know. I know she's a spoiled brat. I know I am too," he says. "But Amelia, she's been through some stuff."

"Stuff?" Baby asks. "What kind of stuff?"

"She was eleven or twelve and went on this canoe trip with this other girl. It was at camp. And they sent the twelve-year-olds off in pairs to do like an overnight adventure. And they kept track of where they sent them and everything, so it's not like it was meant to be unsafe, but there was this freak storm and Amelia and the girl she was with, Mallory Huggens, their canoe was damaged and it was taking on water. And they were just kids, I guess; they didn't know what to do. And apparently Mallory tried to leave Amelia behind. There was some kind of struggle and Amelia just barely escaped. You should've seen her face, the scratch marks. There were these big deep gouges . . . anyway, Amelia got in the canoe and paddled off, thinking she wasn't so far away, that they'd be able to go back and rescue Mallory. She had a life jacket. But they never found her."

Baby exhales, feels her eyes growing wide.

"I know," Peter says. "It was crazy. And Amelia used to be really—I don't want to say lighthearted, but she was a little easier going. After that trip, she became really intense about her life. Trying to make it worth something. I don't know. She has a lot of survivor's guilt. And my dad doesn't believe in therapy; he wouldn't let her get any kind of counseling. Just bought her a gym membership."

"Wow," Baby says. "That sounds like a lot for a twelve-year-old."

"Yeah," Peter says. "Tell me about it."

Baby sits, listening to the water lap against the side of the boat. "But she kept going to camp?"

"Yeah," Peter says. "My parents didn't force that."

"Wow," Baby says.

"What?" Peter asks.

"No, that's just . . ." Baby swallows what she really wants to say, the questions she really wants to ask.

"I know," Peter says. "She's the strongest person I know."

Baby wants to throw up in her mouth, just a little bit, at that. Because it's weird to her. It really is. That Amelia—if she was so traumatized by the summer camp, if a girl had died because of her—would be able to return.

"I think she just wanted to prove to everyone that she was okay," Peter says. "My dad can be . . . he doesn't really tolerate weakness."

Baby sees the pieces coming together in a jumbled mess, none of them fitting quite right.

"She comes by it honestly, is all I mean," Peter says, in his easy way. "Now let's go eat something. You look hungry."

"I didn't bring my wallet," Baby mumbles.

"My treat," he says.

"No," she says. "I'm paying you back."

"Baby, come on," he says. "Why do we have to fight about this?"

"Because it's . . ." She trails off and stares at the bottom of the boat.

"If we've been friends for a long time, it's not pity, is it?" he says, brushing it off. He turns on the motor, puts the engine in gear, and pulls a shirt over his head.

"If it's not pity, what is it?" she asks.

"Baby, it's a date," he says. "A date. You know, like on TV."

"Fine," she says. "But I want my own pizza." She sits down and crushes a smile inside her fist, feeling like she's won something, pushing all the weirdness about Amelia aside. There's a small part of her brain that feels as if this story of Amelia's past has been edited down, the sharp edges of it smoothed away. As if there's something he isn't telling her.

"Deal," he says, then turns up the engine, and they take off.

Baby takes stock, as they fly over water toward town, of all the times Peter hasn't shown up for her, trying to figure out if now is any different. She knows if she tries to talk to DJ about it, DJ'll remind her of what's happened every single August or September for the last nine, ten, eleven years. The fading away. The nothingness, the void of the last text or phone call or IM or whatever method of communication they'd been using that summer, stretching out until Peter was gone, back to the city for September like a sexy sex ghost, disappeared into nothing, making Baby feel like he'd never really existed at all. But when he was there, it wasn't like he seemed to take pleasure in her yearning for him, in keeping her at arm's length.

And there was the time she'd driven Crystal to the city for an abortion and Hannah's car had broken down on the side of the highway and he drove an hour to get them, then waited for six hours for the tow truck and drove Crystal right home, didn't play the radio or ask weird questions or try to force her into conversation. And then the time he went to Dorset to buy them all WrestleMania tickets because everyone else had to work and the line was so long; he apparently bribed some kids to let him skip. And every birthday of hers that he was around for, he showed up with some kind of cake that he drunkenly fed her in the middle of the dance floor at the Parrot, usually after hours, when only the staff and their close friends were huddled around.

One summer, maybe five years ago, maybe farther back, sticks out in her mind. She thinks it was right after Bad Mike went in, but she's not sure. Peter'd gone backpacking in Europe with some friends for the summer and had only come up for a few weeks, middle of August until early September, and she remembers how fast things moved. They'd hang out almost every single day. He'd always show up for her after work, boat parked at the dock, and they'd drive off somewhere to have sex or eat or just lie around or drink. Every single day.

So when he left without saying goodbye, the day that he didn't show up, Baby fell into a real deep hole. And Hannah knew what was going on and just left her to her own feelings, but the summer after, Baby remembers, Peter had come to pick her up at her dock and Hannah grabbed her shoulder, stared into her eyes. "Be careful with that one," she said.

Lakeside isn't busy, and when Peter pulls up to the dock, Baby grabs the rope and stands up, ready to catch the dock. Peter's a lot of things, but a talented parker he is not. "I got it," she says, putting her foot up on the edge of the boat, then realizes just how far from the dock they actually are.

"It's all right," he says, slowing the boat down and putting it into reverse, maneuvering it up against the dry planks. The side of his boat is covered in scratches, divots and cracks. He stopped bothering with bumpers five years ago. But Baby watches, surprised, as he slowly edges the boat closer until it's sidled up tight enough for her to step out.

"What the hell?" she says, looping her rope through the cleat on the dock, grabbing the other that he tosses up after her.

"People change, Baby," he says, reaching out a hand. She pulls him out of the boat, and he slips an arm around her waist as they walk down the dock.

Her heart thumps, the terror of all of it drawing itself together, like their bodies are hovering on the edge of some great sneeze. She's suddenly at a loss for what to say to him. How to act around him. Everything feels incredibly embarrassing.

She walks with him toward the pizza window in silence, incredibly aware of her body, of the sounds around them. She nods at Grace Clutterbuck and her husband Dave, who're parked on the sole picnic table, finishing up slices. "Sorry about the resort, Baby," says Dave, who's been around for ages, has always looked like he was sixty-five to Baby. No younger, no older, for her entire life.

"We're working it out," she says, smiling.

"I hear the new owner is a real piece of work," says Grace.

"Something like that," Baby says, glancing at Peter, whose expression betrays absolutely nothing. Baby knows they want the gossip, and the feeling of knowing, of being important, would usually prop her leg up on the bench, let Grace and Dave feed her pizza while she invented and expanded on the usual drama to make it seem like it was the end of the world. Instead, she keeps on walking, Peter next to her.

"You okay?" he asks.

"Fine," she says. "What do you want?"

"It's pizza, Baby," he says. "Whatever you want. It's all delicious."

"Really?" she says. "Hawaiian? Really, Peter? It's like I don't even know you."

"Not Hawaiian," he says. "That's not pizza."

"Thank god," she says. "I was starting to regret the last decade of my life."

She orders one with everything but fruit, and they go sit on the rocks and wait. The sun has warmed them and Baby relaxes against a large, bleached boulder, the chill from their diving excursion slowly evaporating from her bones as the sun inches closer and closer to the horizon.

"You know, Baby, I think you and Amelia would really get along if you just tried it. Everyone likes you."

"Not everyone," Baby says, gesturing to Deputy Donna and Judy Mork sitting in their pickup truck, chewing. Peter waves to them and Donna nods back, all business, even though she has a napkin tucked into her collar.

"Pretty sure that's your own fault," he says. "Didn't you torture her in high school?"

"I didn't torture her," Baby says. "She tortured me. By existing."

"Asshole," he says, but he doesn't stop smiling, nudges her with his shoulder, clearly glad he's on the inside and not the out. Baby shrugs and watches the fishing boats, little tinnies trolling around, ignoring the environmental edict from Donna. Seems like it's selectively enforced.

"I just wish she'd get over it," Baby says.

"Get over high school?"

"And middle school. And I guess kindergarten." Baby relents. "Still. I've never even seen her crack a beer. She should learn how to relax. Stop taking life so seriously."

"Baby, I barely said anything." Peter laughs. "It's Amelia I want you to be friends with."

"Why?" Baby's suspicious. It doesn't make sense. Not really. But he's pushing it so hard.

"Because it would make your life a lot easier."

"Why do you care about how easy my life is?" Baby spits it out, realizes then that this is a step too far. Peter quiets, looks away. These sorts of questions are exactly what they don't talk about, the fights they've never had. Because Baby always chickens out, is afraid that once she starts pulling at threads, everything will unravel. Even when she starts, Peter usually refuses to engage. Changes the topic or waits for her to calm down.

"Amelia and I are just different," Baby says, covering.

"I swear she's not so bad. My dad was a real jerk to her growing up," he says. "That's why she spent all her summers at that camp. He's kind of . . . old-fashioned."

"What do you mean?" says Baby.

"He . . . I don't know, he definitely favored me," says Peter. "He didn't want to pay for her to go to business school."

"Really?"

"Yeah, he said it was a waste of money."

"She seems like she's smart. Bad with people. But smart."

"I know," he says. "He's just an old prick."

"How'd she pay for school?" Baby asks.

"She has a trust," he explains. "From our grandfather."

"Man, how rich are you?"

He shifts on the rock and shrugs and Baby doesn't push it. She's Googled him, sure she has, Googled the whole damn family. DJ has more than once, danced the numbers in front of her face. More than enough money, too much, even. The kind that should weigh on you, though Baby's sure it doesn't.

"Are there fewer boats around now?" he asks, looking around the lake. Outside the few fishing boats, there aren't many people, no one out on their docks. Just quiet cabins, lights out. Protected by security cameras and motion sensors. No signs of life.

"Definitely," says Baby. "No one uses their houses. Can you imagine? Having a house and not using it?"

"People get busy," he says.

"I'm just saying, if I could afford a house on a lake, I'd live in it."

"That's just nuts," says Peter.

"Me owning a house?"

Peter exhales, frustrated. "Obviously not, Baby. Come on. I was being sarcastic. You know I think the world of you. You could really do something if you just played ball, you know? Honestly, I think Amelia's maybe got a year or two with this resort thing until she'll be looking for someone to manage it, and she'll be onto something new. I bet if you just worked with her, that could be you. You know, if you just . . ." He trails off, and Baby thinks of a million horrible things he could be thinking. "If you just tried," he says instead.

Baby doesn't believe him.

"Besides, you used to live on a lake," he says, changing tactics, dancing away from his own advice. "Your cabin was the best. Why didn't you stay there?"

"Too expensive for one person," Baby says. "I'm fine where I am—right now, anyway."

"Really?" he asks.

"Yes," Baby says, because admitting that she can't pay for herself in front of Peter fills her with deep shame. She starts to feel incredibly angry about it. "I'm fine." Her heart is pounding and she can't escape him right now, and she just hates it, she hates him, the pity that's seeping out of him. "It's your sister you should be worrying about."

Baby gets up and climbs off the rocks, heads over to the pizza window, just begging them, willing the pizza to appear there. Instead, she can see it isn't even in the fucking oven. The idiot teenagers working it, she doesn't recognize them, wants to cuss them out. Probably some city kids up for the summer needing summer jobs, not for the money but for the experience, god fuck them, their parents treating this like a lesson, most likely.

And Baby is just so stuck inside this humiliation that she doesn't notice that Donna's cruiser is gone, doesn't notice Bad Mike pull up behind her in a brand-new black pickup truck. She doesn't hear him crunching through the gravel or across the grass. It isn't until his hand clenches her shoulder that Baby jumps.

"What the fuck?" she says, stepping back, away from him, speaking loudly, clearly. Peter's still out on the rocks, far enough away not to hear them.

"Baby, Baby, Baby," Bad Mike says. "How are ya?"

Baby meets his eyes. "What do you want?"

"Rude girl," he says, gesturing over to the picnic table. "Let's sit down."

"I'm with someone," she says, gesturing toward Peter.

"This'll only take a minute," Bad Mike says. "And then I'll let you get back to your gold digging."

"Oh, fuck you," she says, almost hoping she can get him to hit her, give Donna a reason to haul him back in. All she needs is a reason. And a witness.

"Sit down," he says. Baby takes a few steps to the picnic table, already vacated by the Clutterbucks, then realizes he's probably been watching her for a while, waiting for everyone clear out. She sits. Bad Mike settles across from her, folds his hands together like a businessman.

"What are you diving for?"

"I don't know what you're talking about," she says.

"I see you, Baby. I've got eyes everywhere. Now tell me what you're diving for, or I'll break your arm." The frankness of his voice is the scariest part, because Baby knows he doesn't have to pretend to terrify, knows that he knows she's well aware he'd do it in a heartbeat, that the only thing stopping him was a witness and now it's just the two of them.

"Blow me," she says instead.

Bad Mike watches her, cocks his head to the side, as if he's trying to understand what she said.

"You heard me," she says.

He reaches out and grabs hold of the back of her head and slams her forehead down on the table, presses it into the scratchy wood, the force of his fingers on her throat pushing tighter and tighter. His hand is so giant, she knows he could kill her, so easily, if he wanted to, right now, and Peter wouldn't hear a thing.

"Baby, I could end you here, but I won't because I don't want the hassle. But hear me now: stop looking for whatever you're looking for. I can kill you quickly and I can kill you slowly, and honestly? I like it slow. Got it?"

Baby gasps, but no air will enter her throat. She struggles against his hand but feels so ridiculously helpless, manages to raise her hand in a thumbs-up just before her vision starts to darken. He lets go of her and she sits up, inhaling desperately. Mike's somehow already back at his truck, and without a second look at her, he turns the engine on and roars off.

Baby takes big, gulping breaths in and out, water streaming down her cheeks from the fear of it, the pounding of her heart, the adrenaline surging up toward her head. Dizzy, she closes her eyes and presses fists into them. It's not an empty threat. She knows that, at least.

Baby hears the ding of the bell on the counter inside the pizza hut. She wheels around, searching for Peter, as she takes more gasping breaths, angry tears gathering in the corner of her eyes. Fucking Mike. At least Peter didn't see.

As she walks up to the counter, she knows she can't tell Peter, because then he'll make them stop diving, stop looking. Because if Mike's up here, they must be getting close to something. And Baby's going to claim it before anyone else can.

She takes a minute at the pizza window, breathing in through her nose and waiting for her heart to stop pounding so she can walk back over to where Peter's sitting on the rocks with his eyes closed, oblivious, tanning in the sunset, the light playing and bouncing off the lake, making him look like some sort of bronzed god, relaxed, without a care in the world.

18

Baby takes a tequila shot, the liquor hitting her behind the eyes, the picture in front of her, an idiot in a sombrero, all swoopy edges, glassy. She slams it down and stuffs two limes in her mouth, then grabs the extended twenty and hands back eight bucks, waves when she hears the tip clink in the jar. Drunks are three deep at the bar, money in outstretched fists, but she needs a second and turns around and takes a long swig from the giant glass of Coke she's been sucking on all night, presses the cool glass to her forehead.

The place exploded once they opened, and Baby thinks someone shot a flare from the deck of the Parrot and everyone in a ten-mile radius heard the music blasting out through the windows and followed the trail up into the bar. They'd only been open for an hour and a half and the place was already at capacity.

It happened quickly, and Baby's still worried that Donna'll show up and be able to smell that something's off. Baby doesn't know what the deal is with liquor licenses, whether or not Amelia has told Donna they aren't supposed to open the place. Instead, when Amelia announced she was spending two nights in the city and DJ got the call from the triple bachelor party wanting someplace to party, well, they just decided to go for it.

Amelia wouldn't need to know, they figured. Marco was still in charge of the bar inventory and they figured they could pocket everything and Amelia'd be none the wiser.

Problem was, Marco showed up wasted at seven thirty and was making out with a twenty-year-old by the pool tables, which meant it was Baby and Crystal behind the bar, Johnny at the door. And the bachelors seemed intent on showing their gratitude by buying Baby drinks and shots, and she knows it's about time she starts to wave them off. Crystal next to her, Baby can see she's starting to wobble in her heels, her hair pressed down onto her forehead, weighed down by sweat, smiling and reaching down under the counter, dropping the twenties, then pointing to the next guy.

The dance floor is heaving. DJ had them going minutes after they walked in, rolled out a sub and a single speaker, a small board and her iPod, probably just bumping through her old stuff. No one cares, though, Baby knows. They need the space, the ever-shrinking space, just to exist and be loud and here it is, even temporarily. Between the cover charge, the bar, and tips, Baby thinks they all stand a shot at walking away with seven hundred bucks. They get up early, mop up, and Amelia will never know.

Baby side hops over to Crystal, avoiding eye contact with all the desperates leaning against the bar, money in fist, and hip-checks her. "This is fucking crazy," Baby sings, happy she's wearing her hat. Baby takes it off, grabs an ice chip, tosses it under, then draws the bill back down.

"I know," Crystal says. "I've been tossing shots all night."

"Oh, good idea," Baby says, feeling stupid because the thought of not taking the shot, of not kicking it back, never crossed her mind. "I'm hammered."

Crystal grabs her on either side of her head and tilts her eyes up. "Bless this mess."

"Baby!" a voice shouts, and she looks up. One of the bachelors she recognizes from summers past—she thinks his name is Stavros or maybe George—waves her over.

"What?" she asks. It's hard not to smile at him, all floppy haired and wasted.

"Come here!" he says.

"I've got to work," she says.

"Come greet your subjects." He reaches forward and grabs her arms and she laughs and thinks, why not, and dives over the bar, lets him haul her over, and when he kneels in front of her, she straddles his shoulders and grabs his head as he stands up and starts parading her through the room. A hand emerges from the crowd and passes her a beer and she tosses it back, takes a long swig as the guy dances her across the floor, her arms spread wide. This is the way it should be. This is the kind of fun that matters, not the back-massage, gluten-free, diarrhea-tea bullshit Amelia is peddling. The good stuff.

DJ transitions into one of Baby's favorites, an old rap track from back when they were in high school, and taps George/Stavros on the shoulder to put her down. Instead he tosses her up in the air and catches her and she lands in his arms, laughing. "What the fuck?" she asks.

"I'm a cheerleader," he says.

"A what?" Baby says, not sure she's heard him correctly. The music is really loud.

"A cheerleader," he says, and throws her again, spinning her in the air. Baby lands, laughing, laughing so hard she can feel the tequila sloshing around in her stomach.

"Can you do the worm?" she asks.

"Oh hell yeah," he says, and puts her down. She clears a space in the middle of the dance floor, pushing the bachelors back, the sombrero bachelors and the tie-dyed-shirt bachelors and the business bachelors, and the local girls, the weekenders, who answered the text message and did what they were supposed to do and passed it on.

Stavros and Baby face off in the middle of the dance floor. DJ can see what's happening from the booth and pumps up the volume. Stavros faces off with Baby and they start moving, and when the bass starts to really thump, they drop down and roll their bodies against the floor. The crow erupts around them, but Baby is focused on the task at hand, smells the fresh varnish they used to polish the floorboards, and slips, rolls over, and lies flat on her back, spent. Her record is nine, but tonight she only made it through two body waves. It doesn't matter, though; everyone knows Baby, everyone loves her, everyone is here, feeling the way they're feeling because of her.

Hands reach under her body and lift her up, tossing her up in the air, and she feels as if she's moving in slow motion, feels her body fly up in the air, eyes on the freshly painted ceiling. The crowd catches her and she throws her arms back and lies there, held up by what feels like hundreds of bodies.

When the song ends, she's placed on her feet by one of the business bachelors at the edge of the floor right in front of Deputy Donna and Mork the Dork.

"Ah!" Baby says, startled by the two of them just standing there, not doing their usual side-wall skulk. Donna clears her throat—the human eye roll herself. Baby's sure she's never had fun, not ever, not even when she's breaking up bush parties and booking meth heads for possession. Sure, she enjoys it, sure, but it doesn't make her happy. Not happy like Baby is now, being worshiped as the lord and savior of this joint, the Captain of Snapped Opened Cans.

"You see Mike in here tonight?" Donna asks, which surprises Baby. Usually when they come to talk to Baby, it's about something they're trying to pin on her but can't prove.

"No," says Baby. "Is that something we should be worried about?"

"Yes," says Donna.

Nothing has ever gone down at the Parrot that they couldn't control. They never *really* violated the license. Baby knows the server and bartenders aren't supposed to be hammered on the job, but still, it's just one of those things you can get away with.

"Baby, call me if he shows up," Donna says, putting a hand on her shoulder. "Have you seen him at all?"

Baby knows she should probably narc on him about what happened outside the pizza spot, but then she'd have to explain the chest, the money, what the Parrot is doing open, Amelia, Peter, the dumpster she was born in.

"No, I haven't," Baby says. "Have you talked to Crystal?"

"She's next," Donna says.

"Where's Marco?" Judy Mork asks, looking around the room. Baby clenches her teeth and looks around too.

"He's not working tonight," she says.

"That's weird," Judy says. "He told me he was."

"He showed up," Baby says. "But we had enough staff."

"That's a pretty big line at the bar," she says.

"We're handling it," Baby replies, and it does sound like she's covering, any way you slice it.

"If you see him, tell him to call me," she says.

"You got it," Baby says, purposely not looking at the dark, back corner of the bar where Marco is still probably squirreled away with the girl.

"He's been weird lately. Does he seem weird to you?" Judy Mork asks.

"Lot of changes around here," Baby says.

"Tell him I'm looking for him, all right?" Judy says.

"Sure," says Baby, knowing she won't. Those are the rules of the bar, and Baby abides.

"Don't overserve," Donna says, flashing her light at Baby, but she's clearly got meatier onions to fry. And as soon as they walk off, Baby turns on a flip-flop and heads to the corner where she last spotted Marco, but when she arrives, he isn't there. Probably scuttled off to one of the rooms, the dirty dog.

"Bitch, the toilets are all backed up," one of the Morrison sisters says, grabbing her by the shoulder.

"There's a plunger right in there," Baby says.

"Well, have at 'er," the girl says, clucking her tongue. "I don't work here."

Baby heads back into the bathroom. Even Amelia has had trouble improving them. Years of grime leeches through the fresh coat of paint, and one of the new barn-style doors Amelia had installed is already hanging off its hinges. A girl wearing purple cowboy boots sits on the toilet, her jean shorts down around her ankles. She's playing Tetris on her phone, doesn't even look up as Baby passes by.

Baby heads into the other stall and finds mounds and mounds of paper stuffed into the gray water. Baby grabs the plunger and goes at it—this isn't the first time she's been in here—gets into a real rhythm. It takes five straight minutes of jogging the plunger in and out and in and out of the toilet before a flush diminishes about half of what's inside it. And it's while Baby is standing there, panting as she pushes the plunger in and out and in and out of the toilet, that she gets an idea, the idea, really, that she knows will work, will ruin the big grand opening weekend, will maybe even gross Amelia out enough to abandon this enterprise entirely.

"Fuck yes," Baby says, watching the toilet paper disappear down the drain.

"Get it, girl," Purple Cowboy Boots says from the other stall, the sound of her Tetris game still echoing in the dim fluorescent light. "You get yours."

* * *

When the party ends, Baby and the gang each walk away with six hundred bucks in their pockets and pool an extra four to replace the liquor they sold. "She'll never know," Baby says, looking around the room. Cleanup is necessary. "Should we just start now?"

"I'm beat," Crystal says, forehead pressed against the table.

"It doesn't look so hot in here."

"What happened?" Peter's standing by the front door, looking around the Parrot, at the spilled drinks and empty cups trampled on the ground, a weird red streak against the far wall that almost looks like blood. A hush goes over the employees, all of them acting like they've been caught, and even Baby stands, worried at how carelessly Peter has been straddling both lines, unwilling to separate the two parts of his life that truly need to be held in different hands.

"Hey," Baby says, crossing the room to Peter, grabbing his wrists.

"Did you open tonight?" he says over Baby's shoulder to the rest of them. No one in the room looks at him, no one answers. Instead DJ grabs a broom and starts pushing the trampled cups into a pile. "Baby," he says. "You opened?"

"Yeah, so what?" she says.

"You weren't supposed to do that."

Baby snaps then, knows she needs to make a show of standing up for the room. "Everyone's been hurting for tips and Amelia doesn't give a shit. She's paying minimums, which is good for her and everything, but we saw an opportunity and we took it. We're talking about livelihoods here," she says. "Maybe this isn't something you understand, but working here isn't like a fun hobby, it's necessary."

Peter nods, the expression on his face impossible to read, and it makes Baby feel like she should lash out at him, words forming on her lips, almost out of her mouth. But instead, Peter shrugs. "Okay," he says.

"So you won't tell her?" Baby asks.

"No, this is her thing," says Peter, the other employees peeking up at the both of them as they sweep up around them. "You want to . . . hang out tomorrow?"

Baby grins. "Yeah, maybe you could stay here tonight?" She steps toward him, making sure no one can hear them.

"In the boathouse?"

"No, in one of the cabins?" Baby asks.

"Is that allowed?"

"I mean, sure," says Baby. "If no one finds out about it."

Peter smiles and nods. "Sounds good to me," he says.

"Do you want to just meet me out there? I left cabin four open," she says. "Let me deal with this." She leans in and kisses him and can feel everyone watching behind her, all the judgment rising up behind her like a wave. Peter nods, as if almost grateful he isn't being forced into a position, isn't being forced to pick sides, and heads off.

When Baby turns around, everyone pauses.

"So is he going to narc or what?" asks DJ, putting down her busing bin. Crystal looks up from where she's standing behind the bar. Johnny keeps shoveling trash into bags, clearly just trying to finish up and get out of there.

"Not," says Baby. "We have an understanding."

"Yeah, right," says DJ. "He's just telling you what you want to hear."

"I'm not doing this tonight," Baby says. "We're fine." She shoulder checks to make sure Peter's gone. "And besides, I've got an idea and I think it's really going to work. Two words." She pauses for dramatic effect. "Septic tank."

19

T HE NEXT MORNING Baby and Peter slip out of the cabin
before sunrise. Baby thinks she might still be a little drunk,
can taste the beer and tequila still working their way through
her body. Fog hovers over the field as they cross it and pick their
way down to the boathouse.

Baby slips out of her clothes and into one of the bathing
suits she keeps hanging on nails in the boathouse, shivers in the
morning chill as she grabs both of the wet suits and heads back
out to where *Rude* floats. The fog lies low and thick, and Baby is
glad for it, glad that Mike won't be able to spot them out there,
at least until after the sun rises.

Peter's waiting in the boat, swiping dew off the captain's
chair, then sitting up on top of it, looking adorably rumpled.
Baby tosses in the lines, scanning, paranoid that someone might
be watching. But there's no one around. No Amelia sitting
there, waiting to catch them, no Mike with the brass knuckles,
ready to split Baby's cheek open. Just the two of them in the
quiet. Peter starts the engine and Baby shoves them away from
the dock.

Peter drives east of Oakwood, toward a thin inlet that
cuts along two shorelines, shaped like a very depressing slice
of pizza. Once they're near the mouth of it, he turns off the
engine. Baby still can't shake the feeling of being watched, the

creeping feeling of eyes that can see through the fog. But as Peter slows the boat down near a fallen birch tree, its bent-over white fingers hovering over the water, its roots not quite ready to give up on it, the ends of branches just barely touching the surface, Baby shivers, searching the shore for signs of life, peering through the thick brush and woods bordering the bay. Nothing.

Peter preps the anchor and drops it as Baby squeezes into the Splash Queen wet suit with a strange feeling of anticipation, as if today is the day they'll find it, making all the long mornings spent out here dropping their bodies into icy-cold water worth it. She watches the anchor find ground, causing a cloud of murk to mushroom around it. "Mucky down there," she says.

"Make sure you dig," he says, pulling out the metal detector and booting it up. She zips up the back of her wet suit and grabs her mask and flippers, slides into the water.

"Water's really warming up," she says. "I might not need this."

"Still early," he says.

"Yeah, you're right," she says, treading water and waking up her muscles. He passes down the metal detector and she slides it onto her arm, tightens the straps and pushes away from the boat, staring at the green bottom. The metal detector immediately goes off and she dives, straight down. Nothing's sitting on the muck and she grabs a stick slick with algae and plunges it into the bottom, feels around for a solid hunk of metal. No huge safe, no huge metal box. Just another fork. She grabs it and pushes back up to the surface, tossing it into the boat.

"I just don't understand why people lose so many forks," he says. "What are they eating on boats?"

She shrugs and takes off again, kicking slowly, trying to keep the particles of sludge and sand flat so they don't float up toward her mask, obscuring her view. A fat fish swims along the bottom, past an angry sunken log. Baby sighs, and then static explodes in her ears. She dives, reaches the bottom in an instant, and feels around. Her fingers close around something cylindrical and she yanks it up, an old tin can revealing itself as the muck clears. Swearing, she tosses it to the side and surfaces, taking a deep breath and floating on her back. "Anything?" Peter calls from the boat.

"Nope," says Baby, pulling the mask away from her eyes and spitting on the lens, trying to clear the mist that grows every time she takes a breath. She yanks it back down and takes off again in the opposite direction, away from the shoreline. And then, very abruptly, Baby sees it, just as the detector explodes more static through the headphones. The face of a combination lock, sitting on the bottom.

She throws the metal detector off, leaves it and the headphones floating on top of the water and dives straight down, hands out. At this point, the lake is about ten feet deep and the pressure builds in her ears, and she grabs hold of the front of the lock, smooths away the face and finds it. She finds it. Plunging her hands in the muck, she feels around the outside of the safe for jagged edges, any signs of corrosion, and instead she's met with the kiss of cold, smooth metal.

Her empty lungs start to scream in protest and she rockets to the surface, takes in a giant breath, yanks the mask off, and waves at Peter, the words coming out strangled as she gasps, treading water. "Peter!" she shouts. "Peter! It's here!"

He looks up from his phone and squints at her. "What's here? Oh god," he says, and stands up. "You found it?"

"I fuckin' found it!" she shouts back, and he rips his shirt off, grabs a mask off the floor of the boat, and dives in with it pressed to his face. His body slides toward her and when he surfaces, he puts the mask on and they both take huge breaths and dive together.

They both plunge their hands down into the muck, and it's like quicksand the way it sucks the edges of the safe down, like a magnet. They brace their feet against the ground, look at one another and lift, but instead of the safe moving upward, their feet bury themselves in the soft, endless mud. Baby has to stop herself, use the safe to pull her body out of the hole it's dug before she gets in too deep, and pushes back up to the surface.

The safe disappears in a cloud of brown-green fog. They rip their masks off and grab hold of one another in the water, lips tight, and scream so quietly.

"We did it!" she whispers and pulls him to her, and they clumsily try to hug while floating, their bodies warm against each other, legs churning underneath them.

"I can't believe we did it. I was really giving up there," he says.

"I know," says Baby. "Now we just have to get it out."

They swim for the boat. Peter lifts himself out first and hauls Baby backward, clumsily dragging her onto the floor.

"How are we going to get it out?" she asks, still staring at the point in the bay where the sediment has risen, terrified she's going to lose it. She looks out at the shore and sees the birch tree right behind it, almost like the white branches are pointing at it, trying to direct them to it.

"I can't believe it," she says, sitting down on the bench and peeling the wet suit away from her like an orange rind. It feels crazy to her, that it's even real.

"What can't you believe?" a man's voice asks. A fishing boat appears out of the fog, three men inside it, weighing it down, the gunwales riding close to the water. The boat is filled with trash and the man standing is giant, and she knows right away from the size of him, without seeing the meth scabs on his cheeks and the grime under his fingernails, that he's a friend of Bad Mike's, probably a cousin, and she needs to come up with a good lie and quick.

"How . . ." Baby says, grabbing a towel and wrapping it around her body, pretending she isn't afraid, that they caught her in a bathing suit and now she's trying to protect her innocence. "How beautiful this lake is," she says, trying her best to sound sincere.

"This is the bitch Mike told us about."

"Who?" Baby says, playing dumb, her stomach sinking. She sits down at the back of the boat and reaches behind her slowly, carefully, and pumps the gas bulb a few times. "Who's Mike?"

"You know who," he says, the tip of their boat bumping *Rude*.

"Hey," Peter says, reaching over and shoving their boat away. It's *Rude* that swings away instead, and Peter takes the opportunity to unclip the anchor, leaving it and the chain on the floor of the lake, their boat drifting in a wide arc.

"You're not supposed to be out here," the guy says.

"Then we'll take off," Peter says, turning the engine key. It stalls. The fog is still low over the lake, thick enough that no one on shore can see them.

"Hey now, not so fast," the man says, as the tinny comes toward them again.

"I've got to get back," Baby says. "My . . . uncle will be wondering where we are. We're sorry. We won't come back here."

The tip of the tin boat comes at them again and Baby shoves it away, just as the man starts to clamber forward. He grabs her wrist, tight, and pulls her close. Baby can smell him, thick and sour.

"I'll make sure of it," the guy says, and just as he gets close enough to clamber aboard, Peter starts the engine and Baby twists her wrist in a circle, breaking free. *Rude*'s wake splashes the men as they take off, disappearing into the fog. Peter guns it past Oakwood Hills, doesn't stop until they're on the other side of the property.

"What the hell?" he says once they've slowed down. "What was with his skin?"

"Fucking meth heads," Baby says. "Thanks for getting us out of there."

"Meth heads?" Peter says.

"That's what Bad Mike trades in."

"But wait, if they know where you are, what's stopping them from coming and getting you?"

"He's just trying to scare us off," Baby says, as the sputtering engine sends them back toward the dock.

"Why?" Peter asks. "Does he know about the safe or something? It's not his money, is it?"

"Of course not," Baby says as Peter parks the boat against the dock and Baby grabs hold of the cleat, wraps the rope around it, but before she can hop out, Peter pulls Baby to him, squeezing her.

"Your heart's pounding," he says.

"I've got to get that safe out," Baby says. "I have to."

Peter sighs against her body. She knows it probably seems so ridiculous to him, that she's putting herself in danger for any amount of money. He doesn't understand how much money can mean to someone.

"I don't know, Baby," he says. "Is it really worth it?"

"Yes," she says.

"Right," he says, shifting uncomfortably, and she can tell he's thinking. "You think we should ask Donna to come?'

"No," says Baby, doesn't add that what they're doing, well, she's not sure about the legality of it. Doesn't want there to be any question about ownership when she pulls the safe out of the water.

"Okay," says Peter as they get closer to the dock. She hops off his lap.

"The last thing I'd want is that money in Bad Mike's gross hands," she says. "I think we should go tonight. Around midnight."

"Okay," Peter says, though Baby can hear the doubt in his voice.

"You'll be here?" she asks again, can hear the tone of voice, the same tone he uses on her all the time when he makes promises he doesn't keep. "I'm going no matter what. I'll swim out there if I have to. I don't care." What she doesn't say is how desperate she is at this point, how she'll do anything for it, because she knows there isn't a single part of him that could understand how potentially life changing the money in that safe could be.

"Baby," he says, seems hurt at the intensity in her voice. "Of course."

*   *   *

After she changes back into her jean shorts, Baby walks up the hill toward the main lodge, where she's got an hour to kill before DJ and Crystal show up for phase two. She can't stop thinking about the safe, about the money, about the possibility laid out in front of them.

As she rounds the corner of the resort, she finds Marco standing next to his truck in the driveway, making out again with the twentysomething from the bar the night before. He pauses, feels eyes on him, and turns around, sees Baby standing there, wishing she could be anywhere else.

"Morning," he says. Baby knows it isn't any of her business, the fact that he seems to be cheating on Judy Mork with this girl.

"Hey, Baby." Baby doesn't recognize the girl he's with and realizes then that neither she nor Marco is looking so hot. It's not the hangover, though; there's something about them that makes her pause, squint, horror opening up inside of her. No. He can't be.

"Hey," she says, carefully.

"What happened last night?" Marco asks Baby, with a skittishness she's never seen in him before. She can't believe he's using.

"Could've used you behind the bar."

"Yeah, you know," he says, walking over to Baby and lowering his voice. The girl leans against the door of his truck. "Did Judy . . ."

"I don't think so," Baby says. "Well, check your phone. Cops showed up around eleven."

"It's dead," he says.

"Well, charge it, then."

"How much did you take home last night?" Marco asks.

"Six," Baby says.

"Hundred? Shit, Baby," he says. "Shit."

"Should've worked last night," she says.

"You think we'll do it again? Back open for good?" he asks.

"I'm working on it."

"Can you spot me?" Marco asks. Baby looks past him at the girl, then thinks about the safe, waiting for her out there in the middle of the lake. "Please? I'll pay you back."

She gives him fifty bucks, doesn't know if it's the right or the wrong thing to do.

"Shit, Baby, you're the best," he says, ducking forward and kissing her on the cheek.

"No problem," she says, watching him pocket the cash. She's not used to seeing Marco messed up, can't really imagine a version of him that would take money from her. The Marco she knows usually wouldn't even accept a ride. He gets into his car with the girl, revs the engine once, twice, then takes off down the drive, leaving a cloud of dust behind him before Baby can regret what she did.

*　*　*

"The thing is," Baby says to them, as they push a cart loaded with canned food down the hallway toward the lakeview rooms, "I know she didn't pump the septic out at the end of the season. Hannah told her it was a problem, especially with winter coming. Freezing and then thawing? Come on."

"Louise rigged this place to blow?" DJ asks.

"What a freak!" says Crystal, impressed.

"I mean, I think she was just out of money," says Baby. "I don't know how, but . . ."

"He had debts," says DJ. "She was still paying them off."

"Who?" says Baby.

"You know, her husband," says DJ. "He was a gambling addict."

"I think I heard something about that too," says Crystal.

Baby pauses, a moment of panic. Thinks of the safe sitting on the bottom of the lake, waiting for her, the answer to all the questions about the past seemingly locked inside it, then pushes it aside, focusing on what she can control now. They open up one of the rooms and push the cart in. A mouse sits in the middle of the room chewing on a sunflower seed and doesn't move, just stares up at them as they rattle in.

"Scram," says DJ. The mouse turns around and stares at the window and keeps eating. "So we're just going to clog it up, right?"

"Yeah, sure," Baby says. "We'll take it out of commission for a few days, ruin her grand opening."

"I think it's a solid plan." Crystal picks at her fingernails. "Gross, but solid."

"We just can't take it too far," DJ says. "Right, Baby?"

"Right," Baby says, annoyed. DJ's acting like Baby wants to blow up the building. If Baby wanted to burn this place down, she would.

They walk into the bathroom and Baby flips open the toilet lid. She starts unwrapping tampons while the other two jack open cans of beans. Baby waits until the beans are stewing in the toilet to drop in the tampon, and they watch as it expands and takes on the black liquid, morphing into a thick, cotton slug.

"Weird," says DJ.

"Gross," says Baby.

"It's like art," says Crystal. They flush, head back to the cart, and head to the next room.

"Are the debts clear now?" asks Baby, surprised that Hannah never shared that version of events.

DJ shrugs. "No idea. I mean, she sold the resort, right?"

"Christ," says Baby, thinking about the safe locked at the bottom of the lake and just how fucked up that is, how Terrence sent himself to the deep with the last of the cash tied to his body, screwing Louise even harder in death than he ever had in life.

Baby opens a can of tangerines and dumps them into the toilet, flushes. They swirl slower than usual, half of them remaining, floating behind like dead bugs. "It's working!" Baby breathes down into the toilet and grabs the plunger they brought with them. "Let's finish this bitch." She plunges and plunges until the water begins to swirl again, the oranges eventually disappearing.

"We're close," says DJ.

They head from room to room, flushing beans and fruit cocktail and tampons and condoms, a stale bag of tortilla chips, a maxi pad; they keep at it until they can't plunge anymore. Until the water in one of the toilet bowls creeps toward the edge.

"I think this is good enough," DJ says, watching the toilet water spill, ever so slightly, onto the floor of the bathroom.

"But we want to make sure it's all of the toilets," Baby says.

"What do you mean? This is definitely gross enough," Crystal says. "This looks just like it does in the Parrot. You remember those nights." Baby knows what Crystal's referencing. So many nights over the years, the toilets have backed up and they've had to lead pee patrols out into the woods, industrial-sized rolls of toilet paper slung over their arms. It's alarming to Baby just how many city girls she's had to teach how to hug a tree.

Desperate for this to work, Baby waits until Crystal and DJ leave for the night and walks back into the Parrot. The toilet in there still flushes, so Baby sits there for at least an hour, finishes off all the old dusty cans on the shelves, watching them spiral and disappear, until they don't, until the water stays close to the brim of these toilets too, sure now that whatever happens next will change everything.

20

B ABY SITS ON the dock at midnight waiting for Peter, surveying the crap she loaded into a wheelbarrow to help them get the safe out of the lake: a cinder block, a shovel, a long length of chain, a rusty padlock and a hammer.

Peter drives up, the boat chugging through the quiet darkness, the engine pissing a long stream of water out the back. He's slumped over the steering wheel, resigned, probably nervous, Baby can't be certain. "You ready for this?" he asks as the boat slides up next to the dock.

"Yup," she says, passing him the cinder block first, just barely able to pick it up.

"You're not worried?"

"Nah," she says. It's probably stupid, but she feels bulletproof around Peter, knows that he has a family, he has money, he's worth something to someone. They'll come and find him if he disappears, and that makes him more difficult to mess with. There was a reason Bad Mike waited until Baby was alone the other day. Because Peter, for better or for worse, has influence and they all know it.

"We had a couple of these on the island," he says, showing her three long, packaged glow sticks. "I figure we could crack them and drop them onto the bottom. Probably won't attract too much attention."

"Great idea," she says, pushing away from the dock with her heel. It's a clear night with no moon and she's grateful that at least they have the darkness, though it's dangerous to be out in the boat with no lights on. That's how people collide, how bodies get thrown in all directions, losing consciousness, inhaling, sinking, lungs full of water. So many ways to die out here.

The tarp Peter has folded across the back of the boat rustles in the breeze and he keeps the engine low and quiet, barely in gear as they drift toward the tree. The wind has kicked up behind them and the waves are fighting their direction, pushing them back toward the shore. "I think I should cut it," he whispers. "We've got to drop anchor. It's too wavy."

"Do I need to dive for it?" Baby asks, thinking of the anchor Peter unclipped that morning so they could escape the scab-faced trio. Peter shakes his head and pulls out another anchor, fresh from the marina, tags still on, and when they reach the spot, he slides the anchor into the water as she cuts the engine.

They work silently in tandem, Peter snapping the glow sticks and dropping them, Baby grabbing a mask and slipping into the lake. She feels as if her body is being swallowed up. It looks so different in the darkness, the water thick and black around her, but she pumps her fist, heart in her throat when she sees the edges of the safe lit up in the pale-blue light. She clings to the edge of the boat as Peter tosses the cinder block into the water, the sound of it landing like a small eruption.

Baby dives after it and intercepts, redirects the weight of the block as it drops so it settles into the ground just a few inches away from the safe. Peter slips into the water holding the shovel, legs churning to keep him above the surface, giving Baby time to push up for a gasp of air. They tread water, looking at one another quietly, then both take deep breaths and push off the boat toward the bottom. Baby wedges the shovel under the edge of the safe, and they both try to lever it against the cinder block, pushing against it as hard as they can.

The safe stirs on the bottom, then inches upward, freed from the muck, and flips over to the side. Final bubbles exit their mouths and they surface again, inhaling, gasping. Baby looks around, paranoid, but the lake is empty. No boat engines, no voices carrying through the dark. Just the two of them, a rustling wind, tiny waves lapping at the boat, making it smack lightly against the water. Peter lifts himself up into *Rude*, leans over the edge, and grabs the length of chain and the padlock from the boat and they dive once more, down, Baby now feeling desperate to just finish the job, be done with it.

Peter wraps the chain around the safe in a complex knot, Baby closes the padlock around it, and they both climb into the boat. Peter braces himself against the edge, Baby behind him, and they start to pull. *Rude* dips hard to starboard as they strain against the weight of the safe, the two of them grunting in the quiet. The metal slips in Baby's hands and she leans back with all her weight, bearing down with everything, and feels the metal box slowly start to move.

Peter pants and she stares at his biceps as they bulge out, pulling, pulling up. "Fuck," he whispers as the safe nears the surface and he nods to Baby, bracing his foot against the edge of the boat and leaning back with all his might. He holds on to the weight all on his own. She scuttles over to the edge and grabs hold of the slick box, taking it in her arms in a clumsy, slippery hug.

Cursing, they get the safe into the back of the boat. It's not as big as she thought. As soon as they tip it over, Peter pulls up the anchor and she turns the engine on. It's loud. Too loud. She puts the boat in gear, swinging it around. Neither of them looks back at the land behind them or at the safe, scummy water running away from the metal box in snaking lines, staining the carpet.

They don't head back to the resort, instead take off across the bay to make sure they aren't followed. "Holy shit," Peter says, rubbing his face with his hands, streaking mud and rusty water all over his cheeks. Baby notices then that they're shaking.

"I know," she says, stepping behind him. She's shivering too, but only because she didn't bring a towel and was too afraid to move, to put on her sweatshirt. She grabs it and pulls it over her head, then stands next to Peter, both of them now staring at the safe dripping on the back of the boat.

"You don't know the combination, do you?" he asks.

"No," says Baby. "I figured we'd just take a crowbar to it or something." Peter steps onto the tarp and kneels down next to it. The combination lock is obscured by gray-green goop and he swipes it off, wiping his hand on his shorts, which, Baby realizes, are nice and khaki and not the usual cutoff denim or bathing suit she's used to seeing him in, as if he left a fancy dinner to come and be with her.

"Should we go back to the boathouse and try it?" he asks. Baby looks around the lake, paranoid, searching for anything—signs of movement, sounds, anyone, two eyes blinking in the darkness—but nothing stirs. No lights flash. Nothing. They're alone.

"Yeah," she says. "Let's do it." The safe itself looks intact, solid, and barely impacted for having spent years on the bottom of the lake.

"We'll get it open," he says, squeezing her shoulder,

Baby presses her hands to her eyes, thinking about the septic system and the building and everyone who isn't going to have a job soon because of her. Now that the safe is sitting in front of her, the weight of just how stupid this plan could be hangs helplessly in front of her. So many things can go wrong. So many.

"What if it's empty?" Baby asks, saying the words out loud for the very first time, entertaining this possibility.

"It won't be," says Peter.

His faith in her, in the safe, seems so ridiculous because he doesn't have any consequences to face, really, if it's empty. He'll still leave her at the end of the summer, he'll still go back to his life. The weight of an entire town's future isn't resting on him.

When they pull up at the boathouse, Peter parks in the slip and Baby closes the sliding door behind them, wishing the lock hadn't rotted off all those years ago. And they get to work.

They try crowbars, an ax, a chainsaw, and nothing manages to even make a dent in the metal. Baby swings the ax at it, over and over again, showers of sparks flashing, the vibrating shaking her fingers. "Goddamn," she says, flexing her fingers. "Ow, fuck!"

"It's late. It must be almost three," he says. "Maybe we try this tomorrow."

"Do some research," says Baby.

"Yeah, exactly," says Peter. "You want to just sleep here?" The unspoken subtext is that Amelia will be back soon and he doesn't want to be caught in the cabins with Baby, doesn't want to have to awkwardly explain what he's doing straddling the divide between his family and the future of this town, a gray-green metal box the one deciding factor.

"Sure," says Baby. Peter kisses her on the head and grabs a life jacket smushed between the seats and the edge of the boat.

"Pillow?" he asks, hands it to her. She takes it, absently staring at the box, at the future in front of her.

"Come, lie down," Peter says, pulling her down onto the floor of the boat. "We're not going to fix it tonight."

Baby hesitates but lets him fold her body against his, down again on the scratchy gray carpet, listening to the sound of the water lapping against the boat, echoing throughout the crib.

"Remember that night we went down to the gravel pit?"

"That was really fun," she says, automatically, but she can't close her eyes, just lies there, marooned on this boat, responding in kind as he reminisces. She wants to roll over and shake him, ask him what the point is, of all this shared nostalgia. *I'm right here.* He could love her now, so much better. Instead, she murmurs bland replies until he falls asleep, his breath steady against her shoulder. She lies there, staring up at the ceiling, listening to the waves echo up into the rafters, the slapping of the water against the hull.

21

T HE SUN STREAMS in through the boathouse windows. *Rude* rocks gently, and Baby stands up, back aching. Peter sleeps on. Her jean shorts are undone, just by the button, and she slips them closed and rolls open the boathouse halfway, surveying the lake. Fishing boats putter around the bay. The safe still sits in the back of the boat. She woke up several times throughout the night, panicked, haunted by this feeling like they were being watched, that Bad Mike was just out of sight, waiting for them to nod off so he could come aboard and take it. The crowbar, the ax, and the chainsaw all sit on the dock next to where she and Peter slept. A feast for a murderer, a buffet of weapons, just there, waiting.

Baby's then struck by the stench. She coughs. It's disgusting. Raw sewage. The toilets. She inhales and the taste of it lands on her tongue, buries itself in the back of her throat. "Oh god," she says, coughing, and starts pumping the gas.

Peter stirs as the engine roars to life, the boat vibrating beneath him. "It's too early, Baby," he says, one eye open. "Go back to sleep." Instead she throws the door open wide and busies herself untying lines.

"We've got to get out of here," she says, booting up *Rude* and backing the boat out of the port. Peter smells it.

"What is that?" he asks.

"I don't know," she says, ducking as she backs the boat out of the slip. "It smells like the septic tank."

She worries, then, that'll he'll figure it out. Put three and three together. The septic has always sucked at the resort, she knows. He's been there nights when the bathrooms flooded and the guys all pissed off the deck or, after they closed, into the lake. He knows. It's reasonable that this could happen.

As they back away from the dock, Baby sees it. "Oh, gross!" she says. A river of black sludge runs down the hill to the boathouse, tiny waterfalls of it spilling over the bank and into the lake. Peter stands. "Ew," he says, sniffing, rubbing his eyes.

Baby opens her eyes wide. "Fucking hell," she says. It's worse than she expected, worse than she wanted it to be. So much worse. A fisherman powers over to them, standing up in his boat. Baby doesn't recognize him and he doesn't recognize her. Probably a weekender.

"I called it in to the sheriff," he says. "Dumping into the lake. They should be ashamed of themselves."

"Great!" Peter calls back, and the fisherman stands, waiting for them to pile on. They don't and he seems disappointed.

"There's already that algae bloom."

"We heard about it," Baby calls back. "You're not supposed to troll."

"I'll stop when that does," he says, gesturing up to the resort then sitting back down in the boat, redirecting back out into the bay, safely astride the moral high ground.

Baby and Peter stand next to one another, staring up at the river of human waste running down toward them.

"Shit," Baby says, then looks at Peter sideways. "Don't say literally."

"I wasn't going to," he says. He's not smiling but he's still Peter. None of this is life-and-death to him.

"I don't even have shoes," Baby says.

"I've got to call her," Peter says, pulling out his phone.

Baby looks down at her feet, scrubby as they are. Crystal painted her toes with silver polish ages ago, and the remnants of it still linger. She's got a blister on the side of her pinkie toe already popped, the sore still bright pink and throbbing.

"Maybe we should park at Martin's," Baby says, gesturing to the dock of the weird hermit who lives next to the resort. It's half sunk, but there's a tree near the bank they can tie up to. Come to think of it, she hasn't seen Martin this year. Doesn't mean he's not home, but usually she catches glimpses of him, sitting on the edge of his dock at night, a mug of tea or maybe whiskey or wine in hand, enjoying the sunset.

Peter squeezes his phone, clearly frustrated. "And it's dead," he says. "Can we just go back into the boathouse? I've got to call her."

"Okay, sure," Baby says, not wanting to be found at the scene. But if she's with Peter, she reasons, Amelia can't blame her.

They drive back in, turn off the boat, tie up, and Baby pauses. Peter's almost out the door and they haven't moved the safe yet, haven't cracked it. It's still just sitting there, out of place in the back of *Rude*, weighing down the tail of the boat. Baby closes the roll-top door but still feels like it's too easy, grabs a tarp from the corner and shakes it out, more than one spider skittering back into the shadows.

"No one's looking for it," Peter says. She grabs the edge of the tarp and drags it forward a bit. It rips under her hands as she stretches it over the lump in the back of the boat. Still obvious as the day is long, a rectangle surrounded by green mucky stains and covered in plastic.

"Come on." He grabs her hand and pulls her out of the boat.

The shit river runs slowly down toward the lake and they pick their way across the pavement, on tiptoe up the hill, faces buried in T-shirts. Even then, the smell gets into her nose and her mouth.

"Goddammit," she says, once they reach the driveway in front of the main building. The lawn has flooded, the grass all under a foot of gray, grotesque water. Baby pulls the keys out of her pocket and they head inside to the phone.

"I'll go call the dippers," she says. Tippie Gibbs and her brother Grant took over the septic business from their dad a few years ago. "I'm not sure there's anything they'll be able to do, but maybe they can try."

Peter grabs a different phone, hops on another line, and starts dialing his sister, his forehead creased with worry. Baby stares at him while the dial tone rings in her ears. He's distressed, running fingers through his hair. Baby's never seen him so upset.

Tippie answers on the third ring.

"Baby," Tippie says, "to what do I owe the pleasure? Heard a rumor you were stirring up trouble at—"

"Don't know what you're talking about," Baby says quickly. Tippie never knows when to shut up. "I need you to come over."

"Oh, you got it, Baby. You know I love the Parrot. Fucking city cats coming up here thinking they can tell us what—"

"Exactly," Baby says, her voice now down to a whisper. "Just don't say anything . . . about these rumors. Okay?"

"See you soon," Tippie says conspiratorially, as if they're waging some kind of underground war. Worried, Baby hangs up. This kind of talk isn't good for them. She should've expected it, but she'd have thought people would be considering how serious this is, might try a little harder to mind their business.

"Aw, hell," Baby says, looking down the hallway at the sewage seeping out from under the doors. It's everywhere, the smell getting thicker and thicker as the liquid buries itself in the carpet. If it's in the hallway, it's inside the rooms, the carpets soaked through.

"I can't get hold of her," Peter says. "What happened? Was this because you opened the Parrot?"

"Of course not," says Baby. "They must've hit something when they were renovating. Amelia's been forcing them to hurry."

Peter seems to accept it. He's never dug a septic tank out of the hill, never plunged a toilet for half an hour, his lower back twisting up in knots, arms burning, someone else's shit creeping toward the edge with every desperate attempt at a flush.

The front door flies open and Amelia storms in, tote bags dangling from her fingers, shock and disgust arranging themselves on her face. She drops everything on the floor dramatically, one of the bags falling open, a thick candle rolling across the floor. Baby meets Amelia's eyes and doesn't back down as Amelia rushes toward her. "What the fuck is going on?" Amelia shouts. "What is this? What did you do?"

She catches Baby off guard, the sudden implication, the blame. Baby doesn't understand how she could immediately know Baby was behind all of this—there's no proof.

Amelia grabs Baby by the sweatshirt and shoves her, slams her body against the wall. Her head cracks against it. "Ow!" Baby screams, trying to get some footing as Amelia grabs her again, shaking her back and forth, slamming her against the wall over and over. "What the hell?" Baby manages to yank herself away, pushes off from the wall, ducking Amelia's blows. There's a manic energy to her, as if the veneer has been utterly abandoned. Amelia chases Baby and Baby runs in circles around the lobby, hides behind Peter, who stands, frozen, not sure what he's seeing.

"What the fuck is wrong with you!" Baby shouts, shoving Peter at Amelia and running behind the front desk.

Peter grabs Amelia by the arm, pulls her back. "Amelia, chill!"

"I know she did this. I know it!" Amelia says, screaming and jabbing a finger at Baby. Peter wraps an arm around Amelia's waist and holds her back.

"What are you talking about?" Baby says, annoyed at how fearful it sounds.

"Baby was with me last night," Peter says.

"Don't be an idiot, Peter," Amelia says. "This wasn't an accident."

"You're crazy," Baby says.

The entire scene is interrupted by a knock. A knock that turns into a banging, slamming with a fist. Baby straightens out her sweatshirt. Amelia pauses, arranges her face, takes a deep breath in and out, eyes closed, then opens the door.

"Morning." Donna steps inside, the Mork next to her, both of them wearing knee-high rubber boots with thick soles. Donna has her bylaw violation notebook out and Judy looks like she's about to puke, leans against the doorway, her cheeks pale.

"Morning," Amelia says, a wide smile on her lips. "I guess you've caught wind of our situation."

Judy Mork bursts out laughing. "Good one!"

"We have to issue a bylaw violation," says Donna, flipping open her notebook. "Because raw sewage is leaking into the lake." Donna is soft and kind, and it annoys Baby because she knows Donna's only talking to Amelia like this because she's rich. She scribbles on the pad and tears the ticket off. Baby knows it's for the smallest amount legally possible.

"Of course," Amelia says. "I'm so sorry. I have no idea what happened." She shakes her head, pauses for dramatic effect. "The perils of small business ownership."

"You'll be closing," Donna says. "Until this gets fixed."

"Immediately," Amelia says.

"You don't have any guests here?" Donna asks.

"No. Tomorrow night was supposed to be our big reopening. I'll have to go make some calls, if you'll excuse me."

"Good luck," Donna says, then turns and nods. "Baby."

"Donna." Baby nods.

Amelia waits for Donna and the Mork to leave, listening for the car doors, the engine starting up before she turns to Baby.

"Can you deal with the septic company? Seems like a good job for you," Amelia says, then heads back into the office and slams the door behind her.

"Are you okay?" Peter asks.

"Yeah," Baby says, stretching out, a sort of emotional whiplash overtaking her, wondering exactly what Amelia is going to do next.

"I'm going to go talk to her."

"Sure," Baby says, her voice smaller and more pathetic than usual. "Go ahead."

* * *

Tippie shows up alone a half hour later, wearing coveralls and knee-high rubber boots, a baseball cap tugged down low over her eyes, driving the big ol' truck her dad drove for all those years with the smiling honeybee plastered to its cylindrical tank. She hops down from the driver's seat. She's a big woman with wide shoulders and large breasts she refuses to stuff into real bras, her nipples usually visible through her shirts.

"Where's Grant?" Baby asks.

"On vacation," Tippie says. "You want some boots? I've got some spares in the truck."

"Yeah, sure," Baby says. Tippie grabs a pair and tosses them at Baby. She shoves her feet into them.

"Holy shit!" Tippie laughs, looking out over the field. "Did you do this?"

"Can you keep your voice down?" Baby hisses. "Christ." Tippie's booming alto feels like it's echoing all around them.

"You really fucked this one up. I've never seen anything like this. And I've seen some shit."

"So what do we do?"

"Let's go dig," Tippie says, grabbing a shovel.

Baby follows Tippie and watches her take stock of the damage, continuously whistling at just how much is leaking out. They walk over to the clear mound where the tanks are buried. "She's going to have to replace it," Tippie says, even before she starts digging it out. "What a friggin' doozy."

"How much?" Baby asks.

"Twenty thousand easy," Tippie says. "Plus labor."

"So thirty?" Baby asks.

"I mean, probably," Tippie says. "I've never seen it this bad before. I'm not sure there's any point in trying to dig it out when we're going to have to replace everything."

"What should I tell her?" Baby asks, gesturing inside. "Is there a timeline?"

"I don't know," Tippie says. "With a failure this bad, I don't even know what we're going to do about the lawn. I've got to call my dad."

"All right. I'll go tell her," says Baby, heading back to the front doors of the resort.

If there's a way to lie about this for her own benefit, Baby isn't able to pull it out in time, not before she's made it to the front door, kicked off the boots, and walked through to the Parrot, where Amelia sits with Peter at a table, her face in her hands. Baby loiters outside the bar, unsure if she should go in. They don't hear her.

"The instructions were clear. Open by July first."

"Repairs aren't necessarily a bad thing," says Peter. "If you take everything into account."

"It reflects badly on my ability to run this place," she says. "How am I supposed to prove myself if I can't even fucking open on time?"

Baby slides away from the door to the Parrot and heads back to the front doors and slams them, waits a minute before pacing back over to the bar. They're both waiting for her, Amelia sitting up as if everything is fine, shoulders thrown back, Peter next to her, his eyebrows furrowed.

"What's the damage?" Amelia asks.

"It's not good," Baby says.

"Clearly," Amelia says. "Just tell me."

"Between twenty and thirty thousand. Full replacement."

"Fucking hell," Amelia says, standing up and tucking her chair back in with so much force that it shakes the table. "I should sue her."

"Louise?" Baby asks. "Why?"

Amelia ignores Baby, knits her hands into her hair and walks to the bar, grabs a bottle of vodka off the shelf and pours, takes a shot back.

"Let's just focus on what we can do right now to get this place open," says Peter.

"Are you not listening?" Amelia snaps. "It's not opening. It's over."

Baby backs away, knows it isn't a conversation she wants to be part of, and hurries outside, eyes burning from the fumes, knowing there's only one thing left for her to do to save them all from this disaster. Get the safe open. Make Amelia an offer, now, while the chips are stacked against her, while she's at her lowest.

Despite the cost of repairs, Baby knows that once she gets control of the resort, the Parrot will keep them all afloat. Maybe they won't even deal with guests this summer, just knock everything down and rebuild things slowly, using the money from the bar to fund it. She could just bring in some porta-johns. You can clean those with a hose. It'd be difficult, but Baby thinks they could make it happen. And they'd be free from all of this.

Hope swells in her chest as she pictures Amelia in that bar, head in her hands. Defeated. It's the perfect time, really. Baby to the rescue, with a check big enough for Amelia to walk away with no one even paying attention. Back to the city where she can open up a jazz lounge or something stupid like that, leave the shit-filled lake to Baby.

*   *   *

Baby practically throws herself at the door to the boathouse, desperate to get back to the safe, hope surging through her body. Especially after Amelia smashed her up against the wall. Baby knows the stages of shame that chase you after you've done something like that, gotten physical, the regret. The next few hours, days, will be the time to strike, the time to give Amelia a way out and a way to find absolution, an escape hatch. To leave with some cash and her dignity.

Hope. Weird, blooming hope seems to just be exploding inside Baby as she twists the broken knob and hip-checks the door, simultaneously, to get it open. Years of practice, of timing, have made it so she can enter the boathouse without thinking. This place belongs to her, it's in her bones. It's in her soul.

A cross breeze immediately whips through, slamming the door behind her. The garage door at the front of the boathouse is wide open, making the lake in the background look like a dramatic painting, and the safe that was sitting on the back of the boat is gone.

22

"DID YOU HEAR about the body?" DJ asks. They're all slumped around a table at the Legion, Baby, Crystal, Marco, and Johnny, the five of them, splitting a bag of microwave popcorn and nursing warm beers bought with the bucket of change they rescued from behind the bar at the Parrot, placed in tall towers, nickels and dimes and a few quarters. Not enough for anything real. Not by a long shot. Baby's absently rolling the bottle back and forth on the table, tossing it from hand to hand, the swill in the bottom sloshing against the sides. She stares at it, tries to become hypnotized. None of them can afford the nine, ten, twelve drinks they need to relax, and the mood is already defeated.

"What body?" Baby asks, secretly hoping it's Amelia's but knowing it isn't.

"Was a fresh one. Someone dumped it in the shitwater," DJ says. "Off of Oakwood. Bullet through the head."

"Fuck sakes," says Marco, grabbing his beer and finishing it in one gulp, heading back over to the bar and raising a finger for another.

"What's up with Marco?" Crystal asks. "He looks terrible."

"Whose body?" Baby asks again.

"Well, this is all from Tippie, so take that with a grain or two, but she says it's one of Bad Mike's crew, like from the old days. Don Something?"

"Don Fawn," says Crystal. "Dumb name. Yeah, he used to hang around with Mike. Went straight, opened that frozen yogurt shop in Dorset with Matilda whatsername. You know, the soccer player from high school? Remember her?"

"Oh, yeah." DJ shakes her head. "Damn, she was hot."

"That's the best yogurt," Baby says.

"He always seemed pretty decent," Crystal says.

"Maybe that's what did him in," says Baby.

They all sit in silence, picking at the popcorn kernels. Baby shudders, thinking about Bad Mike, about the threat, his fingers on her neck, her face pressed into the rough wood of a picnic table. How easy it was for him to control her body.

"What do you mean by decent?" Johnny asks. "If he was in with Bad Mike, he wasn't decent."

"I don't know," Crystal says, obviously frustrated. "He was nice. He had a conscience. That's all. They're people. I know they're idiots. But they're people."

Johnny huffs and shakes his head, chewing loudly on a handful of the popcorn kernels, popping them between his teeth. "I just can't really imagine calling anyone who chooses to work with Bad Mike a good guy."

"Well, you didn't know any of them, did you?" Crystal spits back. "And what makes you think they have a choice?"

"We all have a choice, don't we?" Johnny says. Crystal takes out her phone, the pink sparkly thing, and slumps even farther down in her chair.

"Do we?" Crystal asks. "I'm not so sure anymore."

Baby sighs, tries to crush a popcorn kernel under her thumb. The septic explosion was ten days ago and it's been like this most nights, everyone meeting at the Legion, slumping over beers, playing darts, eating bags of microwaved popcorn, and doing their best to avoid talking about the future. No one has told them anything about dates or deadlines. No one knows if the building is done for, what kind of shape it's in, what they're going to do next.

Baby didn't tell anyone about Amelia slamming her up against the wall. Didn't mention all the aggression, the rage, all of the anger directed at her, as if Amelia knew what they've been doing, or at least trying to do. Baby hasn't told anyone about the safe either, finding it and then losing it. Piling that kind of hopelessness on everyone now—she knows it's a recipe for some real shit. The kind of shit they're trying to avoid.

And as far as Baby's concerned, Crystal and DJ don't need to know she went back and doubled down on the toilets, that this is mostly her fault, not theirs.

"So you think Bad Mike killed Don? Why?" Baby asks.

Crystal shrugs. "He's always looking for businesses to launder his money through. Maybe Don turned him down. Or he could've owed him money. A favor."

"Bad Mike's got a long memory," DJ says.

"Did he have family?" Baby asks. "Don?"

"I looked him up online," DJ says, and sighs. "Just had a baby."

Johnny gets up, walks away, over to the bar, and pulls a handful of change out of his pocket, starts counting it out, trying to buy another beer.

"This place is depressing," DJ says.

"They won't let you put any music on?" Baby asks, looking around the room. No windows. The ceilings are high, dusty rafters, a dribbling fan spinning overhead, the rod attaching it to the roof shaking it with every turn, making it look like the whole thing is about to collapse and decapitate someone. A cat lounges on the bar next to three old men, who drink with their heads down. Baby sighs.

"What do you think?" DJ sits up, puts her phone down on the table. "Here, watch." She pushes play, and immediately, before the singer can get three words out, all three of the men sitting at the bar turn around and look at her.

"Turn that down!" the one closest to them hisses. DJ complies and smiles at Baby, almost in jest, a shrug of the shoulders that says, *Well, here we are.*

Baby hasn't seen Peter since the fallout. She borrowed one of the golf carts from Oakwood Hills and shuttles between couches, back and forth between Crystal's and DJ's, the smell anywhere near Oakwood too overpowering for anyone to stand. On days when the wind kicks up, everyone walks around pressing T-shirts and rags to their faces so they can stand to breathe.

"Does anyone want to head out?" Baby asks.

"And go where?"

"Anywhere? A drive?"

"A drive uses gas, which costs money," says DJ. "Which we don't have."

"We could watch a movie," Baby says.

"My internet is out," says DJ.

"Mine too," says Crystal.

"There's no one we can steal from?"

"All the ones around my place are password protected," says DJ.

"Same," says Crystal.

Baby fidgets, slides her bottle back and forth on the table, faster and faster, annoyed at how determined they are to remain miserable. The boredom, the lack of anything to do, the uselessness that's descended on them, they all seem to be wearing it exactly the same way, and Baby feels like she can barely breathe.

The front door squeals open and everyone turns to look, even the cat sitting on the bar, its mouth stretched wide open, fangs bared. "Fuck," Crystal says, flat, and stares determinedly at her phone, flipping through photos at a clip, energy entirely focused away.

Bad Mike steps sideways through the door and stops to survey the landscape.

"Should we go?" DJ asks. "Shit."

"There's no back door," Crystal says. "Maybe Margie will let us out behind the bar. Fuck, he's coming over here."

Baby stamps down about a million reactions as Bad Mike walks over to their table and stands over Crystal, just behind her. She could whip a beer bottle at him, flip the table, grab the cat and throw it at his chest like in a movie. If he were alone, they might be able to get away, but Dirk the Dickhead and Sammy Saltlick are flanking him. There's no way they'll make it out one to one with those overpumped salamis blocking the exits.

Crystal's hand starts to tremble.

"What's cracking, daddio?" Baby asks, looking up at him, not really sure where the phrasing has come from but committing to it all the same, trying to break the tension.

"My three favorite girls," Bad Mike says.

Johnny returns to the table, drink in hand, wordlessly steps around Bad Mike and sits down in the empty seat between DJ and Crystal, filling in a gap, stopping Bad Mike from doing it himself.

"And GI Dickhead," Bad Mike says, slamming a hand down on Johnny's shoulder, then rubbing his shaved head. "Look who made it to the Legion."

"I see that," Johnny says. "Glad you found it."

Bad Mike squeezes Johnny's shoulder, puts his other hand on Crystal's. "I thought you'd be up to visit me."

"I've just been really busy with work," Baby says. "And all my extracurricular activities. You know how crazy the summer can be."

Bad Mike leans harder onto Crystal's shoulder, squeezing tighter. She lets out a tiny whimper. "We'd like a minute alone."

No one moves.

"I think I'm good right here," Baby says, reaching into her pocket for her phone, trying to figure out if she can call Donna without him noticing.

"Me too," says DJ.

"Same," Johnny says.

Crystal says nothing, stares at her lap, taking deep, slow breaths.

"Boys," Bad Mike says, gesturing slightly with his head. Dirk and Sammy step forward, both of them flicking knives open, as if this was all planned. Sammy presses the tip of one blade into Johnny's neck, just below his ear, a tiny pebble of blood appearing in a slowly blooming dot. Dirk stands between Baby and DJ, clearly unsure of what to do, which one he's supposed to be grabbing hold of, and Baby takes advantage of that moment of indecision to stand and flip the table. Bottles go flying, crashing to the ground. She hears Johnny shout, but it's muffled in the back of her mind, and she feels as if she's moving on an entirely different plane of existence as she dives at Crystal, grabs her wrist, and pulls.

But Crystal twists away from Baby, rushing toward Johnny, fixated on the blood dripping on the floor, the shocked expression on his face, his mouth in a wide O shape. Crystal grabs a handful of napkins from the counter, presses it to his neck.

"He missed the artery," Bad Mike says. "Everyone calm down."

The men sitting at the bar keep their heads down. Baby tries not to puke as droplets of blood hit the floor. There's something about the sight of it, the red liquid streaking down his neck. It's a thin cut, but it could've been so much worse. It's enough to make her dizzy, the stupidity of her impulse. The fallout.

"This one'll do; what do I care?" Bad Mike says, gesturing to Baby with his chin. His lackeys grab her by the arms, and no one bothers protesting as they march her toward the door, the bar silent, drunks sitting with their eyes down at their drinks. Even the cat looks on, bored, its tail swinging back and forth like a pendulum. Baby looks around for Marco, who's seemingly disappeared at a really opportune moment, and cusses him out silently, for his timing or perhaps his cowardice. She isn't sure which.

Outside, they let go of Baby and she spins around, adrenaline coursing through her. "What?" Baby asks, pumped up, her heart pounding in her ears. "What's going on?"

"I'd much rather have this conversation with Crystal," he says. "Or that queer in the overalls. But you'll do."

"Don't call her that," Baby says and steps forward, trying to shove Bad Mike. She's terrified, sure, but she wants her goddamn safe back. She needs it and she knows he has it and the fact that he could murder her doesn't even really register; it doesn't feel real. But even as she's leaning against him, trying with all of her might to push against his body, he won't move.

Instead, he grabs the neck of her T-shirt and steps to the side, shoving her past him to the ground.

Baby scrambles to her feet, spins around so her back is to the bar. "What do you want?" she asks again, this time trying to calm herself down.

"You girls have something I need, I have something you need," he says.

"What do we have?" she asks. "We don't have anything."

"I've got your safe," he says. "And you, I'd wager, have the combination."

"You took it from me," she says. "You . . . thief." Even Baby knows it's a lame retort. Mike laughs at her.

"Come on, kid. So here's where we're at. You come up and open it for me, and I'll give you ten percent."

"Ten percent? Ten percent?" Baby feels like she's going insane. "You've got to be kidding me. Do you think I'm an idiot?"

"Absolutely," Bad Mike says, still laughing. "And I know you don't have any options. Now, I could just blast the thing open, but I risk losing money. And I don't like that. I could also just grab you, drag you up there, and beat you senseless until you cough up the combination, but I don't need that kind of attention or trouble right now."

"Why?" Baby asks. "'Cause you murdered Don and left him floating in the shitwater?"

Bad Mike shrugs, careless. "So you understand, then, what happens to people when I don't get what I want."

As if on cue, Dirk the Dickhead steps forward and slugs Baby in the gut so hard so she doubles over, the entire contents of her stomach erupting onto the gravel. She coughs, her eyes watering, hands on her knees. Baby's a good puker, has had lots of practice.

When the liquid stops coming, she stands up, tears rolling down her cheeks from the coughing and sputtering, swipes the back of her hand against her mouth. "Was that supposed to hurt?" She wheezes, a snot bubble blooming out of her nose and popping.

Bad Mike laughs again. His laugh is slow, languid, comes out of his throat like a low cough. *Huh, huh, huh.*

"Always entertaining. You know where to find me," Bad Mike says, walking back to the shiny black truck in the parking lot. Baby sits down on a parking slab, taking deep, wheezing breaths.

And as Baby sits there, alone, her friends inside, her phone starts to buzz inside her pocket. She opens it, thinking for a brief instant that Bad Mike is sending her another threat, but it's not Mike, not even close. It's Amelia.

Baby waits, staring at the number that she programmed into her phone as a defensive tactic the day Amelia gave it out at orientation so she'd know to avoid it, know how to screen the call. She answers. "Hello?" It comes out as a wheeze.

"Baby?" Amelia says.

"Yeah," she says, again wheezing.

"Are you sick?"

"No," she says, "I'm just . . . out for a jog." She angles the receiver away from her mouth and takes a few deep breaths, tries to calm down, spitting bile into the gravel.

"Oh. Weird, okay. Well, I have an offer for you," Amelia says.

As Amelia talks, the group of them come outside, Crystal, DJ, Marco, and Johnny, holding a fresh napkin to his neck, Crystal, an arm wrapped around his back, crying, and DJ, a mixture of anxiety and relief and anger, sort of pacing around the group of them, seemingly not sure what to do with her hands.

Baby squints, listening to Amelia, can't really understand what she's saying. "Can you repeat that? Sorry, I just bumped into everyone."

Amelia repeats the offer and Baby asks her to hold on, presses her cell phone into her shoulder.

"You guys want to waiter a party at Pomoroy Island tomorrow night?" Baby asks, wiping stray puke off her chin. "Two hundred each."

A collective shrug. It's not even really a question of want so much as it is desperation. Need. They agree, and Baby makes plans to meet Amelia at the public dock the following day at four PM. The phone call is oddly cordial, as if the last time Amelia saw Baby she didn't slam her up against the wall.

"What happened?" DJ asks, once Baby's hung up the phone. "Where is he?"

"I took care of it," Baby mutters. "Thanks for the backup, by the way. Really helpful."

"Oh, I'm sorry. You were the one who got Johnny cut. He could've died," Crystal snaps. Baby can't remember a time when Crystal spoke to her like that, her eyes wide open, unblinking.

"And where were you, huh?" Baby asks, turning on Marco instead. "You disappeared."

"I was taking a dump," he says. "But that doesn't matter. I'm glad this happened. Someone needs to slap some sense into you."

"Into me?" Baby shouts.

"Yeah, into you," Marco says. "You're the one who blew up our fucking workplace."

"It wasn't just me," Baby says.

"Oh come on, Baby," Marco says. "As if this doesn't have you written all over it. That idea is about as stupid as they come."

"At least I'm trying!" Baby screams this so loud, it feels like her throat is tearing open. "What are you doing, huh? What are you doing? Getting wasted? I know this isn't just beer that's making you like this. And now, I'll be out there tomorrow night, humiliating myself on Pomoroy Island for all of you. So don't tell me I'm not—"

"Baby, c'mon," says DJ, grabbing her arm.

"No," Baby says. "No. Why are you all up my ass?"

"Because Johnny's throat almost got cut and we're all broke and we're all tired. Marco, shut up, all right? Crystal and I helped Baby with the septic. We never meant for it to get this bad."

"Thanks a lot for bringing Johnny and me in on that group decision," Marco retorts.

"Fair enough," DJ says. "We're sorry. But what's done is done. Let's pack it in for tonight."

Baby takes a deep breath, dizzy, annoyed that she just puked up her dinner, a whole seventy-five cents, out onto the gravel. As much as she'd like to think she's being forced up to Pomoroy Island, that she's too good for it, she's down to her last buck. And if it isn't Pomoroy Island, it's Bad Mike. It's ten percent of what she earned every day out there on the lake looking for that safe. It's Amelia, probably going to spend all of tomorrow rubbing everything they don't have in their faces

The door to the Legion cracks open behind them. "You need Donna?" Margie the bartender asks, throwing out a leg to stop the cat from running out into the night.

"You're a little late," Baby says.

"Well, I'm here all the same," she says. "Do you?"

"No," Crystal says. Baby doesn't know why Crystal's word on this is final. "We're good."

"I think it's time for you to clear off, then. For the night. Always welcome back tomorrow." Margie doesn't wait for them to agree, just closes the door on them. It bangs shut. They all look at one another, helpless, unsure of what to say.

"I'm sorry, Johnny," Baby says, after a long pause, not sure if it's what they want from her exactly. The apology is followed by silence. Baby holds her breath. Terrified at the darkness surrounding them. At the night. At what she'll do if they all walk away now. Johnny shrugs.

"Just a scratch."

"Good," says Baby. "I didn't mean for it to happen." The phrase is loaded. Baby tries to make it sound meaningful, full of regret, but Margie turns the parking lot lights out, letting them know it's time to go home.

It takes too long for them to organize rides, places to go. Baby goes back to DJ's for the second night in the row. Crystal doesn't look at her as she climbs into Johnny's car, but Baby decides not to be too worried about it. Crystal will get over it. She always does.

CHAPTER

23

Pomoroy Island looms in front of them. "I can't believe we're doing this," DJ mutters at the back of Baby's head. All of them are slumped in a pontoon boat, of all things. *A pontoon boat.* Amelia picked them up at the town of Lakeside's sinking dock, cursing and swearing as she tried to park the giant vessel while they all stood and watched. Eventually, the boat's railing got close enough that Marco was able to grab it and pull it in while yelling, "Cut the engine! Cut the engine!" at a flustered Amelia, who accidently revved and almost took him out.

Baby shifts on the bench, hand clutching the flagpole. The speed blows her hair back. A shifting flavor of dread blooms inside her the closer they get to this island, this fucking island. She considers jumping off the side, diving into the water and swimming back to land, the aquatic equivalent of running away screaming. It's not exactly the circumstances under which she thought she'd arrive on the island for the first time. And she certainly didn't envision wearing this dumb uniform. It's like she's holding a sign that says *I don't belong here.*

"We should've done shots or something," DJ says. "Before this bullshit." Even DJ is wearing the uniform. It sits a bit tight on her chest, the outlines of her overall straps imprinting through the fabric.

"Why didn't I think of that?" Baby whispers back, then tries to make eye contact with Crystal, who's been determinedly avoiding her since they set foot on the dock this afternoon. She keeps at it, her chin on her fist, eyes facing toward the opposite shoreline.

Baby plays with the drawstring on her uniform pants, knotting and unknotting the already fraying cord. It's just five or six hours of work. She knows it, can get through it, has had longer days filled with worse guests. But as the boat slows down and Baby sees that Peter isn't waiting on the dock, she starts to worry that Peter doesn't know they're coming. What will he do when he sees her weaving through a crowd of his daddy's friends, a tray of champagne flutes balanced on her palm?

Amelia parks at one of the three docks on the island, this one around the back, away from the house, and everyone piles out next to a run-down little storage cabin, out of place among the beautiful buildings poking through the trees—three roofs of different sizes plopped all over the property, little tiny universes all their own, the entire thing connected by paved pathways snaking through the forest like miniature highways. "There's some crates of dishes and cutlery and stuff . . ." Amelia waves at the little cabin. "Can you grab it? Some wine too."

Baby leads the charge, trying her best to convince everyone she isn't ashamed, but she can feel their pitying looks following her as she throws the door open. Inside she finds stacks and stacks of equipment. She starts passing them back, saving the light boxes, the glasses and cups and water tumblers, for DJ and Crystal, and shouldering the biggest, heaviest box she can find. Baby's determined to remain cheerful, upbeat, to meet any pitying glances with a shrug and a smile. Focused on convincing them all that she's not deluded. She knows who she is, she's always fucking known it.

Amelia leads them up a path through the woods to the main house. It's just as big as the main building at Oakwood but incredibly posh, with storybook windows and plants and flowers pouring out of ceramic pots strategically placed all over the shiny, white wraparound deck. Baby tries to picture Peter living here, barefoot, with that stupid mustache and his ripped clothes, and the reasons he used to sleep in his crappy boat all the time become clearer and clearer. This version of him she knows probably doesn't exist the second he sets foot on this island. It can't.

"I have to go make a quick call. Just put it in there; my mom will show you," Amelia says, gesturing to a woman standing up near the side door to the house.

All of Baby's fantasies about a future with Peter die completely when she sees his mother. She's on the deck wearing soft leather sandals and expensive linen pants with a silk blouse tucked into them, a fat, thick, solid-gold chain around her neck. Her skin is clear and smooth and probably fake. Her hair has been dyed an expensive, warm caramel color, and she talks on a cell phone. "Oh, darling, just try to make it. We can send one of the waiters to come pick you up; just call me when you get to the marina and they'll be right over. No, stop it. It's absolutely no problem at all." Her voice is smooth and present and clear and Baby imagines that nothing terrible has ever happened to her, that her entire life has been spent lying on expensive mattresses eating grapes and reading magazines and listening to uplifting lifestyle gurus coo at her from speakers buried inside plants.

Peter's mom hangs up the phone and turns toward them, brightly. "Hello, hello!" she says, smiling like sunshine. They're struck dumb and halt in a line, like a bunch of six-year-olds meeting their teacher for the first time. "Welcome!"

They all mutter out insecure greetings. Baby thinks she might be blushing.

"Thank you all so much for coming out to help us tonight. I hope those dishes aren't too heavy. Come on up."

"It's no problem," Marco says, smiling. He's the only one who speaks. Baby's embarrassed for all of them.

"It's a bit strange, living on an island," Peter's mother says. "Like I'm some kind of enigmatic hermit. Though I'd probably have to be more interesting to be enigmatic. I probably just seem like a lonely old lady."

No one knows what to say, or if they're allowed to laugh, so they all just stand there, their arms still loaded up with boxes and crates.

"Sorry," she says. "Just a joke. Don't let me keep you. I need to go and greet some guests at the dock."

Baby considers that this woman supposes they all think about her and wonder about her, and she wants to know what that's like—to feel like you're so important that people are day-dreaming about what you're up to. Baby has lived exactly opposite to this, she realizes, acting like a complete moron because at least that means someone is looking at her. When you break it down in the middle of the dance floor, someone is seeing you, they're definitely looking; when you're on the arm of a rich guy, they start to ask questions. It's the same exact thing.

But now, it's all so fucking obvious. They came in the *service entrance*. The two docks on the front are much bigger and grander and probably all lit up and decorated for the guests. There are the people wearing uniforms and the people wearing outfits. And Baby knows that to these people, she'll always be a uniform. She knows it. But there's this other small part of her that she can't ignore that keeps screaming *why, why, why not*. Why not? She's been friends with Peter forever, more than friends for a while. Why shouldn't she get to be inside his house? Why shouldn't his family be kind to her?

And the other voice says, *You're down to your last twenty bucks, bitch. Just smile for the pricks and get out of here with some cash and the remnants of your dignity.*

They put their crates down in something Peter's mother calls a mudroom, then stand around staring at one another, all of them unsure of what to do.

"Should I go find someone?" Johnny asks.

"Nah," says DJ. "Let's delay this freak show for as long as possible."

"Whoa," says Crystal, leaning around the corner and spying a long table decorated with flowers, driftwood, and seashells. The patio doors are open, so the breeze floats in, ruffling the white gauzy curtains framing the window. "Is this a wedding or something?"

"This is just how rich people party," Marco says. "No doubt." Baby can hear the bullshit behind his confidence.

Amelia strides back through the patio door and they all jump, not wanting to be caught peeking like kids at Christmas, all of them trying their best to seem unimpressed. "All right, can you guys, like, line up or something?"

They all stare at her blankly, as if to say, *Seriously*? It's Johnny who moves first, shuffling forward. Everyone falls in behind him.

"No, like, horizontally. God. Haven't you ever seen a movie?" Amelia asks.

They shuffle out of the vertical line, Baby starts to panic. She hadn't realized how big this party would be. On the phone, Amelia said it was mostly old family friends, but Baby can spot at least a dozen people their age walking up to the porch, talking and laughing. Peter has to be around here somewhere, and all of those friends he always forgets to bring to the Parrot must be coming too.

Amelia divides them into teams, sending Marco and Johnny out to the deck with bags of ice thrown over their shoulders, brushed aluminum tubs, cases of wine, flats of glasses. Baby, DJ, Crystal, and the kitchen guys prep trays of appetizers: glistening shrimp, tails off, sitting in little shot glasses of cocktail sauce; paper-thin phyllo pastries stuffed with goat cheese and dates; miniscule hamburgers the size of a silver dollar that make Crystal exclaim, "Oh my god, it's so cute"; stinking cheeses and folds of fancy ham and beef; fresh, shining crudités arranged in spirals. Baby doesn't understand any of it, stares at the tray, at the food, at the thoughtless way Amelia waves it off, as if it's the least important part of the evening, while her stomach groans.

"All right, we'll get you three circulating with trays," Amelia says, pointing to Baby, Crystal, and DJ.

Baby's stomach drops. "Are you sure you don't want us to just set them out? People love grazing."

"What do you think I'm paying you for?" Amelia says, picking up a tray of cocktail shrimp and handing it to Baby.

"Taking out the trash?" Baby asks, helpfully. "The guys back here will need help with dinner and—"

"Just do what you're asked," Amelia says. "Okay? Just do it. And by the way, you're welcome for this opportunity."

Baby shuts up and nods, knows that it's her own fault she's here, that if she'd just stopped and said, "Hey, Peter, let's move the safe somewhere secret; I think there's a wheelbarrow we could use up in one of the landscaping sheds," things might be different. And now all of her friends have to put up with some rich, bleached assholes, all because she doesn't have the guts to tell them the truth, that at this point the only thing that can save them is Baby robbing Bad Mike, a murderous criminal who loves vengeance, a hopeless task in and of itself. Because even if they do rob him, he'll know who it was and he'll make it his job to get it all back, and then they'll just be stuck in this endless cycle of who can get the better of the other until one of them winds up floating facedown in the shitwater off Oakwood.

Baby doesn't have a death wish, doesn't want anyone to get hurt because they couldn't play ball with Amelia Pomoroy, so for now she's going to keep up the facade. It's so much easier than having to admit it's hopeless.

Baby peeks around the corner at a crowd of young people hanging out on the deck, all of the men wearing the same variation of pressed shorts and shirts, sockless feet stuffed into boat shoes. The women all wear some take on the floral sundress, a few of them accessorizing with brimmed hats, strappy sandals, intricate handbags—an entirely different brand of city bitch that Baby hasn't encountered.

Baby watches as Amelia greets three of the women and their voices all go up an octave, different variations of "Oh my god, you look amazing," assaulting eardrums everywhere. "Oh my god, this is so amazing." "Oh my god, you're so amazing."

"Peter!" one of the girls shouts, and Baby's stomach bottoms out. She doesn't recognize the voice, watches as he walks up the front steps, wearing a rumpled button-down shirt, his feet in a pair of worn leather flip-flops she's never seen before.

"Heidi," he says, and gives her a long hug, too long. "Hey."

"How have you been? I haven't seen you since the formal."

"Crazy night."

"So crazy," she says, tilting her head to the side and pressing a finger into his chest. "You never called."

"Oh, no," Baby says, then ducks back into the mudroom as she realizes she's wandered into the middle of the kitchen, has said the words out loud at an open door. No one notices her.

Sure, Baby's been no saint in the winters, but to be confronted by it, to have it walk across a deck and kiss him on the cheek . . .

"Don't torture yourself," says DJ, pulling up next to her holding a veggie tray. "You knew he was doing this kind of shit. Let's just get this over with. They won't even make eye contact with you if you keep your head down."

Baby ignores her, leaning out again. Peter's sitting next to the girl now, on stools at the edge of the deck. Baby's jaw tightens as the girl puts a hand on his shoulder. She knew this was happening, she just never had to actually feel it before, had become very skilled at burying any thoughts of it, and now it's sitting right there, wearing an absurd hat that's a cross between Indiana Jones's fedora and something the world's cheesiest cowboy would own.

"Two hours and we're done. Three hours tops," DJ says.

"Will you trade with me?" Baby asks, offering DJ the tray of shrimp, the tiny cocktail glasses clinking against one another. "No one will want to eat from the vegetable tray."

"True," says DJ. "Sure. Don't say I never did anything nice for you."

Baby laughs and passes her the little shot glasses, then takes the groaning vegetable tray, watching a grape tomato tumble off the side of it, roll across the floor and under the stove. "See you on the other side," DJ whispers, and strides out through the doors and onto the patio.

Baby walks off in the exact opposite direction of Peter, takes a slow path around the deck, weaving through the gaps between sport coats, the occasional partygoer stopping to dunk a carrot stick into a strange green dressing she's been told is a vegan, avocado-based crema, whatever that is.

Once Peter and his other girlfriend are out of Baby's sight, she finds it easy to slip through the crowd. The people mostly ignore her, and she finds a pathway, a loop that makes it easy to avoid the girl who keeps leaning on Peter's shoulder and laughing.

And she's just coming out of the kitchen, her tray reloaded, when a loud voice cuts through the crowd. "Where's my son?" Everyone turns and looks. Baby spots Peter in the crowd, a weak smile on his lips.

"Dad."

Jasper Pomoroy walks up the steps, his arms spread wide. He's taller than he seemed on the internet. Taller than Peter and Amelia. He's wearing a suit without a tie, the collar pried open, his hair surrendering to gray as if it were planned. He strides across the deck and shakes Peter's hand.

"Jasper," Peter's mother says, jogging up the steps behind him, clearly as surprised as everyone else, her hair bouncing behind her. "Darling." She plants a dry kiss on his cheek. "How did you get here? Where's the plane?"

"Surprise," he says, flat, and walks to the bar where Marco is polishing a glass and orders a Scotch. "Client dropped me off on his way up north. You sound disappointed."

"Not at all," she says. "Just surprised. It's not every day you appear out of nowhere, dear."

"Poof," Jasper says, his tone challenging now, knocking back his Scotch. Everyone in the party is watching him, and when he puts the glass down, he lets out a small chuckle. "Oh, as you were." A dismissal, a flick of the wrist, and all the conversation returns.

"Look, the Parneviches!" Peter's mother says, waving over Jasper's shoulder. "They must've bought a new boat."

She hurries off the deck, waving and letting out a moaning "Hellooo!" at a couple struggling to park a baby yacht, a slumping teenager filming the entire thing with his cell phone, sitting in the bow rider and doing nothing to help.

"Man, fuck this," DJ says, once they're all in the back room, trays down on side tables, waiting for the kitchen guys to reload them.

"Just look at them," Baby says, marveling, poking her head out from the mudroom. "What is it that makes them seem so . . . I don't know."

"It's money," DJ says, putting the finishing touches on a cheese plate while Crystal arranges dips. "Fuck money."

"Shit, don't let them hear you say that," Baby whispers. "They'll run you off the island."

"Communism! That doesn't sound so bad!" DJ shouts, a wicked smile on her face. "Man, why'd I let you drag me out here? You know I don't swim. What if they set the dogs on us?"

They hush as Amelia enters the kitchen holding a very full glass of white wine.

"More appies ready?" she asks, leaning her head in. "What are you doing back here? Didn't I tell you to circulate?" Amelia takes a deep sip from her glass, red splotches popping up all over her neck. She grimaces. "Ugh, this town could really use a wine merchant." Baby bites down a snicker. "C'mon, let's go. I didn't think you'd need to be supervised."

They pick up trays and follow her outside. Baby wishes she could close her ears the way she can her eyes. Really shut them tight. What a skill that would be. She thinks about early humans, prehistoric people. It made sense to have your ears open, to know where your enemies were, how close to your cave they'd gotten—you know, dinosaurs sneaking into the cave while you're sleeping and all that. *Now,* Baby thinks, *what peace we could all have if we didn't have to listen to one another. If we could choose.*

She walks past Jasper. "You know how I feel about women in business," Jasper is saying. "I'm not a monster; it's just a bad fit for a lot of their personalities. Now, some are suited for it, for sure, but Amelia just cares too much. It's detrimental to her success. You can see with the resort. She should be suing that older owner—yes, I will, thank you," he says, grabbing a handful of carrots from the tray Baby lowers down in front of him. Jasper's talking to another man in a loud shirt, puffs of black cotton hair whipping away from the back of his skull.

"Got any cheese?" the man asks.

"It's coming around," Baby says.

"Send them over," the man says. "Thanks." Dismissive in the way only men seem to get away with. Baby moves on.

And it's not intentional, but the crowd opens up, by some ugly twist of fate and motion, and Baby is standing directly across from Peter and the woman, that woman who lights up when she sees the vegetable tray. "Oh, thank god," she says. "Excuse me!" she calls to Baby. "Can we have some crudité? I'm starving."

Baby freezes, as if her ankles have sunken into the deck, and it's a nudge from DJ in the center of her back that gets her moving, taking steps toward them. "You're a saint," the girl says. "I've just gone vegan, and this is the only thing I can eat." She grabs a napkin out of Baby's hand, oblivious. Baby studies her. She's naturally beautiful, doesn't wear much makeup, but whatever she is wearing forces the light to play on her cheeks. As she leans forward, Baby can smell her and it's incredible, like a joyful weeping.

And that's when she notices Peter, who isn't looking at her, the embarrassment so obvious on his face that Baby wants to cry. Instead, she moves the tray under his face, says "Crudité?" so loudly she's surprised the party doesn't grind to a halt. Peter flips his sandal off and stuffs his foot back in.

"Babe, don't be rude," the woman says, nudging Peter, grinning hopelessly at Baby, as if to say, *Isn't he just . . .*

"I'm fine, thanks," Peter says, looking up, making direct eye contact with Baby.

"You know, you look familiar," the woman says to Baby.

"Do you have a place on the lake?" Baby asks.

"I wish," she says, then nudges Peter with her elbow, lightly wiggling her eyebrows. "I keep trying to score an invite, but he's so . . . picky."

"I bet," Baby says, pretending she understands and secretly praying there's some faulty wiring in the house and the entire thing is about to explode, blow her body through the air and into the lake—or vaporize her, really; she wouldn't mind. Peter's expression shifts toward terrified, and Baby just wants so badly to be anywhere else. *Prison. Dead, in the ground.* She's blushing, she can feel it, and can't have this girl noticing it. "I should keep moving," she says.

"Are you sure we don't know one another?" the woman asks. Baby looks at her clothes, her hair, takes a deep breath and finds a smile somewhere in the bullshit. A million cutting remarks about this rich bitch live and die in her mouth, and instead she just shrugs, invokes a breeziness that's so unfamiliar it's as if a stranger has commandeered her vocal chords.

"I'm sure," she says, straightening up. "I never leave the lake."

"Wait," the girl says, reaching into her purse and pulling out a dollar bill. "If there's anything else vegan back there, can you send it my way?"

Baby looks at the dollar, at the girl's manicure, thin strips of white swiped across the tops of her nails. Every small detail in place, the entire arrangement of her so perfect she's like one of those giant stores where you walk into it and sigh, seeing everything laid out exactly as it should be. Baby understands now, the value of this sort of woman. She's easy to look at. Relief from the chaos of the universe, this person.

"I'm not supposed to—"

"Take it," the girl whispers, conspiratorial, ducking her head, smiling at Peter. "Right, babe? We won't tell anyone."

Baby wants to puke. Instead, she takes the dollar, crumples it in her fist, knows that it's easier to just take the dollar than to continue the humiliation of arguing about it.

The woman winks at her, then bites down on a carrot stick, and Baby heads off, free from it, finishes her round of the party and ditches the half-finished tray on a table with a carved wooden bear as its base, then rushes inside, brushing two warning shots making tracks down her cheeks. She leans against the wall in the mudroom, forehead pressed against the cool tile, trapping the tears behind her eyes, squeezing the muscles, barely breathing, really, until the threat of a spillover stops. Her face is red hot. Baby knows that if she starts crying now, it'll all come out—the lying, Peter, Oakwood, Hannah. It can't. She can't do that now. She'll never stop.

When she's sure she's held it together, she slips out the back door, grabs two fistfuls of ice from a cooler, and presses them to her face. When Johnny pokes his head out, she looks up from the ice and shrugs. "Hot out, eh?"

It's not at all, but he doesn't push, just finds two pieces of paper towel for her to dry off with. Baby hurries to scrub her face clean because she can hear the sound of Amelia's heels stomping on the hardwood. When she arrives, she stumbles around the corner, a glass of white wine in her hand, the hives now creeping up her neck. "Dinner's coming. Just make sure you serve my father first," she slurs, bracing her hand against the doorframe for support. Baby wonders how the night will evolve now that Amelia is round the bend.

It makes sense now, Baby realizes, so much sense. Amelia pretending she didn't drink at the resort, resolved to keep her professional life and her drunkenness held apart with two hands. But Baby knows a lush when she sees one and watches Amelia find a half-full wine bottle and upend it carelessly into her glass. If there's one thing Baby learned growing up with Hannah, it's that no matter how hard you try to hide it, how hard you try to reset, how hard you try to push it apart, it's so much easier to just let it happen. Because the effort of pretending it doesn't exist is exhausting enough in its own right. All it takes is a bit of stress, a few sleepless nights, and there it goes.

Maybe Amelia will grab Baby the way she did when the septic busted open, throw her up against the wall again. Baby almost wants her too, wants this whole WASP parade to be ruined by one of their own. A big revealing moment that exposes the cracks. Even if it's just for a moment before they find a way to stamp it down, forget about it. Because, it is, Baby realizes—as she watches Amelia try with so much effort to stay on her feet—a small victory for her to see how much they've undone this bitch, this violent, incapable woman.

"I know none of you have formal banquet training, but like, just try not to be total fuckups, would you?"

"Got it," Baby says, and Amelia straightens and drags herself outside to bring people back in.

The catered food is basically a glorified burger, sort of weirdly deconstructed on the plate, with potatoes that really just resemble sour cream and onion chips snugged up next to a small mountain of burned Brussels sprouts.

"Why don't we eat out here?" Baby hears Jasper say. "It's beautiful outside."

"Amelia put a lot of work into the long table," her mother says.

"Just look at that sunset," he says. Baby expects the crowd of them to start clapping at it, as if Jasper painted it specifically for all of them, arranged it like a fireworks show.

"We're eating at the table." Baby peers around the corner and watches Peter's mother walk through the doors, talking to the vegan. "Maybe we could just move it a bit so there's a better view."

"I feel like we could inch it around without disturbing anything," the vegan says. The two women, ignored by the rest of the party, stand at either end of the table and try to pick it up, but it's a giant table, it can seat at least fifty people, is already weighed down by place settings and party favors and napkins and glasses and the stupid decorations. "Maybe we can get some of the catering staff to help," Peter's mother says, looking over at the mudroom. She spots Baby immediately before she can duck behind the doorframe. "Do you mind?" she asks. "Is anyone else back there?"

"I'll get them," Baby says, and turns to DJ and Crystal. "They want some help moving the table."

DJ rolls her eyes but follows Baby and Crystal out into the main area. They all take places around it.

"Where are we going?" Baby asks.

"Just a little closer to the door," Peter's mother says.

"Right," Baby says, and grabs her side.

"On three," she says. "One . . . two . . ."

"Mother, what the fuck are you doing?" Amelia says from the open door. Baby reflexively moves the table in anticipation. So does Crystal, and the glasses on the table topple over, a few of them crashing to the floor, place settings clattering after them. "Baby, what the fuck? Did I say you could touch the table?"

"Darling, we just wanted to move the table closer to the door."

"It's in the perfect place. I measured it with a fucking measuring tape," Amelia says. "And now look what you've done. What are they doing out here?" She points to Baby.

"We asked them to come out," the vegan says.

"They're dirt," Amelia says, examining the table as Crystal tries to put the cutlery back as it was. "Look, they didn't even put the fork on the proper side. They go on the left, you hicks."

"All right, that's enough," says her mother. "I'm going to get a broom and sweep it up, then we'll all sit down to dinner."

"What are you still doing in here?" Amelia asks the three of them. "Actually, I have a question for you," she says, pointing at DJ. "Why do you always wear overalls? I can see them under your uniform. You're an adult. What the hell is wrong with you?"

"Okay, enough," Peter says gently, appearing behind Amelia. He puts an arm around her shoulder. Baby wants to punch her, feels her fist curling up into itself.

Crystal grabs Baby's wrist instead. DJ has hurried off, and when they get into the mudroom, they find the back door wide open. "Let me go," Crystal says, looking outside at DJ's retreating back. "Are you going to be okay to serve?"

"Yes," Baby says, fighting an urge to open up the warming cabinet and start throwing every one of those perfect plates onto the floor.

"She's just drunk." Crystal gestures with her head over to the main dining room, where Amelia's probably chugging wine. "We've seen worse. I'll get Johnny to help you."

He appears as Baby pulls the plates out of the warmer, droplets of Scotch and red wine dotting his uniform. "Man, I fucking hate these people," he says. Baby nods, bites down on her lower lip.

Once the guests are seated, they parade out in long white lines, hot plates burning their fingertips. Baby heads to Jasper first, Peter next to him. Amelia slumps, sullen, staring out at the lake, the view fading minute to minute as the sun disappears behind the tree line. Baby's gaze flickers over at Peter as she puts Jasper's plate down and he notices, looking at his son and then back at Baby, gesturing casually with a butter knife.

"Do you two know one another?" he asks.

Baby stays silent.

"We're friends," Peter says.

"What's your name?" Jasper asks, largely not caring at all if she answers.

"Baby," she says.

"Baby! What kind of name is that?" he asks.

Baby pauses, feels too many eyes on her. "A four-letter one?"

Jasper blinks at her, then lets out a long and barking laugh. "She's sharp! Baby, get me a refill, would you?" He hands her a glass and she walks off, throat burning.

By the time she's returned with his Scotch, everyone has plates and they're eating. Baby puts the glass down and Jasper ignores her, which she prefers, and she ducks back through the mudroom and steps out the side door and takes a deep breath.

DJ is slumped over on a tree stump, drinking wine from the bottle. "We found this," she says, passing the bottle to Baby, who takes a long drink.

"Broken cork." Marco shrugs. "Can't serve it."

"You okay?" Baby sits down next to her.

"Rich bitch." DJ spits on the ground.

"You want me to fight her?" Baby nudges DJ, kidding, and DJ shakes her head, keeps staring at the ground.

"Nah," DJ mutters. "Too many lawyers in there."

They huddle around the bottle of wine, shoulders hunched, not saying much, making sure DJ gets most of it.

Eventually Peter's mom pokes her head out and smiles at them. Johnny steps sideways, blocking the bottle from view. "We're about wrapped up in here, if you want to come in and clear. Thanks so much for all your help tonight."

They descend on the table, desperate, moving too quickly. Most of the diners are gone save Jasper and Amelia, who's barely upright, slumped on an elbow next to her father. She has switched to red wine, which has settled into the corners of her mouth.

"I'm not being confrontational," Jasper says. Baby scans for Peter but can't find him in the crowd back on the deck. "What I'm saying is, running a business takes a certain kind of personality, and maybe you don't have that personality."

"What are you even talking about?" Amelia says. "You're the one who never shuts up about good debt."

"The building has been condemned. You owned it for, what, six weeks?"

"I have a buyer," she says. "I can enact the clause at any time and poof, two million." Everyone in the room freezes, but neither Jasper nor Amelia looks away from the table, from their drinks, from this conversation they're locked into. Baby almost loses her grasp on the stack of plates in her hands, the porcelain clattering together.

Jasper takes a sip of his Scotch, finishing it off, then starts to laugh. The laugh is condescending and loud and lonely, echoing in the room. "Oh please, Amelia, you don't have to lie."

Baby hates him. She hates him for laughing at his daughter. Baby hates it. It's everything she's ever felt, and she knows that years of this festering bullshit made Amelia into what she is.

"It's true," Baby says.

Jasper looks up at her in surprise. "And what does a Baby know about a building sale?"

"I know the former owner always had offers. Big companies. Holiday Inn—"

"Oh, very prestigious," Jasper says, dismissing her. Baby shuts up then; she doesn't have the stones, misplaced them, or maybe just wasn't ever born with them.

Baby, who has faced down drug dealers and murderers and addicts, who spent her life dragging around an alcoholic who vomited abuse at her almost as often as she hurled actual barf, feels this powerlessness gripping her now and the frustration chasing it, that she just can't get through to him simply because he has already decided she isn't worth anything. That anything she'll say to him now means nothing.

Jasper laughs again. "Surely they're going to pay full price for a piece of land that's been turned into a shit swamp."

"They will," Amelia says. "I'm going to sell it. And then you'll be fucking sorry." Amelia slugs back her wine.

Glass shatters. Baby looks up and sees Crystal standing next to the counter, the remnants of a wineglass at her feet, staring at Amelia. Baby knows she's overheard, maybe not all of it, but this last part. The one part that matters.

"Make sure you dock that from her paycheck," Jasper says to Amelia, then stands and walks out to the deck. "And send someone out to pour me a drink." Amelia, slumped at the table, her cheek propped up on one hand, sniffs quietly. A tear overflows out of her eyelid and down her cheek. Baby takes a step toward her.

"Are you finished with your plate?"

Amelia picks it up and hands it to her with such force that Baby struggles to grab it out of the air, steadying the stack as she spins around. She jogs back into the mudroom, past Crystal on the ground with a broom, sweeping up the shards of glass. Baby hurries back to where everyone is scraping plates into a yellow painter's bucket lined with a flimsy, thin white garbage bag so out of place in this paradise it seems like it shouldn't exist.

"What are we going to do, Baby?" asks DJ, as soon as she sets down the stack of plates. So much food left there, left behind, uneaten.

No one had asked her yet, even though she'd been expecting it. Baby with the big plan, and now? Their jobs. Their futures. Rent for their apartments. Amelia's going to sell.

Baby's heart starts to pound. Literally everyone she cares about in the world is standing around a trash bucket, blinking at her.

"I . . ." she says. "I'll figure something out."

"What are you going to figure out?" Johnny snaps. "The building is condemned. The building is condemned. When were you going to tell us that part?"

"I didn't know," Baby says. "I didn't think it would be that bad."

"But what about this summer?" DJ asks. "What about my August rent?"

"There's welfare," says Baby. "Plus she didn't say she was definitely selling. She just said she had a buyer. And she might be lying."

"Why did you defend her?" DJ asks. "What the fuck, Baby?"

"Welfare's not enough for the winter and you know it," Johnny says. "What are we going to do? Baby, my mom's furnace is broken. And Amelia might not be rebuilding. The Parrot. Everything. Baby." He presses his palms into his eyes. "How could this happen?"

"Just give me a minute," she says, her breath coming short, face on fire. Outside, she can hear drunken voices screaming into the night, high-pitched laughter. Never in her life has Baby felt so much impatience for drunks. They're usually her favorite kind of people. Beasts unleashed, dogs at bay, unwound and uncomplicated. But this is something so entirely different.

"We can still figure something out," Baby says. "The money, the safe. There's still the safe."

"It's a big fucking lake, Baby," says DJ. "God, this was such a stupid idea."

The pressure of the lie, the depth of it, Baby starts to feel like she's going to explode. "I did find it," Baby spits out, not quite sure where she's going with it. "The safe. We found it."

"What?"

"Peter and I found it."

"And you didn't tell us?" DJ says, cutting in. "Where is it? What was inside?"

"It's not. I mean, I lost it again." Baby hears the words tumbling out, wishes she thought about how she was going to deliver this information, to lay it out credibly so it wouldn't make her sound so pathetic.

"What do you mean you lost it?"

"Mike took it," Baby says. "That's why he came into the Legion last night. He can't figure out how to open it and wants my help."

The futility of the sentence casts a pall over the group. Silence.

DJ is the first to break it. "So it really is over," DJ says. "If Mike has it, it's as good as gone."

"He hasn't opened it yet." Baby searches Crystal's face for any sort of hope and doesn't get it. "He said he'd give me ten percent if I did it for him. But I think we should go take it back."

"I'm not going up there ever again," Crystal says.

"How did he get it?" DJ cuts in. "Baby, you didn't even bother telling us you were looking for it. All those fucking mornings with the wet hair—"

"Because you were such jerks about it in the first place," Baby says.

"We care about you," Crystal says. "We didn't want you risking your life for something so—"

"Stupid," DJ cuts in. "So you've been lying to us this entire time? What, were you going to run off with it?"

"Of course not. How can you say that?"

"She never found it," Marco says. "Did you?" Baby looks up at the circle of them, Crystal, DJ, Marco, and Johnny, all of them staring at her or at the ground, arms crossed.

"Why would I lie?"

"Why did you?" It's Johnny who speaks, quietly, and makes Baby feels a curling kind of shame, this really fresh, disgusting shame that wants to pull her under, all of it magnified. Because she did lie. She lied every day.

"I don't know." A kind of silent pleading has overtaken her body. Baby stares at her feet. "But I know I was doing it for you."

The entire group of them shifts uncomfortably, looking off in different directions. And it's DJ, again, this time. "Bullshit," DJ spits. "Bullshit, bullshit, bullshit. God, Baby, it's so fucking obvious. You just wanted an excuse to spend time with him. Stop pretending you're doing it for us. It's all for him. It always has been. And for once, we've needed you to just play ball, be there for us, and you couldn't even do that. I bet you went back and messed with the toilets after Crystal and I told you not to. Didn't you?"

Baby doesn't confirm it. She knows she doesn't have to. DJ's already decided.

"You just served his family dinner and you'd still probably go off with him if he asked you. And we're here, Baby. *We're right here.* We've been here the entire time. And that doesn't seem to matter to you at all." DJ pauses and Baby knows she's trying to stop herself, stop the rant, because it's getting hard to hear. "He doesn't want you. He wants that. He wants her. You're never going to fit in here. Why can't you accept it?"

"And now we have nothing." Crystal seems to be realizing it for the first time and sits down on the ground hard.

Baby knows they're betrayed, just trying to hurt her. To derail the conversation. "Why don't you just leave, then? You could've left years ago. Face it. You're just as stuck as I am. At least I tried to change things. To make it better. At least I tried."

"It was a fucking paycheck, Baby," Johnny says.

"You all agreed," Baby says, backing away from them. "We all agreed to do this."

She looks at all of them in turn. They all turn away from her, and Baby, well, she doesn't know what else to do. Anger courses through her. Her fists tighten.

A case of wine sits at the back door, and she grabs two bottles and heads off into the woods.

24

S HE FINDS A rock on the edge of the island and sits down. It's dark now, but the white uniform is making her feel like she's glowing. She tries to twist the top off the wine and swears, seeing that both bottles she grabbed have corks buried in the tops of them. "Goddammit." She reaches down and picks up a small rock and bashes it against the neck of the bottle, the glass cracking but not breaking.

Hannah did this once. Baby came home, found her asleep on the table, in her usual position, her lips slit and bloody, mixed with the purple liquid, making her look demented.

"You want me to open that for you?" Peter appears on a path off to the side, holding a corkscrew.

"Sure," she says. He sits down next to her, takes the bottle of wine out of her hand and starts to twist.

Baby's not sure what to say to him. She knows she can't compete with the vegan hat girl. The Peter she knows wouldn't freely associate with a vegan. It just doesn't make sense to her. It's like she doesn't know anything at all.

"I didn't think Amelia drank," Baby says.

"Jasper Pomoroy brings out the alcoholic in all of us," he says. "Cheers."

Peter hands her the bottle and she drinks deeply, wincing at the taste. "Ugh."

"That's a sixty-dollar bottle you've got there," Peter says.

Baby swipes her mouth with the back of her hand. "I've met a lot of assholes in my day. Your dad is next level." Baby takes another deep swig of wine.

Peter mutters something incomprehensible and takes a sip.

"What was that?" Baby asks.

"Do you wish I called you Jane?"

"No," she says.

Silence again. She watches a boat in the distance chugging along the shoreline, way off in the inlet on the other side of Oakwood. It's too late for fishing, and yet whoever's driving seems to be doing something strange, standing on the edge of the vessel, a long pole in hand.

"Can I ask you something?" Peter says.

"Nope." Baby takes another swig of wine, knows some question is coming anyway.

"Why does DJ wear overalls?"

It's not what Baby expects from him, and she's relieved it's not about her. "She had a . . . well, listen, don't tell anyone. Especially not Amelia."

"Sure."

"She had a stepdad growing up. He did, you know . . . whatever the worst possible thing you can think of, he, well . . . yeah. DJ was really young. It actually ended up being Bad Mike's uncle who drove him out of Lakeside in the end. And she's worn overalls since. Like a security blanket, I guess." Baby slugs back another mouthful of wine. It doesn't taste like it should cost sixty dollars. "I don't know, I'm sure a shrink could unpack it for you better, but here we are."

"That's horrible." Peter takes the bottle from Baby and takes a long drink.

"Yup."

Silence again. The boat in the distance has disappeared around a bend in the shoreline. Baby wants so badly to ask him about the hat vegan, but it's just too much. She can't look at him. It's all too much, this overwhelming fear of actually having an honest conversation for once in their goddamn lives.

Baby wants to do anything else; she'd try to have sex with him in full view of the houseful of rich, drunk idiots just so she didn't have to have this conversation.

He reaches over and grabs her hand. "Baby . . ."

Her face glows red and the fear that has kept her awake during all those lonely sober nights starts to make her panic. She gropes for the bottle next to her and sees that it's spilled over, a red stain seeping into the leg of her uniform pants. She didn't notice.

"Baby, I—"

She looks at the lake. The water is deep enough, though the algae bloom has covered the shallows in a thick green sheen. She slides off the rock, allows her entire body to submerge, gasps a little at how cold the water is. It makes sense, though, the temperature. They are in the middle of the lake.

She waves her arms to keep herself underwater and then hears another body hit the surface next to her and sees Peter there, down with her in the muck.

He grabs her arm and pulls her to the surface and they tread water, staring at each other, bracing themselves against the slippery rock, hands grasping for any kind of hold and finding nothing. It's like a sheer drop off the side of this island. A sheer drop into a cold nothing.

"What'd you do that for?" Peter asks, panting a bit with the effort of having to stay above the surface.

"I'm in love with you," she says, and it pours out in a blurt, the words that have been stalled for as long as she can remember, kept frozen over the winter, thawing out over the summer, but never quite pushing through.

"Baby—"

She cuts him off, keeps talking, afraid that he'll stop her before she can get it all out. "I always have been, and sometimes I think I always will be. But this . . ." She gestures to the island, the lake surrounding them. "I can't find myself in it, and you've never . . ." She trails off and loses it, loses the ability to form the words that DJ has shouted at her over and over again, and she can't finish the sentence, because it hurts too much and he isn't saying anything and hot tears obscure her vision, so she lets herself sink down again and says the words to the rocks at the bottom, says the words to the algae mucking up the water: *You've never made me feel like it could be anything.*

Baby hates that she's still here in the same place she's always been, stuck in love, stuck in this town, trying to save a home and a family that don't seem to want her anymore. Just stuck.

A hand, his hand, grabs hers and pulls her up to the surface. Peter's just looking at her, really, his eyes wide open and confused. "What were you going to say?" he says. He somehow climbed back onto the rock, its slick surface. There must be something he knows and she doesn't about climbing out.

Baby has to tell him. She has to. But instead, she tells him something else. "I sabotaged the septic tanks. Well, Crystal and DJ and I did it. The whole group of us, really. We had a plan to chase your sister off, undermine her confidence," Baby says. "I had this really stupid idea that if I found the safe, I could buy the resort from your sister. But I had to make it worth less. So I could afford it."

Peter drops Baby's hand. "So . . . wait. The safe . . ."

"It was a stupid idea," says Baby. "But I ruined it. I did it on purpose. It was me." Baby breathes, eyes down on the water, her movements causing little waves to lap at the edge of the rock, crash against it, the stone unmoving, unaffected, really.

Peter is silent. Baby looks over at the rocks next to the dock. If she gets up here, she has to walk past the party, around to the other side, and wait on the dock reserved for the help for someone to come and pick her up. She doesn't know who to call. Everyone is out here. Everyone who might've come, anyway.

Peter is silent, his face not moving, eyes suddenly a little deader.

"It was my home, Peter. You know that. She was taking my home away."

Peter lets her hand go, and Baby feels herself start to cry, so she sinks again and waits underwater, holding herself in the dark muck until his feet disappear and she rises, gasping, to the surface, this time alone.

Baby can't stand the idea of climbing up and looking at his big, rich, house, at the people inside helping themselves to chocolate mousse and free wine and laughing in loud, high voices.

So instead, she shrugs out of the uniform, leaves it floating in the water, like she's been raptured, the white cloth tinged green now by the muck. She has a feeling she won't need it again and swims, free of it, all, away from the island, toward land.

B ABY PAUSES, PANTING, in the middle of the bay, and treads water. Night has fully realized itself in the sky over her head, and she lies on her back, floating, knowing that if a speedboat comes to hit her, she'll at least die looking at the most beautiful thing she's ever seen. The cold water laps at her skin, making her shiver. She's in good shape from all her morning swims with Peter, but the resort is still very far away, and even then, she'll have to swim through the shitwater to get back up into the boathouse. She could swim back into Lakeside, but there's nowhere for her to sleep there either.

You idiot. The voice echoes inside her head, loud. Hannah. *It's right over there.*

Her old place. The tiny house she and Hannah rented, the cabin on Betty's property. Betty called it a coach house to give herself the superiority she needed to get through the day. The coach house, parked on the edge of the bay due east of where Baby's paddling, trying to make up her mind.

Baby changes direction, using a breaststroke, her head above water. There's no rush, really. As soon as she starts moving, the shivering stops, her heart pumping warm blood all through her body. She makes her way to the shoreline, the water warming up as she gets closer, the bottom of the lake rising up beneath her, appearing suddenly. A few of the cottages have porch lights on. Most don't. Baby doesn't see anyone, no one sitting next to a barbecue or at the end of a dock, sipping on a beer, no laughter echoing out from porches, no clinking of glasses, no sounds of tidying up, of drunks climbing into boats, arguing over whether they should be driving or not.

Betty's cottage is situated in a particularly wealthy stretch of lake, and Baby knows most of the people who own the homes are weekenders who really only visit for four or five weekends a summer. The cottages are assets. Money parked in place. Just money, growing, so long as they make sure the building stays standing, and even without that, a lakeside property always turns a profit.

Betty's place is in the next bay, just around a bend in the lake. It's particularly quiet. The wetlands across from her property are home to some kind of endangered heron or something, Baby doesn't know, but it earned a government protection in the eighties, so there are fewer properties and less boat traffic.

What Baby's banking on is that Betty isn't home at all. Betty has always hated Baby, and even though Baby knows that if she climbed out of the water wearing nothing but her underwear, Betty'd help her, she also doesn't want to give her the satisfaction of getting to lend charity and feel good about herself. The old bitch. If she isn't home, Baby can squat in her place instead of having to face her old cabin and all the feelings that come with it.

Luckily, when she gets to Betty's dock, the entire place is quiet and dark. The porch lights that are always on are on, but thick cobwebs drip from them, waving back and forth in the air, bullied by an invisible breeze. Baby boosts herself up onto the dock and leans around Betty's house to look at the driveway. Betty's truck isn't there. It's empty.

Baby walks up the stone path, and the security lights flash on, illuminating a *For Sale* stuck in the gravel at the end of the driveway. Of course. Everything is for fucking sale.

Baby knows how to break into Betty's, did it several times in her youth, twice in the winter when electricity went out and they needed to use the fireplace and once in the summertime when their water heater died and she desperately wanted a hot shower.

There are a few ways in, and Baby chooses the side window first, only to find it's painted shut. The next best way is the side door, and Baby rummages through a handful of wood chips in the garden to find the best wedge, and when she finds it, she jogs around to the screen, flips the latch open with the wedge, then sticks it in the gap and jiggles. There's no deadbolt on this door, and when she opens and inhales, she smells stale air and knows that it's been a while since Betty was here. Things were getting serious with her boyfriend after all.

Betty's got a magnificent Jacuzzi. It's old and giant and pink and the head of the faucet is shaped like a swan. Baby strips naked and turns the water up on high, as high as it can go, and waits as it surrounds her body and turns her skin pink, makes her feel a little bit like she's on fire, and she starts making a mental list of things you can't sell. She can't think of one thing. Memories can't be sold, Baby thinks, but surely that Facebook dweeb is circling the drain on that. Any minute now. Memories. Love. Love don't cost a thing, right? Jennifer Lopez really nailed it with that one.

Baby squirts some shampoo into the running water and brings forth some bubbles. She thinks about what will happen, thinks about the feelings that descend in the winter, everyone scraping by on government help, tips from the summer spent by February. Waiting for the thaw. But she doesn't know what will happen now that they have nothing. If everyone will leave, find jobs elsewhere, never come back. Probably. But it takes money to leave, and Baby knows most of them don't have it.

The only thing left is the safe. Baby pushes herself under water. Bad Mike and his safe. It's the only thing left. If she gets the money back, at least they'll have something to help them get through the next few months. Maybe they'll even forgive her.

The water in the tub is a soupy mess of dirt and sand and gross lake water. Baby drains the tub, feels the suckling of the water pulling her down, down against the current as it leaves her surrounded only by sand and white puffs of soap. She makes a bikini for herself out of the suds, rinses out the bottom of the tub, and plugs the drain once more.

She gets out of the tub in her bikini, the water rushing behind her, and pads into the kitchen leaving wet footsteps in her wake, because really, water evaporates, soap disintegrates, but Baby, well, Baby could always use a drink. She finds the stash under the kitchen sink, where it always was. Two unopened bottles of wine Betty'd probably miss and scattered liquor, assorted, that she won't.

Baby pulls all the bottles out and grabs two glasses, roots around in the freezer for ice and finds it, snaps it out of a tray and out onto the counter and starts dumping: schnapps, liqueurs, tequila. She finds a jug of cranberry juice in the fridge only a few weeks past its expiration date and adds a few splashes, shakes the entire thing up, strains it into a martini glass, and takes a sip. A hard bite of liquor, sure, but not the worst thing she's tasted. Not by a long shot.

By the time she's back in the tub, the buzz has started to muddy her feelings and she settles into thinking. If no one has jobs, bank accounts run dry, everyone is poor, depressed, bored. And here's Bad Mike, back on the scene again, clearly cooking, selling—if he puts it out into the community, if everyone's checks just start getting funneled to him, what then? A bunch of addicts with no jobs waiting for time to pass. Baby knows it could happen. It was starting to happen before Mike was put away last time, when Crystal's mom died, the first of nine overdoses from one batch. He was supposed to be going away for second-degree murder. And that was when everyone had jobs. When the lake was buzzing with activity, three marinas up and running, boats being pulled in and out of storage, back when Dorset was chock-full of people on weekends, parents buying kids tall frozen yogurt cones, bags and bags of groceries for their friends and family coming up to join them, when times were good.

And now Bad Mike has her money and the lake is a ghost town, a strange shadow growing longer on the ground as the sun sets on their shared future. She chugs the martini, feels for a second like she might be going blind, then closes her eyes and allows the liquor and the hot water to put her to sleep.

CHAPTER

26

A CRASH, GLASS SHATTERING. Baby wakes with a quiet gasp. The water is icy cold and her neck is pinched to her shoulder. Banging and the voices of men. Baby sinks deeper into the tub, suddenly very aware of how naked she is. The soap bubbles have all popped, disintegrated. She doesn't move, knows that any sound of water, lapping at her body, sloshing against the sides of the tub, will give her away. She starts to shiver in the cold water, tiny waves snaking away from her body.

"This?" the gravelly male voice asks, and she hears cupboards opening, the sounds of pots and pans clanging.

"Microwave," another says. "Get the microwave."

Her own sharp breath is echoing in the cavernous bathroom and she drops lower in the water so only her nose is above the surface, listens as they struggle.

"It's fuckin' bolted to the wall," one of them says.

"What? That's . . . no, it ain't." Sneakers squeak against the hardwood.

"It fucking is. Dammit, dammit, dammit."

"You think she's got any gold?"

"Gold? What do you think this is?"

"Like a fucking necklace or something, you moron. I'm going to check."

At least, Baby reasons, the light in the bathroom is off. But he's in the other room now, she can hear him, tossing the contents of drawers just a slice of dry wall and a half-open door away from her. She watches the faucet as a bead of water blooms, grows bigger and fatter, and she stares at it, tries to invoke some sort of higher power, a form of ESP to stop that bead of water from ballooning and dropping down, keep it from making a sound that could end her life. Tries to keep herself from imagining all the things they'll do to her if they find her there, naked in the cold water.

The house falls quiet. The men stop moving.

"Find anything?" the man in the kitchen shouts.

"Nuh," the man in the bedroom replies. "Nothing good."

She hears his feet pause on the bedroom carpet, closes her eyes and waits. Eventually they leave, or at least it sounds like they do. Baby can't be sure. Nothing drives off, and she waits until the sun rises outside the windows to turn around in the water and peek over the edge of the tub. She doesn't see anyone and moves quickly, grabs her damp sports bra and underwear from where she left them slopped on the bathroom floor, and runs into the bedroom.

She throws open a drawer and finds a Christmas onesie decorated with flying reindeer that has a hood with horns. Betty definitely won't be needing this for a few months. She zips into it and slides her feet into a pair of rubber flip-flops, then runs out the door, bouncing down the steps.

It's hot out already, too hot for the stupid costume, the heat starting to weigh on her. She knew it last night when she swam away from the island and she knows it now, walking down the steaming-hot shoulder, her feet sinking into the soft gravel. There's really only one place left for her to go. To get her fucking money.

*　　*　　*

Once she makes it out to the main road, Baby hitches a ride in the back of a pickup truck driven by two guys delivering a ride-on lawn mower up to a property north of Oakwood, close to Bad Mike's. She lies flat in the bed, staring at the sky, her body sliding back and forth around corners. When it's time to get out, she knocks on the window and the truck pulls over to the side of the road. To the naked eye, there's nothing around, just a driveway, grown over, with a *No Trespassing* sign on it, but Baby knows exactly where it is, because Crystal showed it to her once. The fact that Crystal showed her is the only reason Crystal is still alive.

Baby remembers how crazy things were back then. "If I ever disappear, that's where you send them," she said to Baby in a rare moment of clarity amid the insanity of that relationship.

"You sure this is the right place, Rudolph?" the guy calls out the window.

"Rudolph had a red nose," Baby says, pulling down the hood, ignoring the question.

The guys drive off, one of them waving out the window. Baby peers up the road, then spots it, tiny, up on a tree. A black camera perched up on a branch, peering down at the trail beneath it. She walks fifty feet back down the shoulder and enters the woods to the south. Once she's up the ditch, she picks up the flip-flops in her hands and ducks, creeping through the brush, realizes that the reindeer pajamas weren't the best idea but keeps going anyway, because she's come this far. He might not even be home. She might be able to just waltz in there and roll off with the safe. Maybe he's even opened it himself.

As she creeps through the brush, she thinks about the night Donna's father came up here to pick up Crystal. He hadn't let Baby come, but she and DJ had driven to the base of the driveway and waited, hands crushed together, slumped down in the front seat of her car, engine running. A tough year, that one. They'd begged Crystal; Baby remembers getting on the floor and grabbing her around the ankles and trying to physically restrain her from going up there. "It's just a bit of weed," Crystal would say, but they didn't believe her. The shallows under her eyes, the faraway look behind her pupils, the deadness in her voice. It was like trying to hold on to air. She hadn't OD'd, but the police chief found her locked in a closet, Bad Mike standing outside it, a crowbar in his hand, just about to get through the door.

Baby's not an idiot. But sometimes you have to act like one, she reasons as she follows the driveway, when you've got nothing to lose. A big house appears in the forest, surrounded by trees, crumbling up ahead in a clearing, a decrepit barn off to the side that looks like it used to be painted red, the remnants of the color faded, almost scrubbed completely from the wood, a big black shining pickup truck looming over the driveway, out of place compared to the sagging old house, the trembling barn that looks like even the lightest breeze could collapse it.

Bad Mike inherited it from his Uncle Chester. Chester'd been a different kind of criminal, had modeled his backwoods enterprise after a mafia movie, was seen in all the towns dotting the lake wearing a suit jacket and a gold chain. Baby doesn't think he was Italian, but he had a habit of loaning money out, then disappearing people who didn't return it, especially gamblers. Before the casino opened, he was known to run card games, bring people in who needed cash and then turn the screws.

What Baby likes about Bad Mike is that he wears his darkness frankly, doesn't pretend to be anything else.

Her feet inch forward through the brush. She doesn't really have a plan; it's not like she can just pick up the safe and walk out of there.

A dog starts barking. *Shit.* She wasn't banking on a dog. He's standing on the porch, his collar attached to a long chain, snarling, spittle flying from his mouth, demonstrating an eagerness that worries her. He sprints toward the woods and is yanked backward by his chain, squealing as the metal crushes his windpipe.

Baby crouches, hidden by the thick brush, waiting to see if anything stirs inside the house. It's quiet, dull. Maybe Bad Mike's not even home. She's about to take a deep breath and run for it when he strides outside, a shotgun casually thrown over his shoulder.

"What are you barking at?" he asks in an oddly kind voice, as if the dog is doing something incredibly adorable. A squirrel runs out of the woods and across the driveway, and the dog barks again, a cheerful, happy bark. Still a puppy. Bad Mike laughs, watching the dog's attention. The squirrel hops twice and stops, and Mike pulls his shotgun off his shoulder and fires.

The squirrel explodes. The dog stops barking.

"Great," he says, patting the dog on the head, a little too hard. "Shut up, would ya?"

Baby's hands are shaking, and she waits until the door slams behind Bad Mike to take off, running flat-out across the lawn, hears the dog straining on its chain, snarling at her. There's a jagged hole in the side of the barn, and she dives through it, panting, rolls over on her back, heart thudding in her ears, flat on the ground.

She's shocked to see the safe dumped unceremoniously in the straw, just there.

She rolls over and grabs at it, her hands sweating, heart pounding in her ears. *Think.* She really should've thought this through, how she was going to get in before she came up here. Stupid.

And then she feels hot steel against the back of her neck.

"Took you long enough," Bad Mike says.

Baby tenses, inhales sharply.

"Don't shoot me."

"I just fuckin' knew it," he says. "Baby's such a moron, she won't take a deal when it's offered, is going to wait for an opportunity to ruin her own life."

Baby rummages through her head for something to say, anything, really, to get her out of this, almost goes with *I'm pregnant* but realizes the moment she thinks it that Bad Mike doesn't have many scruples and probably would like it if she were pregnant; it would make beating her up so much more satisfying.

"Now open it," Bad Mike says.

"I don't know the combination. If I did I would've opened it when I dug it out of the lake, you fucking moron."

"I've got time," Bad Mike says. "You'll figure it out."

He pulls the shotgun back and flips open the chamber, pushes a shell into the barrel and flips it closed, pressing it to her cheek this time. She pushes back a little with her tongue, just to feel it, a blush creeping up her neck, tears muddying her vision. She really is stupid.

"Open it."

"Can't we just—"

"Fucking open it," he says. "Or I'll go get your friends and we'll see how long you hold out. Maybe I'll introduce them to Crystal. You saw her on the porch, right? I figured it made sense. Name a dumb bitch after a dumb bitch."

Baby swallows. "I don't know how."

"Well, you'd better figure it out."

She turns the dial to a random set of numbers, tries to push down the lever. Nothing.

Bad Mike drops the gun and backhands her, and Baby tastes copper, falls over swearing.

"Fuck you," she mutters, speaks to the straw. Bad Mike grabs the clump of hair at the back of her head and drags her up.

"Ugh, when was the last time you washed your hair?" he says, letting her go and swiping his hand against his jeans.

"Last night!" Baby says, indignant. The one time she isn't actually disgusting.

"I don't believe you," he says, reaching down next to her and swiping his hand against the straw. "Let's go, c'mon. It must be something to do with that resort."

Baby thinks, as the stinging on her cheek subsides. Louise and her husband. It must have something to do with them. She remembers their anniversary only because Louise would always take vacation days, leaving them without a boss, and tries the date. Nothing.

Bad Mike jams the gun against the back of her head. She wants to puke. "C'mon, Baby, I thought you were good with numbers."

"I don't really see what that has to do with it," she says. Bad Mike walks around to face her and slaps her again, on the same side of her face, and she looks at him, can't quite hide the loathing.

He laughs. "God, I've been waiting so long for this."

She spins another combination, Oakwood's address. Nothing. The first six numbers of the phone number. Nada. The last six numbers of the phone number. Nope.

Baby doesn't know what to do, can feel Bad Mike growing impatient behind her, but on a whim, she tries her own birthday, the date she picked, anyway, the day they pulled her out of the dumpster: 09-01-90. Almost a palindrome. And, to her amazement, the lock clicks. She pulls the groaning door open, has to force the hinge. Bad Mike leans down next to her, peering over her shoulder.

In her mind she pictured neat piles of bills, the way Hannah used to organize them, all facing the same way, uniformly stacked and bound with rubber bands. Instead, brown water cascades out in clumps, one of them landing on her foot. She bends down and picks it up, the lump disintegrating in her hands. Mud. That's what was in here all long. No money, no casino chips. Mud.

Baby starts laughing hysterically, picking up the clumps and squeezing them, brown droplets making tracks down her arms. What an idiot she is. A real idiot. She collapses onto the ground, sits down in the muddy pile and feels it soaking through the crotch and butt of the pajamas. Her laughter is high and uncontrollable and accompanied by tears, her fingers massaging the muck in front of her. Everyone is fucking screwed. Everyone.

Bad Mike hauls her up by the shoulder. "Shut up," he hisses, shaking her. "Shut the fuck up."

But she can't. Not really. And instead of shutting up, a snort comes out of her mouth and she closes her eyes as Bad Mike pulls the butt of the gun backward, like a fist, and brings it down on her head.

Baby cries out on impact, the dull pain making her eyes blot out. Bad Mike starts, thinking he must've knocked her out. But her head is just that thick. He shoves her down into the straw, grabs an old roll of duct tape from a ledge in the barn, and starts wrapping it around her ankles.

"What are you doing? People know I'm up here, you know; they'll wonder where I am."

"I heard that drunk you lived with is dead."

"So?" Baby says. "There are other people who'll wonder."

"Of course they will," he says, pulling her wrists up over her head and taping them to a wobbling support beam. "I'm banking on it." She follows the beam up to the rafters, sees its cragginess and the fact that it's rising tall out of the ground, but really, the roof is balancing on it, almost as if a wish is holding the entire thing together. If she so much as sneezes, there's a chance the entire structure will come crashing down all around her, burying her on this psycho's property for good.

"Don't move too much," he says, pulling his phone out of his pocket and taking a picture of her. He laughs, admiring his masterpiece, seems to be sending a text message.

She leans on the beam just a bit just to see if it moves, and it does, the entire barn groaning. A flap of particle board floats down from the ceiling and lands a few feet from her. Wonderful.

"You don't want to do that," he says, checking his cell phone. He seems to be waiting for something.

As Baby struggles to calm herself in the straw, Bad Mike sits down across from her.

"You know, your boyfriend and I aren't so different."

"You've got, like, eight tattoos and a hundred pounds on him, but sure, okay. Identical twins," she says.

"We both come from drug money," Bad Mike says.

It takes Baby a moment to realize he's referring to Peter's family's money being made in pharmaceuticals. "So?" Baby says. "He doesn't break the law."

"I don't either," Bad Mike says. Baby snorts. "I just don't follow laws I don't believe in. Not all laws serve justice."

"You nearly killed my best friend. You beat women."

"She owed me a lot of money. Still does. And you," Bad Mike says, picking up his gun and tapping her on the head with it, as if he's saying *bad Baby, bad girl,* "you're trespassing on my property."

"Peter would never physically hurt someone," says Baby.

"Because he doesn't have to. The family he was born into made sure of that. Just like the family I was born into made sure I became this. And you? You need to stop fighting it. Come work for me."

"What?" Baby says.

"Come work for me," he says. "You're unemployed. Come work for me. This is where you belong."

"Drop dead," she says.

He laughs. "You're going to have to. This town is drying up."

"I'd rather dry up then murder people."

"It's all fucking relative," he says. "If you haven't figured that out yet, you will."

From where she's sitting, she can see the driveway through the gaps in the rotting wood, and in the fading light, headlights appear, marking a tree. The whine of the engine DJ kept saying she'd get fixed in the new year announces their arrival, and Baby—well, Baby swears.

"I'm going to kill you," Baby says.

"See? You're already getting it," Bad Mike says. "You're a natural." He grabs the duct tape and wraps it around her head three times, ensuring she can't make a sound.

Crystal parks DJ's car in front of the house and gets out. Baby screams against the duct tape covering her mouth, tries to push it away with her tongue, but it's way too tight, it's taking so much effort just to breathe.

The dog goes crazy, and Baby forces herself to watch as Crystal stands and waits at the foot of the porch. Baby understands why he took the picture. And she knows now what he did with it, what Crystal's here to do. And Baby also knows that if Crystal goes through with it, it's going to fundamentally change everything about their relationship, maybe forever. Crystal stands with her arms crossed and waits and Baby starts to cry, wants to call out to her, tell her to just leave her here, to just go.

Bad Mike stands in the shadows of the barn and watches her.

"Mike!" Crystal shouts.

The dog keeps barking, snarling really, and Baby can tell Bad Mike is trying to scare her by making her wait out there, facing the dog as it spits rage in her direction. Crystal takes a few steps toward the dog, her palm up and lowered beneath its jaw. Baby can't hear her, but it sounds like she's whispering to it, smiling, so calm as she inches toward her namesake.

The dog stops barking. Crystal sits down on the bottom step and the dog lets out a little whine, its energy totally changing as Crystal smiles at it, reaches toward it, hands open and outstretched to let it sniff. Baby feels like she's going to piss her pants as she watches Crystal with the animal, just waiting for it to lunge. But the dog doesn't lunge, just leans into her hands, and she scratches behind its ears as it whines and rolls over, its legs up in the air, belly exposed.

Bad Mike chooses that moment to stroll out of the barn, and Crystal jumps off the steps and tries to look defiant, but Baby can tell she's scared, her body shrinking into itself.

"What do you want for her?" Crystal asks.

"Rude girl," Bad Mike says. "Hello, Crystal, how are you?"

"Oh, get on with it. What do you want?"

"What do you think I want?"

"I don't know, Mike, I haven't seen you in years. Maybe you want dick now. I hear prison changes a man."

The punch happens so quickly Baby doesn't have time to dread it, a swift shot to the gut. Crystal falls to her knees, doubled over, wheezing.

"I'm going to enjoy this so much," he says, and grabs Crystal by the arm and drags her toward the barn where Baby sits, crying, hands taped over her head, too terrified to move.

"Baby's going to love it!" he shouts, a perverse joy. The dog starts barking again behind them, and Baby wants to think it's because the animal knows the right and the wrong of the situation. The worst thing about Bad Mike, Baby thinks, is that he's not crushing Baby, he's not going to touch her, because he knows crushing her is easy. Baby already knows she's worthless. It's taking something Baby thinks is wonderful and true and honest and good and tearing it apart in front of her—that's the torture of it.

Mike drags Crystal in front of Baby, on parade, and Baby screams again through the duct tape, the muffled sound so small and ridiculous. Crystal sees her in the dirt and the straw and Baby tries, so desperately, to send her a message. *Just leave me here, just go. Don't do this. Stop it.* She's not worth it. Not worth it by a long shot.

Crystal stares defiantly. Mike squeezes her arm and she cries out. Baby's body starts to tremble so hard the beam starts to sway. "Try not to wreck the place." Mike drags Crystal off toward the house and Baby starts to sob in earnest, doing her best to keep her hands steady, because if the building collapses around her and she's crushed by a falling beam, then what Crystal is about to do will be in vain.

27

Hours later, Crystal walks out of the house, alone, right eye swollen shut, blood dried under her nose, white Keds dangling from her fingers. She tosses them onto the hood of DJ's car and limps across the mottled lawn to where Baby sits. She gets down on her knees in front of Baby's ankles and uses the car keys to slice the duct tape in half, ripping it as it goes. Baby wants to ask her if she's okay, but her mouth is covered and Crystal makes no move to tear it away.

Once Baby's ankles are free, Crystal moves to her wrists, tied to the beam, letting out a little sigh, the exhaustion so pent up inside her Baby can feel it coming out of her in shakes. Baby's hands come free and Crystal stands up, turns around, and walks toward the car without a word.

Baby follows, unsure if she's allowed to get in the car or not. The house behind them is quiet. The dog is nowhere to be seen. Baby tries the handle on the front seat. The door opens and she gets in. Crystal stands at the front of the car, staring off into the woods, looking at nothing. Baby doesn't know how long she stands there, staring. It feels like years. Eventually she gets in and they set off, driving slowly down the path, the car creeping around potholes. Baby starts pulling the duct tape away from her mouth, wincing as the tiny hairs on the back of her neck are yanked away.

"Don't say anything," Crystal says, when Baby tries to open her mouth. "Just shut up. Why are you dressed like a reindeer?"

"It's a long story," Baby says.

"Is it true?" Crystal asks, her words falling flat.

"What?"

"That the safe was empty?"

Baby wishes she could lie to Crystal and tell her she found the money, that everyone will be okay, that they'll get through the winter and there's nothing to worry about. That there's a future here. But instead she just tells the truth.

"Yes," Baby says.

Crystal exhales and closes her eyes, banging her forehead against the steering wheel. She takes the corners from memory. They've been driving these roads for so long, Baby would trust her to get her home in a whiteout.

"It'll be okay," Baby says, and Crystal lets out a bitter laugh.

"How?" Crystal says, her voice turned hard. She hasn't spoken like this since her mother died, since they lost her for a little while.

"We always figure it out."

"We've never in our lives fucked anything up as royally as we have. You know, Peter told Amelia it was all our fault. No one got paid last night. I mean, she was shit-faced, sure, but she refused, and Peter drove us all back. She's going to sell. And it'll take them years to rebuild it, years before we get our jobs back."

Baby sighs and sinks down in the car, pressing a hand to her forehead. "Peter told her?"

"We could go to prison, Baby. What's stopping her from pressing charges?"

"I'll talk to him."

Crystal doesn't say anything to that, lets out a small *tch* sound, gives a shake of her head.

"I'm pregnant," Crystal says.

"What?" Baby asks, shocked. "You're what? Did Mike not use a condom or something?"

"No, you idiot," Crystal says. "It's Johnny's. And I'm keeping it. If it's still in there. Mike was . . ."

"Crystal, I'm—"

"I don't want an apology, Baby," Crystal says. "I want my fucking job back. I want my child to have a future. I'm not having this kid in prison."

"You're not going to prison," Baby says. "Don't be stupid."

"I'm not being stupid," Crystal says. Baby shuts up then, slumps down in the passenger seat even farther, sticks a finger in the tiny cavern imprinted into the door, what was probably once meant to be an ashtray, back when this car was made. "You weren't there. You didn't see Amelia. She was . . . furious."

Baby watches as they drive past Oakwood, caution tape strung up across the driveway to keep unsuspecting tourists without a sense of smell from wandering into the shit-filled bog. *I tried*, Baby reasons. *At least I fucking tried.*

Crystal keeps on into town. Baby forgot to ask where they're going, but Crystal clearly has something in mind when she pulls the car up in front of the Legion. DJ sits on a parking slab, an empty bottle of wine next to her, a double bottle of Copper Moon Shiraz, $11.99, and she runs over to Crystal as they pull up, wraps her in a hug that lifts her off the ground.

Baby stands there in the stupid costume, staring at the gravel, waiting for DJ to open her mouth. Instead of talking, she slaps Baby across the head.

"Ow!"

"What the hell is wrong with you?" DJ shouts.

"I didn't—"

"Clearly," DJ says.

"Why didn't you just call Donna?" Baby shouts.

"Because he sent us a text saying he was going to fucking kill you, idiot, if we called Donna," DJ says. "God. We should've. We fucking should've let him." Baby's not sure she's ever seen DJ this drunk, especially in the daylight.

"The safe—"

"Fuck the safe!" DJ shouts. "We don't all have the luxury of hope, Baby! God. Crystal is pregnant. I have a goddamn dream. We need practical solutions and here you are, trying to gamble our futures on sunken treasure. Gamble your life! Does it mean so little to you?"

"DJ," Baby says. "I was doing it for you."

"Well, stop it," she shouts. She walks up to Baby and shoves her, hands on either side of her shoulders, pushes her back down into the gravel. Baby goes down hard, the stones eating into her hands. She stays on the ground and DJ kicks up the rocks, a shower of tiny pebbles bouncing off her.

"Do you know what you put everyone through last night? We thought you'd drowned yourself," DJ shouts. "And then we find out you sold us all out to the guy you've been fucking who just made you waitress at a party at his parents' house. You should've seen the look on Amelia's face when he told her. We've always had your back, Baby, always. Us. We're here. Where is he? Huh? Where the hell is he?"

The words are slurred, her eyes glassy, tears spilling onto her cheeks.

Baby studies her palms, picks at the sharp little rocks embedded in the skin, blood blooming around them. It hurts. It really fucking hurts. She pinches one between her fingers, watches as the red bead gets bigger and bigger, the pebble still stuck, probably getting pushed deeper into her hands. Maybe she'll never get them out.

"Look at me," DJ says. Baby can't, she just sits there, picking at the rocks. "Amelia's in there and she's got a deal for you, and you'd better take it because if you don't, she's pressing charges."

"DJ," Crystal says, grabbing her by the shoulder. "Let's just go." DJ gets in the front seat of the car and slams the door so hard it bounces open again. Crystal gets into the driver's seat next to her and turns on the engine. Baby waits for her to put it in gear, but instead, the passenger side door opens and Baby hears DJ puke.

When the coughing stops, the door slams and the two of them drive off together, leaving Baby alone in the parking lot, sitting next to a puddle of purple vomit that's already seeping through the gravel.

Crystal, pregnant. Amelia inside the Legion, of all places. Baby should go in, she knows she should. But she can't, really, not yet, and instead lies down in the parking lot and presses her body together like she's trying to disappear and closes her eyes and thinks about trying to evaporate.

And Baby can't help but be a little pissed off because no one seems to remember that it was Louise who up and sold the place, just left them there without any notice. It wasn't Baby. Sure, maybe Louise tried to do some short-term looking out, but she could've warned them. Could've given them some time over the winter to decide what they wanted to do. Instead she fucking up and left without any warning. And Baby's the bad guy for trying to hold it all together?

Baby can't really find it in herself to go inside, where there are likely witnesses waiting for her, a scene ready to unfold, so she just waits and waits and eventually Amelia comes out.

She's really overdressed for the temperature, wearing her fancy jeans and high heels and a blazer, and when she sees Baby sitting down there on the parking block, she lets out a scoff. Baby knows she's probably got bruises now from Bad Mike slapping her around, knows she's got mud streaks. She doesn't even have shoes. She's wearing a dirty reindeer onesie. And this woman, standing over her. Baby sits up on the parking slab, feels like she's in high school again.

"So."

"So," says Baby.

"Here's the thing," Amelia says. "We're going to rebuild."

"What?" Baby says.

"The place needed it and insurance is going to work out, so why not, right?" Amelia says, smiling, Baby wants to disappear, just totally dissolve. "Then I can actually build something that's mine."

"Oh," says Baby.

"So here's the deal," she says. "As a thank-you, I'm going to let you push the button."

"Huh?" says Baby. "What button?"

"The button," she says. "I'm going to let you demolish it."

The button. The button. This is the deal. Baby can see it clearly now. It's all a manipulation, a sick manipulation. Amelia is going to win and she's going to do it by making Baby destroy the only place she's ever really loved.

"And in return, you'll keep everyone out of prison?"

"Yes," says Amelia. "Though if you think any of you will ever work for me, you've got another thing coming."

"Fine, deal."

"Oh, there's just one more thing," she says. Baby grimaces and wants to close her eyes but finds it in her, somehow, to look up at Amelia, look at her face.

"What?"

"You never speak to my brother again."

Amelia doesn't wait for a reply. She's too satisfied. She knows she has her. It's Baby's friends or Peter, who never loved her well enough. Baby has to choose. Amelia walks off, leaving her there alone on the parking slab as the sky darkens in front of her.

Baby stares down at her bare feet, covered in dirt, nearly black, the flip-flops long lost somewhere up at Bad Mike's. She could try walking back to Betty's place, but it's mostly gravel road, which would eat into the bottoms of her feet. They would probably be bloody by the time she got there, would resemble her bloody palms.

Eventually Donna drives by and squawks her horn at Baby, unrolls the window. "You know you're not supposed to loiter," Donna says.

"Can I get a ride?" Baby asks instead, feels shameless now, as if there's nothing she can do that's worse, so why not relax into being a burden?

"Where to?" Donna asks. "Where are you living these days?"

Baby pauses, remembers the break-in at Betty's, doesn't want to implicate herself, chooses a neighbor next to Betty, Randolph Hayes, who definitely wouldn't take her in.

"Randolph said I could stay with him for a few days."

Donna gives her a once-over and Baby can tell she knows she's hearing a lie, but shrugs, nods with her head to the side door. Baby climbs in and slumps down in the front seat, staring very intently out the window, willing Donna to stop asking her questions.

"Where's Judy?" she asks.

"It's her night off. How did Crystal get that black eye?" Donna asks, cutting to the chase.

"I don't know," Baby says reflexively and feels like she's back in the principal's office, covering for Crystal for the eightieth time she skipped bio to make out with whatever turd had called her a slut that week.

"Really? I find that surprising," says Donna as she turns off the main road and down the gravel spit toward Betty's. Baby really could've walked, fuck her feet. They're callused enough. She could've handled it. It'd be better than this.

"You know, I was talking to Tippie the other day."

"You don't say," Baby says, slumped, looking out the window.

"She says the septic thing was really strange, that it looked almost deliberate."

"Why would she say that?" Baby asks, cursing Tippie and her gossiping. People never fucking change; they really don't. Baby's starting to wonder if this town is worth saving.

"I don't know," Donna says. "Does Crystal want to press charges?"

"Is my name Crystal?" Baby asks, and it comes out harsh and angry and mean, and she knows this was what it was like in high school, the angry outbursts, Baby taking out her feelings on people who didn't know how to stick up for themselves. To her credit, Donna pulls over this time, still a ways out from Betty's, and there's probably a good mile of road for Baby to walk alone, through the darkness.

"I think this is far enough," Donna says. And even though Baby could find the way to Betty's after drinking an entire bottle of tequila, stumbling drunk, she's afraid as she steps out of the car and slams the door behind her, doesn't bother to say thank-you and sets out, blinking her eyes into focus, back down the road to Betty's house.

28

Baby raids Betty's cupboards while the sun rises, sidestepping the mess the junkies left when they broke in, deciding that it really doesn't matter if she gets implicated in this. She's already so deep in shit, it's hard to care about yet another thing. She opens a can of beans into a frying pan, scrapes freezer burn off three pieces of bread that brown in the toaster, covers all of it with sloppy hunks of old margarine and carries it down to the water. So many springs, so many nights in June spent lying on the end of this dock on her stomach, her arms crossed under her chin, waiting for the lights to turn on at Pomoroy Island.

She remembers the feeling, the mix of excitement and dread and this ridiculous hope, looking down the barrel of summer, of all that might happen to them once they were together again. It was like waking up from a long nap.

Baby's stomach aches as she finishes the food and knows she needs a life. She needs more. And she needs a shower. She strips off the giant T-shirt she stole from Betty and jumps into the lake, her plate of toast and beans half-finished on the dock. She dives down to the bottom and rubs at her body with sand, under her pits, her tits, her crotch, trying to slough off yesterday, trying to leave it all behind.

Crystal's face, the set of it, the exhaustion of it, the *this again* way her shoulders scrunched up to her ears. Baby rubs and rubs, thinking of that look in her eyes, and realizes she's rubbing her thigh too hard. She pushes up to the surface again and takes a deep breath and all she can think of is Peter.

She doesn't know how to escape him. It feels like the only way out is to charge through him. How can you end something that might've never existed? She wishes she could see it the way DJ does, she really wants to. To be able to hate him. But she just can't. She can't.

She pulls herself up onto the dock and finishes the rest of her toast in her underwear, lake water dripping onto the beans in plops. The sun screams at her from the horizon. It's impossibly beautiful. Maybe now is the time.

She hasn't so much as looked at her and Hannah's old cabin since she moved out, knows it's empty and abandoned. She's strangely nervous as she pads through the forest, the tiny building looking so much smaller than she remembers it. The door is open, just by an inch, and she pokes her head in, listens to the quiet. "Hello?" she calls. Waits.

The kitchen sits quiet, snugged up against the tiny sitting room, facing the ancient television. Hannah wouldn't give it up. Their ratty blue couch is still in there. The old black cast-iron pan hangs on its nail next to the stove. Everything else is gone.

Baby steps inside, the floor creaking beneath her. She looks up and the pine needles are so thick on the skylight that barely any light is getting in. What a fucking dump. She walks to her room, the tiny room where she slept on her single bed her entire life, and reaches up into the closet. Hannah, the remains they gave her after she was cremated, handed to her in thick plastic, sits up there, abandoned. She grabs the bag, feels the weight of her. It's nauseating.

Baby runs out of the cabin. It was too small in the winters. Couldn't contain Baby's confusion and Hannah's misery. The couch had two cushions on it. If they sat down next to each other, their bodies would touch. Neither of them really knew what to do when they did. Baby still remembers nights, their thighs pressed together, watching reality shows where people chased their dreams on that old TV, wineglasses dangling from their fingers, slumping in opposite directions. They never talked about getting a new couch, though. Not ever.

Baby feels like an asshole because she can't afford an urn, a vase, something nicer than this for Hannah. A mantel to put it on, a candle to burn next to it. That's what you're supposed to do, right?

She jogs back down to the dock. It isn't much. But it is a sunrise. Hannah'd stay up for them sometimes. "It's free," she'd mutter, gesturing with a thumb, embarrassed that Baby'd caught her admiring beauty. As if she weren't good enough for it.

Baby upends the entire bag into the lake, watches the clumps slowly dissipate. Hannah loved the lake. Baby wishes she could've gotten them a boat. A canoe, maybe. That would've suited their relationship. Hannah in the back, steering. Baby up front, doing all the work.

Instead, Hannah stayed on the edges, sometimes dipping her feet in. Baby doesn't think she ever saw her swim.

If she still had a cell phone, she'd be able to check the time. Baby knows it'll take her a while to get into town, especially if she's walking. There isn't anyone up here who'd give her a ride. She's sure of it. It's probably time to go.

Baby sighs and stands up. She's got to go blow up her home now. She's got to go push that button.

*　*　*

Everyone is waiting for Baby when she arrives; at least that's what it seems like. The crowds of people all standing behind a line of cones; Amelia wearing heels and jeans in the sweltering heat, a construction vest over her blazer. There's a crew of burly men Baby doesn't recognize ready to clear the property. Baby thinks it's a bit ridiculous, really. Amelia probably had to get permits, everything, all for this stupid little bit of humiliation, of revenge. Baby stands at the foot of the driveway wearing a pair of knee-length cotton shorts and a tie-dyed T-shirt with the logo of a local animal shelter on the back, a fund raiser Baby vaguely remembers attending herself. On her feet, a pair of broken Crocs held together by duct tape. The clothes Betty wouldn't want, that's what she was going for, and hopes she didn't accidentally take her dead husband's favorite shoes.

Crystal and Johnny stand next to DJ, all of them hiding behind sunglasses and passive expressions, though Baby thinks it's probably because they're all trying not to cry. They all did a lot of living in here together.

"You're late," Amelia says. Baby shrugs. She doesn't have a watch or a phone. She might as well be naked, standing there.

"Sorry," she says. Marco is standing over on the edge of the hill at the top of the driveway, staring out at the lake, a beer in his hand, another one in his back pocket. He looks thin, his jeans bagging down around his hips.

"We're ready when you are," Amelia says. Baby takes a deep breath and gags, just a little. The smell of the sewage is really overpowering, the sweet scent of rot. A pack of mosquitoes hovers low over the field between the crowd and the building. It's so thick, Baby can see now that the property probably could never be recovered in its current state. How do you clean up a mess like this? She could smell it before she arrived. It makes sense now, that the building has to come down, the lawn dug up and fresh sod laid. All of what was old, gone forever.

Amelia steps up next to Baby and passes her the button. The button is blue. She thought it would be red. They're usually red.

"Does anyone want to say anything?" Baby says to the crowd, to her friends. No one does. Baby feels like she should say something to this place, a farewell, but she thinks maybe everyone else has closure, or maybe to everyone else this wasn't a home at all, just a place to go for a little while to make some money, just a job. Maybe it didn't really mean anything.

"Thanks for the memories!" she shouts, to no one, to the building, and her thumb presses down before she loses it. At first she thinks it didn't work, but then she hears the click and watches as the building starts to collapse from the inside.

The crowd has a strange energy about it, as if people are thinking they should start clapping, all of them hovering on the edge. No one does.

She swipes a tear away from her cheek and hands the button back to Amelia. "I want you to pay everyone for the catering job." She says this loudly and publicly, trying to get at least a bit of an acknowledgment from her friends, from her people, that she's trying, she's trying so fucking hard, to do the right thing.

"Oh, yes, I brought checks," Amelia says, opening up her purse, deflating Baby's balloon. She's not painting herself as the enemy, not anymore. Instead, she's responsible. An employer. The best thing you can do for a town. Employ people who live there. Baby doesn't need to fight for the people against her. She brought checks. She'll be creating jobs soon. She's going to rebuild.

"Well, good," Baby says.

"Here's yours," says Amelia. "I put a little extra in there, for the delay." Baby takes it and looks around at everyone else, slowly walking over to Amelia, hands out, ready to get paid.

They take their money and leave without any ceremony. DJ, Crystal, Marco, Johnny. Baby knows they're probably all heading to the bank to immediately deposit the money to move it onto credit cards, into the hands of landlords, grocery store clerks, the Legion. No one speaks to her.

Baby stays, alone. She stands up at the top of the driveway and admires the view, a pile of rubble now where the building used to be. Oakwood Hills extinguished from the horizon, making way for the lake and the trees. It really is the most beautiful place. It makes her think of Louise, and how incredible it was that she got to own this spot, even if just for a little while.

Stupid Louise. Why couldn't she just give them more time? Just a little bit more? Baby would never have had to hate Amelia and she and Peter would be together, probably, a least for a few more months.

And the thing that really confuses Baby, that's been bothering her, is this question: Why was her birthday the combination to the safe?

She laughs. Stupid.

Does it really matter anyway? Oakwood is done, and Baby has nothing left. Literally nothing but the check from Amelia in her pocket. She turns away from the remains of the building and starts walking along the shoulder, her feet in the Crocs, sweating, pebbles immediately entering every hole. The sun beats down on her neck. It's a check, but, Baby reasons, she can probably cash it at the liquor store.

She starts thinking of Peter and all the places they had sex. In his boat. In the woods. In literally every room at Oakwood. Showers. Bushes. Trees. On grass. In the quarry. In her bed. In Hannah's bed. In her bathroom. She's lost track of how many times. Just how many. And now he's sold her out to his psycho sister.

She's stopped to empty the stones from her Crocs when a car pulls up beside her on the shoulder, hears a power window unrolling. Baby doesn't look up, waits for the voice, worry descending. It's Betty. "You want a ride?" she asks, leaning out.

"Sure," Baby says.

"Where to?" Betty asks.

"Just heading into town," she says. "Gotta cash this check."

"Okeydoke," says Betty. Baby climbs into the car and she takes off, gravel spitting out from behind the tires.

"You squatting in my house?" Betty asks.

"No," says Baby. "No. Someone broke in, though."

"Someone?"

"I forgot a few things in the cabin. And when I got there, your place was trashed."

"Trashed how?"

"Junkies looking for shit to sell," Baby says. Betty doesn't sound like she believes her. Baby doesn't care. Coming after her won't mean anything. Betty doesn't hate her enough to throw her in prison over a cheese grater.

"Are those my Crocs?" she asks. "And my shirt? And my shorts?"

"Sorry," says Baby, kicking the shoes off. "It's been a weird couple of days."

"It's fine, keep them," Betty says, and turns into the liquor store parking lot. Liquor store, dollar store, convenience store. "I'm trying to sell, so if you don't mind . . ."

"Yeah, got it," Baby says, sliding her feet back into the Crocs because she knows she'll need them to buy the two-four she's going to drink this afternoon. The liquor store enforces their no shirt, no shoes, no service rule, which Baby has learned the hard way many times before. She remembers one particular summer night a few years ago when she and Peter had to wait outside and borrow shoes from Tippie just so they could grab a six-pack.

"What are you going to do now?" Betty asks, pulling onto the shoulder in town, putting on her blinker.

"What do you mean?" Baby asks.

"Now that Oakwood is shut down?"

"It's a little early to be asking that question, isn't it?" Baby gets out of the car and slams the door. Because fuck her. Fuck 'em all.

She charges into the liquor store and grabs twenty-four cans of PBR, gets in line to cash her check. Earl looks up at her over his glasses, cryptic as ever. "Another one?"

"Yes, please," she says. He sighs and looks at the check.

"You got ID?"

"You know it's me, Earl," she says. "Come on."

"Fine," he says. "Fine. Here. Just take it." He slides three hundred-dollar bills over to her and flips the check over for her to sign. "I don't think I can break a hundred," he says.

"You just gave it to me," Baby says.

"You're going to take all my change."

"Just sell me the fucking beer," Baby shouts, losing it. The liquor store goes quiet around her, and everything seems to stop and zoom in on her. Baby closes her eyes. "Sorry," she says.

"It's all going to be fives," says Earl, as if Baby could possibly give a shit about that at this moment.

"Fine," says Baby. "It's all fine." Earl counts out the fives, putting them in little rows, just like Hannah used to do. Baby feels the tears start coming and grabs the wad of cash before he even finishes dishing it out, shoves it into her bra and grabs the two-four, and the second she's outside, she sets it down on the edge of a trash can, rips it open, and cracks a beer. It's warm and thick and it seems to shove itself down her throat. She finishes it in one, tosses the empty can over her shoulder and starts walking.

Because of the stupid way she ripped open the box, she has to carry it in a sloppy hug to keep the cans inside. She waddles down the side of the highway and makes it to the public beach, which is almost always empty because it's the shittiest one on the lake.

It has an old lifeguard chair, from the glory days of the town of Lakeside. It sits rusted out and tall, and Baby lifts the case of beer up over her head and puts it down on the seat, then climbs up, her back to the road behind her, to anyone who might be passing by. Once she settles in, eyes on the horizon, she starts to drink in earnest.

Baby knows that with beer, for her anyway, it's harder to get blackout hammered, the kind of drunk she wants right now, but it'll knock her out for longer. It's the speed that matters, and she's never had a problem with finishing. Snap open, chug, then huck the can into the water. Some of them sink, landing properly, spout down, and the lake sucks them beneath the surface, but others bob in the waves, end up washed back onto the beach in front of her.

Six beers in, she starts laughing, laughing at these cans that, for all her effort, won't go away! Some trash you can't avoid, can you? Can you? She wants to scream, to sob, to explode, and instead she just slumps. She can see, from this vantage point, the remains of Oakwood Hills, perched up high on its cliff, to the east. And to the west, Pomoroy Island, the peak of the cottage jutting out through the trees.

Baby pictures Amelia now, sitting in her fucking hot tub, Jasper gone, back to the world to make money, her tormentor disappeared, just relaxing, eyes closed, savoring this victory, counting her cash and probably investing it in something that will make her richer while the rest of them stay here to rot. Maybe Lakeside will disappear.

All because of a worthless Dumpster Baby and her idiotic dreams about what she could be.

Baby watches clouds blow over her head, the blue sky shift toward gray. It might've been subtle; she's nine beers in. Who knows? Clouds arrive and the skies grows even darker. Baby keeps chucking her empty cans into the lake and thinks about never speaking to Peter again, which gives her this feeling in her throat that's a little bit like being strangled.

It's easy for DJ to diagnose their relationship. She knows because DJ is standing back and looking at a house she's never been inside of. She doesn't know what really goes on. It's easy to condemn something you only know the worst parts of. Baby knows this.

But there was this moment last summer when she was sure. She was sure it was some sort of turning point. It was closing time at the Parrot. Just a normal Thursday night. Baby was staffed on bar and had to stay relatively sober. Peter showed up alone and sat in front of her all night, only venturing out to the dance floor when Crystal dragged him, threw him at a bachelorette party, literally shoving him into a pack of, like, twenty women. The women were all in their forties and Baby stood there and laughed and laughed, and when he arrived back at the bar, she spotted a red lipstick kiss on his cheek and she could barely breathe, tears were running down her face, and she watched him as he got drunker and drunker.

And there was something nervous about him, the way he'd stared at her and slumped on the bar and kept ordering beers, and every time she looked up from what she was doing—cutting a lime, mixing a drink, pulling a pint—he was looking at her with a dreamy expression.

When they left the bar after closing, she brought them a few more drinks and they lay down in his boat and talked about different versions of the future. "Okay," she remembers saying. "Mine is a farm, where there's bears that live on the property, but they want to be there, like every night they walk themselves into a pen and close the latch behind them and I just get to stand there and watch them all day, feed them spaghetti and stuff."

"But who would make the spaghetti?" he slurred. "You can't make anything."

"I can make, like, every cocktail in existence," she said.

"I can make the spaghetti," he said. "It would be my pleasure."

"Oh, thank you," she said.

He was so drunk. She knows he was so drunk. But it's not like he didn't mean it when he grabbed her face in his hands and held it so their eyes were only inches apart and somehow managed to stare into both of them at once. And he held her and stared, and she felt so much like he was trying to force her to take him seriously. "I'll make the spaghetti."

Then he turned away and threw up over the side of the boat.

And throughout all their years together, Baby can think of hundreds of tiny moments like this, where he said something to her, tried to get her to decode a riddle, and whenever she feels like a giant idiot, she just lies down and thinks about all these tiny moments, strung together on a line, and when she does it, she can't see anything but a love story complicated by the fact that she was born in a dumpster and he was born in a really fancy hospital.

Thunder seems to break open the sky before her, and Baby, on her nineteenth beer, the case crumpled beneath her on the lifeguard chair, sits and watches as rain dumps out of the sky, as if her entire life is the trough outside a bar and all the gods are having a piss.

The wind kicks up, the waves coming in and crashing against the beach, the water actually lapping at the earth beneath the lifeguard chair, eating at it. It's very dramatic and Baby clambers down, stumbles onto the beach and thinks about Hannah as she wades into the shallows and pulls off her shorts and starts peeing in the lake. A wave hits her and she falls over.

The world spins. She ends up on the shore on all fours, her ass out, and the puke comes out water and it lands in the waves, foaming, as if her mouth is a tap. She pukes and pukes until the liquid has exited her body, and still just so unbelievably drunk, she falls backward, trying to sink. But the lake doesn't want her, no one fucking wants her, and the waves just throw her back up on the sand. She tries to stand up again and can't.

Thunder crackles in the air, the wind whipping the sound all around her. She screams out at the water, first to the east at Oakwood Hills and then to the west at Pomoroy Island. Why isn't he coming for her? If he loves her, why has he left her here in her own piss? And it's DJ who taunts her in her mind. *He never wanted to make your spaghetti*, she says.

"Yes, he did!" Baby screams so loudly her throat aches. The rain starts to fall thicker, and suddenly she can't see anything in front of her anymore. No Oakwood. No Pomoroy Island. All of it erased, just a towering wall of falling water. She lies down on the ground and shimmies into the shorts, taking all manner of sand with her, and stands up, doesn't even know what direction she's moving in, the entire world is shifting around in front of her, the ground underneath her tilting left to right as she tries to take steps away from the lake.

She trips, flies into a flat-out sprawl on the side of the road, all the air sucked from her body, and just lies there, and really, honestly, she doesn't know if the ground is on her face or on the back of her head. She is just so, so drunk. And it's the obliteration of any kind of reality, it's like a death, and she rolls over and pukes and it tries to run down the back of her throat, and she at least has the experience to roll over onto her side and puke again, this time away from her throat. She lies there for a long time, counts the cars that roll past, that don't stop. She must know the people inside of them, rain still splattering on their windshields, falling in flat splotches on her cheeks.

Eventually, she gets up onto her knees, weakness and pain and her head, oh god, her head. Somehow she stands up and takes two steps. Then another two steps.

She finds her way back to the liquor store, which is now closed, the parking lot empty, and she thinks maybe she was lying on the side of the road for longer than it felt like, because it's dark outside and it wasn't dark outside before. And the rain is still falling. There isn't even an awning in sight to keep her dry.

She laughs when she sees it, feels like a pocket of sunshine has opened up over her head and is pointing her toward home. Where else is there to go? Nowhere. No one wants her. No one will take her. She could probably stumble up to Bad Mike's front door and he wouldn't even hire her to sell fucking meth. What's left?

She drags her feet across the parking lot, the line she walks a staggered zigzag of too many steps, and when she gets there and opens the dumpster, the smell is terrible and overwhelming and she almost throws up. But the lid can be propped up and still give a little bit of cover and she rolls into it and lies down against the garbage bags and the trash and thinks to herself, well, outside of what garbage is—you know, stuff thrown out, unwanted—it's not like this is uncomfortable. It's not a terrible place for a Baby to be, not really. There are worse places for a Baby to end up.

29

There's a loud banging and a bright light in her eyes, and she screams and sits up so quickly she hits her head on the dumpster lid and then swears and lies back down. "What the fuck," she shouts.

"What are you doing in here, Baby?" It's Deputy Donna. She moves the light and Baby sits up again, slower this time, blinking. It's the middle of the night. She's surprised at how sober she feels. Probably all the puking. Donna turns off her flashlight.

"You got any water?" Baby asks, her voice coming out in a ridiculous croak, as if she's aged seventy years in a single drunken afternoon.

"Get out of the dumpster," Donna says, and Baby moves so slowly, every muscle in her body complaining, straining against it, as if she's damaged the connection that exists between her limbs and her brain, something she probably would've learned about in biology had she ever actually attended class. She collapses onto the pavement, slumped over her body, pressing her back against the dumpster, panting.

"Water. Please?" Baby asks, bending forward, her stomach cramping. Donna walks back to the cruiser, opens the trunk, and pulls out a bottle. She hands it to Baby and Baby rips the lid off and chugs the entire thing, feeling so entirely desperate she keeps sucking.

"Baby, even you're not stupid enough to sleep in an open dumpster in bear country."

"Oh, try me," she says. "I think I'm exactly that stupid."

"How much have you had to drink?" Donna asks.

"Not enough," Baby says, tipping her head back against the dumpster, fighting the rising tide of nausea that's growing as the water works its way into her body, her insides confused by this foreign liquid. The dumpster doesn't even really smell to her anymore. Hot garbage has been cooking for weeks in a tight metal box and here she is, not even able to smell it. People can get used to anything. She wonders if maybe her mother leaving her in a dumpster was just her giving Baby a reprieve from a much worse life. She'll never really know, will she?

Baby presses her hands into her eyes.

"Where are you supposed to be tonight, Baby?" Donna asks. Baby just laughs.

"Nowhere," says Baby. "Nowhere is where I'm supposed to be. I don't have a job. I don't have a home. Where are you supposed to be?"

"I'm supposed to be here," Donna says.

"Just leave me alone," Baby says. "Go catch a real criminal."

"All right, get up," Donna says, reaching down and grabbing her by the arm, and when Baby doesn't even bother trying to help her, she gets down in a squat and lifts her up underneath her armpits like a toddler. Baby lets her knees buckle, crumpling her body down to the ground, lying, splayed out. It's not raining anymore but the ground is still wet.

"Baby, why do you do this?" she asks.

"You can't arrest me for trespassing in a garbage can; that's my home!" Baby shouts. Maybe she is still drunk. "I was just visiting my parents." She cracks up.

"Baby, come on, let's go get you some dry clothes and a shower."

"This is about the tuna water!" Baby shouts.

"No, this is about your well-being," Donna replies.

"I think it's probably both," Baby says, then whispers to herself, "but mostly about the tuna water."

"I can hear you," Donna says, sitting down on the wet pavement next to her. "I mean, sure, I don't think there's anyone in the world who would like having tuna water thrown at them."

"I didn't throw it at you," Baby says. "I put it down the back of your gym shirt."

"No, that was Antonella," says Donna. "Don't you remember when you filled up the water gun with tuna water?"

Baby searches her memory. "That was tuna water? I thought it was red food coloring."

"Tuna water dyed with red food coloring. I really enjoyed walking around with everyone thinking I had blood on my butt. That was a great day."

"I'm sorry," says Baby. "I mean, it's a little bit funny."

"No, it's not."

"But, like, if you saw it in a movie, you might laugh at it," says Baby.

"I don't think I would," says Donna.

Baby wants to scream into her fists and instead spreads her arms out wide. "Well, take a big fat look at me now, Donna, then," she says. "Because this is my comeuppance. Enjoy it."

Baby feels Donna measuring her up, deciding if she should say anything else or just load her into the backseat of the cruiser and throw her in a cell.

"Baby, you know why I still hate you?"

"Because I'm a hot bitch with a rich boyfriend," Baby mumbles. Definitely drunk. She tips over, her elbow hitting the concrete sideways, and gives in to it, folding her body in a full fetal position. Donna starts laughing at her, shamelessly.

"Not that," Donna says. "But close. I hate you because everyone covers for you. Everyone. You should probably be in prison. If these rumors about the safe and the septic are true, well, I'd definitely like to know more about that. But seriously. Everyone in this town has your back. Every single person. And what really gets me is that you don't even seem to notice them. You act like your life is so tragic and terrible when the reality is, you're actually really lucky."

"I don't feel very lucky right now," Baby says. "I'm licking pavement." She sticks out her tongue and touches it to the moist rock.

"This is just a blip," says Donna.

"Is it a blip? Or is this the beginning of a very big fucking spiral? Is it the end?" Baby presses her forehead against the concrete.

"You were born in a dumpster," Donna says. "That doesn't mean—"

"And to the dumpster I return!" Baby interrupts, standing up and grabbing hold of the edge of the metal box, hanging on to it for dear life. It really does smell disgusting.

"Oh, just stop that," Donna says. "Come back to the station and have a shower. You can sleep in the holding cell."

"This is a trap and I'm not falling for it," says Baby, one leg up on the edge of the stinking metal box.

"I'm not going to book you for passing out in a dumpster. Half this town would have a charge if that was the case. Come on." Donna leaves Baby, her hands clutching the rusty metal edge, staring down at the imprint of her adult body in the trash bags. The station probably has hot water, she reasons. And food. Baby's stomach gurgles. She counts to three, then turns and limps toward the police car.

*   *   *

Donna helps her into the shower, turns it on hot, and leaves Baby alone to sit, legs crossed, puking directly into the drain. It's almost fascinating to watch the yellow and white globs appears and then disappear through the vent in the floor, gone forever. Washed away.

She empties and fills her stomach with water about nine hundred times during the shower, leaning back against the warm tiles on the walls until she starts to feel a little bit like a human being again.

Donna left her a towel, a sweat suit a few sizes too big, and gray work socks, and Baby gratefully puts it all on, even though it's a hot, soggy summer night, and she slides out into the empty station, where Donna sits at a desk, lit by a single amber pool of light, right next to an oversized radio, her head in her hands. Stacks of paper and junk pile up on either side of her and she's staring at a map of the area, the lake all flayed out and blue, extending in about eight directions, its arms thin and spindly as if it were a person trying to grab hold of eight things at once.

"Thanks," Baby says, and Donna nods, lost in thought. "Everything okay?"

"Three ODs in Westfield County," Donna says.

"Where's that?" Baby asks.

"Just north of Dorset."

"Shit," says Baby.

"Two of them are kids, one is in critical condition," says Donna. "Shit is right."

"It's not your fault."

"When the only known drug kingpin in six counties is on my turf, it is," says Donna. "Just a little bit."

"What do you need to arrest him?"

"He's on probation, so anything really. But what I want is the supplier," she says. "That's why I've held off, because I wanted to see if he would show his hand at all."

"Right," says Baby.

"I know he's cooking, but I don't know where, and I don't know how he's getting the materials."

"I was up on his property," Baby volunteers. "Just a few days ago. There wasn't anyone there but a dog."

Donna sits back in her chair, her finger tapping against her cheek, lost in thought. "What would you do?"

"Huh?" Baby asks, sinking down on a bench by the door next to the half-empty flat of water. She grabs another tiny bottle, twists the lid off, and takes a big swig. Her stomach rumbles.

"If you were trying to catch Bad Mike with his supplier," Donna asks. "If he's selling to dealers in Dorset, it means he's got a supplier, someone getting him what he needs to cook without any suspicion. He's got product, in other words, and that's changing hands somewhere at some point. He knows we're like a three-man operation here, with Dewey on weekends and all that. What do we do?"

Baby sits back and thinks, lightly tossing the bottle of water back and forth in her hands. Her head is muddled and thick and she can barely remember all that's happened in the last twelve hours, let alone problem-solve about criminal justice.

"What would your dad have done?" Baby asks.

Donna heaves herself up from the chair, shaking her head, walks over to an ancient coffeepot and flips it on. "My dad was dirty," says Donna. "Took cash from just about anyone who could cough it up. It wasn't until three people died that there was an inquiry at the county. He retired before they could get anything solid on him."

"I thought your dad put Bad Mike away," Baby says.

"Sure," says Donna. "But only when it worked for him, when he'd taken enough bribes to retire early. He had a case long before you guys made him go save Crystal. He could've put Mike away for a lot longer if he wanted to."

"Where's your dad now?" Baby asks.

"Drank himself to death," says Donna. "Two Christmases ago."

"I'm sorry," says Baby. "I didn't know."

Donna shrugs and heads into the kitchen, where she pulls a bag of bagels out of the cupboard and slices one in half. "You want one?" she asks.

"Thanks," says Baby, and Donna puts two into the toaster. Baby remembers how afraid everyone was of Donna's dad, back in high school, how fast they'd run away from bush parties when the flashing red and blue lights showed up, his deep voice hollering into the forest through a megaphone. If you were a girl, he wouldn't take any kind of crying bullshit from you; if you were a guy, you'd probably get your ass kicked. Didn't stop anyone from breaking the law, just made it more likely you'd piss yourself when he showed up.

The bagels pop in the toaster.

Donna plucks them out and drops them onto pieces of paper towel. "Come and get it," she says, and Baby stands up slowly, the liquid sloshing around in her stomach, and shuffles across the room to the kitchenette, her entire body aching. "Just, sometimes I wonder what my life would've been like if I didn't feel so stuck here."

Baby has never heard a statement she could relate to less, as if Donna has exactly what she wants, but the exact opposite. All Baby's ever wanted is to be stuck here.

"I'm sorry I was such a dick to you in high school," says Baby.

"And . . ." Donna says, handing her the bagel.

"And for all my recent comments," Baby says. "And for the future, when I'm sure I will continue to be kind of a jerk."

Donna smiles a bit, rolling her eyes. "I accept your apology."

Baby nods, taking a big bite of the bagel and paying close attention as it works its way into her stomach. She stands still, waiting to see if she's going to puke or not.

A weird blurting ring echoes through the station, and Donna drops her bagel on a paper towel, licking her finger. "Shit," she says, and runs over to her desk and answers the phone.

She listens, then sits down on her chair, puts her forehead down on the desk. "Goddammit." Baby watches, still chewing on the bagel, still transitioning from the grotesque phase of her hangover to the starving one. Donna hangs up the phone and sits up, staring blankly at the air in front of her. Baby doesn't expect it.

"Marco," she says.

"Marco?" asks Baby, not really getting it. "Marco what?"

"He OD'd," she says.

"What!" Baby says.

"He's at the hospital," she says. Baby leans back against the counter in the kitchen, unable to accept it. Marco barely used to drink.

"Is he alive?" Baby asks.

"He's in critical condition," Donna says.

She knows, then, that it's her fault. The place he's lived and worked for twenty years just collapsed. Of course he went and got fucked up at the Legion . . . god, Baby doesn't even know how it would happen. But it's happening. The panic grips her. It's fucking happening. The town is collapsing around her. She sees it all, moving forward as if someone is skipping through scenes in a film, the flashes of friends dying, families breaking apart, everyone moving away from the sadness, leaving it before they get sucked in. The stopper is out of the drain. They're all fighting a desperate tide.

"Can we go see him?" Baby asks.

"I can't take you right now," Donna says. "I've got to go wake up Judy Mork. They said family only for now. Which, I think she's all he's got in town. Right?"

"Yes."

"Why don't you get some sleep?" Donna says, reaching into a cupboard and pulling out an old sleeping bag. She tosses it to Baby. "There's a holding cell down the hall if you want some privacy. I'm off in a few hours, but you can stay here as long as you want."

Baby stares at the sleeping bag. "You're being really nice to me," she says, and feels herself welling up, probably just the aftereffects of all the beer and the lack of sleep and the news.

"Yeah, maybe figure out a way to deserve it for once," Donna says. Baby shoots her a weak smile, picks up the sleeping bag because she feels very much like everything is caving in, and much to her weird disgust, she just wants to shove her body in the sleeping bag and black out, and so she drags herself down to the jail cell, shrugs her body into the weird, musty flannel tube, and tries to fall asleep.

30

Baby wakes up hours later to finds Judy Mork sitting at her desk, eyes glassy red. She swipes at them with a balled-up tissue, sniffing once, and going back to the computer. Baby's surprised to see her, and she doesn't make eye contact when Baby drops the sleeping bag in a puddle at the foot of her desk.

"Where's Donna?" Baby asks.

"She's sleeping for a few hours, then we're going to drive out to the hospital," says Judy, turning her attention to the computer in front of her, her voice wavering. "Did she tell you?"

"She did," Baby says. "What time is it?"

"About six," Judy says.

"PM?" Baby asks. "Shit. I'm sorry about Marco. I didn't realize . . ."

"He took the whole thing with the Parrot pretty badly," Judy says, tears escaping from her eyelids. She ignores them, keeps doing whatever she's doing on the computer, and Baby watches as they track down her cheeks.

"I know," says Baby, annoyed that Judy Mork's treating her like she doesn't know him, like he was never important to her. "I know he's not like that."

"Like what?" Judy Mork says, looking up at Baby over the computer monitor. "An addict?" The silence hovers, ragged. "It's just the way things go sometimes."

Baby remembers that Judy's cousin Ross Keener, who played lacrosse at their high school, was one of the first overdoses the last time Bad Mike's shit flooded the market.

"You're right," Baby says. "I'm sorry. Tell Marco I'm thinking about him."

"I will," Judy says.

The sun blasts Baby in the face, and she mutters as she leaves the station, starts jogging down the side of the road. Her insides cramp up; her entire body aches, and she immediately starts to sweat all over. It's too hot out for a sweat suit. She pulls the sweatshirt up over her head and continues on in just her flimsy, faded, neon-green sports bra.

The strip mall appears just around a bend in the road and she presses on, despite feeling as if she's about to vomit everywhere. She's only got a few minutes until the general store closes, and she races inside to where they sell the stupid T-shirts, ignoring everyone she knows. "No shirt, no shoes, no service, Baby!" shouts Randall at the till. She grabs the first shirt she sees and puts it on, yanks off the tag and wordlessly hands him a damp twenty-dollar bill from the wad of cash that's still managed to stay stuffed in her sweaty cleavage.

"Ew," he says.

"Now what have you got for shorts?" she asks.

She leaves the store wearing a pair of men's boxer shorts with a fish on them that read *Kiss My Bass!* Then buys herself a whole large pizza and a two-liter of Coke, ignoring the weird look from the kid at the counter when she hands him a soggy fifty-dollar bill and baldly stuffs the change down her sweaty sports bra.

She hikes back up to Oakwood Hills, the pizza pressing into her hip bone, picking her way carefully through the remains of the building, which is now a construction site, half of the rubble already cleared away. The edges of the foundation still exist, crumbling rocks and broken-down beams creating a perimeter. Baby sits down in the Parrot on a large, flat, concrete slab, opens up her box of pizza, and folds two slices into a sandwich and takes a giant bite, trying hard not to moan as the hot, salty grease slides into her empty, cramping stomach, then falls back against the slab.

She stares up at the blue sky darkening overhead. The longest day of the year feels long gone, and she chews and swallows and thinks about all the nothing she has. No money, no place to stay, no one speaking to her, no boyfriend, no job, no family, no nothing, just this pizza, these clothes, the money in her bra, the greasy mop of hair on her stupid head, and the alcohol from the beer still metabolizing in her body.

As she eats, she thinks about leaving. How she wouldn't be homeless, she isn't sure, but there's something unbelievably freeing about the notion, right now, of sticking her thumb out and leaving. Quitting. It's tempting, and, she reasons, people quit all the time.

A flash of glass, a glint of it, shimmers on the ground, and Baby says, "No," out loud, when she realizes what it is. The crushed remains of the giant ship-in-a-bottle that used to hang over the dance floor, now smashed, ruined underneath the giant block she sits on.

Baby reaches down, annoyed no one thought to save it. She touches the mast of the ship. It feels different than she thought it would. She spent years staring up at it, drunkenly fantasizing about where the ship was going, what it might find. Its body is waxy, sticky, years of moisture leached in through the unreliable cork, the sweat and drips from the ceiling congealing on its insides, coating it in grime.

"Baby?" a voice calls. She sits up, looking around, worried it might be someone coming to beat the shit out of her.

"Who's asking?" she calls back, smoothing her hair away from her face.

"It's Peter," he says, and she sees him walking up the hill from the boathouse. "Can I talk to you?"

"I'm supposed to stay away from you," Baby says, hoping he feels the absurdity of it.

"I'm not afraid of Amelia," he says.

"I am," Baby says simply, hoping he'll turn around and leave.

"You want to go sit in the boat?" he asks, picking his way through the rubble in his usual pair of flimsy flip-flops, careful not to step on anything sharp or broken or covered in sludge.

"No," she says.

"All right," he says. "Baby, what's going on? How did this happen? Why are you wearing Crocs?"

"They're comfortable," she says.

Peter arrives, finds a hunk of the foundation, and sits down on it sideways.

"Did you eat that whole pizza?" he asks, gesturing to the empty box at her feet.

"No," says Baby. "That box was there when I got here."

Peter chuckles, fiddles with his boat keys. "I came to apologize." He trails off, the struggle to say the right thing clearly weighing on him. "I just don't think . . . this didn't go the way it should've. She's not. . . . I never thought she'd do something like this."

"I mean, I wouldn't know," Baby says, swallowing a meaty burp. "Because I never met her."

"Yeah, she's not around a lot." His voice is dismissive. "Why haven't we talked like we did at my place before?" he asks.

"When I was a kid, I saw that Indiana Jones movie where he straps his girlfriend to that metal platform and offers her up as a human sacrifice to satisfy those cannibals, and Hannah changed the channel before I saw how it ends, so I don't know," says Baby, "I guess I just have trouble trusting men."

Peter doesn't laugh. "Be serious, Baby," he says. "For once."

"I am!" she says. "That part's really scary."

"Indy doesn't actually sacrifice her, you know," he says. "He snaps out of it."

"Well, I never saw the rest of it," Baby says. "How was I supposed to know?"

"You could've, though!" Peter says. "You could've at least tried, you know. They have movies at the library."

"Have you seen our library?" Baby mutters.

Peter throws his hands up in the air and walks off, makes like he's going to leave, then spins around. "Sometimes I think you just see what you want to see," he says.

"What does that mean?" Baby says, swallowing another burp. Definitely overdid it with the pizza.

"It means you judge people before they can judge you. And that makes you comfortable, because you get to decide who they are."

Baby wants to punch him, to push him off the concrete slab, and instead feels a deadly calm breaking open in her stomach, fear totally evaporated. "You want to know how I see you?"

"Yes," he says, desperately. "Please."

"I see a spoiled little rich idiot who is ashamed of the girl he's been using for sex for almost a decade. He's so embarrassed by her he won't even let her into his house unless she's working for his family. He won't acknowledge her in front of his parents. He won't stand up for her in front of his sister, and he won't bring his friends to the bar she works at because he doesn't want them to know what he does every summer when they're at golf camp." She studies his face while she spits out all the words DJ's been railing at her since they were teenagers, since the very first summer she and Peter started doing whatever it is they've been doing.

Peter sighs and toes the gravel in front of him. He should be getting angry, he should be yelling at her, but instead he just lets her say whatever she needs to say, as if the words can't reach him. He stands up and digs around in his pocket. "I came here to give this to you." He holds out the keys to *Rude*.

Baby ignores him, doesn't move, instead focusing on the darkening of the world around her. He tosses the key down onto the ground and walks off, and she doesn't bother trying to say anything. A part of her wants to beg, to chase after him, to shout, *That's not what I really think. I know you. I know you!* But she lets him leave instead, and sits back on her heels. She looks over at the demolished bar but doesn't move to try to find something to shove down her throat, to keep her from feeling. She's had enough of that.

She's done with crying. It seems like it should be a moment for that, but she feels strangely dull.

And then footsteps crunch through the debris, and it's Peter, coming back, his face red. "I'm not wrong, you know," he says.

"Huh?" Baby asks.

"You're just seeing what you want to see," he says.

"No, I'm not," she says. "I was being honest."

"Baby, you've never, since I've known you, until we talked at my place, told me you liked me. Not once. Not even when you're piss drunk. Not even then."

"So?"

"So how was I supposed to know you weren't using me too?"

"What?" she says.

"Did you ever stop to think that maybe I was embarrassed? That I know how you look at me? You think my life is so easy."

"It is easy," she says.

"I'm still a person, Baby," he says.

Baby rolls her eyes. "Oh come on. You're Peter Pomoroy."

"So?"

"You're a billionaire," she says.

"Did you ever think I was embarrassed to show you my life? And my friends? That mob of snobby, throbbing assholes. You have a life full of people that love you. It's wide open. Did you ever think about that? Of course not. I'm really going now," he says. "And next time someone you love dies, don't just send me an email with the funeral date and a sad face. Tell me you want me to come!"

"You should've showed up!" she shouts.

"I know!" he says. "I'm seeing now that there are about a million things I should've done different. I'm sorry for thinking it was impossible that the girl who once cleared a packed dance floor so she could do an interpretive dance to 'My Heart Will Go On' could possibly be afraid of *me*."

"I think my performance was inspired!" Baby shouts, a stupid kind of hope seeping back in, and she feels herself smiling, remembering that night, remembering how she ran to Peter at the end, and he tried to lift her up over his head like Patrick Swayze in *Dirty Dancing* but couldn't quite get there and they both fell over onto the floor of the bar, laughing.

"It was," he admits.

Baby doesn't know what to do now. Both of them seem to be hanging in the silence, the terrifying reality of *what could be* forcing the quiet. Both feeling deep-seated dread at the prospect of making it real. She grabs his hand. "I want to show you something."

She leads him through the rubble to the remains of the ship-in-a-bottle.

"Aw, man," he says, when he sees it was crushed. "I can't believe no one grabbed it."

"I already touched it."

"Without me?" Peter says, then kneels down and runs a finger along the stern of the boat. "Oh, yeah," he says. "I've been thinking about this for years."

"Right?" she says, reaching down and running her own finger along the edge of the bow, losing her balance as she does it and pressing too hard. The thin wood collapses, her finger going right through, leaving a gaping hole. She swears, but when she tries to pull her finger out, it brushes past a rolled-up bundle that feels like paper. "There's something in here," Baby says, feeling around with her finger, pulling at it.

"What is it?" Peter says.

"It's stuck." Baby pulls out her finger and stands up, closing her eyes. "Sorry, boat."

She pulls her knee up to her chest and stomps on the bow, crushing it beneath her Croc. A wide scroll of paper covered in dust lies in the wreckage, and Baby picks it up, unrolls it.

"What is it?"

"It's a letter," she says, scanning the top of the page. The paper's dusty and the scrawl is a tight cursive.

"*Dear Louise,*" she reads. "*First off, know that I love you. But I can't be part of this anymore. It's gone on too long and people have died. I'm sorry. I hope what I did reminds you how precious life is, how monstrous we've become. Terrence.*"

"Is that a suicide note?" Peter asks.

"What the hell?" Baby says, flipping to the second page, a photocopy of an official document. "It's a deed for Oakwood

Hills," she says, scanning. "PEG Holdings. What do you think it is?"

"I don't know," Peter says, looking at the deed, then back at the suicide note. "Poor guy, sounds like he went a bit nuts, eh?"

Baby stares at the papers, at the handwriting, then out at the water. Something doesn't make sense. She reads it again. If he just hated the business and the money and he was trying to take it away from Louise, that would be one thing. But this feels like it goes deeper, as if he was trying to keep the money from someone or something else.

"You said he had gambling debts, right?" Peter says. "It probably had something to do with that."

"That's just a rumor," Baby says, reading the letter again, then turning around, staring out at the lake, at empty spaces between the shimmering lights, all of the people who aren't here. *People have died. Can't be part of it anymore.* She walks over to where the deck used to be and kicks at the rubble, sees the glint of metal beneath another fallen beam, nudges it aside and finds a pile of quarters and nickels and dimes all spread out across the floor. Cash only. The bar was cash only.

The pieces start to add up and she doesn't like the picture that's forming, not one bit.

"What's that?" she asks, pointing to a cove to the east. A pair of lights sweep the lake. They're dim, but Baby can see them, right around where they found the safe. Where Bad Mike must've seen her diving, must've been worried she'd find something she wasn't supposed to.

"Fishing boat?" he asks. "What's going on, Baby?"

"It's Mike out there. Come on," she says.

"What? Baby, that guy is a menace."

"And he hates me," she says. "But Marco's in the hospital. I'm going." She grabs the keys he left for her on the slab, clutches the Styrofoam key chain, her heart booming in her ears. "We can text Donna from the boat."

"I don't have her number," Peter says. Baby laughs, thinking of all the times she's tortured Donna with dick pics from other people's phones. She thinks of the card taped up on the wall outside the Parrot, right next to Johnny's stool, and can picture the numbers, all ten of them in a row. Whoever thought it would come in handy?

She grabs Peter's hand and pulls him down the hill. "I know it. C'mon. Let's go."

31

T HEY GET *RUDE* started in silence and push out into the bay, the engine chugging louder than Baby'd like.

"Give me your phone," she says. "I'll text Donna."

"What are you going to say?" he asks.

"That we're chasing a lead. I'll tell her where we're going, to look for your boat."

Peter doesn't turn on the lights and heads to the opposite side of the bay, trolling along the shoreline. "What lead?" Peter asks. "What is going on?"

Baby isn't sure what she should tell him but decides some version of the truth can't hurt. "Donna has a case lined up to put Bad Mike away," Baby says. "She just needs some evidence."

"Oh, okay," says Peter. "Just taking on a crime lord, no big deal."

"It'll be fine," says Baby.

Peter trolls slowly, and Baby climbs out onto the bow of the boat and peers through the darkness. As they get closer, Peter cuts the engine and Baby sees a giant figure, definitely Mike, standing in the tin boat, holding a long pole. Not a fishing road though, something much longer. "He's looking for his stash," she says, staring so intensely off that she almost tumbles into the lake.

"What?" Peter says, joining her on the bow. They crouch together, barely breathing and watch as the pole moves around in the water, eventually hooking something on its handle. A black square gets pulled out, no larger than a briefcase. Bad Mike sets it down on the bottom of the boat, and it moves on.

"I knew it. That's why he didn't want us in, diving around there," Baby says. "Because that's where his supplier does his drops!" She wants to yell at him, *Ha! Got you! Got you, fucker!* But she doesn't cave to her most basic instincts for once and instead grabs Peter's phone and dials Donna. The phone rings and rings and eventually goes to voicemail. Baby doesn't leave one and instead, sends a text. *FOUND THE STASH! FIRST BAY EAST OF OAKWOOD, HE'S PULLING IT OUT OF THE WATER NOW!*

Baby turns the screen off so Bad Mike doesn't see the glow of it across the bay. They're far away but not exactly invisible. The boat's still a rotten orange and the moon, well, the moon is high and bright in the sky and betraying their existence handily. If anyone wants to see them, if anyone's looking, they'll be able to.

"This is so fucked," Baby says, watching as the boat moves on, Bad Mike putting the pole in the water, trying again, feeling around in the depths of the lake.

It's the ding of the text message in the dark, the singing chime that echoes across the bay and into their ears, that betrays them, and it happens so quickly—the gunshot cracking through the night, burying itself in a tree behind them in an explosion. "Fuck!" she says, diving off the bow and scrambling for the wheel, trying to turn the engine on. Peter's dropped down to the floor, facedown, not moving. "Are you hit?" Baby asks, nudging him with her foot while she tries to turn the key in the ignition, the roar of the motor trying to start so incredibly loud.

"Don't flood, don't flood, don't flood," she says as she turns the key. The engine sputters, then dies.

"We've got to go!" Peter says, crawling toward the stern, pumping the gasoline bulb as another shot zips past, this one hitting the water a few yards away, exploding. "They're coming over here!" he hisses, and she turns the ignition again, the engine still protesting.

"Oh for the love of God!" Baby says, letting the key fall slack. *Don't force it.* "Come on!"

She waits for what feels like eons, then turns the key and slams down on the throttle, the engine roaring to life, the boat taking off. The wheel's cranked to the left and they start spinning in a tight circle and she throws the wheel to the right, pointing the bow out toward the black expanse of lake in front of them. She looks over her shoulder and sees the bow of the boat holding Bad Mike and his two hunching cronies has risen, the wake behind it building. "He's definitely got a new engine on that thing," she says.

A third shot whips through the air past them, and Baby jams down the throttle.

"Their aim sucks," says Peter, crouching next to the captain's chair, grabbing a life jacket from the bottom of the boat and shoving it half onto her body as she drives. "Buckle it up," he says, picking up the other one and throwing it on. Another bullet whistles past them.

"Shit!" Baby screams and starts driving back and forth in wide swoops.

"What are you doing?" Peter shouts.

"Trying to throw them off!" Baby shouts back. "I don't know! I've never been in a speedboat chase before."

Baby's sure Bad Mike knows all the fingers of this lake as well as she does and knows their only hope is getting witnesses out on their docks, people to see what's going on, let Donna know where they are. Maybe then he'll give up. She leans on the horn as they drive, hitting it over and over, the wind whipping past her.

"What's the most populated part of the lake?" Baby asks, thinking out loud more than asking a question.

"What? What do you mean, there are cottages everywhere," Peter says, and Baby knows he doesn't see the lake the way she does, doesn't see the emptiness everywhere. She heads closer to the shoreline, leaning on the horn. Hoping that one of these rich idiots out here, somewhere in the middle of this lake, can come out on a dock and take a video, call the police, will do anything, even if they're just annoyed. Even if they just want Baby to shut the fuck up.

Baby loops around an island with the lights on, desperately pummeling the horn, the sound pathetic compared to the weird stillness of the night. They whip past a floating red buoy, its lone light flashing mournfully slow. Baby looks over her shoulder. Bad Mike's getting closer to them. "Take the wheel," Baby says, stepping to the side, keeping a hand on the steering column until Peter takes over. "And head toward the dock in Lakeside. That's where Donna usually launches her boat." Peter takes over and Baby starts rummaging around the bottom of the boat, tries not to panic at how close Bad Mike is getting.

He's standing tall, seems unbothered by the circuitous route they're taking and cuts across their wake, pushing down on the throttle, getting closer and closer. Baby can see him, see the expression on his face. He's laughing.

"Can you go any faster?" Baby asks.

"It's flat out," Peter says, looking over his shoulder. "Shit!" he shouts, when he sees the boat inching up on their rear.

"He's still got more throttle," Baby says, and then, to her horror, sees Bad Mike's fucking brother, Dirk the Dickhead, sitting right there next to him, reloading a gun.

Baby reaches down into the hold and grabs an empty beer can and throws it back at them. Bad Mike ducks, laughing as the can, caught by the wind, spirals off into the darkness behind him.

She digs around at the bottom of the boat and finds another one, this time it's full and she takes aim at Dirk, winds up and throws. It hits him square in the face, the gun falling out of his hand. "Yes!" she says.

"Pull over, Baby!" Bad Mike shouts. "You're done." He pours on speed and the tip of his boat bumps *Rude*'s engine. Baby stumbles and almost falls out of the boat, bracing herself against the windshield.

"Swerve!" Baby says in Peter's ear. "We've got to move."

"There's a buoy coming up," he says, and Baby scrambles around on the bottom of the boat, picking up more empty cans, throwing them backward, one after the other. Mostly she's just trying to confuse Bad Mike, distract him. Tucked beneath the anchor, she finds a garbage bag, and she sends that backward and hits Mike square in the face, the plastic wrapping around his eyes.

Bad Mike screams and swerves sharply, the side of his boat scraping against the red buoy with an almighty screech, metal on metal, and one of his idiots flies through the air and lands in the water. The boat doesn't flip, seems to hover on its side for an instant and then slaps the water, the engine barking out a strangled yelp but roaring to life as he takes off again, after them. Baby screams in frustration and once again goes to the bottom of the boat for something, anything, to pitch back at him.

Her fingers find the line for the anchor, and she picks it up, weighs it in her hands.

"What do we do?" Peter asks, turning around another island, swerving. Baby doesn't know. If they go somewhere desolate, Mike will just corner them, kill them.

"I don't know," Baby says, feeling the weight of the anchor. "Just keep going." She holds on to it. Bad Mike's got more speed than them and probably more gas, more time.

He gains on them and Baby doesn't have to see his face to know the expression on it, that tonight she's got a better chance of ending up dead than alive. She shouldn't have brought the suicide note with her, the deed. She should've left it for Donna, left a trail for someone to find, just like Louise's husband. Now it'll all be for nothing.

Mike gains on them and Baby holds the anchor in two hands, knows she'll have only one shot. "C'mon," she whispers as he creeps up on them. "C'mon!" she shouts, raising the anchor up over her head. "C'mon, you dickhead!"

And it's then that they're both jerked out of the boat and thrown through the air. Baby feels like she's dying, the air emptying from her lungs so quickly, she gasps and can't quite scream, can't hear or see anything, she just feels the collision; her shoulder hitting the lake, a moment of intense pain and then the quiet of water lapping against her. Mouth full, she inhales, then coughs, sees and feels nothing but water all around her, dark water, black.

32

B AD MIKE YANKS open a garden shed door, Baby thinks, by
the sound of its whining metal, and shoves her inside. She
collapses to her knees, groaning, her head pounding, her neck
almost incapable of righting itself. The pain isn't agony, exactly,
but it's enough for her to moan into the dirt, press her forehead
flat against it. Her vision is blurry, as if she's looking at the
world through the bottom of a glass.

The last hours have been impossible to track, her mind slipping in and out of consciousness. She remembers getting yanked
out of the lake by the life jacket and dropped onto the bottom
of Bad Mike's boat, where she proceeded to puke out lake water
and stomach acid, an entire pizza, bile spreading, cheek pressed
into the mess. The puking got her a kick to the stomach, which
only made it worse. They moved her from the boat and into the
back of a pickup truck, where she passed out until they turned
off the highway and drove up a bumping country road.

She reaches up to try to wipe her eyes and remembers she
can't move her hands. At some point Mike or one of his idiot
cronies duct-taped them behind her back. "Shit," she says,
blinking her eyes over and over again to try to clear them. The
boxer shorts cling, damp, to her thighs. She remembers being
catapulted out of the speedboat. They must've hit something. A
sandbar, a rock. "Peter?" she whispers into the darkness, but she

can feel that she's alone. The walls are corrugated metal, and the roof seems to be too, a light rain falling onto the ceiling, making the drops sound bigger than they are, and her voice bounces around it, echoes back down at her.

"Fuck." Her ankles are taped together. She rolls onto her back and sits up, pushing up on her knuckles until she can lean back against the metal wall, her eyes finally coming into focus. She seems to have lost the Crocs, probably when she flew out of the boat; pictures the shoes floating among the wreckage, imagines them one day washing up onshore, without a foot attached to them. Like a real baby, she's now incapable of hanging on to her shoes.

The fact that Peter isn't next to her, Baby reasons, as she feels around on the floor for something to rub against the duct tape, means he's either dead or he's betrayed her. To Baby, it's obvious now. Louise never owned Oakwood Hills; she and Hannah managed it for someone who needed to launder money. A lot of money. Through a cash-heavy business. And Amelia taking it over? It just makes so much sense, Baby feels like a complete moron that it took her this long to put the pieces together.

And she knows, now, who's been dropping the cases. Who has a seaplane? Who makes frequent trips to the lake from the city? Who owns a fucking pharmaceutical company? Who made sure his charming son Peter befriended the locals, fucked one of the resort's most loyal employees for years, making sure the investment was sound, the small-town hick idiots too happy with the cash lining their own pockets to question where it came from?

Louise's husband must've wanted out. Baby doesn't know what he did with the money that was in the safe; maybe he burned the cash or dumped it, then strapped the safe to his ankle, wanted to make his death mean something to Louise, to shake her morality loose. But of course, the money he took trapped Louise at the resort, kept her and Hannah in the Pomoroys' employ. Louise probably thought he was drunk and insane, hadn't been able to cope, that he wasn't in his right mind. Convinced herself of that over the years, believed the money was still out there. They probably promised the Pomoroys it was, were forced to look for it, to pay them back. Said it so many times she believed it to be true.

Baby hops on her butt, fingers desperately scraping the floor for anything sharp. If she's right, she knows she just became expendable. The soggy deed that connects the resort to a holding company, that can probably be traced back to the Pomoroys, that she can feel stuffed in her bra, the smoking gun—it will be buried with her.

Her eyes get used to the darkness, and she surveys the shed. She's surrounded by trash. Empty two-liter soda bottles with tubes sticking out the top; cans of paint thinner stacked by the wall, held in place by strips of duct tape. Used rags heaped next to a small pile of dead batteries in the corner. And then she spots it, a rusty nail, curled up inside itself.

She rolls toward it, wiggling until she feels it with her fingers, grabs it. She hears voices outside, muffled, male. She takes a deep breath and passes out again, eyes closed, doing her best to look relaxed, unconscious. The metal door screams open, the beam of a flashlight crossing her body. Baby stays frozen, worried the pounding of her heart is visible through her shirt.

"Can't we just do it now? I hate this bitch," a craggy voice says. One of Bad Mike's dipshit cronies. Definitely.

"They want her awake," another voice says. "That bitch wants her fully conscious."

"God, what a fuckin' psycho. We should've just let her drown."

They shine the light on Baby's face, and she does her best to stay relaxed, keep her eyes closed, tongue lolling slightly out of her mouth.

"Still out, eh?"

"Guess so."

"She not dead, is she?"

"Nah, still breathing."

The door to the shed closes behind them, and Baby waits until the footsteps disappear before she lets herself breathe, her body relaxing. She's got to get out of here.

Baby fiddles with the nail in her fingers, flipping it over so the sharp, pointy end is scraping against the silver duct tape.

DJ was right. She knew. Baby remembers one rare night where DJ was the drunkest of all them. It was the end of the summer last year. And Peter was doing his disappearing act, the slow, odious escape, that left Baby hooked on the end of a line, waiting until the following summer, forgetting her anger over the winter like she was trapped in a goddamn vaudeville routine. Peter was supposed to come by the Parrot, had been saying he would for the last week and kept ducking out, making excuses about his family.

"It's tribal with these people. Family. The things they get sucked into," DJ says. "Oh, this boy is full of shit, I know that, I bet half of this was made up. But goddammit, Baby. The money, the prestige, the name. They hide behind it, all of them, and they're stuck, by this name, the invisible meaning that's been strapped to it. From where I sit, it's a fucking anchor that'll drag him down; boy, it's going to eat him alive. Just like it does all of them. Everything that's wrong with the world, you can bring it back to the name and what these people will do to defend it. Fuck!"

DJ puked that night, right in the middle of the dance floor after closing, passed out in the back seat of her own car and wouldn't let anyone drive her home, just lay there with the door open, facedown on the upholstery. At the time, Baby thought she was angry. In hindsight, DJ had never made more sense in her life.

Baby keeps working the nail, feels the tape start to give, her relationship with Peter now thrown into focus, like the lights have all been turned on at the end of the night at the Parrot, revealing the sloppy drunks, the puke, the broken glass. What she's always clung to is the truth of the two of them, the moments where they lay together in the bottom of the boat and their relationship was a tiny universe that had its own reality, outside all this. It existed in that place; it was real. She knows that. But what she doesn't know anymore is if what's here, now, is bigger than that. If it's going to do what DJ said it would and eat them alive.

Her wrists are almost free when she hears footsteps again, and she forces her body to go limp, eyes closed, tucking the nail up into her fist. The door creaks open again, the beam of a flashlight flickering into the room. "Oh, get up." It's Amelia, and there's a brief moment of silence, then a splash of ice-cold water hits Baby and she screams in surprise.

"I knew you were faking it." Baby rolls over, keeping her wrists squeezed together. Amelia kneels down and cuts the tape holding Baby's ankles and drags her upright by the shoulder.

"You know, you could've just gotten out of the way and none of this would've had to happen," Amelia says, pulling her out the door. Baby takes a beat, steadies herself as they walk.

"How long have the Pomoroys owned Oakwood Hills?"

Amelia smiles. "You figured it out. My father bought it in the early eighties. He was going to build a cabin on that cliff, but then a business opportunity presented itself, and well, the rest is history."

"Business opportunity," Baby scoffs. "You know how many people have died?"

"If people can't control themselves when they use our products, that's not our problem," Amelia says. "We're just reacting to the market."

"Jesus," Baby says, stopping on the path, trying to delay. She knows that if Amelia keeps talking, she'll be distracted. "What did they teach you at that summer camp?" Amelia yanks on Baby's shoulder, simultaneously pulling a handgun out of the back of her jeans, and forces her along a path through the dark woods.

"When I was twelve, they sent us out in pairs," Amelia says. The path around them is surrounded by thick brush, branches reaching out and dragging at them as they walk down it. These woods Baby doesn't recognize. "A survival exercise. To spend a few nights camping in the middle of nowhere, just the two of us. I don't even remember the girl of the name they sent me out with. Catherine? Kate? Something boring. On the second night, a storm hit and a tree fell at our campsite, damaging our canoe. We tried to patch it with supplies from the first-aid kit, but it was a long journey and halfway through our trip back, water was seeping through the bottom. I knew that the canoe couldn't support the weight of two people and the supplies we needed."

They round a bend in the trail, and Baby sees a fire up ahead. She considers pushing Amelia to the side, making a break for it into the woods, but she needs to see Peter, make sure he's alive, she needs to know whose side he's really on.

"You killed her?" Baby says to Amelia.

"I left her," Amelia says. "In any given situation there's an outcome. There's a measurement. Who deserves to live? Who deserves to thrive? Who earns it? I earned it that day, and that's when my father knew I was the one he could trust to take over his business, to make the kind of choices necessary for the growth of his empire."

"Wow. Okay," Baby says. "Great work, crazy."

"Thank you." Amelia shoves Baby into a clearing, in front of a roaring bonfire so hot her clothes immediately start to dry, the moisture evaporating, her skin warming. "It was easy then, and it'll be easy now." Amelia jams the pistol deeper into Baby's neck. "I should just shoot you, get it over with, clean up this mess Peter was supposed to have in check. But I'm not allowed."

Baby blinks in the bright light, getting her bearings. A small canopy tent is set up across from her between two paths leading off in all directions, deep into the thick brush. They're definitely far from the road. Baby feels the duct tape holding her wrists together start to give for real, and she straightens up, pushing them together. It's all over her body, this aching, and it's taking so much for her to just stay standing.

Still, she's had worse hangovers.

There's no telling which direction she should run in, which direction holds a cook site and the rest of Bad Mike's cronies, which direction will take her to safety. Baby looks up at the sliver of moon through the trees, but it's directly overhead. Where it rose, where it'll fall, Baby can't tell.

Voices float through the air, and Baby tries to calm herself. Amelia's standing behind her now, still pressing the gun into her neck, almost bored, as if this is just an inconvenient turn for her. Baby hears rustling in the trees and it's Jasper, first, who steps into the clearing. He looks totally out of place in his expensive suit, the shine of dress shoes reflecting the firelight. Peter's next, behind him, eyes on the ground, incapable of looking at her, Bad Mike with a heavy hand on his shoulder. "I'm going to enjoy this," he says, leaning toward her, spitting at her across the fire, the glob of saliva falling short, landing on one of the hot rocks in front of her, sizzling.

"Ugh." Baby wrinkles her nose in horror. "That was a real gross color. You should definitely get that checked out."

"What did I say?" Amelia pushes the gun into the back of her neck harder. It's so surreal, she can't quite capture the fear she's supposed to be feeling, the agony they're trying to inflict on her. Maybe it's the fact that her future was so fucking dire already, that she doesn't mind sitting here, mouthing off. If she's going to die, at least she'll know the truth. At least she'll know who she is.

Amelia keeps her gun trained on Baby while Jasper takes out a phone, flips through it, untouched by the situation in front of them.

"Are we doing this?" Bad Mike asks. Jasper nods, scrolling through emails.

Baby screws up her eyes, but it's Peter who Mike turns to.

"This is from your father," he says, then draws a fist back and brings it down on Peter's jaw, a clicking sound on contact that makes Baby want to hurl. Peter lets out a grunting cry and falls to his knees, punching the ground. Baby watches across the fire, trying to figure out if this is a punishment for disobedience, for a small moment of rebellion, or if Peter's in the same ignorant boat she is, having finally put the pieces together. She tries to find his eyes from the other side of the fire, but he's still on the ground, swearing.

Bad Mike straightens up and flexes his fingers as Peter whimpers. She's been hit like that, she knows the feeling, the betrayal and the powerlessness of being on the wrong end of a fist that heavy, the emotional weight of it.

"You okay?" Baby asks, calling on this decade of the two of them, trying to summon it in her voice. It might be her only escape from here.

"No," Peter says, his voice gruff and heavy.

"Oh, shut up," Amelia says, kicking Baby in the spine, throwing her toward the fire. It takes all the strength she possesses to roll out of the way, keeping her freed wrists held tight together behind her back. The heat from the fire is fierce and raging, and so hot on her face, she looks down to make sure her hair hasn't caught.

Jasper looks down at Peter and nudges him with a dress shoe, careless, disappointed. "Stand up." His voice is crisp and deadly angry. Peter does what he's told. As Jasper moves, Baby spots piles and piles of money behind him, sheltered by the canopy, bills banded and stacked in pyramids.

"Now you," Jasper says, looking to Baby. "Where are the files?"

"What files?" Baby says, confused.

"Hannah and Louise's files."

"I don't know what you're talking about," she says, then remembers the locked cabinet Louise had Baby help her load into the back of her wood-paneled truck the night she made a run for it.

"I know you're lying." Jasper stands and walks around the bonfire, grabbing a stray stick from around the edges and pressing it into the embers. "Think for a moment about who you're protecting. A dead woman and someone who abandoned you."

"I'm not going to talk," Baby says simply, her voice conversational. "Because I have nothing to tell you."

"It's her mother who was doing the books, correct?" Jasper asks Peter.

"Yes, it was," Amelia says.

"Was I addressing you?" Jasper says, his eyes focused on Peter. He kneels down next to him, puts an arm around his shoulder. "Just tell your father."

"Yeah." The resignation in Peter's voice, the failure in it.

"Peter," Jasper says, turning around to face Baby. "Thank you."

Baby knows now she really doesn't have a chance. Amelia drags her up by the shoulder. Jasper stares into her eyes. She's afraid but doesn't look away, stares back at his dull pupils. unblinking.

"This isn't how I wanted to spend my summer holiday," Jasper says, mostly to himself, but Baby can tell Peter pricks up when he speaks, and she wonders what they went through as kids, with a father like this. If he ever showed up, ever treated them like they were worthy of him. "There's a chemical called methyl iodide, a common ingredient in most pharmaceuticals." Jasper pulls the stick from the fire, stares at the bright, glowing ember at the end of it. "An overdose of this chemical can cause a severe pulmonary embolism. It mimics a stroke. So, say, you want to get rid of an old alcoholic who's starting to act like she wants to talk. There's a way to do it cleanly."

Baby realizes now, all of it exploding in front of her. Why Louise ran off so fast. *Hannah.* Baby wants to scream, but realizes the full weight of just how stupid she was, to think she ever had a chance at taking down these moneyed dipshits, just her, alone, this idiot orphan, this piece of nothing.

"You're a fucking psycho," she said.

"It's too bad you're so annoying. We could use more people in the family who can count. I hear you're a bit of a human calculator. An asset. Could've been," Jasper says.

Baby wonders what kind of alternate path her life could've taken her to bring her here, to a place where she could be auditioning to count money for a drug lord. She wonders what separates her from them. Bad Mike and Baby. What's the difference? Both born trash, treated like trash. What's stopping her?

"Can we get it over with?" Peter asks, eyes on his father now, the glowing red ember at the end of the stick. Baby can't tell if he's trying to save Baby from the additional torturous pain Jasper might inflict on her or save himself from having to watch.

"Peter, Peter, Peter," Jasper says. "I don't begrudge you your fun. I don't. I never have. But now it's time to grow up."

Peter doesn't move, but Baby can see him trembling.

"Here," Jasper says, and reaches behind the stacks of cash and picks up a handgun. "Do it."

Baby sucks breath into her teeth. She looks up and counts. Amelia is still standing behind her, the tiny handgun pressed into her shoulder. Bad Mike, arms crossed, but probably not holding, it's not his style. And Jasper. Only two guns Baby can see.

"You're sick," she says, her body shaking, trying to find a way to delay. To figure out what to do.

Jasper turns to Baby and tilts his head to the side. "My dear, I don't want you to die thinking we're feral. We don't enjoy this. This isn't fun. This is business. This is what it takes. This is who it takes. Peter needs to become someone else tonight. And your death is efficient that way. It serves more than one purpose. It'll help him move on from whatever this is . . ." He gestures with a hand at Peter, who's crying, his clothes mussed. "And it'll help him become someone we need him to become by way of disposing of you, the only idiot in this nothing town that's managed to figure out what kind of operation we're running here. Now, you, boy, get up." Jasper taps Peter on the head with the butt of the gun, as if he's knocking on the door. "Get up and do what you're told."

"Do it, Peter," says Baby, her voice wavering. Starting to break. "Just do it." She'll take the gunshot. Better than having to sit here and wait for it.

Peter stands up with a heavy breath and takes the gun from his father. Baby knows it's coming. She thinks of all the dumb, idiotic bullshit she's been doing for the last few years. Sleeping through housekeeping and getting into fights and pushing Crystal and DJ away. All amounting to what?

The gun hangs from Peter's hands, and she watches him and it's a different look behind his eyes, like he's trying to access something in his genes that doesn't sit well with the rest of his body, his heart. She stares at his fingers, the loose way they hold the weapon, as if he doesn't believe what he's holding, isn't ready to fully comprehend it.

"Do it, Peter," Amelia says, and it comes out taunting. Baby can tell Amelia wants him to fail.

Baby opens her eyes, raises her chin, and presents her forehead. He walks over to her and stands in front of her, trembling, raising the gun. Baby leans forward, pressing her forehead against the barrel. It's not cold, the steel, it's oddly warm, like it was recently fired.

"Don't disappoint me again," Jasper says, and Baby wonders what conversation preceded this. What was the first disappointment? Befriending the locals? Spending a decade fucking a girl born in a dumpster? Kindness?

Baby wishes she could see these things clearly. She presses her head harder against the gun, *just do it, just do it, just do it*. Her eyes close. The moment seems to stretch through an entire lifetime.

"Look at me," Peter says, his voice wavering. Baby opens her eyes, but she can't look at him. "Look at me," he says. She can't. He pushes the barrel of the gun against her forehead, shoving it back. "Look at me!" he shouts, hysterical, and she thinks Amelia might've just laughed. Baby looks up. So quickly his lips move, his mouth in the shape of it—*run*. "Go!" he screams, and fires over Baby's shoulder.

CHAPTER

33

B ABY BLINKS AT the gunshot, catches a glimpse of Peter, a
wild look in his eyes, the pistol hovering in the air, smoke
whispering out of the end of it in slow motion. She scrambles
up off the ground and takes off, ripping her wrists apart and
flying into the forest. Branches drag at her body as she claws
her way into the brush. Pine trees grow so thick here that Baby
understands why they're using this land to cook. No one would
bother trying to find it. More gunshots echo behind her and
she pushes harder, deeper into the darkness. The light from
the moon overhead isn't reaching her, not anymore, and Baby
feels blindly forward, throws her body at the woods and somehow, somehow manages to stay upright as she stumbles over
tree roots.

An eerie silence behind her. Peter's dead, she reasons. Baby
swears, pushing on, trying to keep out thoughts of Hannah,
the confessed murder, the truth of her entire existence trying
to pull her down, keeping her in these woods, dead next to the
reality that everyone who lives in this town, who's worked at
that resort, deserves to hear. What they all did. What they were
complicit in. Peter. It's a mess, all a mess, and she needs to focus
on something else now. On getting away.

Rustling in the brush behind her forces Baby faster on, and
she prays wildly that Bad Mike didn't bring his dog tonight,

didn't crawl through the mud to unchain her, to send her out into the world to rip her neck out of her body. Baby knows she has an opportunity, some luck, and she doesn't want the reality of what probably happened to Peter back there, what he did, what it could mean, to drag her backward.

"Shit," Baby whispers as she whips through the woods, pausing to listen behind her. Nothing. If it was a dog chasing her, there'd be crashing in the brush. She'd be able to hear something guttural. Barking, foaming at the mouth, the ragged breath of its pursuit. She pauses, trying to hear, her own breath and the pounding of her heart in her ears. Thudding like a fist against a door.

It reels around her, the truth of it. Hannah, Louise, the Pomoroys, Bad Mike, all deadlocked together, siphoning money, blood money, and Baby right in the thick of it, a drunken idiot on the dance floor every night, reaping the rewards.

Snapping branches. Swearing. A woman's voice. Amelia. Of everyone standing around that campfire, she's the only one psychotic enough to give chase through the darkness with gun in hand, the one person who really wants Baby gone, who would be crazy enough to do it now. Peter must've fired past her, just enough so scare her, to give Baby a chance. Three gunshots. Baby counted. Probably one for Peter, two at Baby's retreating back.

All that's left is Amelia needing to settle something personal. Baby keeps running blind, her eyes slow to adjust to the inky blackness.

She's so desperate to widen the gap between them that she looks over her shoulder at exactly the wrong moment, doesn't feel the incline of the earth changing beneath her feet or smell the musk of the trickling water, doesn't hear the tiny waterfalls, and loses her footing and falls, screaming in surprise as she hits the hill and rolls over rocks and sticks and dried old leaves down a steep embankment, her breath leaving her body, arms flailing out at all sides as she clumsily rolls and rolls, the forest flashing all around her.

When she finally lands in a puddle at the bottom of the incline, her ankle pinches so sharply she cries out again, reaches down and finds a sharp stick buried in the skin, just in front of her Achilles. "Fucking shit," Baby says, trying to stand up. The pain is so intense she lets out another sound, a desperate yelp, then crushes her lips together, trying to take a deep breath.

Hannah. She can't help but think of Hannah, dead. Hannah who did wrong for so long, who drank herself to sleep every night because she couldn't bear the truth. Hannah, pushed out of the way, elegantly, quietly, it seems, because she didn't want to cook the books for a family of sociopaths anymore. They probably found out she was going to confess, turn them all in.

Get up, bitch. Baby tries to and lets out a whimper, then pauses. In the quiet, she can only hear the trickling of the water in the shallow ravine. She looks up and around her. The stream cuts through the forest, steep embankments on either side of it, like a trench.

"Baby, come back. We were just kidding."

Amelia shouting, somewhere behind her. "It was just a joke. Kind of like a hazing, welcome-to-the-family thing. I know my dad has a sick sense of humor. Where are you?"

Get up, bitch. Baby wrestles herself into a standing position and limps down the edge of the ravine, her feet slipping over rocks. Water always runs downhill. If she follows this, she'll have to end up at the lake. Or dead.

"Peter twisted his ankle; otherwise he'd be out here too. Come back!"

Baby almost laughs at how psychotic it is. That after everything, Amelia thinks she's so desperate for Peter that she'd throw aside her better judgment and trust them again.

Baby reaches down, grits her teeth, and yanks the stick out, a harsh and desperate *fuck* ripping out from her lips. Amelia's blond hair flashes at the top of the ridge she fell down, just a hundred yards back, scanning the brush.

Baby throws herself behind a pine tree, ducking out of sight, its long branches swooping low to the ground. She crawls up under them, nestles against the trunk in a strange crouch, and tries to calm her breathing, pressing hard against the blood leaching out of her ankle. Amelia sidesteps down the steep slope and looks around, a grin on her face, white teeth flashing in the darkness.

"We just want to talk. I admit, the joke about Hannah was a little insensitive. But that's all it was. So come back, Baby!"

Amelia steps into the water, her feet sliding over the smooth stones, takes wobbling strides, her ankles giving out under her. She casually looks all around, up at the trees, and Baby detects just the smallest, tiniest note of surprise, that Baby was once here and now has disappeared. Baby squeezes her lips together to force her breathing to quiet. Amelia pauses right next to her, looking up the hill, then presses on.

Baby waits, but knows she won't be able to run on her ankle. Not faster than Amelia. Blood's pouring out of it, thick, sticking to her thumb. She leans out and checks, sees the blond hair far enough down the ravine, and in that second, decides to risk it.

She dives out from under the branches, crawls up the hill as fast and as quiet as she can, makes it to the top and crouches behind a large boulder. Amelia sensed something and whips around to look at the tree, where Baby was, moments ago, a wide smile crossing her lips when she sees the branches wobbling.

Baby panics. Thick, tall pines, surrounding her on all sides, block out the sky. Following the ravine is her only chance at getting out of here. These woods stretch for forever on all sides. She could wander in them for the rest of her short life.

Baby faces back up the stream, back to where she fell, her heart thudding in her ears. At least she has the high ground, a few meters of space to make up for the giant chasm of difference that keeps her and Amelia on totally different planes.

Baby reaches down onto the forest floor with her free hand, fingers grasping at dried-out pine needles and forest scrub until she finds a smooth stone the size of her palm half buried in the dirt. She picks it up and throws it, hard, across the ravine at another boulder, where it bounces and then hits the water a few yards behind Amelia.

Amelia spins around, paranoid, her chest rising and falling, panting through adrenaline. "Come on, Baby. Stop wasting time."

She seems to have locked onto a spot a few yards in the opposite direction, heading up the trickling river, momentarily duped. Baby scuttles through the brush toward what she thinks is the lake, just out of sight at the top of the bank. As soon as the trees have grown thick enough behind her, she stands up and breaks into a limping jog.

Amelia's on her almost immediately. "Moron." Baby's shirt is yanked backward, the cheap cotton stretching out behind her, the momentum causing her to tumble over and fall down again, this time taking Amelia with her. The two of them flail through the air, bodies rolling over one another, dirt flashing beneath them as their legs and arms lock and unlock, twist and bend in every direction.

They land intertwined in a shallow pool, thrashing, fighting for leverage. Amelia rolls hard to the right and gets on top of her, pressing Baby's shoulders down, her blond hair hanging around them like hands, blocking out the light. It's weird, staring at her like this. Baby almost wants to close her eyes and give her a kiss.

"I've been wanting to do this, ever since Peter told me who you were to him," says Amelia, putting all of her weight on Baby's body. "You think you're good enough for my brother?" Amelia grabs a thick branch from the ground next to them and places it across Baby's neck. The wooden knobs, the bark scratches against her skin.

Amelia shifts all of her weight so she's bearing down on Baby's windpipe, her breath exiting her body. Amelia keeps rambling and Baby panics, tries to gulp in air, but can't, her hands grasping on either side of her, dipping into the water. Nothing but pebbles, sand. She tries to move, to squirm. Baby feels her throat begin to collapse.

"And stupid too. With those useless friends. They're next, you know. You think we don't know how to tie up loose ends?"

Darkness laps at the edge of her vision, and Baby closes her eyes and lets it come, leaning into the bitter truth that she did it again. She failed. Just like she always does. She thinks about the smell of the dumpster, the feeling, lying there, drunk, body on the bags, shivering in the cold. Useless.

"You're nothing," Amelia says.

No, I'm not. The voice arrives, almost in surprise. A whisper, a female one, right in her ear, and Baby blinks. There's no one else there. It's just the two of them. And yet.

"A waste of skin."

Not true.

"Worthless."

"No." It comes out garbled, stuck in her throat, and Baby decides then that this feeling, that this knowing, that what she understands right now is about as good as it's ever going to get.

And Baby knows Amelia's wrong. She's fucking wrong. *The bitch.* Baby lashes out with her leg and kicks Amelia square in the crotch, surprises her enough that she drops the stick. Baby shoves her aside and scrambles away, dragging herself to her feet, panting, gasping for air, the sudden relief bringing tears to her eyes that cloud her vision.

Amelia dives at her knees and Baby stumbles backward, the pain in her ankle throwing her off-balance. She just catches herself as she falls down to the ground on the edge of the riverbank, her head flying backward, almost hitting a rock. Baby struggles to stand up.

Amelia pulls her gun out of the waistband of her jeans. "I was hoping I'd get to enjoy this more." Baby stops and freezes, raises her hands as Amelia cocks it. There's a thick cut on Amelia's forehead, dumping blood down into her right eye. For once her blond hair is matted and out of place, dirt scrubbed all over her. The smirk has abandoned her lips, and instead, a blind rage seems to have taken over, her entire body shaking with it.

"You got me," Baby says, doing her best to keep the fear out of her voice.

"Get down on your knees!" Amelia shouts, then shoots one in the air, giving Baby the opportunity she was looking for. She dives at Amelia, grabbing her left hand and shoving it high. The gun fires, another bullet at the sky, and Baby feels the kickback, the power of it, as the two of them land back in the stream. Baby grabs Amelia's wrist and brings her hand down against a rock, once, then again. The pistol falls from her grasp and sinks into the water, disappearing.

Baby stands up and dances away, panting, then sees the thick branch that was just moments before pressing down on her windpipe. She grabs it. It's heavier than Baby thought it was, feels weighty in her hands.

It starts to rain, water falling through the trees, the sound of it hitting the river a strange contrast to the adrenaline throbbing all through Baby's body. "It's over," Baby says. "Come with me and turn yourself in."

But Amelia laughs at her, high and insane, looking up at the little bits of sky peeking through the treetops, as if she's waiting for a ride, for her father to swoop down in his plane and save her.

"I don't want to fight anymore," Baby says, and to her surprise, she means it.

"Too bad." Amelia jumps to her feet and runs at her, and Baby winds up and swings, the branch connecting with the side of Amelia's head, the force of it driving her head to the right with a sickening snapping sound. Amelia's body spins like a cartoon, and she goes down, settling face first in the water.

Baby drops the branch, watches Amelia's blond hair playing in the current, her bloody gash turning the water red. She isn't moving. Baby waits for what feels like an hour, trying to decide if she should roll her over or not.

The rain pours thicker down on them. Her ankle throbs.

She turns away, takes a deep breath. Then reaches back and grabs Amelia's shoulder and rolls her body over, watches her chest rise and fall, a tiny smile playing on her unconscious lips.

Baby sighs and limps off, down the edge of the river, the water running toward something, at least hopefully. Something else.

34

Baby stumbles out onto the highway, the winding road shining from rain that's since stopped falling. Her ankle is still bloody and drags behind her, and as soon as she reaches the shoulder, she sinks down onto the pavement, lying flat on her back. A passing pickup truck stops and a concerned couple climbs out, hikers wearing matching puffy jackets, a catalog model of a golden retriever barking from the back seat. "Should we call 911?" the woman asks, and and Baby wrestles herself to her feet and takes the cell phone from her hand.

"I'll do it," says Baby, quickly navigating through the phone, her hands shaking as she texts Donna their location, then dials to ensure she picks up. Donna answers and their conversation is quick, terse.

"I'm on my way," Donna says, and Baby's knees buckle a little, the man grabbing her to keep her from falling into the ditch.

He guides Baby over to their truck, lets Baby sit and pet their dog until Donna shows up. The dog's name is Norm. It licks Baby's face, gets some of the grime off it, and she finds herself hovering on the edge of tears but keeps her cool, eyes trained on the woods, paranoid that Amelia is going to drag herself out of there like a ghost from a Japanese horror movie. Instead, the rain stays steady and quiet, the wind rustling in the trees, the huge, tall trunks swaying back and forth and back and forth. The couple keeps offering to drive her to the hospital, but Baby shrugs them off. She's not leaving this spot until she finds out if Peter's alive.

Donna arrives after what feels like a lifetime, though according to the clock on the woman's cell phone Baby is holding, it only took sixteen minutes. They aren't as far away from Lakeside as she thought. Donna brings Baby a sweatshirt and a blanket and she moves into the police car, sitting sideways with legs poking out of the car door, feet in the gravel on the shoulder, staring into the woods. Donna takes statements from the couple and they leave, and that's when Baby finds herself breaking down, on the very edge of her own sanity.

"Have you got backup?" Baby asks.

"On the way," Donna says.

"It's the Pomoroys," Baby says, sitting up and barely able to contain herself, relieved to be speaking the words out loud. "It's the Pomoroys."

"I know," she says. "I just needed proof."

"What?" Betrayal arrives, faster than Baby'd have liked, a feeling of being worked by Donna, tricked in some way. Used. But Baby takes a breath, steadies herself. Waits.

"We had a tip a few weeks ago. A float plane was seen dropping cases into the water just over there." Donna gestures to the bay on the other side of the road. "We were able to obtain one of the cases and found large amounts of recently expired drugs containing pseudoephedrine. No labels. But c'mon, right? Who has access to a plane and drugs?"

"Is that why you were nice to me?" Baby asks. "To see if I was in on it?"

"I mean, partially," she says. "But I'm also not a monster."

"Fair enough," Baby says, sitting up and looking at her ankle with one eye. The blood flow has slowed down to a light gushing.

"But the cook site? I've been petitioning the state guys to let us use the helicopter to search for it for months and nothing. They must be paying someone off."

"Well, you've got at least one living eyewitness," Baby says. "Oh, and this." She roots around in her sports bra and pulls out the damp letter and deed she found inside the ship in a bottle. "You might want to let it dry off a bit," she says. "Oh, and don't smell it."

Deputy Donna looks at the hunk of paper, the ink still visible. "What is this?"

"Proof connecting the Pomoroys to Oakwood Hills. And a letter from Louise's husband confessing. The Pomoroys owned the resort, and Louise and Hannah had been cleaning their money."

Donna lets out a choking sound, eyes bulging. "They what?"

"It's all there."

"Where the hell did you get this?" Donna asks.

"I found it in the ruins of the Parrot. None of us knew," says Baby. "They kept us happy. They kept us stupid. And it worked."

"Jesus," Donna says. "Let's keep this between us for now, okay?" She ducks into her car and grabs a plastic evidence bag, slides the papers inside, then locks them in her glove compartment.

"What do we do now?" Baby asks. The rain has stopped and the silence of the evening settles eerily. She watches the trees for movement, for blond hair, but knows deep down that Amelia won't be walking out of the woods. Not on her own.

"We wait for backup," Donna says. "I called. The state is sending a whole team of assholes."

Baby jumps, hears a familiar squealing growing louder and louder. Donna's hand goes to her pistol, and they both look at the bend in the road, but Baby grabs her shoulder. "Don't worry," she says, as the familiar purple car rounds the bend, one headlight shining through the darkness. "I know who that is."

"WHAT HAPPENED TO your ankle?" Crystal asks. They parked on the side and ran over to Baby, slumped over in the police car, Crystal with a hand pressed over her mouth.

"Stick got me," says Baby. "I think I need stitches." The wound is still dripping blood, the punctured hole a darker red than the skin surrounding it.

"Ew," says Crystal. "Can I touch it?"

"No," says Baby.

"It might not hurt," Crystal says. "If you're in shock or something."

"I'm not in shock," Baby says.

"You look like you might be in shock," DJ says, passing Baby a bottle of water.

"Am not," Baby shoots back, grinning up at her.

"What happened?" DJ asks. "Did you get stabbed by a really short person?"

Baby takes a deep breath and lets her head fall to the side of the car, the prospect of telling them about everything that happened so incredibly daunting that she feels dizzy.

"I fell," she says, "when I was running from Amelia. She tried to kill me."

"I knew it!" DJ says.

"Are you okay?" Crystal leans down and hugs Baby, pulls her close.

"I don't know," says Baby, then realizes where she is, who she is, what she's been doing. "Shit," Baby says. "What about Peter? *Donna!*" she calls, trying to stand up, the pain almost crippling, her body having relaxed, and it all seems to be catching up to her. The speedboat crash, the stick in her foot, the wrestling match with Amelia, all of it arriving at once, cramping. "Donna! We've got to go up there."

Donna's sitting inside her cruiser now, the passenger door open. "I need to create a perimeter," she says, turning the key in the ignition and starting the engine so the blue and white lights flash in the darkness, lighting up the forest on all sides.

"Donna, we have to go help Peter," Baby says. "He could've been shot."

"Baby, no," Donna says. "We have no way of knowing who's up there. We're outgunned and outnumbered. Stay here." Donna climbs out of the car and opens the trunk, grabs pylons and walks them down the highway.

Desperate, Baby turns to DJ, who's turning off the car, pocketing the keys. "Hell no," DJ says.

Crystal grabs Baby's wrist. "Why don't you lay down in the back seat of the car?" Her voice is so kind and quiet, as if she's trying to talk Baby down off a ledge.

"I'm not a child," says Baby. "I don't need the baby voice."

"But do you maybe want the baby voice?" Crystal asks.

"No," Baby says.

"I don't believe you," says Crystal.

While they talk at her, they coax Baby into the back seat of the car, lying across the bench, and she knows what they're doing and is happy to let them. "You're not a cop, Baby," says DJ. "You're just a person."

"Am not," says Baby, because she feels contradictory, but she leans into the caring this time instead of away from it, and it feels so good, she lets it happen, lets Crystal put her head on her lap and stroke her hair away from her forehead, lets DJ pull her ankles across her knees and elevate them.

"I saw this on *Baywatch*," DJ says, grabbing a hunk of fast-food napkins off the floor and pressing them to her ankle. "Rest, elevate, direct pressure."

"Thanks, Hasselhoff," Baby says. "Thanks a million."

* * *

Eventually, police trucks, ambulances, cars, and onlookers all gather around Donna's perimeter, the world erupting in a sea of blue and red and white flashing lights, of hubbub and questions. Some captain of the state police leads a team up into the woods, troops in tactical gear and German shepherds rearing up on the end of leads, barking, all heading up in the direction that Baby can only point to vaguely. Near where she is, there isn't a road; she's got no idea how someone like Jasper Pomoroy in his suit and wing tips could get up there without tearing the silk.

"Can we take you to the hospital now?" DJ asks from the front seat.

"No," Baby says. "Peter saved me. I'm not leaving until we find out what happens."

And so they wait, in the quiet, to see who gets wheeled out of the woods alive. Baby keeps tensing up when she hears a rustling in the trees, as if some of Bad Mike's cronies have been waiting for opportunities to make it out of here, and she doesn't doubt that there's at least one or two meth-scabbed saggy-pantsed dipshits wading through a bog somewhere. But they have Donna and they have each other, and Baby's starting to feel a whole lot calmer.

So when Donna's door slams and her boots click against the pavement of the highway, Baby isn't prepared for the news. "Two dead," Donna says, poking her head down into the car. "One down with some pretty rough injuries. They found an old logging road and they're taking an ambulance up now."

"Who?" Baby asks.

"They haven't identified any of the bodies over radios," Donna says. "These aren't local guys. They don't know who they're dealing with."

Baby folds in half, sits with her head pressed between her hands. Two dead. Jasper? Bad Mike? There were others, she remembers, the two men who came into the shed while she was knocked unconscious. There could be any number of people up there she didn't know about. It doesn't mean it's Peter.

"I've got to go up there," Baby says, sitting up too quickly, a dizzying bout overtaking her, forcing her to lie back down on the seat, swearing and thinking about Peter bleeding out onto a pile of dead leaves, the image of it seizing at her, even though she doesn't know for sure that Peter had no idea about any of it. That he didn't know about Hannah. That his hands are clean.

"Say, Donna," DJ says, leaning out of the driver's side window. "What would you do if this car drove off right now?"

"I wouldn't like it very much," Donna says. "But under the circumstances, I'd turn a blind eye. But you had better go straight to the hospital. You hear me?"

"For sure, definitely," DJ says, turning on the engine, the squealing of it echoing out through the dark.

"You better not be going up there!" Donna shouts, realizing too late what they're doing as DJ executes a near perfect three-point turn and starts following the ambulances down the highway, away from the scene of the crime. "I order you to not go up there!"

"You got it!" DJ shouts out the window. "We're just going to go up there. See you later!"

Baby laughs as DJ follows the ambulances down the highway, around the bend and then up through the brush. Piles of bushes, branches, and twigs lay haphazard in the ditch. "I don't know if this is a logging road," DJ says. "Looks homemade to me."

"Mike had a new truck," Baby says, shifting in her seat, sitting up as they follow the ambulances' flickering lights.

"Of course he did," says Crystal, pressing her fist to her cheek.

"How did you guys find me?" Baby asks. "I don't even know where we are right now."

"We heard the boat honking," DJ says. "It was echoing all over the lake. I can't believe there wasn't a bigger stink about it, to be honest."

"But by the time we got down there, Donna was out there and she said the boats had flipped—"

"We thought you were dead—"

"Not actually—"

"We followed Donna—"

"She'd been surveilling Bad Mike's cousin Redneck Dave in town—"

"He was at the liquor store and got a phone call—"

"But what the fuck do the Pomoroys have to do with all of this?"

Baby tells them everything, about the safe and lying to Peter, about finding the deed, about the suicide note, about her birthday being the combination, about waking up in the woods, about Jasper and Amelia and Peter pressing the gun to her head, about them admitting they killed Hannah, about running off into the woods, about some records that went missing, about helping Louise load the filing cabinet into the back seat of her car. By the time she finishes, the ambulances are easing to a stop in front of them and Crystal and DJ sit in a stunned silence.

DJ is the first to break it. "It makes sense, in a way. We always had too many staff. I just always thought it was the bar, you know? I mean, I don't know many people who can make that kind of money in five months."

"Yeah," Baby says. "I know. I just can't believe . . . *Hannah*."

"Bad Mike was back in the game. She must've wanted out. Same with Louise. They must've wanted to quit."

The truth of it is difficult to digest, that they've all played a small part in this, that they never asked questions that needed asking, that people died all around them, everyone trapped by this need to stay in the same place, to not change, to not move, to not grow.

Baby sits up, bites down on the dizziness that gasps her all over her body, and climbs out of the car. Dogs barking, lights sweeping all over the place, the same rhythmic flashing of the red and white and blue they experienced down on the highway. Baby shuffles away from DJ's car, feels them get out behind her, and hurries forward, toward the clearing. She sees the canopy, the remnants of the bonfire, and Judy Mork, taking off her jacket, standing over someone lying flat on the ground.

Baby sees him and rushes to the body, Judy Mork intercepting her, pushing her backward. "Baby!" Mork shouts.

It's Peter. He's not moving. A fist-sized blob of red stains his shirt, just over his heart. *He's dead.*

"No!" Baby says, the horror rising inside of her, thinking about nothing but the splotch of blood on his chest and how she was the one who dragged him out here, forced him to confront all of this.

Mork grabs her by the shoulders and shakes her. "He's not dead, Baby," she says.

"What?"

"He's breathing. He hit his head and got knocked out. That's not his blood."

Baby stops thrashing and finds Judy Mork's eyes, looks directly into them and steps back.

"Weak. Idiot."

Baby follows the voice through the commotion, finds Jasper, handcuffed on the other side of the extinguished bonfire, sitting in the dirt, the arm of his suit jacket torn clean off, smudges of dirt and grime and blood all over his dress shirt.

"You shut up," Judy Mork says in a voice so commanding that Baby freezes. She remembers Marco then, lying in the hospital, hooked up to machines, and Judy Mork out here finding the man who in many ways is responsible, having to just stand there in wait while this police operation digs up what put him there.

"Hey, Mork, do you mind going and checking on the ambulance?" Baby asks.

"Sure," Judy says. "I'd love to do that." Except she doesn't. She stands there and Baby takes her cue and winds up, thinking about all the times she's decked girls in the bar. This is her first adult man. The punch lands so hard, Baby curses, her fist screaming in pain. The force of it sends Jasper onto the ground, swearing at her. She still doesn't have shoes on and she feels the wet dirt squelching between her toes, and she lifts some up and swipes it across his cheek.

"You'll pay for that! My lawyers—"

Baby cuts him off, rubbing her muddy foot over his lips, muffling his threats.

"Pay for what?" Baby says. "No one saw anything. Right, Judy?"

"I was doing paperwork," Judy says, dragging Jasper up out of the mud, and tries to lead him toward the police van.

"Do you honestly think I'm going to forget this?" Jasper whispers to Baby as he walks past her, pausing. She can smell his expensive cologne through the mud and sweat.

Baby shrugs. "I'm not the one in handcuffs."

Mork shoves him off to the back of the van, where he steps up and sits, crosses one leg over the other, as if he's seated in some five-star restaurant and not in the back of a police van in the middle of meth country.

Crystal puts a hand on Baby's shoulder. "We should get you to the hospital," she says, gesturing at Baby's open wound, now covered in mud. "That got more disgusting."

"If it's even possible," DJ adds. They all pause and watch as two paramedics push Peter Pomoroy past them, digging in their heels as they wrestle the gurney through the muck.

"I bet he wakes up tomorrow," says Crystal.

"And still doesn't text you," DJ cuts in.

Baby can't help it, she lets out a soft chuckle and keeps watching as the paramedics lift his body up into the back of the ambulance and close the doors behind him. Thinks of the moment back in the wreckage of the Bloody Parrot before the truth wrenched their relationship in half. Baby considers how hard it must've been for him to help her escape. At the same time, she can't abandon the questions that nag at the back of her mind, the tiny voice that wonders if he knew. If he knew what his family was doing, if he was a part of it.

"Let's go, Baby," Crystal says, pulling on her arm.

Baby turns back to the car, then spots the canopy shelter, near the charred remains of the bonfire. The table is cleared, the money gone, but she spots six big duffel bags tucked underneath the gray folding table.

"Go start the car," Baby says. "I'll be there in a second."

"What are you—"

"Please?" Baby says.

"Okay," Crystal says, heading off after DJ. They have a clear getaway. They could drive off into the sunset with this kind of cash. Go somewhere new. Start something honest. Baby sidesteps around the clearing. Everyone seems to be busy enough that no one notices her bend down, unzip a corner, and peek at the contents.

There's enough going on that Baby just goes for it, reaching down and grabbing two handles, then running off back to the car.

36

I T SEEMS ONLY fitting to hold the final staff meeting at the Parrot. Baby, Crystal, and DJ show up early and set up chairs, cart out a barbecue, and fill coolers with ice and beer, bite open packages of hot dogs, peeling the tubes away and slapping them onto a hot grill. Construction halted on the property when the Pomoroy assets were frozen, the company hauling off its machines, leaving crap everywhere. They hadn't had a chance to do much to the wreckage of the bar. Baby sweeps away the loose debris, the tiny rocks and stones, splintered bits of wood, to leave an open spot on the floor where they can talk.

Johnny shows up with a box of tiki torches from his uncle's garage and they prop them up using rocks DJ finds in the woods. The whole thing looks a bit demented, but when cars start pulling up and people get out, smiling and happy to see one another again, the jankiness of the proceedings floats away and Baby feels a little closer to home.

She wants to apologize, sure, but she has a bigger plan for all of them.

When Marco arrives, he walks up to Baby and she braces herself, unsure of how he's going to react, but he wraps her in a giant hug, holding her body for a long time, rocking back and forth.

"What happened to your damn foot?" Marco asks, gesturing to the gauze and bandages around her ankle.

"Got stabbed by a stick," she says. "Real dramatic. How are you?"

"I'm fine," he says. "I'm doing good. Judy's got me going to meetings. I can't believe I broke my one rule."

"Don't do meth?" Baby asks. "It's a good rule."

"I was blackout," he says. "And pathetically sad. Whatever. Judy says your boy is still unconscious."

"Just my luck," says Baby.

"I mean, I'm sure he wouldn't mind if you wanted to hop on." Marco gives her that pervy look she hates, wiggling his eyebrows, and despite herself, Baby laughs.

"Gross."

The silence pauses, and she stares at the center of his chest. "I'm sorry about all of this," she says. "It's not the way I wanted things to happen."

Marco shrugs. "That's life, I guess," he says. He wraps an arm around Baby, pulls her into another side hug. "Besides, Judy let me move in with her. Do her laundry, you know. I'm the house boy."

"That's great," says Baby.

"We'll see how long it lasts."

"I'm sure it'll be . . . great," Baby says, unable to come up with a better word. She grimaces at the idea of forever. Too greeting-card. Marco smiles down at her awkwardness. "Has Judy mentioned anything about—"

"Amelia? No, they never found the body. Apparently, they took dogs up, followed the ravine just like you said. Nothing."

"Huh," Baby says. It's not like she wants Amelia dead or anything. There's just something creepy about knowing she's out there. That she could come back one day. Baby isn't afraid. She's ready. But it's creepy nonetheless.

"Want a beer?" he asks.

"Always," says Baby, sighing, grateful that he can navigate through the detritus so easily. She sits down on a hunk of the Parrot's foundation, her ankle throbbing. They wouldn't give her any of the fun painkillers. Not even the suggestion of codeine. It's like the baby-faced emergency room trainee who stitched her up knew what she was after. Didn't even blush when she asked him what time he got off.

She ducked into Peter's room on her way out. He'd been cleaned up and seemed very much alive, just with eyes closed. She touched his hair and whispered, "Peter, wake the fuck up!" but he didn't move. "Quit faking!" Nothing. She reached up and parted his eyelids, stared into the blankness of his eyeballs, and only then did she really, truly believe that he was out, unconscious, and not just doing what he did at the end of every summer but this time in a grand, dramatic fashion. It was their last summer, after all. Time for a big finish.

Baby watches as almost everyone shows up, grabs beer and hot dogs. She heard a lot of them had moved on. The teachers all went to another resort a few hours away, because a summer paycheck is a summer paycheck and they're getting by all the same, just with a longer commute and a creepier manager. But there's a large group of them, too, who aren't doing anything, and Baby can see the differences in how they're talking to one another.

"Are you sure you want to do this?" DJ asks, sliding up next to her and handing her a hot dog wrapped in a piece of paper towel, a single wobbling line of mustard down the center of it. "It's not too late to drive this over to Tina's."

The offer came to Baby by way of DJ, who heard it from Super Steve. Tina had a hunk of land she wanted to offload. The perfect place to set up a tiny house farm, Baby's Bed and No Breakfast. The entire property sloped gently toward the lake, a big red barn sitting at the top of the hill, where they could probably open a bar if they could get the right permits, and if they couldn't it looked like a wedding destination, the kind of thing people post on the internet. Baby went up to the property and walked around, saw her future laid out in front of her.

And Tina was willing to just take the cash and walk away, no questions. It was tempting. It was so fucking tempting. But Baby knows it would have been a cheat and a mistake, and she can't keep making those. She has to do something right, for once.

"Yeah," says Baby. "I'm sure. But let's get this show on the road before I change my mind."

DJ turns around and cups her hands. "Everyone listen up," she says, and the crowd pauses, people sitting down in chairs, a few opening the cooler, rooting around, looking at a few different beers before they choose one, wiping the icy cans and bottles against their pant legs. But listening all the same.

Baby waits until they're all quiet, tries to look everyone in the eye in turn. "I just want to start off by apologizing. Obviously, what I did was incredibly stupid and also very selfish. A real one-two punch of being a big idiot. You're all my friends and you're the only family I have left, and I screwed you. And I'm sorry."

The silence isn't exactly stunned, necessarily, but they all blink up at her, and Baby has this feeling of extreme embarrassment. But she knows what she has to do.

"I know there are a lot of rumors and half-truths floating around. And I'm fortunate to know what happened and I want you to know too, because we were part of it."

And so, Baby tells them everything, every embarrassing tiny detail, speaks to the horizon over their heads, feels her cheeks burning, hives creeping up her neck as she does it. She chokes up when she tells them about the safe, how her birthday ended up being the combination, that the only reason she could make of it was that Hannah made the deposits, that Hannah loved her and probably got entangled with Oakwood because she was a single parent who needed to make ends meet.

And when Baby finishes, wiping tears off her cheeks, she says, "I totally understand the argument. That we didn't commit the crimes. We are, in many ways, innocent. But we also benefited from it. We benefited from not asking the tough questions. From staying out of it. It's not an easy thing to admit or to feel, and I understand if this whole thing pisses you off. But I want to make it right."

Baby limps over to the duffel bags, both of them just sitting casually next to the barbecue. She drags them out to the center of the rubble and opens them up, revealing stacks and stacks of bills, hundreds of thousands of dollars. "This is drug money I took from the scene. It's maybe a third of what was sitting up there. I want us to decide, together, what we do with it."

A stunned silence, necks craning over one another. There's probably twenty people in total, standing up in front of seats, looking at the money. "How much is it?"

"I think it's close to a quarter of a million dollars," says Baby.

"Jesus," says Marco.

"Not bad," says Baby. "The way I see it, we have options. We turn it in to the police, we keep it and divide it up, or we give it to the families of the people who overdosed."

Voices all erupt at once, and Baby knows it's a rough choice. A heartbreaking one, even. She sat up at Tina's farm a long time, looking out at the lake, at this town she's loved more than anything. But she knows that someone has to lose if things are going to get better around here. And if that someone has to be her, it's not the worst thing in the world.

"I don't want us to fight," Baby says. "And I don't want this money to ruin our lives. I just know that this place, this town, all of us could do better. So here's a chance, I guess. This isn't up for debate. We vote once, and that's that. And no one tells anyone. If you cast a vote, you don't tell a soul. Deal?"

The group murmurs its assent, and DJ and Crystal hands out slips of paper, handfuls of golf pencils they stole from the Legion. Baby thinks of all that's she's giving up. But she realizes, as she watches people scribble things down on pieces of paper, that the giving up is the point. It's everything.

Baby sits on the bags of money holding out her old, battered, Oakwood Hills baseball cap. The back of it ripped apart this morning when she was trying to yank her ponytail through it, the strap tearing off in her hand.

Everyone walks up and places their votes in, a few of them straggling, sitting behind in chairs, staring up at the sky.

Johnny saunters up and tosses a crumpled piece of paper in. "You're a real jerk, you know that?"

"And you love it," Baby says, grinning up at him. He laughs and shrugs, smiling more than he wants to.

"Peter's going to wake up."

"Thanks," says Baby. What she doesn't say is that she's not sure she wants him to. That would force a conversation she's not ready to have, decisions she's not ready to make. Did he know? Did he know what his family was doing?

Did he know about Hannah?

The sick look on Baby's face must scare Johnny off, because he doesn't say much else, just lightly punches her shoulder, walks over to the cooler, and fishes out another drink.

There's no rush, just beers to be unsnapped and drunk, bodies to hug. Baby sits on the bags of money until Cory the Cranky Kitchen Guy walks up to her and puts his scrap of paper into the hat, shaking his head.

"I wouldn't do this for anyone else," he says.

"I know," she says back, smiling at the regret on his face. "I get it now. Thank you."

Baby counts them and there's a lot of swearing and cursing written on the pieces of paper, but once she's read all the slips, she lets her head fall back against her spine, stares up at darkening sky. Baby's always been good at counting. Good with numbers, so the tally comes quick.

Of course, it's unanimous.

ACKNOWLEDGMENTS

THANK YOU . . .

To Janine and Lou for their love and support and for helping me maintain the confidence I've needed to pursue this career.

To Abby Saul, the best agent in the world. Thank you for reading so deeply and approaching all of this so fearlessly.

To Sara for her incredible editorial vision, for helping me find this book's heart and for loving these characters.

To Melissa, Rebecca, Dulce, Madeline, Ben, and everyone else at Crooked Lane Books for all of their hard work.

To Michelle Kaeser for your notes and for your friendship.

To the folks at Corner Gas, especially Brent Butt and Andrew Carr, who I learned so much from.

To Tomi who had to live with me while I wrote two novels. I will admit here in print, I am the slob. It's me.

To Tony. I couldn't have gotten here without you.

To all of my family and friends in Toronto and Vancouver who are so generous and lovely. Thank you, thank you, thank you.